LAUGHING
AND
DANCING
Solo

Let the little children
come onto me
Matt: 19:14

Do likewise

Judy Fruek

LAUGHING AND DANCING Solo

a novel

JUDY BUCHHOLZ FRUEH

TATE PUBLISHING
AND **ENTERPRISES**, LLC

Published by Tate Publishing & Enterprises, LLC
127 E. Trade Center Terrace | Mustang, Oklahoma 73064 USA
1.888.361.9473 | www.tatepublishing.com

Tate Publishing is committed to excellence in the publishing industry. The company reflects the philosophy established by the founders, based on Psalm 68:11,
"The Lord gave the word and great was the company of those who published it."

Book design copyright © 2011 by Tate Publishing, LLC. All rights reserved.
Cover design by Kristen Verser
Interior design by April Marciszewski
Author photo by Lifetouch National School Studios Inc.

Published in the United States of America

ISBN: 978-1-61346-721-3
1. Fiction / Family Life
2. Family & Relationships / Adoption & Fostering
11.11.02

DEDICATION

Josh, Jeff, Chris, and Beth, and all the other
children who have passed through our home.

CHAPTER I

Call it selfishness, weakness, or just plain nonsense—no matter, the child was coming. It wouldn't be long now. He hoped—no, he prayed—he was making the right decision.

Black hands on the steel-rimmed clock stretched purposefully to two thirty. Thirty minutes more.

His leather work shoes, scuffed with wear, the rubber mud boots freshly scrubbed clean, and his well-worn tennis shoes stood straight as a shelterbelt, lined up at the door. The scatter rug was shook free of the field and pasture dirt he'd unintentionally tracked into the kitchen. No coffee-stained mugs or a fried egg skillet lingered in the sink. Slate-speckled countertops gleamed from the thorough scouring of a scrub pad. Newspapers usually spilling off the end table had shrunk to today's *Daily Forum* to be enjoyed at day's end. Even the nuts, bolts, pliers, coins, and whatever else the washing machine siphoned from his pockets, filling a plastic ice-cream pail, had been patiently sorted and returned to the workbench cubbyholes in the farm shop.

Joel Linton gave his approval to the kitchen-dining area of his North Dakota country farmhouse, his home for twenty-three years. A meticulous farmer he was, but behind the paned windows of his two-story dwelling, his finical, detailed workmanship ended. Why hide cereal boxes behind cupboard doors to be retrieved again for the morning's breakfast? Why smooth bed sheets and quilts to army perfection at sunrise, only to tunnel under them again at night? Clean stacks of laundry never made it to the dresser drawers, and the discarded soiled clothes avoided the hamper altogether.

But today was different. When forced to polish the porcelain and dust the ivories, Joel could rise to the challenge. Glancing about, he grunted his satisfaction with his efforts. Maybe he'd hire a cleaning lady to start coming weekly. It did look rather nice, the way it used to look.

His eye caught the ticking timepiece—two fifty. He'd wait on the porch. They should be pulling up anytime now.

Although the cushioned porch swing looked inviting, its wide seat envisioned loneliness. It was meant to be enjoyed by two. Joel opted for the porch steps, lowering his lean frame onto the top step. His new blue jeans creased stiffly.

At the age of forty-six, he'd already planted twenty-eight crops. Agriculture was his life, having been born and raised country. Like John Denver's song of the seventies, he'd always "thanked God he was a country boy." At times, his love for the land overwhelmed him, humbled him, to think he was one of the privileged few to own some of this God-created dirt.

Leaning his back against a porch post, Joel scanned the gravel road in the distance, looking for a hint of movement between the ash trees lining the road. Nothing.

This was a good place for a boy to grow up. Wide open spaces to run and yell in, wildlife galore—the cottontail rabbits darting across the grass wet with dew, deer daintily nibbling on the delicate apple tree blossoms in the spring and later the leftover apples after the frost in the fall, the constant twitter and swoop of birds of every size and fashion, the raccoons notorious for stealing his sweet corn the night before it was ready for his dinner table, and even an occasional skunk to stalk. A kid could pedal his bike along the dirt road marking the section line, scaring the gophers down their holes, and sit and watch the muskrats paddling across the slough adjacent to the yard. There were the billowing trees to climb, forts to be built in the grove, and marshmallows and hot dogs to roast over a fire after the dried leaves of fall were raked.

Couldn't a boy find worth in all the tasks pleading to be done on a farm—checking the cattle, especially in the spring for new-born calves, planting the crop and watching it emerge from the warm soil?

Joel's small grain crops of wheat, barley, and oats were already nestled into the warm earth this spring, some of it sprouting and pushing tender green hairs out of the black earth. Tender rows of corn were just peeking through. Only the sunflowers remained to be planted. The weather today would have been perfect for the job. It was the last week of May, time for the sun seeds to be shoved into their soil beds.

But not now. The sunflowers would wait.

Sighing, Joel brought his right foot up one step and used his knee as an armrest. Maybe he was wrong. Living twenty miles from the nearest town might seem boring or even frightening to a youngster from the city; there were not many kids close by for playmates either. His closest neighbors, Ed and Arlene Bautz, a retired couple, lived two miles across the pasture from him. Arlene had agreed to babysit for Joel when his hours out in the field prevented him from having a child with him all day. Would a young boy enjoy following his steps around the farm, or would he beg to stay indoors, engrossed in the animated characters on a monitor screen? The old farmhouse had sheltered kids before. It wasn't like this was all new to Joel.

Running his hands through his salt-and-pepper hair, Joel sighed with frustration. There never seemed to be any easy answers. He'd weighed the possibilities, the pros and the cons, and tipped his weight in favor of the placement. It was too late to back out. He'd see this through—unless the child wanted out.

The honk of a horn startled him out of the tug-of-war pulling in his gut. Meagan Ritter's wheels stirred up eddies of fine dust. Slowing her compact vehicle at the end of the slough, she passed the mailbox, the nameplate clearly reading *Joel Linton*, and swung into his driveway. Always pleasant, Meagan waved cheerily at him as she brought her car to a halt a few yards distant from his perch on the porch steps. Only the top of a white-blond head could be distinguished in the rear seat.

Joel eased himself off the steps, purposefully moving slowly, not wanting to alarm the youngster still strapped in the back-seat. Pushing her car door open and sliding out from behind the wheel, Meagan, with her curly head and contagious smile, put Joel at ease, burying his earlier negative thoughts for the time being.

"Hi, Joel. I've brought you a little friend." Her dimples sank deeper as she spoke. "We talked farming all the way out here. Carson thinks he'll be a big help to you." She winked as she tugged on the backseat door.

Six-year-old Carson Reynolds blinked up at them, grinning sheepishly. Relinquishing his seatbelt, he climbed out to stand stiffly beside Meagan. Dressed in knee-length nylon shorts and a T-shirt with a football player's name printed across the front, he rubbed one of his tennis shoes against the other foot nervously. He took in Joel's relaxed pose and the friendly crinkle lines at his eyes momentarily before averting his gaze to his sneaker scuffing the stones of the gravel, his smile still fastened on his face.

Laying a hand lightly on his shoulder, Meagan made the pre-liminary introductions. "Carson, this is the nice man I told you about. His name is Joel. He has a whole ranch for you to play on," she said, sweeping her arm out for emphasis. Carson's eyes peeked from under his straw stack of blond bangs up at Joel.

Lowering himself to his haunches in front of the child, Joel took in the sky-blue eyes and little nose sprinkled with freckles, a fair-skinned child accompanied with a heap of golden hair. He was thin but tall for his six years. Potentiality fluttered through Joel's chest.

"I'm glad to meet you, Carson. I've been waiting for someone just like you to give me a hand out here on the farm. Have you ever been on a farm before?"

Carson shook his head. In a clear voice, he asked, "Do you got any animals? I saw a pig at the zoo once and a horse in a parade." The boy's blue eyes looked straight into Joel's gray ones.

City bred for sure. "You know anything about cattle, son? I have a herd of cows and calves ready to move out to the pasture for the summer." His head turned to draw attention to the line of fencing extending between two red metal barns fifty yards from the house.

Carson followed the direction Joel was looking. "You mean like a cowboy has?"

A chuckle erupted from deep within Joel's throat. "Kind of like that, only I wear a baseball cap instead of a cowboy hat. I've got lots of caps. You can pick one out for yourself if you like." Crow's feet at the corners of the man's eyes crinkled as his grin broadened.

Carson let the words soak in. "Don't cowboys ride a horse?"

Reining in his amusement, Joel glanced up at Meagan. "Yup, some cowboys do. But I guess I'm not a very good cowboy. I use a four-wheeler instead. You might say I'm a ranching farmer."

The youngster nodded, as if he didn't think it was weird at all to be a cowboy with no hat nor horse. Craning his head upward to find Meagan's face, he asked, "Can we take my stuff out of the trunk? It's okay if I stay here."

The absence of fear often exhibited by foster children had always amazed Joel. Actually, it saddened him. Had Carson already been in the Social Service system so long he knew the routine, that moving to a new home was no big deal? How many people had paraded through his life in his six short years, most never to be seen again? Joel's heart tightened.

Joel's gaze followed Carson's up to Meagan. Meagan was young yet. She'd only been a social worker for a handful of years. Did she find child placements commonplace, all in a day's work? Or did her heart tear a bit too each time she packed up a child and transported him on to his next provider, trying her best to match the youngster with the right caregiver, a temporary Band-Aid, knowing someday she'd be back packing him up again and moving him on to the next station ordered by the courts? How did life get so mixed up for a little fellow who had no say in the matter?

Squeezing the youngster's narrow shoulder, Meagan agreed with his suggestion. Pressing the trunk button on the car keys still dangling between her fingers, she caught the lid as it snapped upward, disclosing a fairly full load of boxes, suitcases, and lumpy garbage bags.

After disentangling a stick horse from the side department, she handed it to Carson. "Here, you can ride Black Beauty up the steps, and we'll let the big cowboy carry the heavy boxes."

Carson swung his leg over the toy horse, clutching its plastic reins. "I forgot. I do have a horse. He can help us with your cows." He looked to Joel for approval.

Letting out a long, admiring whistle, Joel rubbed his hand on the pony's furry muzzle. "She is a beauty, all right, partner. All you need now are some cowboy boots."

Carson smiled in agreement then whopped his horse up the porch steps at a trot.

After hefting two boxes from the trunk, Joel stepped aside to let Meagan grab a backpack and the first of the garbage bags. "Now, cowboy, if you'll hold the screen door open for us, I'll lead the way to your bedroom and Black Beauty's stall."

Bouncing the stick horse's head in assent, Carson gave out a high, mimicking whine. The merry trio filed through the kitchen and dining room to the oak stairway edging the family room. *Thwack, thwack, thwack* went the end of Carson's stick horse thumping up each step, trailing Joel and Meagan to the second floor. Two doors on each side of the hallway stood open, disclosing three bedrooms and a bath.

"You and I being bachelors, I thought you'd want to bunk down right next door to me," Joel said, bumping the door of the far room wide open with his elbow as he entered. After setting the boxes on the round, braided rug, he turned to help Meagan with her bundles then stood back to watch Carson examine the room.

Having climbed off his stick horse, he dropped the reins over the doorknob before proceeding farther into the room. Running his small hand over the red and grey squares of the homemade quilt covering the single bed, he caught sight of a sizeable toy chest on the far wall.

Quickly Carson scooted to the chest and lifted the lid to peer inside. "Whose toys are these?" he inquired wistfully.

What child wouldn't be enticed by a toy box? Joel knelt beside the boy, pushing the lid up and back against the wall. He reached in and brought out a dump truck. "They belong to me, but I'd sure be willing to share them with you." He pressed the hoist lever on the side of the toy, letting the truck dump its imaginary load.

"Cool!" He reached for the toy to try it himself. "I brought my toys with me too."

"Great! There's lots of room in this chest."

Grinning up at him, Carson offered, "I'll share my toys with you too."

"Thanks, buddy. I'd like that." Joel was already dismissing his previous worries as he felt a swelling in his chest.

"Do you want to play now?" Carson's head almost disappeared inside the huge chest as he bent over, attempting to snag the pail of blocks in its corner.

Clearing her throat, Meagan interrupted them. "You two men need to help me finish unloading the trunk. Then we have some paperwork to do before Joel can even think about doing any serious playing."

Catching Carson's eye, Joel shrugged his shoulders. "I think we'd better listen to the lady. She's the boss."

"Okay, but you aren't staying here with us, are you, Meagan?" Carson cocked his head to one side, biting on the inside of his lip.

"No, my little friend. After I have you situated here, I have to head back to Norbert."

"Good, then you won't be the boss anymore."

Smirking, Joel and Meagan guided the imp to the stairs.

An hour later, Meagan stood with her hand on the car-door handle. "I'll be in touch. Carson, you know you can call me if you ever need to tell me something." Although he nodded, his eyes were busy flitting about the expansion of the farmyard.

Jovial as always, Meagan threw her three-ring binder across to the passenger seat and climbed into the driver's seat. "I'll be out next week to check on you," she called through the open window before doing a neat loop and driving off the yard. Joel and Carson watched until she disappeared in the dust.

This was it, he and the boy. It was what he had prayed for, some company to liven up the place. So why was he as scared as a gopher running for its hole?

"Are you ready for a jaunt around the ranch, partner?" Joel gave Carson a sideways look, motioning with his head toward the barns.

"Yeah!" Carson had already sprung into a run. "I want to see the cows and their babies."

"Whoa!" Joel's long strides quickly brought the two abreast. "Not so fast there, young man. We are going to stick together on this tour." Carson brought his feet to a walk. "I want to show you where it is safe to go and where it is not safe. Some things on a farm can be dangerous if you don't go about them the right way."

"You mean I could get hurt?" His blue eyes widened, slowing his steps even more.

"Not if you listen to me. You look like a fast learner."

"I am. I can spell my last name, and that's a hard word. Want to hear me spell it?"

Joel swallowed his amusement, letting it tickle his throat. "I sure would."

Carson sucked in a deep breath of air before reciting, "R-e-y-n-o-l-d-s. Was that good?"

"Yes, it was, Mr. Reynolds. Now I know who to ask when I get stuck spelling a word."

Together, the man and boy ambled toward the corral fence and the inquisitive cattle peering at them over the top railing.

"I don't know how to spell all words," Carson admitted, "but I can spell cow. C-o-w." The sun turned his eyes to slits as he sought Joel for his reaction.

"If you look straight ahead, you'll see the c-o-w-s watching every move you make."

His head swung forward; his feet came to a standstill six feet from the fence separating him from the herd of cattle. Thirty or more inquisitive heads had heard human voices and had pushed toward the railing to investigate. Their large, black eyes riveted on the man and child.

Carson nervously reached for Joel's hand. His soft hand felt secure as Joel's larger calloused hand engulfed it. "Why are they all looking at us?" he whispered.

"Oh, they heard a new friend was coming to live on the farm with them. They want to meet him." As Joel squeezed the miniature hand to instill confidence, he slowly brought Carson up to the fence. He lifted him until his feet found the second board of the four-railed fence. Hugging the top board, Carson stared back at the coal black creatures with the sable eyes. Joel put his chest to Carson's back, an arm resting on the railing on each side of his new charge.

"Girls, this is Carson Reynolds. He spells his last name R-e-y-n-o-l-d-s. He is my new partner living with me out here on the range. He is going to be my right-hand man. Carson, meet some of my cows."

Carson's initial bravado had left him. Whispering into his ear, Joel redirected his attention. "Look down. See the baby calves?"

Carson flitted a downward glance. Baby calves were all over! Some nestled in the dry straw at the cows' feet while others frisked about the enclosure. Two white-faced babies pulled at their mothers' udders, getting an afternoon lunch. Their round eyes imitated their mamas': big and velvety and soft. Carson giggled as a lively black calf gamboled close to the fence before diving behind its mother and disappearing.

"Baby calves like to play just like little boys do."

"Can I play with them?"

"No, the mother cows are watching over their babies. They wouldn't understand you only want to play. They might come after you and butt you right out of the pen. This it the first rule about living on a farm: never go into the cattle pen alone. If I am with you, you are safe. Do you understand, little buddy?"

Carson moved his head up and down, his eyes mesmerized by the creatures before him. Pointing to the nearest calf with charcoal coloring from head to tail, he inquired, "What's that one's name?"

A grin split Joel's tan face. "That's your job, Carson. You get to name them all. Come on, I want to show you the rest of the farm." Side by side, the two walked through the calving barns, now empty, with the calving season over. Carson explored each piece of farm machinery parked inside the massive metal storage shed and climbed the ladders on the tractors parked outside. They continued on through the shop, where a hay baler was presently being repaired, to a few smaller outbuildings.

Viewing his ranch through a child's eyes, Joel was seeing the farm he'd lived on for over two decades in a new light. He would have missed the ladybug daintily balancing herself on the fuel cap of his John Deere tractor and the dandelions poking their sunny faces up through the jagged crack in the cement pad out in front of the shop, had Carson not pointed them out. The bird nest holding three tiny white eggs expertly woven into the spare tire under the workbench would not have earned his attention, nor the hundreds of ants in the middle of the yard going busily about their day's work. Carson's fascination with the details of creation heightened Joel's awareness of nature's gifts.

"Would you give me a push on your swing?" Carson asked, his attention span shortening. This time he motioned to the homemade swing, ropes dangling from an overhead iron railing fastened between two wooden poles.

"Sure, let's do it! Race you!" Joel took off in a light jog, glancing over his shoulder to see if Carson was accepting the challenge. He was. His legs churned into gear, surprising the older man with his swiftness. Joel had to lengthen his strides to keep even with the youngster, who was giving it all he had.

Moments later, Carson was clinging to the swing seat swooping into the heavens, calling, "Higher! Higher!"

Giving the wooden board seat another shove, Joel wondered when he'd last taken a work day—a perfect work day when the weather was in full cooperation for field planting—to do absolutely nothing but enjoy it. Watching a child fly high into an azure sky, listening to his squeals of delight—God must have known this was what he needed. How else could he account for choosing to return to foster parenting? Only solo this time.

After playing outside until the sun's shadows lengthened, Joel coaxed Carson into the house, where they sorted through the boxes and bags waiting in his bedroom. Pajamas for the night were laid out on the bed, along with a fuzzy white rabbit. Joel had never done this part before in caring for a child. Melissa had. He wondered how long their careful male organization would last.

Joel was certainly no chef by profession but by necessity had learned to cook up the basics. A frying pan, a Crock-Pot, and "time bake" on the oven were his saviors. If Carson could survive on potatoes, meat, and noodles with some garden vegetables thrown in, they just might make it. Licking the ketchup off his fingers, Carson had made no complaints over the fried sausage and hash browns the two had shared for supper.

Bedtime went smoothly as well. After reading his new charge a story, Joel tenderly tucked him in for the night, sticking his furry hare under his arm. Sitting beside him on the edge of the narrow bed, Joel asked, "Do you want to say your prayers?"

Carson shook his head. "No."

"Then I'll talk to our best friend for you." The middle-aged man folded his rough, chapped hands and rested them lightly on the youngster's chest. Closing his eyes, he prayed, "Dear Jesus, thank you for bringing my friend Carson here today. Be with him tonight as he sleeps in a new bed in a strange house. Let him know he is safe and loved by you and by me. In your precious name, amen."

Opening his eyes, Joel found two round, sapphire eyes watching him. "Good night, little buddy. I'm leaving a nightlight on in here and another one in the bathroom across the hall. If you need anything, you just call ol' Joel. Got it?" The freckled face continued to stare at him. "Good night." Joel tweaked his nose lightly then stood. Walking to the door, he stopped to turn once more and give Carson the thumbs-up gesture before disappearing down the hall to his own bedroom.

Usually Joel sat in his easy chair in the living room with the newspaper propped in his lap until the ten o'clock news came on. Tonight, he opted to remain upstairs close at hand in case the little guy needed him. Switching on the bedside lamp, he then pushed the pillows against the bed frame. Settling into a comfortable position, Joel gave the *Daily Forum* a sharp snap to hold it erect in his hands. Scanning the headlines, he turned a couple pages to the grain and livestock markets.

Minutes ticked by; the eyelids grew heavy, and the newsprint slumped in a crinkle of paper, followed by a light snore. Night sounds gathered in the farmhouse like relatives congregating for a family reunion: the creak of a yawning stair step, the soft thump of the evening breeze lifting the "Welcome" sign hanging on the front porch, a cricket singing off key from a hiding spot under a baseboard, the heavy breathing of a man who had earned his slumber. Down in the family room, the clock chimed ten, and later, eleven.

A new sound broke the nocturnal harmony. Bare feet padded across a braided rug to the hardwood flooring of the hallway. A muted sob leaked out. Hesitantly, the footsteps proceeded toward the doorway exuding the beam of light illuminating a square of the hallway darkness. Softly, the muffled tread crept into the sleeping giant's domain.

Joel could sleep through the nightly creaks and groans of his prairie home, but tonight, something had intruded on his dreams and brought him fully awake instantly. Momentarily disoriented, Joel found himself fully dressed, lying on his bed, the newspaper now crumpled on the floor. His eyes sought the digital clock radio on his nightstand: 11:47. He listened to the silence. Ah yes, he remembered now. He'd chosen to set vigil for a slumbering six-year-old next door.

A hiccup followed by a choked sob brought Joel to a sitting position, lobbing his legs over the side of the bed and crunching the newspapers at his feet. His eyes caught a tear-stained face clutching a snowy bunny to his cheek. Rumpled tiger pajamas, red eyes, and trembling lips seared Joel's chest. How could he have missed Carson's stress? Of course the little guy couldn't sleep. He was homesick for something familiar. Nothing was familiar here, not the feel of his bed nor the blankets against his skin. Not the scary sounds of the house or the man sitting in front of him on his bed. Only his rabbit showed any semblance of recognition, and he clung to it like a piece of gum matted in one's hair.

Moisture seeped into Joel's eyes as well. He chastised himself. *Why didn't I check on my little friend instead of falling asleep over the paper?* With a heavy heart, he opened his arms to the miserable form in front of him.

Tear gates broke open, sending a steady flow of water droplets crookedly down Carson's cheeks, but his body remained rooted to the spot on the floor. Slowly, Joel slid to his knees, folding his arms around the trembling child. Although Carson did not return the big man's hug, his sobs ruptured into full strength, making it difficult for him to breathe. His breathing was punctuated with ragged hiccups.

"I'm so sorry, Carson," Joel murmured, rubbing his hand up and down the quavering back.

The boy had tried to be strong for too long, huddled in the single bed next door, tugging the quilt over his head to erase the shapes and grotesque faces leering at him from the shadows of the room. Joel's shirt soaked in the tears and the snot draining from his nose.

Resting his graying head on the sun-bleached hair, Joel recited his apologies, assuring Carson he'd take care of him. When he ran out of words, he sang the first verse of "Jesus Loves Me" in a hushed voice. When he couldn't recall any more stanzas, he hummed, continuously stroking the thin back.

As Carson's weeping lessened, Joel pulled away from him far enough to look into his wet face. Holding a blue handkerchief around Carson's nose he'd fished out of his back pocket, Joel ordered, "Blow." Carson obliged. Wiping the last tears off his cheeks and chin, Joel engulfed him once again, rocking him back and forth in his strong arms. At last, the long-lashed eyelids closed, his chest rising and falling evenly, his head resting in the crook of Joel's arm.

Ignoring foster care guidelines, Joel used his free arm to fold the covers back on his own queen-size bed. With utter gentleness, he lifted the frail, weary body, depositing it in the middle of the mattress. Pulling up the top sheet and smoothing it over the boy, he was careful not to awaken him with the change of position. Lying down beside the child, he tucked the child close to his chest. The bedside lamp would burn all night, chasing away any fears that might steal in unwanted, and finally, the lonely man and the lonely child slept.

CHAPTER 2

Soft rays of dawn filtering in the east window blended with the iridescent glow of the bedside lamp, making it difficult for the lethargic farmer to distinguish whether the night had yet faded into morning. His arm felt stiff and numb stretched over the slumbering cherub beside him. Carson slept soundly, both arms thrown up over his head, his chest rising and falling in even meter. Mussed golden hair crowned his flushed face; his long eyelashes endowed an angelic pose.

Like a warm mist settling upon the covers, the morning air felt uncomfortably damp. Joel sleepily eyed the window, thinking he must have opened it last night to coax in the evening breeze, but the glass remained tightly sealed.

Carefully he lifted his deadened left limb and shifted onto his back, rubbing the numbness out of the taut muscles with his right hand. The sheet's coolness seemed to seep right through the jeans he still wore. When he slid his hand under his pants leg, his fingers met a definite dampness. First he grimaced—then smiled, chuckling to himself. It appeared his new charge was a bed wetter, and a smart one at that! It was Joel's bed soaked with urine, not the single one next door. A sour stench wafted upward when he lifted the bedcovers to view their predicament. Yup, a three-foot circle of sodden sheet caught the brunt of the leaky exhaust pipe, saturating the tiger pajamas of the child and the side of Joel's shirt and pants. *Yuck!* Looking at the ceiling, he imagined Melissa grinning at his predicament.

Should he awaken the child or wait for the last of the sand sprinkled by the Sand Man to wear off? He'd had a rough night, the little trouper. Gingerly, Joel slipped off the bed with the least movement possible, grabbing clean clothes off his dresser and tiptoeing to the bathroom for a badly-needed shower.

Fifteen minutes later, fully dressed, Joel ran his hands through his clean hair, holding the blow dryer inches from his head. Air skimming past his ears drowned out the click of the bathroom door opening a crack. A blue eye pushed to the opening. Finished with his hair, Joel opened a drawer below the counter and dropped in the hair dryer.

He smeared a generous spiral of toothpaste onto his toothbrush, dipped the bristles under the faucet, and sent them back and forth, up and down across his teeth. White lather foamed over his lips.

A giggle squeaked through the crevice of the door.

Joel's toothbrush stopped in mid-motion, his eye catching the peeking Tom teetering harder now. Joel reached for the knob, tug-of-warring it away from the grasp of the hand on the other side. "Who do you think you're spying on, young man?" Joel's stern question was belied by the twinkle in his eye and the toothpaste painting him a clown's mouth. Carson's eyes twinkled back at him as he shrieked in delight. "Haven't you ever seen someone brush his teeth before?"

The boy laughed back at him, pointing at the glob of foam about to fall from Joel's chin. Checking his reflection in the mirror, Joel grabbed the towel previously dropped haphazardly by the sink and swiped at his wet chin. He finished his toothbrushing escapade by making faces at his audience in the doorway. Loudly he banged the toothbrush against the side of the sink to shake any remaining water from it and then tossed it back in the cup holder. Joel said, "Your turn. Do your 'jamies feel a little wet?"

"Un-uh." Carson shook his head from side to side.

"Feel them, Carson. I think somebody turned the hose on last night in my bed."

"Un-uh." Carson continued to shake his head no, but his dancing eyes said otherwise.

"Oh yes." Kneeling down in front of him, Joel made a quick one-armed swoop around his middle before Carson could bolt to escape. Giggles shrieked out of the wiggling form like a siren on a cop's car. "Oh yes, somebody turned the faucet on in my bed, and I say it was you."

Carson's towhead bent back, letting another tinkling of laughter start climbing up his throat, beginning all the way from his belly button. "And do you know what we do with guys like that?" Joel walked two fingers up the tiger's chest.

"No," Carson spit out between twists and gurgles.

"Well, I'll tell you what we do. We throw him in the shower to get all that stinky smell off of him." Pinching his nose shut, Joel demonstrated the foul aroma. Rubbing his forehead against Carson's forehead, he started peeling the drenched pajamas off of the wiggling worm.

Carson settled down enough to help, suddenly aware his wet clothes didn't feel very comfortable. Joel showed him how to adjust the shower spigot and turn the water on and off. Laying out a fresh towel, he reminded the youngster to use the soap and shampoo. After sliding the shower door shut, he picked up the pajama puddle on the floor and left the room to tackle the wet bed.

Stripped sheets and a mattress pad were rolled into a ball and stuffed into the washing machine on the main floor. On his return trip, he brought a soapy pail of water to wipe off the mattress. To prevent future seepage, he'd put a plastic or rubber cover underneath the mattress pad on Carson's bed—maybe he'd better do the same to his own bed, in case he got another midnight visitor. Joel grinned.

High-pitched singing drifting in from the shower interrupted his thoughts. "Rub-a-dub-dub. Three men in a tub. And how do you think they got there? The butcher, the baker, the candlestick maker. They jumped out of a soaking wet bed!" A refrain of giggling followed.

Knocking on the door, Joel called above the rainstorm in the shower, "How are you doing, buddy? Are you about done?"

"Yessiree." Carson was a happy guy.

"Did you shampoo your hair and use soap on your private parts?"

"Yessiree."

"Then turn off the water and dry yourself. I'll bring you some clothes."

Sitting across the breakfast table from each other, chugging spoonfuls of soggy cornflakes into their mouths, each studied opposite sides of the same cereal box. "Did you know you're supposed to use cornflakes to make chicken?" Milk dribbled down Carson's chin. Joel flipped the box around to see what he meant.

"It's a recipe for baked chicken. It says to crush the cornflakes then roll the chicken pieces in the flakes before baking," Joel read. "Sounds pretty good."

"Aren't the chickens supposed to *eat* the corn, not *roll* in it?"

Smiling at his cleverness, Joel agreed. "Nice deduction, Watson."

Without missing a beat, Carson corrected him, "My name is Carson."

A continual expanse of black dirt disappeared under the huge tires of the farm tractor towing the sunflower planter across the field, seeding a dozen rows at a time.

Carson, buckled into the buddy seat beside the driver, was fascinated by the sounds and scenes inside and outside of the tinted glass enclosure. This was his first ride in a John Deere tractor. He attentively scrutinized every move Joel made, the lever he pulled back at the end of the field to raise the planter off the ground before swinging the tractor and its trailing implement a half circle and then starting back across the field. Carson watched him push the lever forward to set the planter firmly back on the ground.

Full of questions, the boy wanted to know what every button, dial, pedal, and lever was for. What color of tractor did Joel like best? Why did the birds poop on the window? Had Joel ever played the video games in the arcade at the mall? Those games had steering wheels and blinking lights too. Joel answered each question patiently in simple terms the inquisitive child could comprehend.

Carson embodied a miniature farmer, dressed in his faded blue jeans and a hooded sweatshirt, replacing his nylon shorts from yesterday. Pulled low on his head was the red billed cap advertising the local grain elevator where Joel sold his grain that the child had chosen from the collection of caps hanging on pegs in the entryway. Joel smiled inwardly. Having a companion in the cab took away some of the monotony imposed by the continual trips back and forth across the land.

Arlene Bautz had offered to babysit Carson today while Joel planted sunflowers, but Joel thought he should keep the youngster with him the first day, letting Carson get adjusted to his new environment, nurturing the germination of a bond between the two of them.

It had been seven thirty before they'd left the house that morning, far later than Joel's crack-of-dawn schedule normally entailed, but he wasn't troubled by the delay. He too would have to generate some adaptations in his routine; Carson couldn't be expected to do it all.

In all actuality, Joel was fortunate to have a social worker willing to accommodate foster care regulations with his farming operation. Some counties strictly forbade foster children from riding on any of the field equipment, even going so far as to include recreational vehicles on the taboo list. Families who regularly enjoyed boating, jet skiing, snowmobiling, or using an ATV with their own children had to exclude a foster child placed in their home from such activities.

Joel had always introduced their previous foster children to friends as his son or daughter to include them in his family nucleus. Barring a youngster from a family activity sent a negative message. Sure, there was risk involved in allowing Carson to ride on a tractor with him, but everything in life held a certain amount of risk. Getting in a car or an airplane, shopping in a mall amongst strangers, even pedaling a bicycle could be exposing one to peril. Yes, accidents sometimes happened, but they happened everywhere. Common sense and safety went hand-in-hand. If he and Carson were to bond, they needed to spend as much time as possible together—even if that meant sharing the cab of a John Deere tractor. Period.

As the sun climbed steadily in the fair sky, the hours slipped past. The steady drone of the motor and the lulling motion of the machine gently rocked the newest farmer until his head rested against the sleeve of Joel's sweatshirt. Although the eyelids were putting up a valiant fight in the battle against drowsiness, they were losing ground. His head slipped forward, his eyes hidden underneath the cap's visor; his body went limp. Slipping his arm around the sagging sack of skin and bones, Joel brought the tractor to a halt.

Carson jerked awake, looking incoherently about. "Are we done?"

"No, we're taking a break. It's time to play ball." Joel reached behind the seat, magically producing a soft rubber ball. After pushing the cab door open, he snapped Carson's seat belt open. "Out you go."

After clambering down the tractor steps, the two quickly engaged in a game of catch, lobbing the ball back and forth across the rows of seeded sunflowers. As the throws became wilder, Joel had to do some quick back stepping, jumping high to catch the throws aimed over his head. "Hey, what do you think I am—a baseball jock? Easy does it. I'm an old man. Now, get your hands ready. It's coming your way."

Carson easily caught the gentle underhand toss. With a sly look, he wound up and hurled the ball sideways, sending it skipping over the lumps of dirt before coming to rest thirty feet from either of them, caught between a small rock and mound of soil. Joel started sauntering toward the stationary toy when Carson decided to make it a race. Taking up the challenge, Joel lunged forward to reach the ball first. Falling on top of it, he clutched the rubber ball to his stomach, while a miniature backend tackled him with a loud guffaw.

While throwing the tackler off as he struggled to get up, Joel fell sideways back to the ground when Carson's arms wrapped around his leg. The ball rolled free. Quick as a mouse, Carson shrieked and pounced on it, scrambling away with the ball hidden in his armpit, until a man's arm reached out and grabbed his knee. This time, Carson landed with a thud on Joel's chest in a fit of laughter, knocking the strength out of both of them.

The sun poured down its warmth on the man and child lying where in three months' time sunflowers would stand erect, holding their yellow heads up to the sun. It was nice to have a friend.

When the next wave of sleepiness crept over Carson, Joel opened his lunchbox, sharing peanut butter sandwiches and grapes with his partner while the tractor and planter continued their trek across the land. Mid-afternoon, another ball game ensued, and when the blond head bobbed yet again, Joel cradled it protectively in his lap during a two-hour nap.

The sun was slipping from the heavens when the final round of sunflower planting was completed. Wearily, Joel raised the planter out of the ground for the last time and headed home to the farm.

Although the boy had never complained about the long day, he was eager to be free of the close confinement of the cab. Hastily he jumped to the gravel below him and scampered across the yard to the swing. "Can you give me a push, Joel? Send me to the moon."

Having set the lunchbox and water jug on the porch, Joel strolled over to oblige. With the boy clinging to the wooden seat, each push sent him soaring skyward, reeling higher and higher, until finally Carson declared he'd had enough.

"Are we going to eat some supper now?" Carson asked, slipping his hand into Joel's as they trudged back to the house.

"Pretty soon. We just have to feed two bottle calves first." The older man peered down at the youngster who was trying to match his strides.

"How come? Don't their mamas feed them?"

"These two mothers don't produce enough milk, so I have to help them out."

In the garage, Joel stored a fifty-pound bag of milk replacer. He dumped a cup of the powdered milk into a pair of foot-tall milk bottles topped with rubber nipples.

"Wow!" Carson's eyes filled with wonder. "Is that what you use to feed the calves? They're awfully big!"

"Yes, but calves are a whole lot bigger babies than what you were when you were born. They need a lot of milk to grow."

Carson carried one of the bottles to the corral fence, and Joel the other. Two calves were already expecting their past-due supper, their heads sticking through the rails of the fence, bawling out their frustration and hunger at the tardy farmers.

When each calf had been born in the spring, Joel had fastened an ear tag on its right ear to keep the mother and calf pairs straight in his computer records. Numbers eighteen and thirty-three waved at Carson from the twitching ears.

The calves' eagerness to have the milk intimidated Carson. Backing away from the bawling babies, he clasped the container to his sweatshirt. Having set down his own bottle, Joel held Carson's bottle with him. "I'll help you. Hang on to the bottle tightly, or the calf will tug it right out of your hands." Together they leaned the bottle sideways, offering it to calf thirty-three. Greedily, her wet mouth captured the nipple, her nostril holes flaring as she guzzled down two quarts of milk in less than a minute. She continued to suck on the nipple, not wanting to let go, until Joel jerked the bottle away from her.

Calf number eighteen bumped the head of the first calf, wanting her share of the milk being offered. Handing the second bottle to Carson, Joel asked, "Do you think you can do it, buddy?"

Awkwardly he tipped the vessel toward the bobbing head of the calf but then stepped back nervously when her nose bumped the nipple. "She's too jumpy. I can't feed her."

"Sure you can." Joel put a hand back on the bottle, directing the boy back to the fence. The calf nuzzled the nipple before sucking it into his mouth. His shiny eyes hooked with Carson's as he gulped down each swallow. Calf thirty-three stuck her head through the space between the two railings again, her nose still frothy white from her drink.

Carson giggled. "She wants some more."

"Yup, but she can't have any more. This milk belongs to number eighteen. Okay, she's done. Pull hard." Carson did, and the nipple popped out of her mouth, spraying milk droplets through the air.

Joel lightly scratched the top of her rough nose. Wiggling, she pulled her head away from the fence opening. Carson laughed, stretching his fingers out to touch number thirty-three. The calf abruptly lurched upward, wetting the boy's fingers with the foamy milk. Squealing, he wiped the foam on his jeans. "She licked me! I think she likes me!"

No objections were expressed at bedtime when Joel tucked one tired little boy into his single bed, along with his faithful rabbit. A story was read and prayers said. Smoothing the blond hair back from the forehead still damp from a shower, Joel sat on the side of the bed reviewing the day with Carson. "Thanks for helping me today, buddy. It got pretty long out there in the field, but you stuck right with me."

A sleepy nod of the head followed by a huge yawn made a pause in the conversation. Joel smiled lightly, rubbing Carson's cheek with his knuckle.

"You and I have a really nice neighbor. Her name is Arlene Bautz. She only lives a couple miles away. She's invited you to come over to play. Sitting all day in a tractor is too hard on a fellar like you. Tomorrow, I have to plant another field of sunflowers, so I thought maybe we should accept her invitation."

Two eyebrows bent together above a frown. "No, I want to stay with you. I like it here."

"Absolutely, you are staying here with me. This is your home now; you would only go over to Arlene's while I'm working. When I'm done for the day, I'd come and pick you up. Then we'd feed the calves together and read a bedtime story and say our prayers, just like tonight. Arlene would be like a babysitter— no, you're not a baby. She'd be a *kid* sitter." Carson's eyebrows bent deeper, his eyes studying the gray specks in Joel's.

"I promise I won't fall asleep tomorrow if you let me go on the tractor with you." Carson's lower lip quivered slightly as he propped himself up on one elbow in consternation, anxiety etched on his face. Joel's arms slipped underneath his slight frame and gathered him against his chest, rocking him soothingly until his heartbeat slowed again.

"Hey, it was good you took a nap out in the tractor today. When a man is tired, he has to rest. You're only six years old. That is pretty big, but I don't expect you to be able to work as long as I do. Someday you will. Someday you will be bigger and stronger than me, but right now, you are still growing up. Your eyes told you to rest, and you did. I liked your head nestled in my lap." Stroking his back, Joel kept the gentle rhythm of their bodies shifting from side to side as he held the child.

"But little boys also need lots of time to play. Your legs and arms grow stronger when you chase a gopher to its hole or climb a tree to see a bird nest or pull a wagon up a hill gathering pinecones." Joel waited for a retort.

Carson made no response. Joel bent his head sideways to discern if his eyes had closed in sleep—but no, Carson was quietly absorbing the older man's words.

Gently Joel lowered him to the bed and kissed his forehead. "We don't have to decide now. You get some shut eye, and we'll talk about it in the morning."

Carson's eyelids slid shut in assent then popped open again. "Are you going to bed, Joel?"

"Nope, I'm staying right here until I know you're off in dreamland."

A smile played ever so slightly on Carson's lips. His eyelids went from half-mast to closed. What a beautiful child he was—the translucent skin dusted with the sprinkling of freckles over the tiny nose, the whisper of eyebrows so light they disappeared into his skin coloring, the soft protruding lips above a small chin. Another miracle of God's creation. Perfection.

Barely out of his toddler years, the boy was forced to acclimate to wherever Social Services stuck him. How could such a little guy be expected to do so much? To leave his home, everyone and everything he knew, and all on his own move into a stranger's house. Couldn't parents fathom what an awesome gift a child was?

Frustration clouded Joel's thoughts. Kissing the cool forehead a second time, he murmured, "You're safe with me, little buddy, I'll protect you."

Peeling back the skin of a banana, Carson, on his own, came up with the answer to their dilemma. "I think half and half would be fair."

"Hmm?" Joel raised his eyebrows in puzzlement, continuing to shovel spoonfuls of cornflakes into his mouth.

"I spend half the day with you in the tractor and then half the day at that nice lady's house." He bit off the top third of the banana, his cheeks bulging like a pocket gopher.

"Pretty big bite there, young man. Are you half monkey?" Joel teased, admiring the child's ability to give and take on a decision. "Yeah, that could work. You could help me plant sun seeds until lunchtime, and then I could buzz you over to Arlene and Ed's place."

"Cunn I puc lunc?"

"Hold on, buddy. Chew the banana and swallow it before talking. You don't want to choke."

Carson did as instructed. "I said, 'Can I pack my lunch?' I want to eat with you in the tractor."

"You got it." Joel winked at him, remembering when he was a kid. Often the best part about riding with Dad was Mom packing him fried chicken and mashed potatoes in his own individual metal container with a slice of rhubarb pie for dessert. Something about eating out in the field had made him feel more like a full-fledged ranch hand.

"Peanut butter and jelly sandwiches in a lunchbox with a can of orange soda. How does that sound?" Carson gave him a high five.

Flat, wide open spaces cut only by shelterbelts of neat rows of trees encompassed the North Dakota landscape. Cerulean skies licked the horizon, displaying a panoramic view of sky and land meshed continuously into a sphere of credulous majesty. Travelers witnessed an unlimited visibility crossing the plains, a feeling of exhilarating freedom at the immenseness of the miles mapped out through their windshield.

In the distance, Joel Linton's green and yellow tractor was a mere speck in the diorama of wispy clouds drifting over verdure grassland. Emerging crops contrasted with the dark ebony of patchwork squares still being seeded.

Although the farm implement appeared miniature from afar, for the pair of farmers enclosed in its cab, the 200-horsepower tractor generated adequate power, towing the light sunflower planter in its wake. An inch of seat separated the two comrades, but their minds were farther apart than the years interspacing their ages.

Calculations of the rising expenses being incurred in getting his crop into the ground occupied the man's thoughts. Diesel fuel prices had skyrocketed, followed by the surge in fertilizer and seed costs. With adequate moisture, and providing no early fall frost prematurely ended the growing season, what kind of tonnage could he expect on these sun seeds? Would there be enough income to offset the expense column on the balance sheet?

Thoughts juggled about in the boy's mind as well, the past and present colliding with each other. Some of the images pirouetting through his head he understood after a fashion, and other reflections only as a child would evaluate them. He knew not whether they were right or wrong, only that they'd occurred.

His last foster home was a temporary one—he'd been explained this from the start. The family already had a teenage foster son and two children of their own. The teenager often yelled at the mother and father, using bad words. He'd sneak out into the garage to smoke, warning Carson he'd beat 'em up if the youngster told on him. The mother smiled at Carson sometimes, but she was always busy doing dishes and cleaning the house. Sometimes at night Carson would cry himself to sleep, but he always cried into his rabbit, smothering his wails from listening ears.

He remembered his mommy and daddy too, although he hadn't seen them for a long time. They'd given him his rabbit. Rabbit was his best friend. He didn't know why he didn't live with his real mommy and daddy. They were tired a lot, he recalled. Sometimes they slept all day, and he got hungry. Maybe they were sick and had to go to the doctor. Carson was reminded of the time he had to go to the doctor when his head bled. There was lots of blood. The doctor had to sew stitches in his head to make the blood stop.

Soon after that, Meagan came and packed up his clothes and his rabbit. She even took him to McDonald's, and he got to play on the jungle gym. Now that was really fun! It seemed like there was another place he had lived too. It was all too hard to remember.

Joel's big hand reached over, squeezing Carson's knee. The youngster looked up at him. Carson liked Joel from the very first moment Meagan brought him to the farm. He could tell by Joel's eyes that he wasn't a mean man. Something in his eyes glittered like shiny paper on a Christmas present. And when he smiled, the glitter spilled out all over the place.

He wondered why Joel didn't have a mommy. Was his mommy sick too? It seemed they were just the same. Carson placed his small hand on top of Joel's rough hand, cupping his knee. Joel winked at his pint-sized friend. Carson tried to wink back, but both eyes flashed shut, sending them into a giggling frenzy.

Joel sent the tractor and planter back in the opposite direction, signaling toward a red-tailed hawk flapping its wings. The two witnessed it dragging a mouse clasped in its talons across row indentations to a safe place to devour its morning catch. Then, directing Carson's attention to a clump of pine trees adjacent to the far right side of the field, Joel explained, "That's the Bautz farm where Arlene and Ed live. Do you see how close you will be to me? If you stand in front of the tallest pine tree, you will even be able to wave at me!"

Carson's eyes searched the spot. "And then you can wave back at me. Who is Ed?"

"Ed is her husband. He doesn't farm his own land anymore since he retired. Now he helps his nephew farm when he needs help."

"Is Ed home today?"

"I doubt it. All the farmers are busy getting the last of their crops seeded. I only have one day left after this myself."

"Is it lunchtime yet?" Carson asked.

"Is your stomach growling?"

Carson gave a vigorous nod.

"Then it must be lunchtime." Joel opened the small cooler disclosing peanut butter sandwiches for the second day in a row. It tasted as scrumptious as fried chicken and rhubarb pie. Almost.

Arlene looked like the grandma who used to come to Carson's kindergarten class and read stories to the students when his teacher was busy getting papers ready. Her white, snowy hair had soft curls, and her arms and tummy were kind of chubby, just the way a grandma was supposed to be. Flowers lined the sidewalk to her front door, more spilling out of pots hanging from the roof. It looked like a pleasant place, although the real selling point was the chickens squawking and flying out of the way of Joel's pickup truck when they arrived at the Bautz farmstead at midday.

After getting Carson acquainted with Arlene, Joel knelt down to give the boy a bear hug. "Remember, I'll be back for you when I finish the field." To Arlene, he added, "It could be eight or nine tonight."

"Don't worry about a thing. Carson and I will be fine. Whenever you return, we'll be here." Joel drove away, the dust eating up Carson's view.

"Well, what shall we do first?" Arlene asked. "Would you like to play a game of croquet on the front lawn or entertain the baby kittens in the barn?"

"Can the chickens play?" Carson spotted a cluster of birds pecking at the ground outside of a red wooden shed trimmed in white.

"They aren't the most sociable creatures. No doubt you, being a boy, though, would find the chicken coop an interesting exploration site." She led him to the open doorway of the shed. Peering inside, Carson saw a scattering of multicolored chickens. Some were pure white, others brown, and some black and white speckled. Red wattles flapped below their beaks.

Eying Carson and Arlene alertly, the birds' heads turned from side to side, carefully lifting their four-toed feet with each step they took. A dozen wooden boxes lined one wall of the coop opposite a railed roost for the chickens to perch on at night. Spotting a brownish egg in one of the boxes, Carson excitedly scampered across the floor littered with bird droppings to examine it. His quick, impromptu actions startled the chickens, sending them flying in every direction, dust and straw twirling about, scaring the boy as well. Involuntarily, Carson covered his head with his arms, breathing in the dusty whirlwinds left in the birds' absence.

Arlene rushed to the cowering figure, brushing the straw from his hair. "Oh, Carson. I should have warned you. These flighty creatures panic easily. You're okay. The hens and roosters are all outside now."

Slowly, Carson lowered his arms from the protective stance; a hardy sneeze echoed inside the henhouse. "Let's get out of here." Arlene reached for his small hand. "It's too dirty in here."

Although the chickens' sudden flight had startled the child, it was a momentary alarm. "Can I touch the egg first?"

Arlene breathed a sigh of relief at his ready reversal. She hated to frighten him in the preliminary minutes he was on their farmstead—not a good beginning.

Reaching for a metal pail hanging from a hook that was screwed into the cobwebbed, draped ceiling boards, she readily appeased her guest. "Ed keeps this pail here to gather the eggs each evening. Let's feel in each of the nests and see how many eggs our hens laid for us today."

Bowl-shaped nests, stuffed with straw, had been hallowed out by the hens in the middle of each box, fashioning a comfortable hollow to lay a daily egg. Carson fingered through the scratchy straw in each enclosure, squealing with glee over each egg he found, depositing the fragile treasure in Arlene's pail. It was even better than the treasure hunt his kindergarten teacher had hidden in his classroom. In all, they toted nine fresh eggs to the house.

Croquet was next on the afternoon's agenda. Not familiar with the game, Carson found the mallets and wooden balls intriguing at once. Whacking the balls like a professional golfer, the colored balls were quickly scattered over the lawn, one hidden in the petunias.

Retrieving the equipment, Arlene suggested they engage themselves in the house, where she had lots of books for him to leaf through. She had mixed up a batch of chocolate chip cookie dough and needed to get the cookies baked. Books and chocolate chip cookies were a fine combination to bait a young whippersnapper. Carson was right at her heels, opening the screen door to the Bautzes' one-story, ranch-style house, when he stopped.

"I have to do something first." The boy dashed off at a full sprint down the gravel driveway, his toes digging into the loose sand. "I'll be right back!" Reiterating their performance earlier, the chickens darted out of his way, too fat to fly higher than his head before resurfacing, scuttling away with their wings outstretched for balance.

Surprised at his sudden deviation, Arlene shouted back, "Where are you going?" When he didn't answer, she followed him as fast as her waddled walk would take her. Straight as an arrow, he headed to the end of the driveway then turned at a right angle, tunneling down into the tall grass of the ditch to the nearby pine trees. Stretching his head back, he peered up into the sky, searching for the tip of the tallest tree. Finding it, he followed its camouflaged trunk to the ground, threading his way to it as the weeds and bulrushes tickled his armpits.

Planted in front of the tree, his hand crept up to shield his eyes from the sun, staring off across the cultivated ground searching for a John Deere tractor. At last, picking the slow-moving diesel machine out of the vast ocean of sky and land before him, he raised his arm to wave. Fluctuating his hand in a childlike wave, he willed the man in the cab a half-mile or more away to see him.

Huffing to a stop by the mailbox post, Arlene too sought a figure; however, not in the distance but in the tall grass surrounding the pine trees, marking the corner to the Bautz farmstead—a frail boy with a red-billed cap. With one arm thrown up across her forehead to break the sun's glare, Arlene felt her heart pounding in her heaving chest. *Where did that little rascal run off to?*

At last, she caught his feeble wave going out across the fields to his new hero in the farm machine.

Carson's six-year-old mind told him his hand was only a feather blowing in the wind attempting to get the man's attention. Seesawing his arm in a 180-degree semicircle, he waved with all his might. Unsatisfied with the response, he ripped his red farmer's cap from his head and extended it into the sky, pummeling the air as he jumped up and down. "Hi, Joel! It's me, Joel!"

Carson wasn't one to give up easily. When his right arm tired, he switched the red hat to his left arm, churning it in windmill fashion. "Hi, Joel! Can you see me, Joel?"

Although Carson was not physically in the cab of the tractor with Joel, he might as well have been, for the man's thoughts were not on his planting but on the child he had only known for three short days, a child who was already drawn to him like a magnet attracted to a metal bar. He could say the same for himself.

His eyes shifted to the Bautz farmstead in the distance, a grove of trees hiding the house and the barn. He hoped the child was accepting of Arlene, for Joel knew he needed the woman's assistance.

A silhouetted figure appeared on the road running past the Bautzes' home. Narrowing his eyes, Joel could barely make it out, but he focused on the spot, trying to detect a second figure. Maybe Arlene and Carson had walked out to get the mail from the box at the end of the driveway. But only one person was paused on the horizon.

Joel's tractor continued to advance in the general direction of the Bautz farmstead. Suddenly he saw a flash of red from the base of the tall pine tree marking the grove. A bird? There it was again.

Like the sun coming up in the morning, it dawned on Joel that the splash of red was a little boy's cap sending his love to him across the black field. Snapping the light switch on the dash of the tractor on and off, Joel sent the same message back to his new partner.

Arlene cupped her hands around her mouth to yell to her charge, to signal for him to come to her, to give up this foolish fruition, when Carson started jumping straight up and down in a jovial jig, his joy plain to see. A whole bar of lights along the top of the tractor's cab were flickering on and off in whites, reds, and yellows!

"He sees me; he sees me!" Carson screamed, his smile stretching from ear to ear.

Now he was ready to help Arlene bake those chocolate chip cookies.

At seven, Ed came home. In contrast to his short, stout wife, Ed was tall and lean, his bib overalls giving him more mass than he'd earned. He was more subdued than his talkative wife, but he smiled easily, his wrinkled face rippling into multiple creases.

Arlene set three plates and blue-rimmed glasses upon the blue-and-white checked placemats, hemming in a bouquet of fresh tulips from her flowerbed in the center of the table. Carrying a platter of fried pork chops and a bowl of mashed potatoes dripping with a melting glob of butter in the center, she ordered, "You guys, get washed up. The food's hot." Ed readily complied. Sprawled on the floor, propped up on his elbows, Carson was paging through a book of nursery rhymes.

"I can't eat here. Joel and me will eat at his house when he comes to get me."

"Honey, it's getting late. You eat here, and Joel will eat when he's done in the field." Arlene cajoled the youth. "These men farm, farm, farm. I think sometimes they forget to eat." Ed winked at him, pulling out the middle of his overalls to display how much extra room he had inside. His wife might be right in her summation.

Shaking his head no, Carson stubbornly held his ground. "I have to help Joel fix supper."

Ed laid his hand on Carson's straw head. "I got a better idea. We'll get another plate and set it on the table. You fill it with food for Joel when you are dishing up for yourself. Then when he comes to fetch you, he can take the plate home and warm it up in the microwave."

A growl from his middle nudged Carson. Arlene handed him an extra plate, which he set right beside his own plate before climbing onto the chair.

In unison, the couple humbly recited the same table grace they'd prayed for years. Hungrily, the three did justice to Arlene's well-prepared food, Carson and Ed making sure Joel's plate received generous portions.

Seated beside Arlene in the loveseat, Carson missed the last two pages of the Berenstain Bears book she was reading out loud as drowsiness over took him. Seeing he had drooped like a pulled-out weed, she quietly set the book aside.

Sharp raps at the door brought the limp form instantly awake. He wriggled off the loveseat and hightailed it to the door. "Did you see me wave?" he said to Joel, wrapping his arms around the farmer's dirty pants legs, tilting his head backward.

Grinning, Joel replied, "You betcha. Did you catch the kiss I threw you?"

"You didn't throw me a kiss. You're teasing. You went like this with your lights." Squeezing his eyes shut and then popping them open brought a chorus of laughs from the three adults.

"Thanks for taking good care of Carson for me," Joel acknowledged the couple. "I'll get him out of your hair now so you can go to bed. I have one day of planting left. What does your schedule look like tomorrow, Arlene?"

"I'll be home all day; he can come again."

"We'll make it about the same time it was today then. It should be a shorter day. I only have sixty acres left." Joel reached for the doorknob, taking Carson by the hand. Abruptly, Carson twisted out of his grasp and skipped to the kitchen counter. Carefully he pulled the supper plate, now covered with plastic wrap, into his hands. Balancing it cautiously, he carried Arlene's dinnerware to Joel.

Ceremonially bestowing the gift he had lovingly filled, he announced, "You don't have to cook tonight, Joel!"

CHAPTER 3

Referring to the notes she had written herself, Meagan checked off the points already covered. According to both Joel and Carson, their first week as a foster care placement had gone exceedingly well. Carson gave her step-by-step instructions on how to bottle-feed a calf, even insisting she follow him to the garage to appraise the bag of milk replacer. His next exhibition was the oversized, stained bottle and nipple, setting it squarely on the kitchen table next to their glasses of cold lemonade and the store-bought cookies Joel had managed to scrounge up.

"Ah, why don't you put the bottle back under the sink. It's not an exactly appetizing centerpiece," Joel directed, eyeing Meagan for her reaction.

Easygoing Meagan was undaunted. "Or we could drink our lemonade from it," she suggested, nudging Carson with her elbow. He smirked but obeyed Joel's instructions, storing the objectionable object out of sight, and then returned to the chair beside Joel.

As a social worker, Meagan was mandated to meet face-to-face with her caseload of foster children twice a month. One of the visits had to be in the foster home, but after an initial placement, she preferred to drop in frequently until the child was comfortable. Carson had been on the Linton farm a little over a week now and seemed to be nestling like a wren in a birdhouse.

Joel looped an arm over the back of Carson's straight-back chair, a natural gesture for a father with a child. And Joel Linton was a natural. His slow, easy gait, his soft words, and the ready smile drew children to him trustingly, enveloped in the safety he permeated. Meagan had seen it happen before: first a friendship then a bond of steel. Youngsters prior to Carson had followed Joel Linton's footsteps, soaked in his attention, savored his acceptance, basked in his unconditional love.

It took patience, bushels of it, to be slowed down by a kid who had no concept of time, to tend to needs as trivial as wiping a nose or tying a shoe when the demands of his farming operation shouted from every direction. Being shadowed by a young fellow meant keeping a generous supply of toys in the box of the pickup truck and having a coloring book in the cab of the tractor and crayons in his lunchbox. It meant extra repairs: the window broken from a flying rock, the smiley face spray-painted on the shop door, the flat tire on the bicycle, or the hole in the bedroom door. Frustrating? Yes, but Joel always managed to turn those impediments into teachable moments for the youngster, while the two of them used teamwork to rectify the damage.

"Are we done yet?" Carson wiggled on his wooden seat.

"You mean I drove sixty miles out from Norbert to see you and you want to know if I'm done yet?" Meagan teased, laying both of her forearms on the tabletop, a mock hurt clouding her face. Carson smiled timidly. "Well, tell you what; you're excused while I visit with Joel."

"Why don't you check and see if the cats liked the scrambled eggs we put out for them this morning?" Joel suggested.

"You have cats?" Meagan's eyebrows arched. "I didn't see any."

"They're wild," Carson explained. "I try to catch them, but they always run too fast." Within seconds he escaped to the porch.

"Evidently the felines enjoy the buffet table we spread more than our company," the man commented, listening to the bang of the screen door.

Meagan wasted no time getting down to business, not sure when Carson would reappear. Her amiable disposition made a professional turn. "Level with me, Joel. Are you going to be able to handle being a single father?" Her eyes nailed him to his chair. "He's your charge twenty-four-seven. Is rearing a child not conducive with your farming schedule? Be honest; Melissa isn't here to do the mothering."

Joel picked up a paperclip lying on the table, having fallen off Meagan's papers. Turning the clip over and over in his calloused fingers, he did likewise with her question. This very query had dogged him constantly prior to Carson's arrival.

Some aspect of farming crept into every hour of his day, whether he was operating a piece of machinery in the field, working with the cattle, fixing an implement in his shop, doing paperwork in his office, or attending agriculture-related meetings. It wasn't possible for a six-year-old boy to be with him all the time. Arlene's offer to watch him whenever Joel needed assistance had alleviated many of these worries. But what about the rest of the parental responsibilities, not just the cooking and the laundry? There'd be clothes shopping and haircuts, schoolwork in the fall, eye and dental appointments, foster care meetings and paperwork, sore throats and colds, snacks to contribute to class parties, and holidays to celebrate. Could he really do it all?

"*My grace is sufficient for you*" (2 Corinthians 12:9a, NIV).

Where had that come from? This verse had helped him through the last two difficult years, assuring him he was not traveling the road alone. But wasn't this assurance for someone plagued with adversity? Carson wasn't bringing adversity into his life—more like healing, more like joy, more like a *new* life. He wasn't sure if Carson needed him or if he needed Carson.

Accustomed to Joel's long pauses, Meagan waited him out, letting him sort through the files in his mind.

"Refresh my memory about his birth parents." Joel had previously scanned the portfolio of information accumulated by Social Services.

Meagan briefly summarized the facts. "Presently, his father is incarcerated on a drug sentence. Both the mother and father still face charges on neglect and abuse. This is Carson's third foster home. He was returned to parental care between the first and second placement but was removed from the home again when his birth parents, high on drugs, repeatedly left him to fend for himself. The parents have not fulfilled any of the mandated requirements for reunification. Social Services is seeking termination of the parental rights. There are no known siblings."

A sigh escaped Joel as he rubbed his brow. "It seems there's only one choice: the boy needs me." He glanced at Meagan, well aware nothing got by her.

"He doesn't need pity, Joel. He needs structure. He needs relationships that don't end. Yes, he's a sweet little boy who will crawl into your heart and make himself at home. But if it isn't good for you, Joel, it is not going to be in his best interest in the long run. Farming is a sunrise-to-sunset occupation of grueling work. It's not a day care." She was driving him hard, wanting an answer he could live with.

"There are lots of single fathers raising children. I'd hardly be the first."

"Farming is not a nine-to-five job. It isn't as simple as dropping him off at a babysitter before your shift and picking him up afterward. You won't be pulling into the closest fast food restaurant at the end of the day with the town of Elton twenty miles away." Her unblinking stare crowded him.

One parent performing the dual roles of Mom and Dad. Could he do it? Day in and day out?

"My grace is sufficient for thee: for my strength is made perfect in weakness" (2 Corinthians 12:9, NIV).

Strength in weakness. A faint sensation of rejuvenation pulsed through his veins. Indecision was replaced by decisiveness. God wouldn't have allowed Meagan to bring Carson here if he wasn't meant to stay. Looking up, he met Meagan's firm, unwavering stare. "He stays."

Their eyes held for a long moment, solidifying his resolution in stone. Suddenly, her hard-line stare thawed, draining the unrelenting shades from her dark eyes and replacing them with the usual twinkle living beneath her long eyelashes. A friendly countenance once more invaded her face. "I knew you'd say that."

Amused, Joel smiled back. "You're one tough chick when you want to be."

Her dimples reappeared. "Whatever is in the best interest of the child." She doubled back to her list of items on the notebook pad. "The hospital in Elton is a member of the Rural Health Consortium. A therapist comes from Norbert weekly. I'll check into getting Carson set up with her.

"Next item: his kindergarten teacher in his former placement indicated signs of ADHD. He had a hard time staying focused in school, short attention span, disruptions on the playground."

Joel was aware Attention Deficit Hyperactivity Disorder was common with foster children and yet suggested, "Could have been the insecurities in his home life."

"Perhaps, even likely, but I'm scheduling an evaluation for him with a pediatric neurologist this summer."

"You're talking meds?" Joel only liked to see medication used as a last resort in controlling behavior.

"I'm sympathetic with your aversion to meds and even agree with you to an extent. If a child's lack of concentration hampers him from excelling in his studies or establishing peer relationships, it can be to his advantage though."

Joel listened, not commenting. They'd driven on this side road with previous foster children.

"Anyway, school is still three months away. This summer will tell the story," she continued. He brooded, wishing that sometimes Meagan wasn't so thorough.

"He's a good kid," Joel finally asserted, letting the paperclip drop to the table.

"You're well aware this is the honeymoon period. The first weeks of a placement tend to go well. The child is feeling out the waters, deciding what parts of his personality he wants you to meet. Eventually, he will test the perimeters, and you'll be introduced to the real child."

"That's true more for older kids, junior high and teenagers. Kids Carson's age aren't so adept at hiding their idiosyncrasies."

"Granted, but as Carson becomes more relaxed here on the ranch, the bucking bronco in him might come out." Meagan smiled. "Any bed wetting?"

Reluctantly, Joel nodded. "Every night so far. Hopefully it will quit when he feels more secure."

"It may; however, that doesn't always happen." With a snap Meagan closed her three-ringed binder and then drained the last swallow of lemonade from her glass. "Thanks, Joel. You two are off to a good start. If anyone can make a difference in Carson's life, it will be you. I'm out of here, and you can get back to farming."

Carson was already doing just that. Emerging onto the porch, Joel and Meagan caught him absorbed in pushing dirt with a toy loader tractor beside the steps. A box of machinery was kept under the porch for such activity. *Putt, putt, putt.* An imaginary motor accompanied his actions. Raising the loader heaped with dirt, he dumped it into the growing pile of black soil at the base of the porch foundation.

"I see Melissa's flower garden has become another field. He is increasing your acreage. Better get him some certified seed." Meagan flung the words back at him as she slammed the car door.

"Not a bad idea," Joel mused under his breath.

Haltingly jouncing over the holes and rocks embedded in the prairie trail winding its way to the pasture, Joel and Carson patiently crawled along in the pickup truck towing the stock trailer and the nine Angus cows it harbored. Twin-wheel track indentations raced ahead of the truck, clumps of sweet clover interlaced with crested wheat grass stretching tall down the middle and sides of the path.

"You like this road?" Carson asked, the bill of his cap bumping the passenger window.

His eyes twinkling, Joel nodded. "Yup, it's my favorite." He lazily kept contact with the bottom of the steering wheel with one hand.

"Why is it so bumpy? It makes my tummy hurt."

"It's not really a road. I use it to get the cattle out to the pasture, and a couple other farmers use it to get to their fields back here. It would cost too much to fix it up."

"I could fix it with my loader tractor," Carson offered.

"It'd be a big job, but if anyone could do it, it would be you." The rancher reached over to rub Carson's shoulder, realizing he'd repeated Meagan's words. The social worker had more confidence in his parenting skills than he did.

Adjoining the Linton farmstead, a four-hundred-eighty-acre pasture yielded enough grass to feed seventy cow/calf pairs for four or five months over the summer. The remainder of the herd had to be transported to a rented pasture seven miles from the home place. Fearful the young calves could be trampled by the mother cows when loaded into crowded, enclosed trailers for conveyance, Joel separated the adults from their offspring for the trip.

Out of his peripheral vision, Joel caught sight of a sleek, white-tailed deer bounding toward them on his left. Joel motioned for his comrade's attention. With simple grace, the deer leaped majestically across their trail ten yards in front of the truck, disappearing into a clump of cottonwood trees seemingly painted into an artist's landscape scene of prairie grass. Breaking through the entangled maze of vegetation, a spotted fawn emerged timidly, turning his velvet eyes in their direction.

"A baby deer," Carson whispered, sucking in his breath, caught in the thrill of this unexpected gift. Joel braked gently.

The skin beneath the cinnamon fur quivered, rippling down the front legs, unveiling the baby's panic. Extending its head toward the trees where the mother deer had seconds ago disappeared, the fawn took a tentative step, and in a flick of a white tail, it too was gone.

Quiet for a moment, Carson digested what he had witnessed. "It was *so* cute."

"That's why I like this bumpy trail. It's like looking at the spectacular images in a picture book, only it's a live book." Joel inched the vehicle forward again. "Can you see Ned and Rae behind us?"

Hanging on to the armrest for stability, Carson twisted in his seat, attempting to detect Ned's pickup and trailer behind them. His view was blocked by their own trailing wagon.

"Check your side-view mirror," Joel directed.

Peering out the passenger window, Carson scrutinized the reflection in the exterior mirror attached to his door. The right side of Ned's silver truck swerved in and out of the square reflection. "They're catching up to us; drive faster."

"Can't. Did you forget we're on a bumpy road?"

Ned Schultz, in his early twenties, farmed with his father but was always willing to give Joel an extra set of hands and legs when needed. Today, his girlfriend, Rae Ann Lentz, had been an added bonus, speeding up the sorting and loading process. They had run the cows and their offspring through a long, narrow alleyway, splitting cows off into one pen and the calves into another. Rae, likewise raised on a cattle operation, could swing a gate in a cow's face and cut a calf off from its parent as efficiently as a seasoned cowboy.

The first two trips to the pasture conveyed the cows bawling stressfully at the absence of their babies. On the third and final trip, the stock trailers were loaded with the baby calves.

The trailers jolted to a stop in the pasture for the last time. Hearing the telltale baying echoing from its interior, the cows came bellowing. Lifting the latch, Joel didn't have to give the calves any encouragement, as they readily tumbled off the raised floor of the trailer. Each mother singled out her own baby in a joyful reunion.

This was the best show on earth. Leaning against Ned's silver pickup box, the three ranchers reveled in the homecoming display. Playing it safe, Carson opted for clamoring inside the box. Whether it was by sight, smell, or the sound of the calf's bellow, somehow the mothers mysteriously beelined it to their own offspring.

Nuzzling its calf, a cow turned dark eyes on her audience, as if daring them to pull such a kidnapping stunt again. Her calf quickly found its mother's udder, pulling greedily on the teats.

"Hey, Carson, how about a glass of warm milk for lunch?" Rae smiled at the youngster propped up on the spare tire.

"Only if it's chocolate," Carson declared.

Ned joined the exchange. "Chocolate? Then you need to get your milkshake from one of those black bossies. The white Charolais are the only ones with white milk."

His matter-of-fact tone confused Carson. He looked to Joel for confirmation. "Is Ned right? Do the black cows have chocolate milk?"

"Since Ned seems to be the authority on milk production, why don't you give him the pail, holding those tools at your feet, and we'll let Ned go milk one of those black cows for us. If it's chocolate, we'll all enjoy a chocolate shake. If it's white, we dump the pail of milk over Ned's head. All in favor, raise your hand."

Joel and Rae shot their hands into the air. Following their lead, Carson waved his fingers above his head too. "Three to one. You're on, Ned." Rae conspiringly leaned over the side of the pickup box to confiscate the bucket of tools. Wrenches from the upturned pail lay strewn on the box floor as she thrust the container to his chest.

With his faded farmer's cap in his hands, Ned made a big show of wiping the sweat from his red hair smashed against his forehead. "I was afraid if we used the democratic process it would come to this. You win." He fitted his cap back on his head and held up both hands, palms out, in front of him. "I surrender."

Playfully Rae punched him, pulling one of Ned's hands down. "Repeat after me, 'I, Ned Schultz, do solemnly swear to buy the persons assembled in this pasture a chocolate shake the next time we're in town.'" A round of "Hurrahs!" exploded, startling the nearest cattle.

Winking at Carson, Ned confided, "Carson, never get yourself a girlfriend. Girls are a pain in the butt."

But Carson was thinking about the promised chocolate shake.

CHAPTER 4

The honeymoon was over.

Initially, foster parents often experience a honeymoon period when a new child is placed in their care. That is, all the negative behaviors documented in previous homes and schools seem to evaporate or are so subtle they aren't an issue. It is an easing-in time; the child is discovering what the foster parents are like and their expectations, and the guardians are learning the uniqueness of the youngster.

Change can be beneficial for a child, especially when pulled out of a life of turmoil, but it also holds some trepidation. Having left the familiar and moved into the unknown, the youngster hasn't sensitized exactly what he can or cannot do in the new home. Although the boundaries are stated, how rigid are they? Does one get in trouble for the first offense? How stiff are the consequences? He feels no closeness to the adults he has been assigned. As days and weeks pass, both the child and the parents become more comfortable with each other, and the suppressed behaviors begin to leak out. The days, weeks, and months following the honeymoon are the true test of the relationship.

And the honeymoon was over for Joel and Carson. Joel knew exactly when it ended: thirty-six days after Meagan had deposited him on the Linton farmstead. Even though Joel had encountered this orientation before, its arrival still staggered him.

Heavy, dark clouds had rolled in at sunrise, threatening rain. North Dakota farmers are habitually on the begging end when it comes to moisture, wanting more to make their crops flourish, to boost the pasture growth.

Even so, Joel had some pending chores to tend to before the rain hit. The crib feeder out in the pasture needed to be filled with a mixture of ground corn and oats for the growing calves. An electric fence kept the cattle contained in the pasture acreage, giving a straying cow a shock if she touched the electrified wire. At twilight the evening before, Joel had used a handheld fence tester to determine the voltage the fence was putting out. It was precariously low. This morning, he needed to follow the fence line and find the cause. Sometimes a deer was the culprit, jumping through the fence and tangling the wire. Other times, it was too many weeds touching the wire. If the cattle discovered their barrier was disarmed, he'd be rounding up cattle all over the county.

"Come on, Carson, eat up. We have to get moving." Carson's toast still lay untouched on his plate. Preoccupied with blowing bubbles into his milk through a curvy straw, the child ignored Joel's prompting.

Joel began cleaning off the table, returning the milk carton to the refrigerator and the sugar bowl and cereal box to the cupboard. With a wrung-out dishcloth, he wiped away the crumbs, picking up the glass Carson was still attending.

"Hey, I'm not done with my milk."

"I know. I'm wiping the table off underneath it. Eat your toast. We gotta go. If we don't get out to the pasture and get the feeder filled before it rains, the feed will turn gummy." A roof on the feeder protected the ground feed once it was augured into the storage bin.

"I don't want any toast." Carson resumed blowing milk bubbles when Joel set the glass back in front of him.

The rancher could feel impatience rising within him. "Fine, get your hooded sweatshirt and tennis shoes on."

"No, I'm not going. I want to play with my toys," Carson declared, not budging from his chair.

"Okay, I'll drop you off at Arlene's and pick you up when I'm done." Joel was tugging on his own leather work shoes. "Let's go."

"No! I'm staying home!" The tone of the child's pitch stopped Joel in mid-action of tying his shoe. Never before had Carson refused a request. Granted, sometimes he was pokey and distracted, but not once had he ever dug in his feet like a stubborn mule and emphatically held his ground.

Pulling the reins on his own irritation, the man tried to be reasonable. "You're right. You do need some play time. When the rain hits, we'll delve into your toy box."

Plucked off his chair by the older man, Carson squirmed and wriggled out from Joel's hold. When his feet touched the floor, he spun into action, streaking across the linoleum floor, knocking his chair over in the wake. Like a torpedo, he charged through the dining room, grabbing the pile of newspapers sitting on the round oak table, scattering them helter-skelter, veiling the hardwood flooring. Photographs of Melissa from the center of the table followed. Racing pell-mell into the living room, he dove onto the sofa, whipping the decorative pillows aloft. Tumbling off the couch, the blond whirlwind bumped the rocking chair against the end table, sending the TV remote and the contents of a candy dish over the gray carpet.

Next he seized the Bible storybook Joel read to him nightly and spun it across the room. All the while, a wailing scream howled from his throat, like a mournful coyote crying for its mate. The magazine rack was flipped on its side as he hurled the farm periodicals to the ceiling high over his head, ripping the pages to shreds.

Shocked at the whirling human tornado destroying the room in a matter of seconds, Joel froze, his jaw dropping in disbelief. When Carson torpedoed toward the glass cupboard holding Melissa's antique dishes, Joel plunged in to stop him, sandwiching the boy's back against his broad chest, clasping the rascal tightly in his arms.

Carson hit and kicked like a wild bobcat, his thin body writhing, alternating humping his back or projecting his stomach. His heels pounded backward into his captor's knees. Outmatching him in strength, Joel managed to pin his flailing arms to his body in a bearlike hug. Hissing and snarling, the child bit at the man's hairy forearms, scratching jagged trails down the darkly-tanned skin.

Foster care parents are certified in crisis intervention and take a refresher course annually. Practicing in a staged setting with other parents was no match for a real-life situation when being fought tooth and nail by a struggling tiger.

Accustomed to hard physical work, Joel had a physique of steel in comparison to the frail child. He held the struggling bear cub, amazed at the brawn the angry youngster exhibited. Joel's arms were a ring of iron until the fight drew to completion. Joel could feel the battle leaving the youngster, his energy spent, his body growing limp.

Throughout the wild frenzy, the youngster had remained dry-eyed. However, he now literally collapsed in the man's embrace. The energy he had spent in his reckless tantrum dissolved into a torrent of tears cascading down his cheeks, dripping off his chin. Joel tugged his handkerchief loose from his back pocket and gently turned the sobbing child around in his arms. He sopped up the tears as they spewed like twin geysers. He carried the distressed child to his overstuffed chair and lowered the two of them into it.

Joel was troubled. Somewhere Carson had witnessed uncontrolled rage, maybe numerous times. He wondered if the person had ever turned his anger on this frail child—if Carson had been the target of the fury. The big man wished he could erase the splinters in his little friend's memory closet.

Minutes earlier, Joel had been frustrated by his inability to accomplish his agenda because of Carson's slow-paced breakfast ritual. Now his impatience was replaced by a protectiveness, a desire to shield the tyke from all the mean people in the world, particularly those in his past.

Patting the weeping youngster soothingly, Joel waited as the sobs lessened. Tear droplets clung to the light-colored eyelashes like a spider's web stretched across the wet blades of grass after a morning dew.

Encasing the runny nose with his man-sized handkerchief, he ordered, "Blow." Carson blew, then sucked in a trembling breath of air through his nose.

Lying back on the strong arm holding him, he looked up into Joel's gray eyes. Staring intently, he studied the eyes and creases surrounding them. The boy softly brought his index finger up to Joel's right eye, tracing his cheekbone below it. Silently, the man endured the examination, the boy's own clear-blue eyes mesmerizing his. The little boy lips quivered as if to speak, but instead, his finger moved to Joel's left eye, tentatively etching its outline.

Love billowed within the farmer. His wee friend had only shared his dwelling for a little over a month, and yet in the short space of time, he had captured what was left of Joel's heart.

Joel missed Melissa desperately. Her parting had torn chunks out of his heart, never to be whole again. Lodged within him was a terrible ache, a daily reminder of all he had lost two years ago. But with Carson's appearance, the edges of the ache had been sanded off; laughter had returned to reverberate through the house, the deathly stillness pushed back. Even today's unexplained outburst, the animal-like whining, the deep, guttural wailing, was better than silence. Silence was too overpowering, too loud. How does one converse with something that never talks back, never makes a sound, yet is always there, its presence weighing heavily?

Carson's finger had moved to Joel's prickly chin. In his haste to get some chores done before a possible morning downpour, the farmer hadn't taken time to shave. The finger then traveled to the hewn lips, pausing at the cleft below the nose. Carson's eyes displayed no timidity as his lone finger road mapped the darkly-tanned face. The fingertip returned to Joel's left eye. When the eyelid blinked, eyelashes faintly brushed against the satiny finger. Joel blinked several times in succession, tickling the sensitive skin of the youth's index finger.

"How do you get that glitter in your eyes?" Carson asked, breaking the spell.

Joel's smile widened. "I think you glued it there."

"No, only God can do that."

After folding the child into one more hug to paint the finishing touches onto this memory, Joel loosened his grip and set the child erect on his knee.

Surveying the disarray of the room before them, Joel sent out a feeler. "So...uh...can you tell me what this is all about?"

The previous rascal sat stone still. Did he too wonder what was going on inside of him?

"Is there a reason you don't want to go out to the pasture? Are you scared of something out there?"

The unyielding youth shook his head.

"Come on, bud, talk to me. I'll listen," Joel prodded, bumping a finger down the boy's spine.

Looking down at Joel's big work shoe, Carson stammered, "I—I just wanted to work on *my* farm today." His fist swiped at an errant tear.

"My farm is your farm; you know that." Joel's hand worked its way back up to the slight shoulders.

Flipping his yellow head around to find Joel's eyes, he reiterated, "No, *my* farm is up in my room. I have fields and hay bales and a pasture for *my* cows." The boy's blue eyes were resolute before the eyelids hid them and his head twisted the other way.

Joel understood then. Each evening, Carson lay on his bedroom floor surrounded by the farm he had built from the blocks and fences in his toy chest. He had created a barnyard of plastic chickens, pigs, and cows. There were even a couple of horses and a bull with a broken leg. The braided rug had become his imaginary wheat and cornfields, seeded with the red Case International tractor and an eight-row planter. The harvest machinery along with a semi-truck was lined up under his window.

"Mmm, I see. You spend so much time helping me do my work that you don't have enough time to do yours. Is that it?"

Carson's head bent in assent. "How come we always have to play what you want instead of what I want to play?" He twisted his torso to look at Joel.

"Guess I've been rather selfish. I'm sorry. Can you forgive me, partner?" The man was humbled, being taught such a basic concept by a mere kid—something he'd learned way back when he was in school but had somehow forgotten: take turns, don't always be the boss, or the other children won't want to play.

Carson flung his arms up and circled Joel's neck, initiating a hug. "Sure, Joel. You're my best bud."

"Thanks, buddy. I love you."

"Me too."

"Then we'd better hightail it upstairs and see what needs to be done on your farm." Joel pushed Carson off his lap and stood up.

"First, we have to feed *your* calves and make the fence work right." Carson scurried to the kitchen, grappling for his sweatshirt from an overhead row of hooks.

Confused, the older man called, "I thought you needed some chores done on *your* farm?"

"Yup, as soon as we get back from the pasture." Carson was out the front door, leaving his guardian shaking his head.

The eave troughs caught the summer rain drumming on the roof, pouring it onto the lawn at the four corners of the house. Water droplets cascaded down the bedroom windows.

With all the cultivating, planting, and spraying a farmer did in anticipation of a bountiful crop in the fall, his hands were tied when it came to rain. Moisture at the right time was a blessing from above.

Joel was totally at ease, thankful for the precipitation seeping into his land, nourishing his crops. Sprawled out on the circular rug in Carson's bedroom, he steered a toy tractor towing a hay baler over the braided ridges of the rug. Round plastic bales ejected from the toy machine every couple of feet. "How am I doing, boss?" he addressed the pint-sized farmer.

"Good. When you're done with that field, you can use the flatbed trailer to load the bales and bring them home," Carson instructed, lowering his voice to imitate a man's, busying himself auguring popcorn kernels into a truck.

Dutifully, Joel sputtered a motor sound from between his lips, advancing the tractor and baler across the rug.

Putting a toy cell phone to his ear, Carson ordered in his best bass voice, "Joel, I need you to come home right now. The auger quit. I need your help to fix it."

"Be right there, boss." Joel tottered his tractor toward Carson and parked it. "What seems to be the trouble?"

"The auger is plugged."

Joel picked up the auger and gave the long tube a couple of taps on the side dislodging the popcorn kernels. Once again, the seeds traveled up the cylinder as Carson turned the crank.

"Do you think I should start stacking the bales now?" Joel asked.

"Yup. You've rolled up enough hay for today." Carson had heard Joel refer to the bales he made on his hay land as "rolling them up."

Joel made a big show of backing the baler into line with the rest of Carson's implements below the window. After pulling a metal pin in the hitch to unhook the baler, he puttered the tractor over to the flatbed trailer, backed up to it, and hooked it to his tractor.

Lumbering back over the dips in the braiding, he paused at each bale, hoisting it onto the trailer until the round plastic bales balanced a foot above the trailer.

Carson gruffly cautioned him, "That's a pretty high load. Be careful on the corners."

"Will do, boss." Joel inched his load to the barn, amused at the copycat performance Carson was dramatizing, recognizing many of the expressions as his own. Bringing the trailer to a halt beside the barn, he restacked the hay bales on the floor.

"What are you going to do with your truck full of corn?" Joel asked, puttering the tractor back to the field for a second load of hay bales.

"I have to go to the pasture to fill the crib feeder for the calves." Carson had mimicked what Joel had told him earlier that morning.

"What should I do when I'm done with these bales?" Not used to lowering his big frame to the floor, Joel's muscles and joints were objecting to such treatment, especially the elbow taking most of his weight.

"It will be quitting time soon. Park the trailer beside the rest of the machinery."

Joel was playing the part of a hired hand well, following every instruction he was given. Carson's truck disappeared under the bed; the bottoms of his stocking feet followed it. When it reappeared, the truck box was empty. Evidently, he'd filled the calves' feeder. Joel didn't bother to ask about the pile of corn kernels under the bed.

"Quitting time," Carson announced. "We'll go down to the kitchen and see what the cook baked us."

"Hallelujah, I'm starving!" Joel used the windowsill for leverage, dragging his numb limbs to a stance. *What the cook baked us.* He was 100 percent sure the oven was empty, but he'd whip up some grub. At least the "boss" wasn't a fussy eater.

Joel came to a standstill on the bottom step, his surveillance of the living room refreshing the incident of the morning.

Lowering himself to the boy's level, his rump finding a step to hold him, he spoke to the youngster.

"You were really mad today. Sometimes I get mad too." His arms rested on his knees.

"You do?" Carson's voice held a hint of unbelief. He hadn't ever heard the larger man raise his voice in anger.

"Yes, I do. Like when the deer messed up the fence and we had to put it back up."

"I didn't hear you yell." The boss was becoming a six-year-old boy again.

"Even though I didn't yell and swear, I was frustrated in here." Joel thumped his sternum. "It's okay to get mad—even Jesus got angry—but we can't let those mad feelings talk us into doing something bad."

Carson listened but didn't reply, biting the side of his lip, his hand still on the stair railing.

"What if the two of us had gotten so angry at the deer,"—Joel rolled his hands into two fists—"that we took hold of the wire fencing and tugged and twisted it all over the place? Then what would have happened?" He paused, hoping Carson would supply the answer he was seeking.

"We would have gotten a shock because the fence is hot," Carson said solemnly. Inwardly, Joel smiled. It wasn't the reply he had anticipated, but it was certainly true. This little guy was sharp!

"Yes, and we would have made even more work for ourselves, having to fix a whole lot more fence than what the deer went through."

The boy nodded, busily rubbing the banister.

"Next time you feel anger building inside of you, stop and think: what should I do to get rid of my bad temper? One of the best ways is to talk to someone about what is bothering you. Anyone you think you could talk to?"

Gazing up at the ceiling as if giving the question serious thought, Carson finally decided, "Arlene."

"She'd be good," Joel agreed. "Anyone else?"

"You?"

"I'd like that. I'd like to think of the two of us as friends. Friends help each other with problems." Joel stuck out his right hand, attempting to close the discussion the way two men would.

Comprehension showing in his eyes, Carson shook Joel's hand. "Okay. Can we eat now? We should have packed a lunch-box when we went upstairs to farm."

Chuckling, Joel messed up the youngster's golden hair with his coarse hand. "You see what you can do about cleaning up this mess, and I'll check on the cook in the kitchen."

Sunday was the annual church picnic, held in Elton's city park. Pastor Lance conducted the morning worship service under a canopy of birch trees, the customary wooden pews replaced by lawn chairs and blankets spread over the patchy ground blotted with grass and sand.

Joel had taken Carson to the weekly service at the church each Sunday since his relocation in May, initiating him into the Sunday school class for five- and six-year-olds. Intimidated by the new faces and surroundings on the first Sunday, Carson had kept his hand embedded in Joel's bigger hold when introduced to his teacher, Mrs. Saar. She tried to put her newest student at ease with her friendliness. Nonetheless, when Joel tried to leave the small classroom to attend the adult study group, Carson stuck to him like scotch-tape, refusing to be left behind. Finally, Joel had squeezed his body into one of the primary chairs and listened to the story about the lost sheep Mrs. Saar had prepared.

"A shepherd had one hundred lambs. When night descended, he called them to bed down in the barn. As they entered the sheepfold, the herder counted them: one, two, three, four, five, six … ninety-six, ninety-seven, ninety-eight, ninety-nine … ninety-nine …

ninety-nine? One was missing! What did the shepherd do? Did he say, 'Well, at least I have most of them. Only one is gone. I don't need that sheep.' No, the kind shepherd went looking for his lost lamb and didn't give up until he found him. Jesus is our shepherd. He doesn't want anyone to be lost. He wants us all to be safely with him in heaven."

Mrs. Saar had her class of five students act out the story while she narrated it. Joel was appointed the lead role of shepherd for the five lambs. Each child had a chance to be the lost sheep that shepherd Joel had to search diligently to find. Eagerly, the children stretched their hands high in the air, wanting to be the next one chosen to be lost—except Carson. He had no intention of being lost. He wasn't about to let Joel out of his sight.

During the church service following the Sunday school hour, Carson had sat stoically planted beside the farmer in the pew. Even when Pastor Lance invited the congregation to turn and greet their neighbors, he remained still as a frozen ice cube, staring straight through the people attempting to shake his hand or coax a smile from his lips. On the succeeding Sundays, he had loosened up one notch, at least allowing the ice to thaw from his cold stare.

Now five weeks later, the transformation in Carson's behavior had turned 360 degrees. Everything in the park was a distraction: the traffic flowing by on the highway adjacent to the park, the squirrel scampering along the edge of the three-sided picnic shelter, the barn swallow mud nests stuck to the rafters, the breeze rippling the song sheets held by the parishioners. Using the chair as a merry-go-round, he checked out action on all sides.

Leaning over, his lips touching the wiggle-worm's ear, Joel instructed in a whisper, "Turn and sit straight on the chair. Listen to what the pastor is saying."

Carson obliged, tucking his hands under his knees on the front edge of the metal seat, swinging his lower legs back and forth. Tiring of the sport, he pushed his weight against the back of the seat, elevating the front chair legs. Catching hold of Joel's arm, he balanced on the two back legs, mightily pleased with his acrobatic stunt. Joel firmly placed a heavy hand on the seat, pushing the front legs forward to the ground. The boy, smirking, angled a look up at the older man. Silently, Joel shook his head no, ever so slightly. For a minute, Carson sat properly, leaning his elbows on his thighs, resting his chin in his hands.

Pastor Lance was comparing the life they lived in Elton to the words of God in Deuteronomy.

> For the LORD your God is bringing you into a good land—a land with streams and pools of water, with springs flowing in the valleys and hills, a land with wheat and barley...
>
> Deuteronomy 8:7–8 (NIV)

"All of us have been given comfortable homes to live in. Some of you have been given businesses to operate for the LORD. And those of you who farm the land have indeed been entrusted with a great treasure."

There it was again—the reminder of God's goodness. Closing his eyes for a second, Joel felt washed in blessings. He loved his farm, his neighbors, and now little Carson. Yes, life had dealt him some blows; however, God had promised to be with him through all tribulation.

Movement at his elbow suggested Carson's angelic moments had passed. Bending over at the waist, he lay with his chest on his lap. Reaching down, he yanked handfuls of grass from the tufts growing at his feet. A quick toss sent a spray of green blades floating in the breeze to land on the shoulders of the people sitting nearby.

Brushing the stems off his shirtsleeve, Joel felt irritation prickling within. Drawing an arm about Carson's lean form, he slid him against his side, keeping the squirmy body captivated for the remaining minutes of the sermon. Carson's behavior broke his concentration, making him grateful the pastor wouldn't be distributing a quiz after the last amen.

While standing with the rest of the congregation for the final hymn, Carson's view was blocked by the crowd surrounding him, especially the towering figure of Bill Vance directly in front of him. Boosting himself up six inches on the back rung of Bill's chair, he was oblivious to the words of the song, except that they signaled the end of the service. Play time was moments away.

His neck stretched, his eyes hunting for the boys and girls he'd met in Sunday school. He couldn't really call any of them his friends, having only spent five weekly class periods with them, and yet kids meant action. His toe thumped on the chair rung; his fingers drummed on the chair back. His head checked out every opening in the human wall to glimpse the park's playground equipment.

Joel could see the excitement mounting within his little friend. Placement of his hand on the bony shoulder was twofold: one for the acceptance and love he felt for this child estranged from his own family, the other to make sure he didn't bolt before the concluding notes.

This sudden change in Carson's behavior bothered him. Yes, he had witnessed the metamorphism in prior foster children—the initial tranquility when he and Melissa had wondered how a child yanked from his own home and placed in foster care could display such docile temperament. Then the dam would break, spewing forth hostility and resistance. Lying, stealing, aggressiveness, defying authority, self-mutilation—they'd seen it all.

Contrary to all he'd learned from past placements, Joel thought his relationship with Carson was distinctive. A bond had welded the two of them together almost instantly, the boy trusting him blindly, latching on with no letting go—and he, a grown man with no children of his own, thought he'd found the missing puzzle piece to his life. Based on mere inner emotions, he perceived he knew more than all the child experts. Meagan hadn't been snowed under like he had. She kept her sentiments in check, using knowledge to guide her decisions, not using children to fill her own personal shortcomings.

The last note of an a cappella harmony resounded, bringing the outdoor service to a conclusion. "It's over," Carson shouted, bringing a chuckle from the gathering. Joel winced at his boisterous outburst, nevertheless reminding himself what treachery an hour of quiet time was to a child when the swings and tunnel slide beckoned to him from where he had been corralled. Carson was just a normal kid.

A tug on his arm brought him out of his reverie. "Joel, look. Sam and Eric are up in the fort. Can I go too?" Without waiting for a reply, Carson raced off, dodging in and around legs and feet to get to his destination.

Bill Vance turned at the boy's inquiry and saw him streak in and out of the twisted rows of lawn chairs. "Can't say I blame him. At what age did we trade climbing the monkey bars for sitting at a picnic table? Watching those boys shimmy up that ladder looks like pure work to me." Joel grunted his agreement even though the retired insurance agent had years on him.

Barely reaching the base of the rope ladder, Carson ground to a halt. Sticking a hand in his front pocket, he watched as a swarm of children slid a downward course on the fireman's pole attached to the fort before chasing one another to the monkey bars. Carson remained rooted to the ground.

Three of the park's picnic tables were being aligned to use as a buffet line for all the potluck dishes materializing from car trunks and Styrofoam coolers.

Sheepishly, Joel added his contributions to the country feast: a bag of potato chips and a couple of two-liter bottles of soda. He wasn't even going to attempt vying his culinary skills against the experienced chefs of the county.

Seven-year-old Spencer Miller, critiquing the laden serving tables, noticed the plastic bottles. "I hope you brought root beer, Mr. Linton."

"You can bet on it." Joel winked at the inquisitive redhead. At least if he couldn't cook, he'd done something right.

The clanging of a pot and spoon centered everyone's attention on the noon meal. Two lines formed on each side of the tantalizing cuisine; conversation flowed, sprouted with laughter and goodwill.

Joel sought out Carson by the tunnel slide, beckoning him to join him in the lunch line.

"Not yet, Joel, I'm not hungry." Joel shrugged his shoulders, figuring when his playmates slowed their activity long enough to fill their plates, Carson would likewise. Observing the boy, Joel noticed the boy was content to be a vigil rather than a participant in the play.

Later, while refilling his coffee cup from the oversized coffee urn at the beverage table, Joel met Suzy, Pastor Lance's wife, assisting her toddler in filling her cup with lemonade. "I admire you for taking a child into your home again, Joel. You have all the qualities for being a great father. So many kids these days are lacking a positive male role model."

"Thanks, Suzy, but don't overdo the praise. It wasn't because of my parenting skills that I chose to return to foster care." Black coffee trickled into his cup from the spigot at the base of the pot.

"Oh yeah? So are you telling me it was because you needed another ranch hand?" Her brown eyes jested. She bent down to attend to Erica, who insisted on holding the paper cup by herself.

"Maybe I should have opted for a teenager rather than a six-year-old if that was the case," Joel mused.

"Maybe not. Some teenagers would classify being stuck twenty miles out in the country as cruel and unusual punishment, let alone having to pitch manure out of a barn with you." Erica slurped lemonade while her mother held the cup.

"You might have a point there. Carson pretty much sticks with me, and when he can't, Arlene and Ed help me out. If it wasn't for their willingness, I wouldn't be able to do it." Joel sipped the tepid liquid.

Straightening up, she swung her eyes back on him, resting a hand on her hip. "Give, big man. Why *did* you return to foster care?"

He glanced away. Should he be honest with her or give a generic response? Was selfishness a legitimate reason for foster parenting? Drawing a tired breath, he looked back at her. "Loneliness." There, he had confessed his less than exemplary choice to someone other than himself. Having once been married, he did not cherish the solitariness or freedom of bachelorhood.

By her discerning expression he could tell she understood. "You and Melissa had a special relationship. She would hardly approve of you joining the ranks again."

Both of them caught sight of Carson's surveillance of the gang on the merry-go-round, his head tilted back in laughter.

She reached over and squeezed his arm. "No matter. Carson will benefit exceedingly from the days he spends with you. God bless you both." Turning to retrace Erica's toddling steps, she left Joel with his thoughts—which were perpetually the same: Melissa.

Her facial expressions, her touch, her no-nonsense mannerisms always lingered on the edges of his mind. Sitting on the nightstand was the photograph of her sitting on his lap in the porch swing. Her smile wished him good morning at sunrise and bestowed sweet dreams when he snapped off the lamp at the end of the day. And no matter where he went in the hours in between, she sneaked along, riding at his side in the tractor or the pickup truck, herding or vaccinating cattle, sitting in a pew at church. To others, he seldom talked about Melissa anymore, but her memory was as fresh as yesterday's rainfall.

When he left dirty dishes piled in the kitchen sink or his pants and shirt on the floor where he'd stepped out of them, he mentally apologized to her. When an advertisement for a musical performance in a nearby town was announced, he knew how much Melissa would have loved a date.

Farming decisions he had once discussed with her—should they buy hail insurance on this year's crop? Some of the harvest machinery was becoming old and unreliable. Should they spend the money to replace a piece with a newer model?

He found himself still asking her these questions, only he never received a reply.

Of the two of them, Melissa had the stronger faith, never doubting the LORD's provision to carry them through what life sent their way. When he would wrestle with the rights and wrongs of a situation, she'd always scold, "Give it to the LORD and leave it there." Even after following her advice, he would often pull the problem back into his quarter section and worry about it some more.

And then the medical tests had come back—positive. Cancer. The sound of the word itself had thundered death, a thick, smoldering cloud of doom, a slow, torturous good-bye. Doctors quoted statistics, giving the odds as if playing a game of dice. They praised new breakthroughs in treatments and drugs, building false hope within them.

The first round of treatments left Melissa a pale shell of her former self. Had not the glow in her feeble smile remained, his hope would have been extinguished instantly. She rallied. Each new morning gifted them with another day to love and dream and hope. Her frailty gave way to strength inch by inch, as if each uphill triumph had to be earned. Winter had crept into spring.

One evening, while bringing the air seeder home from the newly-planted wheat field, a continual ticker tape of prayer paraded through his head. The trees by the slough obstructed his view of the house. Turning into the yard at the mailbox bearing his nameplate, he could see her on hands and knees in front of the porch transplanting flowers into the warm soil. A panorama of petunias, tinted in every hue the way her grandmother used to plant her garden, interspersed with dusty millers and bright-red salvia, and tiny white alyssum dotted the embedded border of rocks.

At the sight of her slight form crouched on the ground wearing an old, long-sleeved button-up shirt of his own as a jacket to ward off the cool spring breeze, his heart had soared, ready to believe the proclamation of new life heralded at the Easter service weeks prior.

He had brought the tractor to a standstill, leaving the engine turning over as he jumped off its step, running to her and sweeping her up in a joyous dance. She had flung back her head, chortling at his uncharacteristic jubilation. And when the joviality settled, he'd kissed her warmly and completely folded her in his arms, breathing in the smell of her, feeling the softness of her body.

Releasing his hold, they had knelt side-by-side in the freshly-dug dirt to finish bedding the last of the greenhouse seedlings into her flower garden. Six weeks would pass before he realized that the very flowers he had so gently pushed into the ground, his heart brimming over with the promise of healing and love, were the clusters of blue petals begetting the forget-me-nots.

"Hey, Joel, grab your sidekick and hustle over for the balloon toss." Ned slapped his back as he moved on to encourage others to join the game.

Carson stood alone, an arm wrapped around the fireman's pole, his peers having deserted him for the new attraction.

Two lines of contestants facing each other were forming in the open grassy area in front of the picnic shelter. A clothes basket full of sagging water balloons awaited the annual challenge.

"Come on, Carson, we get to throw water balloons at each other, and if we are good, we won't even get wet!" Carson's face lit up in the excitement of a game he'd never played before. Sam had asked him to be his partner; however, anything new posed a certain amount of anxiety for the child. Even now at Joel's prodding, he shook his head no.

"You'll love it, Carson. The balloons are filled with water. You have to lightly throw the balloon to me so I can catch it. Then I toss it back to you to catch."

"What if I miss?"

"That's the fun part: the balloon breaks, and you get wet!" Joel chuckled. "That's why it is important to be careful." Seeing the consternation mounting up in the youngster's face, Joel quickly affirmed, "Really, Carson, it's fun, even if we do get soaked. It will cool us off!"

Nervously, Carson took his place in line facing Joel. Rae Ann and Ned were in charge of the afternoon activity, handing each pair of contestants a rubbery balloon. Carson's eyes lit up in recognition when Ned handed him a balloon slopping and slipping like a bowl of gelatin not chilled long enough.

"Hey there, Carson. Have you been drinking any chocolate milk lately?" Ned continued down the line handing out the water balloons.

"When I yell, 'throw,' all of you to the right of me will throw your balloons to your partner." Ned was almost yelling already in an attempt to have his voice carry down the lines.

"Throw!"

With both hands Carson lobbed the wobbly balloon over to Joel, who easily captured it. Carson jumped up and down, clapping as if Joel had caught the winning out in the World Series.

"Now, step back one giant step!" Ned ordered.

The contestants complied.

"Okay, Carson." Joel brought the boy's focus back on the catch. "Get your hands ready. I'm going to send you a nice, easy underhand toss."

Carson stood with his feet apart, both hands stretched toward Joel. The older man cast the orange balloon as gently as possible yet still gave it enough momentum to fly it across the intervening space.

Carson was prepared. Although he was not skilled in ball-handling like his peers, he managed to hang on to the juggling balloon, clasping it to his stomach. A look of triumph was written across his freckled face. Joel gave him a thumps-up, when unexpectedly a water balloon torpedoed into him, hitting his knees and drenching his pants legs. He flinched at the impact of the cold liquid. Embarrassed, the teenage girl on the other side of him flung her hands to her mouth, hee-hawing hysterically. "I'm sorry, Mr. Linton. I missed!" Her cheeks flamed red.

Joel winked at her. "That's one of the casualties of this game."

"Are you ready?" Ned shouted. "Take another step backward and throw your balloons again!"

Well aware they couldn't last long as the breadth between them widened, Joel cautioned, "Think before you throw, Carson. Make the balloon go up in the air and over to me."

Carson tried to do his best in replicating Joel's advice. The "go up" part sent the balloon up but not over. Joel dashed into the intervening space, swooping up the balloon inches before it slammed to the ground.

Cheered by spectators, Carson was elated!

Splat, splat. Balloons burst on each side of them, sending screeches into the air as the cold water dumped on participants.

The line had shrunk to half its initial length. Ned's command, "Take a step back!" was met with a groan.

"Now, heave those balloons!" he roared, expecting the end of the game soon.

"Get ready, Carson." Carson nodded.

The jovial crowd set up a chant for the remaining competitors: "Get ready, get set—and next, you'll be wet!"

This time Joel gave the orange glob less altitude in order to heave it across the expanding distance. Its shape stretched as it plummeted, elongating itself. Carson held up his hands, but as the ball of gelatin lobbed closer, he sunk to the ground, crossing his legs. The water balloon slammed right into his lap, miraculously not dumping its contents!

The sidelines roared appreciatively. Carson couldn't have reenacted the catch no matter how long they practiced.

One high school boy purposely drove his water bullet straight at his partner's belly, drenching him in a spray of liquid. The second teenager dove for a leftover balloon in the clothes basket, chasing his friend around the picnic shelter until he could break the balloon on top of his head.

It was wild. No one was surprised. The water balloon toss was always a boisterous event.

Four pairs of opponents remained. Carson's last catch had been pure luck, so when Ned ordered, "Take a step back," defeat was already seared.

Another father must have thought the same. When Ned shouted, "Throw," he took the balloon he was supposed to toss to his son and instead projected it fast and hard at Ned, hitting him on the left shoulder, splattering the frigid water down his side and back. Startled, Ned screeched before heading for the remaining two balloons in the laundry basket. Two teenage girls beat him there, scooping up the rubber torpedoes and flinging them back at him. Dodging the first one, he took the second blast high on the thigh.

In the reckless turn of events, Carson too forgot about tossing the balloon back to Joel. Instead, he beelined it for Ned.

Ned saw the miniature quarterback targeting him. He grabbed the boy by his forearms, lifting him off his feet, the balloon still held to the boy's chest between them. With a mighty squeeze, he slammed Carson hard against his own chest. The water balloon burst, soaking the fronts of both of them. Carson's eyes widened when the chilly water washed over his tummy. Then the giggles tumbled out of him, bubbling up into guffaws of comical squealing.

CHAPTER 5

"Make hay while the sun shines." An old farmer's proverb summed up the month of July.

Cattle grazing in pastures required less care by the ranchers during the summer months—providing there was adequate vegetation, the water holes didn't become stagnant, and the critters were content chewing their cud and swishing the flies off their backs with their long tails.

It was a workable exchange, for July was set aside by ranchers for making hay—hay to feed the animals over the winter when the cattle would be brought home, close to barns and windbreaks. Blizzards and subzero temperatures discouraged ranchers from leaving herds far from the ranch without adequate protection.

Over a lunch of chicken noodle soup and toasted cheese sandwiches, Joel was met with resistance when explaining the afternoon's agenda to Carson, who'd be spending the greater share of the afternoon and evening with Arlene.

Joel used a double mower to cut the tall grass and clover that would then be left to dry before being raked and rolled into twelve-hundred-pound round bales. He would be using his older Oliver tractor to propel the mower, the only tractor he owned without an enclosed cab to protect the operator. Bumping over the rough terrain of hay fields with a child on board was far too dangerous on an open tractor. A wheel jolting into a badger hole or rocking over the helter-skelter dirt mounds formed by the excavation of moles could easily result in a deadly accident. A youngster jarred from his seat would fall either in front or behind the rear tractor tire, making him a sitting duck for the razor sharp mower knives. No, Joel would not place Carson in jeopardy.

"But I want to go with you!" Tears welled up in the blue eyes.

Joel was firm. "I've already explained to you why it is not safe when I'm mowing hay. I don't want you to get hurt."

Carson gripped the edges of the table, leaning toward the man. "Please. I won't fall off; I'll hang on tight."

"No, buddy. I just can't chance it." After grabbing his cap and water jug from the stool beside him, he pushed back his chair and stood up, ending the discussion.

"Come on, champ." Taking the youngster by the hand, he led him through the porch door to his pickup truck.

The arrangement with Arlene was ideal. The Bautz farmstead was close by and the housewife incredibly flexible. Whether Joel sought her assistance early or late, one day a week or five in succession, she always warmly received the mite, as if his visit was exactly what she had been waiting for. In her late sixties, Arlene embodied enough energy to keep up with a six-year-old and had a lifetime of wisdom to nurture an orphan.

Invariably, Carson would have a new snippet of knowledge to share with Joel after spending a morning or afternoon with the grandmotherly sitter.

"It's gonna rain soon," Carson reported one evening.

"Oh yeah? How do you know?" Joel asked, heading out of the Bautz yard, cueing in on the western sky.

"Don't you see those tiny black piles of dirt on the road?" Carson pointed through the windshield.

Joel recognized the two-inch dark rings as ant piles scattered across the roadway.

"The ants are building walls so the rain doesn't flood their house."

Joel smiled, speculating whether the information was an old wives' tale or actually had scientific backing.

When they'd passed the slough marking the entrance to the Linton driveway, a mallard duck and its mate had flown off the water, upset they'd been disturbed from their leisurely swim.

"The one with the green head is a daddy. He is a drake," Carson announced.

"You are one smart kid." Joel had given him a thumbs-up affirmation.

"Arlene helped me make a chart for her 'frigerator."

"What's the chart for?"

"Every time I see a new bird, I color in a box."

"That's a good idea. How many boxes have you colored in so far?"

"Eight!"

"Hey, alright! Arlene has turned you into a birdwatcher."

"Yup, and guess what I get to do when I have fifteen boxes colored on the chart?" He'd stopped, waiting for the man to guess.

"Let's see." Joel had scratched deep, struggling to come up with a plausible reward.

"Guess!" Carson had repeated.

"Ah, ah…" He came up blank. "You get to have chicken for supper." *Boy, was that dumb. We have chicken often*, he'd thought.

"Nope." Unable to conceal the prize any longer, Carson had blurted, "I get to paint Ed's garden gate all by myself!" His face had beamed from one ear to the other.

"Really?" Joel had been amused but wondered why he hadn't thought of giving Carson realistic rewards. Affirmation didn't always have to be in the form of toys, treats, or entertainment. Acquiring another responsibility was bestowing the gift of trust upon the boy aspiring to be a man.

"Yup, and Ed isn't even going to help me."

Then Carson had asked the million-dollar question: "Joel, if I find five more birds after that, can I paint something on our farm?"

What farmer would refuse an offer like that?

Dropping Carson off at the Bautzes,' Joel had no qualms about Arlene being able to bolster him out of his woefulness. When the man bent down to plant a kiss on the boy's temple, Carson reached up, encircling Joel's neck with his scrawny arms. Tears still hanging close by had leaked out when the heartthrob tried once more to change his hero's mind. "I love you, Joel. Please take me with you."

Rubbing his cheek against the child's smooth skin, Joel gruffly countered, "I love you too, and that is precisely why I can't take you. I'll be back tonight." Straining behind his neck to unlock the tightly-bound fingers, Joel kissed the tip of the freckled nose. "Love you truckloads."

He hopped into his pickup, one elbow sticking out the open window. "Bye, Carson." He waved to the forlorn figure, but Carson didn't even raise a finger.

The tall grass of the hay meadows had to be dry to cut. When the sun fell and evening approached rapidly, the condensation of the cool air on the warm foliage forced the cutting bar to jut back and forth harder. Wisely, Joel decided to quit for the night before he'd have a repair job to perform on the mower. He set out at a stiff jaunt for the pickup parked at the corner of the field, hitting his cap against his thigh to dislodge the day's accumulated grime. The mosquitoes kept pace.

Ed, in his bib coveralls, met Joel at his truck door when he rolled to a stop on the Bautz yard. They exchanged greetings. Glancing furtively toward the house, the elder man leaned into the cab. "The youngin' had rather a tough time today, so I wanted to get to you first."

Joel's ears perked up, seeing the concern embedded into Ed's facial wrinkles. "Is he all right?"

"Oh sure. He's fine. Arlene said he was rather bent out of shape this afternoon, having to stay here and all, not getting to go with you."

"I can't risk taking him on an open tractor when I'm mowing. Too dangerous."

Swiping the back of his hand across his chin to dislodge a mosquito, Ed agreed. "You're right, but you know the boy; he thinks he can do anything you do. The missus tried to amuse him when you left, divert his thoughts from you. He got powerfully mad—she's never seen him like that." Ed's speech was nervous.

"He didn't hurt Arlene, did he?"

"No, no nothing like that. See, she'd been to Elton right early today for groceries. Car's still sitting there where she parked it close to the house to haul the bags in. Arlene always drives the Chevy. Usually it's parked in the garage over yonder." He gestured to the unattached garage on the far side of the driveway.

"When you headed out to the hayfield, he ran over to the car there, madder than a bucking bronco in a rodeo. He started kicking away at the driver's door with everything he had in him, wilder than a badger caught in a trap, she said." Irritated by the the bugs flying about his ears, he waved his hands at his ears. The mosquitoes backed off six inches.

After a yank on the door handle, Joel stepped onto the gravel. "You have a dent in the door?" He walked toward the vehicle.

"There's not enough skin and bones to that little shaver to do any real damage; however, the driver's door is a bit sunken in." Joel could tell the old man hated having to tattle on the tyke. He'd been a father of young boys once too. Disciplining and correcting was part of a parent's duty.

Dusk had laid a blanket over the earth, and yet Joel could easily distinguish the mar in the glossy metal surface.

"How did she get him to stop?"

"She called out sharply to him to knock off the nonsense. Without a word, he dashed into the trees of the windbreak behind the house. He sat behind a tree for a good, long time. She seen him there, but she left him alone till he was good and collected."

Joel breathed out a sigh. "I've seen him angry. He turns into a snarling baby tiger at the snap of a finger. I think he has witnessed someone's fury. I only hope he hasn't felt it. Does he realize what he did to your car door?"

"Yup, Arlene said much later he was outside by himself. She could see him through the kitchen window. He knelt down by the car and softly rubbed his hand over the dent. Then he went and got a rag wet by the garden hose. He tried to wash it away." The buzzing mosquitoes were out for blood. "Come on, let's get in the house before they carry us away."

Joel agreed, clamping an arm on the old farmer's back. "Thanks for telling me, Ed. You get your car to a body man, and I'll pay the deductible on the insurance." The screen door banged shut behind the two men.

The sound brought the scurrying steps of Carson from the living room. "Did you cut all the grass?" he asked, throwing his arms around Joel's middle.

"Not all. The air got too damp." He tousled the blond hair.

"If you have to go again tomorrow, I'll stay here. Can I bring my baler along?"

Joel's eyes connected with Arlene's and Ed's above his head. "You won't mind?"

Pushing his chin up to let his eyes travel up to Joel's face, Carson answered the question meant for the farm couple. "Well, I do like to farm with you, but I don't want you to worry about me getting hurt."

"Thanks, bud. I missed you a whole bunch." He hugged the child. "We have to see if Arlene and Ed want you tomorrow. They could be busy." He wasn't merely asking permission for another day of babysitting. In addition, he was releasing them from their commitment to tend to the boy if they now had second thoughts about being able to handle him.

Arlene moved in, adding her hand to Carson's shoulder. "I always love having Carson here to help me. He is good company when Ed is gone."

On the ride home and later while Joel devoured a frozen pizza he'd baked in the oven, Carson was his old self. Refusing a slice of pepperoni pizza, he said he'd eaten supper with Ed and Arlene.

His stick horse cantered and whinnied through the dining room, encircling the kitchen table. His cowboy hat clamped to his head; Carson reined Black Beauty in at Joel's elbow. "I forgot. I don't want any pizza, but Black Beauty is hungry."

"Sorry, buster." Joel stuck his index finger into the horse's muzzle. "The pizza is mine."

Carson made the horse bob its head as if it understood, and then the two of them galloped away.

Joel waited until bedtime to broach the reprimand he knew he had to deliver. Blue eyes followed him as he entered the child's room. Carson and Rabbit were already in bed, the top quilt pulled up to their chins. For lack of a better name, the much loved stuffy had simply been christened "Rabbit."

Joel never tired of looking in Carson's sky-blue eyes. They were startling, vivid, but tonight, the sparkles were dancing a full country polka, proof the rascal was up to something. "Hmm. Tucked yourself in tonight, I see."

"Yessiree." Carson giggled, lying motionless.

"What's up?" Joel inquired, one eyebrow forming a question mark.

"Nothing." His tittering rose a few notes on the scale.

Lowering himself to the edge of Carson's bed, as was his custom each night, Joel's buttocks met resistance. "Hmm. What in the world?" The bed was hard where it should have been a soft, squishy mattress.

After regaining his stance, the farmer bent and plucked the quilt back from the whippersnapper's comical face.

Black Beauty was nestled under Carson's arm, his sturdy, wooden stick protruding from his stuffed head.

"To the barn, Black Beauty," Joel firmly ordered, lifting the stick horse by its halter. He trotted the steed to the door, looping his rein about the knob. "No horses allowed in bed."

Carson shrieked, believing he had played the best trick ever on his friend.

When the joke had played its course, the father figure got serious. "Carson, do you recall last week when anger got the best of you and you let a wild bull loose in the living room?"

Smirking, Carson blinked in agreement.

"When we talked about it man-to-man, do you remember what I suggested you might do when you feel yourself beginning to boil inside?"

Carson was attentive. "Yes, you said I could talk to someone."

"That I did. After lunch today, you weren't very happy about not being able to go out in the field with me. Were you mad?" Joel watched the changing scenes slide over the pale face.

The youngster fiddled with Rabbit's paw.

"Did you find someone you could confide in so you wouldn't do anything you'd be sorry about later?" Figuring he knew the boy's answer, he mentally started rehearsing his lecture.

"Yup, I did just what you said."

"You did?" Surprised at his answer, Joel followed it with another question. "Who?" Joel had the sensation he was losing the upper hand in the conversation.

"I was mad right in here." Carson patted his chest. "I ran behind Arlene's house and sat behind a tall tree and talked to God. In Sunday school, Mrs. Saar told us God is never too busy to listen to our prayers. I talked to him the way you talk to him."

A taste of ineptness had laid a sour bite in Joel's mouth, knowing it was his responsibility to guide his charge through this bump in his character. Frustration and anxiety building within the foster parent ever since Ed's report suddenly gushed from him as if a suction hose was sucking the tension from his forehead, the tightness from his muscles. Why hadn't he prayed about it? Carson had more sense than he did. Joel could almost hear Melissa chiding him.

"And what did God say?" The firmness had evaporated from his voice.

"He was glad I talked to him before smashing the windows out on Arlene's car." Carson's countenance was dead serious.

It took all the strength within the man's muscular chest to subdue a howl of mirth from ruining this teachable moment as he hightailed it out of the room.

Had Joel been able to read the thoughts invading the small mite's dreams as sleep stole over him next door, the farmer wouldn't have been laughing.

In the back closets of the drowsy child, a familiar but unwanted figure appeared. He'd seen him before. Distorted in anger, the man's face was an ugly red. He was mad at the mommy. The furious man lifted a big, heavy hammer over his head, banging it down on top of the car hood over and over and over. Frightened, the little boy crawled into a wheel barrel in the back of the garage to hide, clapping his hands tightly over his ears, futilely trying to block out the piercing whacks. His mommy was shrieking, "I'm sorry; I'm sorry. I didn't mean to leave the bag of groceries in the car." In his nightmare, the boy could see the decaying hamburger package. Long, white, squiggly worms wriggled beneath the plastic wrap. It made him gag.

Haying season continued. Mowing days found Carson at the Bautzes,' fetching eggs, picking beans in the garden, pedaling an old toy tractor the Bautz children played with when they were young, and generally following Arlene about her daily work.

But whenever Joel allowed it, the budding farmer occupied the tractor cab with the man he worshiped, patterning himself as closely as possible in attire, mannerisms, and the farming lingo of his hero.

He was keenly observant when the wheel rake's iron fingers swiftly swept the cut grass into long, neat coils of hay snaking over the meadow. Finishing up the raking of a hay meadow, Joel would switch machines, drawing the hay baler behind his tractor next. Rubber teeth ate up the twisting windrows, packing the coarse hay tightly into giant, round bales. When the baler was packed solid, Joel would come to a halt, the tractor engine idling, while the baler wound twine around the hay bale holding it secure. Once the tying was complete, the back end opened, pushing the bale out onto the ground. Then forward they'd creep again, the baler devouring the loose hay lying in its path.

After cutting and baling the lowlands and ditches of his property conducive for haying, Joel moved his equipment to the rolling sixty-acre plot of wildlife land he'd rented from the government. Likewise, the Schultzes, Ned and his father, Clem, had rented a seventy-five acre chunk cattycorner from his piece. Over a cup of coffee at the local grain elevator earlier in the week, the three had agreed to combine forces in mowing, raking, and baling the two plots.

Although Carson missed out on the mowing aspect of the job, he loved the hours in the field he spent raking and baling with the guys—and an occasional female when Rae would show up to drive another rake. Then there was action on every side of him: two rakes whirling the dried mixture of grasses, reeds, and clover into neat windrows. Clipping along at their heels were Joel and Clem Schultz feeding the twin balers as fast as the machines could inhale the pungent, withered stalks.

His red hat brim cocked to one side, the way he'd seen Ned wear his cap, Carson attempted to count the number of bales scattered over the shifting landscape from his perch on the buddy seat in the cab. However, before he could put a number on each bale in the circumference of their implement, the tractor would descend a slight incline, obliterating the round forms from sight, while a new set of bales started hugging the stubble. In frustration, he gave up tallying the bales and in its place began waving to Ned, Rae, or Clem when one of them would pass Joel's tractor and baler.

By mid-afternoon, he could see the bottom of their shared lunchbox. "What time will it be when we go home?" Carson asked, rummaging through the empty sandwich bags in the cooler.

"Oh, I suspect nine or ten o'clock tonight. Gotta make hay while the sun shines," he reminded the boy.

"Are you hungry, Joel?" Carson asked, closing the cooler.

"I'd say those sausage sandwiches haven't made their way out of my stomach yet." The farmer's eyes crinkled.

"Mine must move faster than yours," the growing youngster said with a sigh.

About seven o'clock that evening, a wine-colored van parked on the approach at the far end of the government land. "Who's that?" Carson squinted into the windshield's glare.

"Hmm. Guess we'll have to wait and see." Joel stopped the tractor, waiting for another bale to tie.

The straw head never bothered to turn sideways to observe the process. His attention was centered on the van before them. Rae had finished the raking on this side of the field. Her machine was parked near the van. Her lithe figure and bobbing ponytail could be depicted crossing the stubble to visit with the driver of the vehicle.

"Does Rae know who it is?"

"If she didn't, she does now." Joel gave the baler time to eject the bale before moving forward.

Forgetting all about baling, Carson studied the cluster of people and machines forming up ahead. Now Clem's baler had joined the knot. Ned and his rake were hastening to the spot as well.

"Why don't they keep going? We want to get done. I'm getting hungry." Carson shielded his eyes with his hands against the western sun. "Do you think they're quitting and leaving all the rest for us to do? We'll never get done then!"

The formation of each bale brought the twosome closer to the boy's point of intrigue. He could distinguish Ned's quick gait crossing the stubble to the Schultz pickup truck parked fifty yards south of the approach. After Ned disappeared into its cab, the truck began bumping its way toward the assemblage of machinery and van.

"Yup, they're leaving." Disappointment drooped from his prediction. Instead, the truck came to a standstill near the van, Ned reappearing from its interior. Opening the end gate of the pickup box, he lifted out five-gallon pails, setting them on the ground upside down.

The John Deere tractor and baler were now almost upon the assembly, clarifying the scene for the eager youngster. Mrs. Schultz was handing a roaster to her husband. Rae held a pitcher in one hand and a cake pan in the other.

Fog lifted, allowing Carson's comprehension to dawn with it. "We're having a picnic! A picnic in the field!" Carson exclaimed, alert as a puppy wagging its tail at the expectant food scraps being dropped in its feeding dish.

Toting a basket piled with kitchenware, Irene Schultz brought up the rear of the processional headed to the open tailgate.

The moment Joel flicked off the key, Carson flung the tractor door open wide and leaped to the ground, skipping the two iron steps. Sitting back in the padded seat, Joel's lips bent upward at the corners. Having Carson in his care hailed every day as a holiday.

Rubbing the dirt off his hands the best he could, Joel sauntered up to the semicircle hemming the back end of the truck.

Carson was ready to burst. Not only did he get to work with the men, but he was getting in on supper in the field! That was even better than a lunchbox! Growls ebbing from his middle kept him hopping from foot to foot, wanting to delve into Irene's pots.

"What's the matter? You got ants in your pants?" Ned joshed him.

Clem stuck up for the thin boy. "A man's gotta eat when he works."

"Okay, it's ready," Irene declared, opening a final container of buttermilk biscuits.

"I'll pronounce the blessing." Clem removed his hat, unveiling his bald head. Ned and Joel followed suit. Copying the men folk, Carson held his red hat over his midsection, forgetting to close his eyes.

"The hungriest should help themselves first." Irene's eyes swiveled to Carson.

Getting a jumpstart on the lad, Ned rushed to the stack of plates. "That would be me!"

Squeezing his slim form in front of Ned, Carson objected, "That would be me!" Laughter erupted as everyone took their turns filling the plates and then sitting on the overturned pails to feast.

Melted butter dripped from Carson's chin, his two front teeth chiseling into a golden cob. On the pail next to him, Joel was finishing off his second cob of the sweet, succulent corn, a wayward kernel clinging to the side of his cheek. "This is corn heaven," he said, appreciatively smacking his lips together. Whipping the bare cob out into the grass stubble, he took a long drink of cold cider.

"Now you won't have to cook tonight, Carson. It was your turn, wasn't it?" Joel cocked his brow at the boy, who had gnawed a clean swipe encircling the middle of the corncob.

"Nope, it was yours. I don't know how to cook."

Balancing her half-eaten plate on her knees, Rae asked, "Does Joel know how to cook?"

"Yessirree." Carson switched from the corn to the moon-shaped slice of watermelon. "Last night he cooked hot dogs."

Not recognizing why the circle of neighbors found his retort funny, he added a postscript. "Hot dogs are my favorite. Joel makes good pizza too, don't you, Joel?" The remark only added to the banter, but the loyalty of the child warmed a spot within the man.

"So, chef, what is the gourmet's choice of frozen pizza?" Ned teased the older man.

"Doesn't matter. We eat them all, although we are especially partial to the ones on sale," Joel admitted, his eyes twinkling. "By the way, weren't we promised a chocolate shake?"

Ned groaned. "I was hoping you had forgotten."

The easy conversation continued, a light breeze keeping the bugs at bay.

The last crumbs of fudge cake devoured, the men and Rae headed back to their tractors. Joel called to his parting comrades, "If we finish up the wildlife land tomorrow night, supper is on me."

"Oh yeah?" Ned was quick with a comeback. "Will the cuisine be boiled hot dogs or cardboard pizzas?"

Carson yelled out an answer for Joel. "Hot dogs! They're my favorite!"

"We'll be there." Clem chortled, enjoying the youngster amongst them.

Haying went even better than hoped the next day.

Upholding his promise, Joel reminded the Schultzes and Rae they were to be his guests at Naomi's Diner in Elton as soon as everyone could clean up and meet there.

Naomi was heralded throughout an expansive agricultural community for her Friday night buffets. She catered to the hardworking class of people who knew the true essence of physical labor, living by the sweat of the brow. A fancy person's croissants and clam salad might be on her buffet table, but in addition, there'd be a choice of three meats, potatoes, pastas, a full salad bar, homemade breads, and a selection of desserts.

"Doggone it," Ned complained with tongue in cheek. "My mouth has been salivating all day at the thought of a boiled hot dog."

Rae gave him no sympathy. "You can have a whole pack of them if you like, but I'm banking on Naomi's broiled lemon fish with wild rice."

"Fish!" Clem pretended disgust. "Not me. I'm chomping these false teeth into a thick, juicy beef steak."

"I'll put a second on that," Joel agreed. "How about you, partner?" He clasped his large hand on top of Carson's red-billed cap.

Pausing to contemplate an answer, the boy felt all eyes zeroing in on him. "I think I'll be the same as Ned and have hot dogs!" Ned twisted his face into a disfigured ogre, crossing his eyes and hanging his tongue out one side of his mouth.

Laughing, Carson looked up at Ned. "Why do you do that?"

"The thought of the exquisite taste of wieners turns him into a fiendish glutton." Rae knowingly flashed her eyelids.

Naomi's Diner was packed as usual this Friday night. Joel had called ahead to reserve a table, which had proved wise. Their table was the only one empty when the six of them entered.

Naomi greeted the group as a handful of high school helpers bustled about, replenishing empty bowls on the buffet line and removing dirty dishes.

"This must be a celebration to see the Lintons and the Schultzes out for a night on the town." Naomi's hospitality was another reason her restaurant was renowned.

"We've been haying together," Joel responded. "Irene cooked last night, so tonight's my turn."

"I'm not sure I can keep up with Irene's culinary arts, but I guarantee you won't go away hungry. Help yourself whenever you're ready." The gracious hostess moved on to an adjacent table.

Carson wanted to cut into the front of the line, but Joel's hand restrained him. "We are the hosts. Irene, Clem, Rae Ann, and Ned are our guests. Guests go first. Our spot is right behind Ned." Carson obeyed.

Doing an overview of the smorgasbord, Ned gazed down at the handsome kid behind him, his yellow hair neatly combed. "Sorry, champ. No hot dogs," he said, feigning disappointment.

"No hot dogs?" The blond head stretched to see for itself.

"Not a one. Guess we'll have to settle for fried chicken, a tenderloin steak, or a fillet of grilled fish. What will it be?" Flipping a steak onto his own plate and then a thigh of fried chicken, Ned winked. "I couldn't decide."

"Are there Jell-O jigglers?" Carson was on his tiptoes, craning his chin upward to get a clear view of the iced containers under the salad's plastic sneeze guard. Spying the red cherry squares of gelatin, the youngster squealed in delight.

"My sentiments exactly. Since you like them so much, I'm going to leave them all for you, pal." Ned dug a serving spoon into a pasta salad.

Copying Ned's lead, Carson used the cup-shaped spoon to tackle the jigglers. Only one square fell into the scoop. Transferring it to his plate, he then dug the spoon into the bowl again. One more. Patiently, Joel waited while the line ahead of them moved on. After five squares wiggled on his plate, Carson proceeded through the length of the buffet table, giving each dish a once-over before continuing to the next. Seating himself at the table between Ned's and Joel's place, he propped himself up on his knees to gain some height.

"Whoa, Carson! Aren't you going to eat any more than that?" Joel's dinner plate in his right hand was stacked high. A smaller salad plate in the other hand was in danger of dripping a tomato dressing off the side as he carefully set them on his placemat before pulling out his chair.

Nibbling on a Jell-O jiggler, Carson eyed the remaining four squares of gelatin on his plate.

"That's not enough for a farmer like you." Across the table, Clem was lavishly smearing butter on his bread. "A gopher's got you beat."

"This is all I want." Carson folded one leg under his rump.

Rae's eyebrows lifted. "I think someone swiped too many goodies out of everyone's lunch pails this afternoon."

Carson grinned back, using his knife to cut a wobbly cube into quarters.

Conversation turned again to farming and how many days before the first wheat would be ready to harvest. The ripe heads were turning a golden amber.

"Is Ben helping you with harvest again?" Clem asked. Ben Fillmor, a retired farmer, had lent a hand to Joel the last couple of harvest seasons since he no longer had Melissa's assistance during the busiest and most stressful weeks of the farming year.

"He's up in Canada for his annual fishing trip. Should return next week, right on time for harvest," Joel spoke between forkfuls.

Sitting side-by-side, Rae and Irene chatted between the two of them, letting the men indulge in their ongoing subject of agriculture.

Glancing over to Carson's chair, Joel found the chair empty, one lone gelatin cube guarding the place setting. Deep in conversation, he hadn't even noticed the little guy slip out of his seat.

Turning his attention to the buffet table across the room, he expected to see his towheaded urchin laying claim to a few more tasty vittles, at least a dessert. Other than a petite lady in a pink suit, probably in her eighties, ladling herself a cup of broccoli cheese soup, the lane was empty.

Slowly canvassing the diner, his eyes inspected each table and corner, perplexed as to where the scamp could have gone undetected. A couple of video games in a glassed-in section were occupied by a cluster of junior high kids and one tiny preschooler cranking a steering wheel. No Carson.

The "restroom" sign posted on the back paneled wall seemed like a plausible answer. Excusing himself from the table, Joel bunched up his cloth napkin, dropping it by his plate, and started to rise. The pink-suited lady passed behind him, carefully hobbling back to her table.

An unmistakable, high-pitched *arf, arf* of a dog cut through the rumble of voices bouncing off the walls and ceiling from the cliques of conversation bubbling in the establishment. Booming laughter would sometimes break the drone, intermixed by scraping chairs or the tinkle of glass on glass from a busboy clearing tables.

No one seemed to notice the bark of a canine. A sign on the front door clearly stated "No Pets Allowed." Perhaps he'd been wrong. Standing to his full height, Joel again surveyed the dining area, but his mischievous companion was not to be found. Turning, he headed toward the restrooms in the rear.

"*Arf! Arf! Arf! Arf!*" Louder now, it was the unmistakable bark of a mongrel somewhere in the building. Others were hitching about, poking under tables, proof that Joel was not alone in his detection of the whelp.

Short, explosive yaps seemed to be emanating from the tables to the far right. Naomi entered through the swinging door from the kitchen, a puzzled expression pasted to her face. No one ever brought animals into her eating facility.

"*Woof, woof!*" The barking had crossed to the left side of the family diner. "*Woof, woof.*" An amicable bark at best.

Soft chuckles began three tables to the left from where the Schultzes and Joel Linton congregated. Polite chuckles waxed momentum rolling toward Joel as one by one the tables recognized the source of the yelping. The movement of people, the noise in the restaurant, and the howls of mirth kept Joel from pinpointing the dog. It was Rae Ann who spotted the pooch first, pointing the culprit out to Joel.

Unprecedented in Naomi's Diner, a sandy-haired *dog* with striking blue eyes peeked out from under the decorative cloth draping the table where an elderly man and his pink-suited wife ate alone. Clearly frightened by the yipping arising from below her table, the woman sat frozen in place, her lips trembling. Patting her hand in consternation, the man simultaneously lifted the corner of the tablecloth to peer under its canopy.

"*Arf, arf,*" the playful dog yipped at him. His eyes grew even larger in size than what his thick lenses magnified them to be. Then a toothy countenance of delight transformed his somber facial expression. Reaching under the table, he patted the friendly canine.

The friendly *arf* changed to a menacing growl, warning the gentleman he did not like to be petted by strangers.

Joel's heart sunk to his boot tops. Juicy bites of steak now lay like chunks of cement in his stomach, anchoring him to the floor.

"Carson!" The exclamation was drowned out in the uproar Carson's portrayal was causing as a cocker spaniel with mottled straw-colored fur.

Leaning over, the old man shouted in his wife's ear. She too cocked her head to see under the table, pressing three ringed fingers on the round O her lips were forming, taken aback by the child on all fours using their table as a doghouse.

Fire burnt within Joel's chest, rising to a flame-red coloring in his neck and creeping into his face. It was not the blaze of anger but rather of embarrassment. A man never to make a spectacle of himself in action or word, he was now exactly the dead center bull's eye of the diner's uproar. He and his pet canine.

Purposely he strode over to the couple's table to apologize and dognap the hound. He reached under the table to grab Carson's hand and pull him to his feet.

He missed. Continuing the dog routine, Carson scrambled on all fours down the aisle toward the front door.

"*Arf, arf. Bow-wow-wow.*" Fueled by the diner's laughter, Carson yapped louder, "*Woof, woof!*"

Joel could only follow him, hoping he'd be able to corner the boy, but the howling mongrel kept three feet in front of his master's cowboy boots.

Baffled, Joel had no idea how he was ever going to correct this ludicrous situation gallantly.

"When did you get yourself a cattle dog, Linton?" a voice in the crowd yelled out, bringing down the roof in howls.

Rae had hastily taken the other aisle winding between the tables reaching the front door before Joel and Carson. Pushing the glass door wide open, she called softly, "Here, boy. Here, boy." Acting the part, Carson padded right through the door opening on his hands and knees, Joel a step behind him. The glass door closed in his wake.

Two descending steps outside the diner brought them to the sidewalk. Sitting on the bottom step, Joel closed his eyes, drawing his hands through his hair. Rae sat beside him petting the docile pooch. All was quiet, except for the panting of the mongrel.

Joel pulled several bills from his wallet. "Rae, would you go back in and finish your meal? And when you are done, pay for it. I need to take my dog home." Rae nodded, giving Carson's ear a little tug.

Carson could tell by the sound of discouragement in Joel's voice the game was over. Sliding the boy's hand into his, Joel got up feeling way older than his forty-six years. Hand-in-hand, the boy and the man strolled down the sidewalk to their pickup truck, hopped in, and drove out of town.

CHAPTER 6

Swooping barn swallows played tag, slicing through the morning breeze, demonstrating an air show for the occupants of the Linton porch. Meagan Ritter and Carson shared the softly creaking porch swing. Holding down an old, spindle-backed wooden chair, Joel rested his arm on the railing enclosing the roofed platform, listening to Carson's version of the haying season.

"Cows eat grass, but grass can't grow in the winter. It would be under the snow. So Joel and me made great big hay bales." He stretched his arms, showing the colossal size. "You wouldn't even be able to climb on top of one. It is too big for you," Carson explained matter-of-factly to his social worker.

"That's too bad. Romping on a stack of bales could be fun. Now that haying is about over, I suppose you two farmers will loiter here on the porch playing checkers," Meagan suggested.

"No way." Carson hopped off the swing, sticking one hand in a side jean pocket, the way Joel often did. "See the combine over by the shop?" Meagan took in the harvest machine parked across the yard. "I have to help Joel combine wheat. Right now, we are fixing on it."

"No rest around here, is that it? You had better be careful. Joel is teaching you so much that pretty soon he'll expect you to run the farm," she teased.

Moving over to Joel, the youngster hung his arm about his friend's neck. "Then you can relax, Joel."

"Sounds good to me, buster." A look of pure delight passed between the two, which didn't go unnoticed by Meagan.

Changing the subject, she nonchalantly inquired, "Any more problems with your anger exploding?" At her last visit, she'd gotten the particulars on the living room incident and the Bautz car door. Concurring with Joel's prognostication, she thought it highly likely Carson's outbursts were a learned behavior from someone in his past. Carson had been seeing a therapist in Elton biweekly, but after the rage reports, the appointments had been bumped up to weekly.

The boy shook his head, not desirous of delving into this topic.

"Maaaa." A plaintive bleating sounded below the porch. Carson peered over the porch railing at the far end of the porch.

"Hi, Brush. Are you missing me? Where is your friend, Spit? For Meagan's benefit, he explained, "My calves couldn't go out to the pasture. They still need milk to drink."

Updating Meagan, Joel clarified, "Calves eighteen and thirty-three now have names: Brush and Spit."

"Interesting." Her dimples dented in.

"It had to do with a teeth-brushing demonstration held in the bathroom one evening."

"Hopefully Carson was having the lesson and not the calves." The curly head snickered.

"Seems he'd been faking the ritual. A man-to-man session of brushing and spitting ensued. Thus the names. Brush and Spit have free reign of the yard now. They are off the bottle, eating a mixture of calf starter pellets and oats from a tub in their pen. The gate is left ajar, giving them grazing privileges." Joel watched Carson sticking his hand through the porch rails, petting the inquisitive, bawling heads.

"Would that be the reason for the woven wire fence guarding Carson's fields?"

When his toy machinery dug up Melissa's flowerbed at the base of the porch, Joel had gotten the young farmer several packets of garden seed to sow. Peas, beans, and sweet corn filled the narrow area.

"Yeah, hate to have his crop wiped out by the predators. I don't think crop insurance will cover a flowerbed."

"Joel, I'm going to see if Brush and Spit have water in their tank." Carson clunked down the porch steps in the pair of cowboy boots Arlene had found in her attic from a bygone era.

"Okay, bud." Brush's wet muzzle butted up behind the child, nuzzling his back pocket.

"Stop that, Brush." Carson giggled, breaking into a run, the calf close behind his heels.

"So what's the latest?" Again, Meagan hastened to the business at hand with Carson out of earshot.

"Oh, I don't know. Things have been going pretty good." Joel rubbed the stubble on his chin.

"School is only three weeks away. I've scheduled him for a full evaluation with a pediatric neurologist on August fifteenth in Norbert. His previous school noted problems with attention, staying on task, and social struggles with classmates. Since it was his first school experience and he came from a dysfunctional home life, they were hesitant to put any diagnosis on his behaviors. The school psychologist did have his teachers fill out observation forms on how he acted in their classes. Once he came into foster care, he was given a physical by a pediatrician to ensure there wasn't some other cause for his inattention and hyperactivity. Now we are at the next step.

"I'm aware you'll be busy with harvest, so I will be here bright and early to pick him up. The date corresponds with our Foster Care Play Day when all of the children under our jurisdiction meet for an afternoon of activities. I purposely scheduled the appointment to coincide with the play day so we'd be able to hit two birds with one stone." She jotted a few words on her pad.

Looking up, she peered full into his face. "Do you still think we're wasting our time and the taxpayers' money going this route?" When the state had custody of a child, his medical bills were often met by Medicaid. She poked the pen's clicker into the side of her chin, waiting for his response.

As usual, Joel was slow with his rejoinder. "Ah, no, it might not be a bad idea. Maybe the guy will find something we've missed." A fly landed on his knee. He flicked it off with his little finger.

"Actually, *he's* a woman: Cary Richards. Her receptionist has sent along a behavior observation sheet for you to fill out before the appointment. But you're not sounding like yourself. No closing arguments?" Silence met her question. "So…what happened?"

Meagan always had a way of getting information out of the reserved foster parent. Before her arrival, he had been debating whether or not to fill her in on the canine scene at Naomi's Diner. His hesitation in itself was a signal to the social worker. Having worked with Joel and Melissa on previous foster placements, she knew when the guy was holding out on her.

"It seems I've acquired a mutt." Slowly, Joel began reiterating the story to Meagan. Retelling the youth's odd behavior in the diner came out a whole lot more entertaining than it had been for Joel the evening it occurred. Both he and Meagan first smiled over the picture he painted of the scamp yapping from his hideaway beneath the table, his tongue hanging out, panting between barks. However, when Joel described the little old lady dressed in her pink polyester suit sitting primly, her mouth round as a doughnut, it became more difficult to give a serious account. Portrayal of her bald-headed husband attempting to pacify the charming poodle, who'd suddenly transformed into a snarling Rottweiler, turned their chuckles into a jovial roar.

Meagan blew her nose and dabbed at the tears running down her face. "The most comical things happen to you, Joel, and no doubt you handled it in a most proficient manner. I would have died of embarrassment if that had been my child, or probably not have claimed the kid at all." Meagan blotted her cheeks, hoping her mascara wasn't smearing. "How did you handle it?"

Leaning back against the spindles of his chair, he said, "I did the only thing I could do under the circumstances: I tucked my tail between my legs and got myself and my dog out of town." His admission sent Meagan shaking like the spin cycle on a washing machine.

"Now I understand completely why having Carson tested for ADHD isn't striking a discord in you," she said with a hiccup.

"God works in mysterious ways."

"Yes, if He can move you, He most assuredly can move mountains!"

Carson sauntered up the steps. The loud thumps of his cowboy boots crossing the porch flooring imitated the stride of a full-grown man. "Aren't you guys done talking?" Agitation colored his voice. Sticking both of his hands in his side pockets, he swaggered up to them. "You know, we can't sit around and talk all day. There's work to be done around here."

Meagan and Joel howled like two coyotes. The social worker clutched her middle as she dismounted from the swaying swing. She reached out to twitch Carson's nose as she stepped past him. "You're right. And when there is work to be done, I vanish!" She almost added, *Lassie*, but held herself in check, grinning to herself.

Joel caught her eye. "A good watch dog chases away the riff-raff."

The Dakota farmer's year is comprised of a continuous cycle of differentiating facets of labor. Each page flipped on the kitchen calendar is significant, embodying its own timely contribution to the annual agricultural cycle.

On the first day of harvest, the excitement pulsed within Joel as he mounted the side ladder to his combine cab. His harvesting machine was in tip-top shape, as well as his two tandem grain trucks. Ben Fillmor saluted him from the truck window, allowing the combine to proceed out of the driveway first.

His young apprentice at his elbow had never experienced a harvest, or more precisely, ridden in a combine and experienced it in action. Carson was about to learn another concept of farming. Both the teacher and student couldn't wait to get started.

Emerald heads of wheat from two weeks ago had matured into a sheet of white, gently swaying in the light breeze. Carson was mesmerized by the huge dragon-like combine eating its way through a wide swath of standing wheat, leaving an evenly-mowed roadway in its rearview mirror. Whichever way Joel swung the steering wheel, the hungry machine sheared off the stalks and swallowed them, the wheat disappearing from sight.

Elbowing Carson, Joel pointed to the window behind their seat, indicating for the boy to take a look. Swiveling about, the boy was again hypnotized. A pipe was dropping a stream of wheat kernels into a square tank, or hopper, while the stems and leaves of the wheat plants were jutting out the rear of the combine, spreading an even mass of chopped straw over the stubble ground. Wow! Carson was enthralled. He'd never seen anything like it before.

Kernels of wheat elevated into a peaked pile above the hopper. Having reached the end of the field where Ben waited with an empty grain truck, Joel brought the combine alongside the truck box. A gush of wheat kernels poured out of the auger's spout, dumping the hopper's load into the truck box.

Fascination lit up Carson's face at all the functions the remarkable harvester could perform.

Joel allowed his charge to share his extension seat the entire length of the first day of grain harvest, even though it was deep into the night when the headlights illumined the roadway taking them home.

Carson thought he would never tire of the adventure of riding the combine, but Joel knew better. Invariably, the newness would wear off, stretching the hours longer, and monotony would set in. Thereafter, Carson was dropped off at Arlene's door mid-afternoon.

At first, the boy was obstinate, always thinking the field was the place to be. Moving into the second week of harvest, two of Arlene and Ed's grandchildren came to spend some vacation time with their grandparents. As far as age, Carson fit right between Jared and Jane. Afternoon hours passed swiftly, kicking a soccer ball amongst them on the south lawn or sailing Frisbees over the low hedge of Dogwood bushes.

Catering to its farmers in the area, the implement dealer in Elton carried an expansive inventory of parts for nearly every type of equipment used in an agricultural operation. Before turning the key off the prior night, Joel had heard a slight knocking in the inner workings of the harvester. He and Carson were on their way to town to pick up the combine parts he needed. Ben was at home in the yard unloading the last two trucks filled the night before.

If ever the widower had reason to believe in angels, it was because of the appearance of Benjamin Fillmor. Prior to him volunteering his help with the harvest two years ago, Joel had hardly known the older man, a mere acquaintance at best. Back when Ben still farmed, the Fillmor ranch was located ten miles east of Elton, whereas the Linton headquarters were twenty miles west of town.

Melissa had died in mid-July that summer. Cancer had slowly squeezed the life from her body bit by bit.

On her good days, when she'd felt strong enough to leave her makeshift bedroom in the living room, the two would fulfill another mini-dream, an "I wish" murmured by his wife. When her health was so transparently frail, she could only envisage the immediate future in tiny bubbles of pleasure in her mind. If her wish was within her husband's ability to reach up and grasp for her, he did.

While he held her against his chest, floating down the Missouri River on the Lewis and Clark Riverboat near Bismarck, the wind had whipped the tails of her scarf against her cheeks, hiding her bald head. In the mall in Norbert, they had chortled endlessly over the scarlet slippers they'd purchased, a simulation of Dorothy's footwear on the *Wizard of Oz*. She'd been in a merry mood that day, choosing a bright-red scarf to match her dazzling slippers.

Standing on the hill in the middle of their cattle pasture, they'd released helium-filled balloons to the heavens. Their favorite Bible verses, written on postcards, twisted and twirled from the strings as they ascended out of their vision. She had insisted the verses be written in their own script, not typed on the computer or clipped from a devotional booklet, and then read to each other before freeing them to the vast universe.

Hers was Exodus 19:4: "You yourselves have seen what I did to Egypt, and how I carried you on eagles' wings and brought you to myself" (NIV).

She had recited it without looking at her postcard but rather staring into the sky as if she could see God sitting on his throne listening to her recitation. Then, riveting her stare on her husband, she'd joyously declared, "That's exactly the way I want Him to take me home, on eagles' wings." The thought had brought her happiness, contentment, but it had seared Joel to the core. On nights like that one, when she'd seemed to be the Melissa he'd married a score of years ago, healthy and whole, he hadn't wanted her carried away in any mode.

The fulfillment of her next wish had been in the cemetery. He'd tried to reason with her and sidestep memories and prophesies it would invoke.

"Don't be silly, Joel. All of these graves mark a living soul. I'll see them in heaven." Begrudgingly, he had led her through the gate of the wrought-iron fence hemming the burial grounds. They'd planted two bushes of baby breath on the pair of mounds representing the miscarriages she'd had early on in their marriage. He'd surmised the visit would bring renewed grieving; on the contrary, it brought peace. "See you soon," she promised the girls, taking his hand and walking away. In his mind, he saw the empty plot next to their daughters waiting to snatch his wife.

The final wish she'd had the energy to execute had been packaged in a shopper's plastic bag on the Fourth of July. Since she was bedridden in her last weeks, he'd carried her diminished form to their pickup truck. She'd sat in the truck parked on the bridge expanding the stream meandering through their farmland while he lit fireworks, sending the explosions out over the water into the night sky. Sunbursts of color spattered the heavens, blending in with the trillions of stars already hanging in the firmament. She delighted at each splash of light in the geometrical compositions of pinwheels spilling sparkles out of paradise. And when his bag was empty, he joined her on the seat, embracing her tightly, enthralled with nature's natural show of stars.

Heck, he'd had a whole year to prepare himself for their last day, the final hour, but it had come as a hailstorm—quick and devastating. If only he had given her what she'd asked for.

And then it had been harvest. Sitting on the porch swing, he could see the ripe fields of wheat and barley in the distance gesturing to him, reminding the farmer in him of the season. It was time to go to work.

Yet Joel Linton didn't have the physical stalwartness to order his muscles to lift him off the swing. The combine and trucks parked by the empty grain bin all awaited the farmer.

The harvest is plentiful but the workers were few.

Matthew 9:37 (NIV)

Jesus was teaching his disciples about the spiritual harvest of men's souls. Yet the verse held truth for the Linton operation as well—the workers were not *few*; they were nonexistent.

That is, until Benjamin Fillmor drove into the Linton farmyard the second week in August.

No wire halo graced his head; no wings were attached to his back. Instead of white, he was dressed in the usual attire of a farmer: denim, a dull cotton shirt, and a billed cap with a seed company's logo imprinted on the front. Striding to the porch where Joel sat, the man uttered no condolences nor expressed any empathy for the grieving husband. Jacking up one leg to rest on the second porch step, he'd leaned his elbow on his knee. Looking straight at Joel in a no-nonsense way yet speaking in a voice rich with compassion, he directed his question in a forward manner, indicating he expected a direct and honest answer.

"Do you prefer to drive the combine or truck the grain at harvest?" Ben's bold eye contact didn't waver. Not knowing the white-haired man well, Joel wasn't sure of his intention.

Clem Schultz had stopped in to express his sympathy. Neighboring farmers were organizing a harvest bee and would appear with a fleet of combines and trucks, taking his crop off in one day. Joel had turned him down flat. The proposal made him feel weak and incapable. He couldn't accept charity, even if it was given in an act of neighborly love. Had it been someone else's sorrow, he would have been first on the spot offering his assistance, but not vice versa. No, he would do it himself; only, he hadn't.

Opening his mouth to speak, he formed the words, yet nothing came out. Clearing his throat, the stoic farmer tried a second time. "I combine."

"Suits me," Ben replied, lifting his foot off the step and turning on his heel. "I prefer trucking." Not once looking back, he paced the interspacing yards to the nearest truck in full strides.

Jarred out of his futility, at least for a term, Joel had pushed his weighted body off the swing, feeling a refreshing strength invading his bloodstream.

Hurriedly Joel alighted from his vehicle out in front of the Farm Supply Store, concentrating on his mental list of tasks requiring attention before the combine would roll today. Carson had to trot to keep up with him.

Once inside, Joel purposely set his aim for the parts counter. A couple of farmers already occupied the high stools adjacent to the front desk. Joel would have to wait his turn.

Waiting idly for any amount of time was not a strong point of Carson's character. Strolling through the aisles of farm merchandise, he fingered the bins of bolts, the bales of baler twine, and the variety of towing chains.

Reaching the end of a row of shelving, he was intrigued by a showcase of riding lawnmowers. One step bolstered him into the driver's seat of the closest model, where he admired its slick paint job and wide-cutting platform. Pretending he was operating the stationary implement, he twirled the steering wheel to the left and then to the right. One by one, he made the full circle of mowers.

Hopping off the last one, he gazed over a display of booklets with large showy pictures of farm machinery. This store must sell everything!

Peeking at the parts counter, he saw Joel still there, only now hunkered down on a tall stool.

Heading toward another aisle of shelving, the inquisitive youngster's eyes wandered up and down the products for sale: spray cans of paint, mud flaps, hitch pins, buckets, rain gauges, electric fence testers, fencing supplies, and grain shovels.

Rounding the corner to scan the backside of the display stand, Carson froze dead in his tracks. Holy smokes! Why hadn't he checked out this store before? From the floor to the ceiling was a whole host of toys—*farm toys*! This wasn't plastic junk. This was the real thing! Metal machinery just like Joel's and the same colors of the real machinery brands. Tractors, alone, there must have been at least twenty sizes to choose from: red ones and green ones, blue ones and yellow ones. He found Joel's front wheel assist tractor and his smaller tractor for haying. Cultivators, harrows, and plows set in a row. Gravity boxes, balers, and air seeders were one shelf up.

Shifting his eyes to the bottom shelf, he saw it—the very machine he needed for the farm spread out on his bedroom floor. He had seeded all the same agricultural commodities that Joel had, but how was he going to harvest his crop? He didn't have a combine! There it was: shiny and green. Kneeling on the tile floor to scrutinize the intricate parts close up, he admired the toy. It was a beauty! And a big one—at least a foot high. Caught up in the fascination of a young farmer's paradise, he was oblivious to Joel's summon. Why, even the unloading auger folded out from the hopper to dump his wheat into a truck! Lovingly, he stroked the cool, sleek coat of paint.

"Hey, Carson, I'm leaving." Joel's voice reached the boy still squatting on his heels. Pivoting his blond head, his eyes brighter than a search beacon, he saw Joel at the far end of the aisle.

"Come here a sec, Joel. I gotta show you something." His head bent over his treasure again, like a hungry man tantalized by a plate of food.

"Carson, I have to get home to get the combine put back together." Impatience gnawed on his words.

The boy was glued to his spot on the tiled floor. Acquainted with Carson's tendency to do things in his own timetable, Joel strode quickly toward him, determined to hurry him out of the store.

Reaching the mite, he paused long enough to scratch the yellow stack of hair. "We have to go, Carson. I have work to do."

"Look, Joel." Carson said the word *look* as one seeing the magnificence of the Rocky Mountains for the first time.

Zeroing in on the object trapping Carson's attention, even the annoyed farmer drew a long breath of admiration at the spanking brand-new John Deere combine.

"It's the same as yours, Joel." Rapturously, the boy's eyes caressed the piece of harvest equipment. Crouching onto his haunches beside the little jigger, the man whistled.

"That's even a newer model than mine. I'd say this is the top of the line, the biggest combine the company makes." Joel tilted the box to read the print on its side.

Continuing to marvel over the enchanted toy, Carson softly pleaded, "I need a combine for my farm, Joel."

Glancing at the pricey tag stuck to the box, the farmer pushed himself back to his feet. "Maybe for Christmas." He scratched the top of Carson's head a second time. "Let's go, partner."

Twisting his head around and up to reason with the giant standing over him, he implored, "Christmas will be too late. Harvest is now." His eyes like two pools of quicksand drew the tenderhearted man in.

"You're right." Bending over to slide the cumbersome box off the shelf, he added, "A farmer doesn't combine wheat when it snows."

Happily, the boy placed a small hand on the box, helping to transport it to the sales counter. "Joel, you don't have to give me another present. This is all I want for Christmas." His sincerity tore at the man's heartstrings. What a gift the child was to him, and it wasn't even Christmas.

August fifteenth arrived: Carson's appointment and Play Day in Norbert.

Obvious to Joel, Carson was being purposely sluggish. In slow motion, he'd chewed his apple slices and pushed chunks of a fried egg in a circle on his breakfast plate. Joel had called up the stairway twice asking if he was finished brushing his teeth. When the sound of Meagan's tires crunching over the loose gravel penetrated the walls, a third message was addressed to the top of the staircase. "Time's up. Get down here. Meagan's here."

Instead of the youngster's usual thundering gallop descending the oak flight and jumping from the second to the bottom step, the slowpoke tentatively took one step at a time in toddler fashion, stretching the minutes as far as he could.

Meagan and Joel chitchatted on the porch marking time while Carson tied his tennis shoes, redoing them a second time to get the laces the exact tightness he liked them.

Finally, he approached the car, hugging his prized combine. Joel stood waiting for him, the back door already wide open, motioning for Carson to get into the vehicle. "Okay, Mr. Turtle, in you go." Meagan waited, checking her wristwatch.

Carefully setting the piece of toy machinery inside on the floor mat, Carson froze before lifting a foot to follow. Gazing up at Joel, he softly murmured, "Did you pack my clothes?"

"No, I didn't think you needed any. Do you want your hooded sweatshirt? It is supposed to be in the nineties today."

"What will I wear then?" he asked with a confused expression furrowing the light-colored eyebrows.

Giving his chum a friendly pat on the rump, Joel inspected the six-year-old figure. "What's wrong with what you have on? Shorts and a t-shirt look good to me. Come on, Carson, Meagan's waiting." He patted the back of the cushioned seat.

A stifled sob escaped before the youngster could cap the outburst.

Joel was immediately concerned. "Hey, bud, what's the matter?"

The fair-skinned face clouded up, two pink circles rising in his cheeks. "Where…where am I going?" He brushed a wayward droplet off his eyelashes with a clenched fist.

Lifting the smooth chin in his rough, calloused hand, the farmer spoke gently. "Remember, we talked about this yesterday. Meagan is taking you to see a doctor in Norbert. A nice doctor, no shots, no pokes. She's just going to talk to you. And then for the whole afternoon, you get to do fun things with other kids your age." Beseeching help from Meagan, the foster father raised his eyes to her. "What kinds of activities are the kids going to be doing?"

"Oh, let's see. When I left the office, there was a big table set up in the activities room piled high with craft materials. And I saw some tickets for the zoo. How does that sound?"

Carson didn't even bother to rotate his head to face her. Pleading with Joel, he insisted, "No, *where* am I going?" His voice raised one notch in volume; he was obviously agitated.

"Honey, we told you. A doctor's appointment and a Play Day and then home again." Joel's hands had moved to the boy's shoulders, grasping one in each hand, attempting to fathom what was bothering the dole-faced elf.

Suddenly, the dam broke, and Carson screamed, squeezing his eyes into slits; he yelled full into Joel's confused face, "*Whose home!*"

Cognizance hit Joel and Meagan simultaneously, like a bowling ball impacting the remaining two pins and knocking them flat. Since Meagan was picking him up, Carson had assumed she was moving him to a new foster home. Every time he had moved to a different placement, Meagan had done the transporting. Joel felt horrible, no worse than if a bullet had blasted his stomach. He was the adult, the parent. Why couldn't he ever get it right?

Tightening his firm grip on the bony shoulders, compelling the boy to look him in the eye, Joel slowly and clearly stated, "*My* home—*our* home. This home right here. This is where you live—with me."

A pair of hands reached for the man's sides. Joel folded the child into an embrace, wallowing in the feel of the urchin's chest against his. Speaking directly into the child's ear, he softened his tone. "When Meagan brings you back, she is going to drop you off at Arlene's because I will be out in the harvest field. Meagan doesn't know anything about farming like you and I do." He winked at Meagan. "She wouldn't be able to find her way out to our fields. So she's going to take you to Arlene's, and I will pick you up there." Holding the boy back from his chest, he tried to read his pale face. "You got it?"

Carson's blond head bobbed. Rubbing foreheads together, Joel tried to erase any last smudging of doubt in the tyke's mind. "If for some reason Meagan can't bring you home this afternoon, like..." His mind went momentarily blank, trying to come up with reasons why Meagan wouldn't make the trip. He snatched whatever came to mind. "... like maybe her car breaks down, or she gets the flu, she'll call me on my cell phone, and I will drive to Norbert and get you." Carson's head bobbed a second time, a timid smile rising on his face.

One last hug, and Joel scooped up his precious charge, depositing him on the cushioned seat. Carson reached to the floor, tugging the combine onto his lap before Joel fastened the seat belt for him.

"Don't forget: the combine stays in Meagan's car. I don't want you to leave it in Norbert. We have harvesting to do," Joel sternly warned.

Having to wave at his prodigy through a pane of glass tore at his heartstrings. Sure, he did it all the time when leaving him with Arlene, but the Bautz farmstead wasn't a distant sixty miles. "Bring my partner back to me," he instructed Meagan.

Watching her taillights until they disappeared in the dust, the man swallowed.

Someday he would stand right here again doing the very same thing, waving good-bye, for foster kids didn't stay forever.

CHAPTER 7

Flipping another pair of jeans over his arm, Joel thumbed rapidly though the piles of folded pants stacked in the display cubicles, hunting for labels printed with a size eight.

"I'm not eight; I'm six," Carson contended, drifting over to a child mannequin decked out in camouflage dungarees and matching jacket.

"Yes," Joel agreed, "but you tried on a size six, and you looked like a house on stilts waiting for a flood to wash in. You might be the tallest kid in first grade this year. Ah, here's one." Deftly, he slid the pair of denims out from the middle of the pile. "Back to the dressing room, captain."

"I like these camouflaged ones. Jared has ones like these." His little fingers felt the stiff brown and green mottled material of the mannequin's pants leg.

Was this the first hint of peer pressure creeping in? Combat in the style zone? What did a middle-aged farmer know about fashion? How enlightened could he be about the apparel of kids these days? "So you want to go to school incognito, do you? Your teacher won't be able to find you."

"Huh?" The span of years was placing the two in separate time zones.

"Look in the pile by GI Joe," he said, referring to the fake model. "Is there a size eight?" His terminology was lost on the younger generation. He let it slide.

Sidestepping another shopper, Joel advanced to give the youngster some assistance. "Yup, here's one right here. Six pairs of jeans, two dress slacks, and a dozen shirts should do you." He dropped the pile on a checkout counter.

"Back-to-school shopping?" the clerk asked. "Will you be needing socks, underwear, or tennis shoes?"

By the time the sought items were paid for, Joel and Carson had shopping bags in each hand to lug through the parking lot.

"Are we going home now?" Carson asked, clicking his seat belt.

"I'd like to; however, since we're in the big city of Norbert, we may as well pick up the groceries we're short on." Driving the short distance, the two spouted off what they'd depleted recently. "Milk, bread, orange juice, breakfast cereal, and salad dressing."

"Ketchup," Carson added to the verbal list, having been forced to eat his French fries plain at supper.

"Right, and we popped the last bag of microwave popcorn," Joel recalled. "And eggs."

Minutes later, the man was wheeling a metal cart through the wide grocery aisles, throwing items into the cart as they passed by them. Without a written grocery list, Joel knew he was making impulsive purchases: cream-filled cookies, cinnamon crackers, a dried fruit mixture.

"Let me push the cart," Carson demanded.

From past grocery trips, the bachelor was well aware of the rapidity with which the boy could motor a cart. More than once, Joel's arms had been mounted high with food items and had nowhere to set them. The speed demon had propelled the cart half an aisle ahead of him, always gaining velocity.

"I can manage it." Joel kept his left hand adhered to the handle while capturing three cans of vegetables with his right hand.

"You put the food in, Joel, and I'll push it." Already the child was gripping the bar.

"You go too fast. Last time I couldn't keep up with you."

"I won't this time. I'll stay right beside you."

Glancing back, Joel saw the macaroni noodles on the top shelf. Releasing his hand from the cart, he walked back three steps to retrieve the boxes of pasta.

Dutifully, Carson waited for him to set the articles in the cart before proceeding. "There's the ketchup, Joel." Joel grabbed three plastic bottles, adding them to the contents of the cart, followed by salad dressing and croutons.

"Do we have peanut butter in the cupboard?" the miniature shopper asked.

His partner wasn't sure; he didn't think so. Clasping the largest jar on the shelf, he saw a selection of jellies next to the peanut butter. They liked strawberry best. Scanning the laden shelves, he detected grape, peach, and raspberry. Strawberry had to be here somewhere, or was it out of stock?

Carson scrutinized the display shelves too. Up ahead, he saw the popcorn Joel had mentioned. As the cart wheeled forward, he threw in a box. Right beside the popcorn were bags of sunflower seeds. Sometimes when they were working out in the field, they cracked the seeds together. He added two bags to the cart.

Coming to the end of the aisle, the driver maneuvered the corner to the next lane. An array of breakfast cereals greeted him. Oh yeah! They needed a bunch of these. Joel didn't buy the sugared cereals, only the boring ones. He said he didn't want Carson's teeth to fall out.

Far ahead, a mini-display of chocolate-colored boxes stood on its own stand, darting out into the aisle. Pictured on the front of the box was a cartoon caricature of a chipmunk dropping balls of cereal into his mouth. It appealed to the young customer. Speeding up the cart, the rollers warbled a *clink, clink, clink* each time they vacillated.

A lady with a curly-haired tyke strapped in the child seat of her cart was rambling straight toward him. Veering his cart to the right, he tucked it into the shelving as he *clink, clink, clink, clinked* past them, gravitating toward the chocolate chipmunk. Picking up speed, he hopped on to the oscillating cart, his feet riding on the back axle, his tummy clenched over the handlebar. *Clink, clink, clink.* There was a certain freedom in riding a loaded grocery cart over the smooth flooring.

Oops! The chocolate display case jutted out directly in front of the sailing cart. Jumping off the axle, Carson quickly jerked the contraption to the left, narrowly missing the cereal rack, the cart leaning on two wheels. Bumping the shelving across the aisle, the out-of-control cart couldn't right itself. *Crash!* The runaway shopping cart tumbled over sideways, hitting the tile flooring. Canned goods, plastic bottles, and boxes scrambled over one another, cascading to the square tiling. Cans of beans and corn ricocheted against one another; a lone can of tomato soup spiraled through the length of the long aisle. Roller bearings in the wheels sang a *clink, clink, clink*, continuing to rotate in midair.

Holding a pound jar of peanut butter in one hand and two jars of jelly in the other, Joel appeared at the far end of the aisle, irked because his cart had vanished. Mentally, he wondered why he had given in to the youngster.

Clattering noises from the metal container spanking the hard floor brought curious customers from nearby aisles peering around the corners to the source of the calamity. Looking ahead, realization blasted Joel in the chest. It was *his* cart lying on its side. They were *his* groceries spilled out in a scattered mess for shoppers to tiptoe through. And the foster boy in *his* care was the cause of the growing crowd of spectators.

Gritting his teeth, the peeved parent trotted toward the crash site of the delinquent cart. Tucking the peanut butter jar underneath the arm holding the jelly, he swooped up an orbiting can of corn in his free hand. Nodding apologetically to the woman with the baby, he swept past them.

A store employee arrived out of nowhere. Cheerily, he righted the cart and began retrieving lost groceries. "Did we have a slight mishap here? No harm done. We'll get this straightened up in no time."

Joel's anger was pounding at his temples. Why had he allowed the twerp to maneuver the cart? Hadn't he learned his lesson from the previous shopping trips? Grunting an apology to the male shelf stocker, he placed his articles in the metal carriage then pitched in to help collect the remaining groceries strewn across the aisle.

"There you go, sir. You have a good day." The store employee strolled back to where he had been stocking shelves.

Perspiration beaded on Joel's forehead. Thankfully, there hadn't been any broken glass bottles or smashed cartons of eggs to clean up.

All this time, Carson stood to the side, his arms locked behind his back, biting on his bottom lip, carefully avoiding eye contact with the angry man.

Humiliated beyond what he could endure, Joel took off pushing the cart in rapid motion, bent on getting out of this store just as fast as it was feasibly possible. With his teeth clenched, he jerked open the glass doors of the cooler, seizing cartons of milk and eggs. Not slowing his pace, he plucked two loaves of bread from the bakery ledge then hit a straightaway course to the closest checkout lane. The guilty culprit stayed two paces behind him.

Carson knew better than to ask for a candy bar or a pack of gum exhibited on the racks next to the cash register, and Joel didn't offer to buy him one. Hoisting the bulging pair of paper grocery bags, Joel turned on his heel and was out of the store, expecting the cause of his frustration to tag along.

After storing the perishables in the picnic cooler he kept in the truck box for the sixty-mile trip back home, he pressed the button on his keychain, unlocking the pickup doors. The man and child climbed in, slamming their doors concurrently.

Silence. Pinching his lips together, Joel fought for control.

Silence. This was the second time the scamp had mortified him in public. What had he gotten himself into going back into foster care? Loneliness was beginning to feel mighty good—like something he could handle after all.

Silence. Frustrated, he was provoked to the max. If Carson would just obey. He had said he'd stay right beside him, so why didn't he? The kid couldn't be trusted farther than an arm's length away.

Silence. Leaning his elbow on the door's armrest, Joel chanced a sneak peek at his vexing charge, who was deliberately keeping his head turned to the parking lot scene out the passenger window.

It wasn't school shopping that had brought them to Norbert. Another appointment had prompted the hour's drive that morning. After evaluating Carson a week ago, the pediatric neurologist had turned her test results over to a highly-recommended child psychiatrist to handle the treatment from here on out.

Brent Halliger, reading from the file of papers on his desk, had confirmed the diagnosis of ADHD. On a scale from low-to-high charting behaviors exhibiting inattention, impulsivity, and hyperactivity, Carson had scored in the midsection.

Mr. Halliger was detailed in his discussion, wanting Joel to thoroughly understand Carson's disorder and how he could be helped. Using layman terms, he'd explained, "Brain cells are known as neurons. When messages pass through the brain, they travel from one neuron to the next. In a child with ADHD, the chemical needed to keep the messages moving is not performing adequately. Thus, the child appears unfocused; however, he is actually focusing on too many stimuli.

"The teacher may be at the board writing the word c-a-t, sounding out the word letter by letter as she writes. Initially, the child sees the action, but he becomes sidetracked by the earring dangling from her ear or the pretty shoes she's wearing on her feet. A noisy car on the street passes by the classroom window, redirecting his focal point. Looking back at the teacher, he notices the pipe cleaner spiders the students formed in art class now suspended from the ceiling. Their wiggly eyes fascinate him, like the eraser and pencil setting on his desk. In seconds, he has the eraser chasing his pencil across the smooth surface. In other words, the ADHD child is being bombarded by stimuli in his environment, making it difficult for him to differentiate which one he should choose to focus on."

As if exemplifying the psychiatrist's words, Carson had slid off his straight-backed chair, attracted by a rubber tub of toys in the corner of the room, unconscious of the annotative discourse presently taking place on his conduct performance. Intrigued by a plastic basketball hoop from the tub, he stuck its suction cups against the wall. The foam ball hit the rim, knocking the whole contraption off the wall. Losing interest, Carson had gravitated back to the collection of toys, confiscating a dollhouse. Swinging it open, he'd been pleased to discover miniature furniture to manipulate.

"Maybe you've noticed an undue amount of fidgeting and squirming in environments where everyone else is sitting properly." Mr. Halliger had resumed his description. Joel could picture Carson tossing grass into the air during Pastor Lance's sermon. "Or possibly he goes beyond the wiggly-worm state to actually climbing on top of or under furniture, executing physical activities not appropriate for the situation: running up on a front platform at a program, throwing his empty soda bottle out onto the basketball court during a game. Are you getting my picture?"

A barking mongrel peeking out from under a restaurant table had accosted Joel's vision. Or the incident Arlene conveyed of Carson perched on the chicken roost in the henhouse flapping his arms and crowing like a rooster for the mailman. Joel nodded to the psychiatrist.

"An attention deficit child has problems taking turns or interrupts when others are conversing."

Right on cue, Carson had blurted out, "Joel, this is my room, and this is your bedroom." Rearranging the furniture in the doll-house, Carson had placed beds in two adjoining rooms.

"The type of meds an ADHD child benefits from are actually stimulants. Rather a contradiction, wouldn't you say? You'd think these youngsters are already overly stimulated; they shouldn't need another energizer. But the medication boosts the brain chemicals, helping the messages to be sent from neuron to neuron properly. In other words, the child is better able to focus on one stimulus instead of responding to numerous points of attention. Do you understand what I am saying?"

"He doesn't seem to have any problem sitting still when he's watching his cartoon shows on television," Joel had commented. Meanwhile, Carson had discovered a red cord in the rubber tub and was twisting the ragged end to thread it through the chimney into the top floor of the dollhouse.

"Ah yes, the media. Kid-oriented movies, television, video games. These all have an extraordinary amount of action racing across the confines of a screen. Lots of stimuli to hold attention! ADHD kids are transfixed by them. Colors flash, scenes change, characters fly in and out. Normal life isn't like that. School will be better for Carson this year with the assistance of medicine. His concentration level will increase, he'll be more attentive to directions, and bonds of friendship will more easily be formed.

"I'm going to start Carson on a rather low dose, partially to ease his body into the change it will create, but also, I don't want to overmedicate him. Since it is a stimulant, the prescription will be a thirty-day supply. I want to see Carson once a month to closely observe his behavior. There may be some side effects: loss of appetite, sleeplessness. If we find we are not getting the desired results, there are a variety of meds that might be more suitable." Mr. Halliger had scribbled the prescription on the pad, torn off the top sheet, and handed it to Joel.

Blowing out his breath, Joel stuck a hand through the open space in the steering wheel, jingling the extra keys on the keychain hanging from the ignition. He didn't expect Carson to be perfect, but a bit of compliance would be nice. Breaking the awkward stalemate, Joel stiffly asked, "Got anything to say about what happened in the store?" The usual glitter twinkling in his gray eyes was snuffed out.

Carson's solidified figure across the seat was pressed up against the passenger door in an effort to put as much space between him and the disgruntled man the cab width allowed.

Repeatedly, Joel battled the inept awareness of his shrinking parenting skills, or better yet, lacking altogether. What route should he take this time? Sternness? Punishment? Consequences? Compassion? Out the front windshield, vehicles streamed past his parking spot, but he didn't see them. Contradictory conjectures collided within his head.

When the high-pitched child's words flowed from the tadpole in his truck, he almost didn't recognize the speaker.

"Yes. I was thinking…maybe you need somebody to talk to…about the mad puppies fighting inside you."

It took Joel a moment to digest the suggestion, to realize his own advice for anger was being fed back to him from the mouth of a babe. Supposedly it was Carson who had anger issues. Maybe Joel did too. He peered deeply into the sky-blue eyes. "You do? And who would you suggest that someone be?" Joel's anger was melting like a double-dipper ice-cream cone dripping on a scorching harvest afternoon.

"Well, since we're the only ones here, it would have to be me or God."

Accepting the conclusion as logical, Joel partially angled his position on the seat. "For now, I choose you. I need advice." He dropped his hands in his lap, as if to say he had a problem he didn't know how to solve.

"Let's say you were shopping with a fine young man who had promised you he would stay right by your side with a shopping cart, but instead, he ran ahead and tipped the cart over onto the floor. If you were the father, what would you do?"

Carson seemed to have acquired Joel's trait of taking his time to think before he spoke. Two of his fingers jogged a path to his knee. Finally, his small voice attempted to convey the confusion inside of him. "I really want to be good. I really want to obey you. But sometimes I see things before you do, and so I quickly do it. Didn't you see the popcorn and sunflower seeds I put in the cart for us?"

Brent Halliger's information flashed back to Joel, doing a replay in his cognitive sector. *"The ADHD child is being bombarded by stimuli in his environment, making it difficult for him to differentiate which one he should choose to focus on."*

Could it be like the psychiatrist equated—that many stimuli were vying for Carson's attention? He, as his guardian, certainly was. He had wanted Carson and the cart to be his shadows. Then the microwave popcorn beckoned to the boy, and the bag of sunflower seeds added its invitation. Chocolate cereal boxes positioned in the aisle fairly shouted at him. The boy wanted to obey, he wanted to be helpful, so he tried to react to all the voices summoning him. And in the end, he became the inattentive, hyperactive, impulsive child that was driving Joel nuts.

"I believe you, buddy. I do truly believe you want to obey, but sometimes it is hard for you. And yes, I did see the popcorn and sunflower seeds in the cart. Thank you for helping."

"You're welcome, Joel." An ounce of color was returning to the boy's fair complexion.

"But I want you to understand where I am coming from too. Most people in a grocery store are merely strolling along picking up a box here, a jar there, and placing them in the cart. Did you see any shoppers whizzing the carts as fast as they could go, ramming and jamming them into other shoppers or shelves?"

Carson shook his head. "No."

"Did you see anyone using the cart like a scooter, jumping on the back of it, getting a free ride?" Exemplifying the action, Joel bent over the steering wheel, gripping it on both sides and pretending to drive at a breakneck speed.

A smirk lifted the corners of the boy's mouth. "No, but it was really fun, Joel. You should try it!"

Joel couldn't refrain from letting a bit of glitter ooze into the corners of his eyes. Carson saw it immediately and let out a shaky laugh.

"How do you think I felt when I realized the fine young man I was shopping with and to whom I had entrusted my cart had it turned upside down in the middle of the floor?"

Nervously, Carson reached for the release button on the glove compartment in front of him. *Ping*. The door flopped open, thwacking his knee. Using both hands, he slammed it shut again. "Bad? I wouldn't like it if some kid banged up my combine."

Although Carson didn't seem to grasp the concept of embarrassment, he did comprehend that his behavior was not acceptable. Joel wondered if embarrassment was an emotion one grew into. Children didn't seem to have the inhibitions adults possessed.

"Let's call it a truce." He stuck out his hand to his small-sized friend for a shake. "Hopefully our next trip to the grocery store will go better, or the two of us are going to get powerfully hungry with no food in the cupboards."

Pumping Joel's hand in an exaggerated handshake, Carson, relieved that Joel had returned to his good-natured self, piped up, "I know a nursery rhyme: Old Mother Hubbard went to her cupboard/To get her poor dog a bone/But when she got there/The cupboard was bare!"

He leaned his head back, giggling.

The friendship of the widower and the orphan had been restored. Crawling into the rear seat, Carson fastened his seat belt.

Miles of pavement swept under the tires, crossing the North Dakota landscape, returning the country boys to their ranch. A comfortable quietness invaded the cab.

"Joel."

"Yeah, buddy."

"You said you wanted my advice."

Reversing his thoughts, Joel reflected on their earlier conversation. "Hmm, I did. Do you have some for me?"

"You wanted to know what to do about the boy who tipped the cart over when he had promised to drive nice," Carson reminded him. "I got an idea."

"I'm listening." Joel had thought the handshake was the conclusion to the discussion. Evidently not.

"You should make the boy go to bed a half hour earlier tonight." Carson was studying the man's profile intently.

"Hmm. Why should I do that?"

"So he learns his lesson." Carson's retort was decisive.

"Do you think it would help him to remember how to act in a store?" Joel raised one eyebrow.

"Yup."

"I accept your advice." Lacing his words with firmness, he ordered, "Young man, tonight you will be in bed a half hour earlier than usual. You got it?"

"Yes, sir!" Carson saluted.

Peaceful tranquility returned, each submersed in his own world. Approaching the slough marking the Linton driveway, Carson came back to life.

"We forgot something, Joel."

"What?" he asked, glancing at the face in his rearview mirror.

"Orange juice. We don't have any orange juice in the 'frigerator!"

Joel wondered if Carson's mind ever rested.

CHAPTER 8

Aa, Bb, Cc, Dd, Ee, Ff … Deftly, Jasmine Kirmis stapled the manuscript penmanship cards to the strip of cork bulletin board running above the white marker board the width of the classroom. Every six letters, she dismounted from the six-foot stepladder, moved it a space to the right, then ascended it again. *Gg, Hh, Ii, Jj, Kk, Ll* …

With school starting next Wednesday, Jasmine had used every forenoon of this prior week to prepare her first-grade classroom for a new group of six-year-olds. At the onset of her arrival, she'd opened the five window panels to welcome in the cool, early morning breeze belying the hot, sultry August afternoon certain to ensue. If the temperatures remained in the upper nineties, the initial days of the school year would be sizzlers. Sweaty children, their clothes clammy on the plastic chairs, wouldn't be prime candidates for learning.

As a teacher, she couldn't control the weather; however, she could create an attractive learning environment for her students.

Xx, Yy, Zz. There. She stepped down and back a pace to critique the alphabet border. Fine.

Jasmine was embarking on her twenty-third year of teaching, all right here in Elton, although only for the last two years had she been a resident of the town as well. Previously, she'd commuted the fifteen miles between Elton and the smaller town of Prairie City to the east twice a day.

Rummaging behind a self-standing bookcase, she slid out the signs painted three summers ago to suspend from the ceiling. *Reading Fever* would hover over the reading nook. Having procured the stepladder to the spot, she alighted as high as she dared to go, balancing the lightweight sign on top of the ladder.

A tapping sound on the open classroom door momentarily startled the lithe figure clinging to the ladder. Principal Peterson stuck his head through the opening, catching Jasmine posed in her precarious position.

Sauntering in, he feigned a reporter broadcasting the biggest story of the day. "And the headlines of the national paper read: 'Exemplary Teacher Crashes to Floor Seeking New Innovative Heights to Reach Her Students.'" His finger was in the air, pointing to each word in the imaginary newspaper.

Rolling her green eyes, Jasmine tucked her short, wavy, chestnut hair back behind her ear. She scolded, "You scared me! The headline below it should say, 'Principal Sends Teacher Plummeting to Her Death.'"

Outlined in the doorway, a second male form went unnoticed until her peripheral vision detected movement. A stranger. Flustered, the lady wished she could reel in her hasty retort. A faint blush highlighted her cheeks as the striking middle-aged gentleman advanced slowly into the room, a towheaded blue-eyed youngster attached to his side.

Swallowing, she strove to compose herself as best as she could, perched three feet off the ground with one end of a sign about to slap her in the jaw.

"I have a new student for you to meet, Mrs. Kirmis. On second thought, you'd better take care of your business in the crow's nest before workman's compensation gets another client."

Sometimes her boss could be unbearable. After hooking the sign, she descended the stepladder, smoothing her raspberry knit top back into place.

Children were her profession. No matter how she felt inside, it was her duty to administer to the child. Putting one knee to the floor, she lowered herself to the boy's level. His hand was clasped in the man's, and by the looks of it, the thin replica of the older gentleman was not letting go anytime soon. Both the father and his son were attired in blue jeans, button-up yellow shirts, and the typical farmers' caps. She mused inwardly, *Like father, like son.*

Mr. Peterson did the introductions. "This young chap is Carson Reynolds. I'm sure he is looking forward to the start of school. Carson, Mrs. Kirmis will be your teacher." No acknowledgment came from the child, only a vacant blue stare that seemed to pierce a tunnel through Jasmine to someone standing behind her.

"Hi, Carson. I'm excited for school to begin." She gestured at the desks pushed into pods of three. "I'm getting our room ready. Would you like to look around?" The blue stare was the answer.

Shuffling his feet, Principal Peterson headed toward the door. "I'll leave the two of you to get acquainted. If you have any questions, Joel, Jasmine will fill you in." With an inclination of his head, he disappeared.

Having not introduced Joel to her, it was as if the principal expected her to know him. The man with his dark tan and gray-tinged hair neatly clipped below the line of his cap did have a vague familiarity about him, but she couldn't place from where. Even though she had not lived in this community long, she had taught here. She should have seen everyone somewhere, even if names didn't stick to faces.

He spoke now in a slow, friendly drawl. "Carson is a bit stiff in new environments. It takes him awhile to open up." Letting go of the youngster's hand, he placed his large hand on the boy's shoulder instead.

Jasmine smiled into the blue stare. "Why don't we take a tour of the room together?"

Rising from the floor, she led the pair through the maze of boxes still needing to be unpacked. Opening an empty flat-topped desk, the teacher explained, "You will have one of these for your school supplies. Have you gotten some crayons and pencils yet?"

The cute blond head peered into the desk while the attentive father responded. "We went school shopping, didn't we, Carson? On the first day of school, you'll have to unpack your school items into your desk." Gently, he massaged the boy's shoulder.

Jasmine unlatched the door to the bathroom in the corner of the room to show where the closed door led. Then the three filed into the cloakroom concealed behind the back wall of bulletin boards. The narrow hallway was lined with hooks to hang coats and schoolbags below a shelf for hats and mittens. Upon exiting the other end, they sorted through the books, toys, and math manipulatives lining the bookshelves.

Next she demonstrated the listening books setting on a small table. "All of these CDs have a voice reading one of the books in the caddy." She dropped a CD into the player and opened the picture book that corresponded with it. A lady's voice softly flowed from the headphones, "Once upon a time..."

Mrs. Kirmis asked the shy child's permission. "May I position the headphones over your ears?" His eyes on the book, intrigued with the reader's narration coming through the headphones, the schoolboy inclined his head, already caught up in the story. Gently, the lady covered his ears with the audio set and then pulled out a small, wooden chair for him to sit on. Agreeably, Carson folded his leg underneath his tailbone, turning the pages of the book in sync with the audio.

Back at her desk, Jasmine rolled her cushioned chair out from behind the worktable, gesturing for Joel to have a seat as she claimed a miniature student's model. Reaching for a notepad and pen, she was ready to address the parent.

"Mr. Reynolds, why don't you tell me about your son."

Clearing his throat, Joel felt slightly out of place. First, sitting in the instructor's chair, and second, being interviewed by a female professional were not his normal agenda. Darting a glance at the child who was growing more dear to him with each passing day, he sat back to concentrate on Carson's teacher. Thus far, he was impressed with the attention she gave a new student.

Aware of the unease he was displaying, Jasmine ventured a second time. "Maybe he has certain likes or dislikes. What are his strengths, his attitude toward school?" Crossing her legs, she leaned forward.

Her green eyes were too much to hold, so centering his attention on Carson instead, he measured out his words in a low voice. "My name is Joel Linton, and while I would certainly claim Carson as my kin, he is not. He is my foster son. I never use the word *foster* in his earshot. To me, it sounds a bit demeaning." His gaze flitted back to her.

Realization dawned on Jasmine. Yes, she had heard of the Lintons before. None of their foster children had ever been on her class roster. In recent years, though, there hadn't been any foster children in the school system that she could recall. Yes, she may have seen Joel Linton before, but never had she conversed with him.

"I apologize. I should not have assumed." She tucked her hair behind her ear again. "You look alike, you dress alike…" She flung her hand into the air then dropped it back to her lap.

"That's all right. Today is 'yellow day' at our house. Sometimes Carson names a color and then insists we wear the same colored shirt."

Mrs. Kirmis grinned at their color scheme. "Evidently the child is quite attached to you. I'll be quiet and let you do the talking before I put my foot in my mouth again."

The amiable foster parent smiled, overlooking Jasmine's blunder.

"Carson arrived at my porch step last May, after school had been convened for the summer. The statue with the blue-eyed stare is his initial reaction to anything new. It is not the real Carson Reynolds. Once familiar with his surroundings, you will find him quite active." He paused, smirking at the energetic rascal his charge had transformed into.

The teacher understood what *active* meant. Many first graders made a marked change after the primary shyness wore off.

"In fact, the real Carson Reynolds needs reminders on how to handle his temper. He can become very excitable and animated. Eventually, you will probably wonder if this reserved little turtle pulling into his shell today is the same tiger cub that streaks into your room in October."

Watching as the woman jotted notes on her pad, Joel continued, "This past month, Carson was diagnosed with ADHD, not the most severe case scenario, somewhere in the middle. I am not one to run for the pill bottle; however, in Carson's case, it may be a benefit. Just three days ago, he started the medication. I'll give it to him at home before he comes to school so you won't have to deal with it."

Looking up from her pad, Mrs. Kirmis held her pen crosswise between her index fingers. "Attention deficit is a disorder we are well acquainted with in the education world. I have seen extremely severe cases where the child absolutely could not focus enough to function in the school setting without medication. Others have had much milder difficulties in concentration and have done quite well with behavior modification techniques. For students on meds, I like to use a combination of methods. The place his desk is positioned in the room can make a difference. Decreasing the number of tools he has on his desk at one time helps. Sometimes I have a private signal only the child and I are aware of—my signal to him to give me his attention."

Mrs. Kirmis's experience was easing Joel's trepidations on whether Carson would fit in at school. Again, he assured himself that Carson wasn't a misfit because he had ADHD anymore than a diabetic child was kept in an isolated bubble because he needed insulin.

"Now give me some ideas of what fascinates Carson. What motivates him?"

"Let's see." Joel's hand stroked his jawbone. "He has acquired the farming fever this summer. I don't think he had any prior knowledge of farming before coming to my ranch."

"With your Siamese twins getup," Jasmine suggested, implicating their attire, "it appears he's quite taken with you and aims to copy your every move. Quite a compliment."

Lifting his eyes to the ceiling, the man blinked several times in quick succession before visibly swallowing.

Jasmine, an ol' softy herself, sensed the foster father's sensitivity when it came to his new charge. A film of moisture wet her eyelids at the magnetism between the man and boy, complete strangers to each other until three months ago. This foster parent had met his calling.

Joel waited until he trusted his voice to be firm and steady. "And a responsibility. I hope I won't disappoint him."

"Every kid needs a male role model. They just don't all get a good one. Being in foster care, it's quite possible Carson has already had the negative prototype. He's a lucky boy to get a second chance with you."

Joel's lips pressed into a tight line. Why did the little guy move him almost to tears? Where was the macho independent farmer he liked to depict to the general public?

Jasmine couldn't believe her conversation with this new acquaintance had sliced away the chitchat façade and gotten right to the heart of the matter. Unmistakably, Joel Linton was in the right profession, and it wasn't farming. Farming was only a sideline.

The snap of the CD player automatically switching itself off reduced the atmospheric pressure. Carson tugged off the ear-phones and migrated straight back to Joel, leaning both elbows on the man's lap. Kneading the thin back, the foster father asked, "Good book?"

Nodding, Carson rested against the muscular legs, indulging in the man's touch on his back. "Can we go now?" It was the first time the teacher had heard the child speak.

"Pretty soon," the man agreed. "Anything else, Mrs. Kirmis?"

"All of the basic information the school secretary will give me from the registration forms you completed. If necessary, what's the best way to contact you during a school day?"

Joel felt his chest pocket for a ballpoint pen. "Why don't I jot down my cell phone number and e-mail address? I'm not usually in the house during the day, but I carry my cell phone with me all the time, and if there is a less urgent message, I read my e-mail in the evening."

The pre-school visit was over. Joel and Carson made their way out of the school.

In neat script, Jasmine added Carson Reynolds to her class roster, for a total of sixteen pupils. It was a perfect size. She'd had as many as thirty and as few as eleven.

Booting up her computer, she realized she was lacking the birth date, foster mother's name, and the emergency home for Carson. She'd leave those areas blank and get the missing infor-mation from the secretary another day. Minutes ticked into hours as she immersed herself into long-range planning for the first semester.

Damp hair tendrils on her forehead and a trickle of sweat between her shoulder blades finally brought her back to the real-ity of a hot, stuffy room when a preprogrammed buzzer in the school's clock system rang at 2:25 p.m., the signal for the junior high classes to switch to their last period class. She'd print off her class list of names to tape beside her door and call it a day.

As she lifted her hair off her neck, she stood up and stretched. Her clammy Capri pants stuck to her legs. Pinching a pants leg, she wiggled her hips in an effort to dislodge the clinging denim.

Looping the cloth handles of an oversized tote bag over her arm, she slid her fingers into her front pocket for her keychain. Once her class list was taped to the hallway wall, she secured the door and headed down the vacant corridor, her footsteps echoing on the polished tile.

The shock of the sultry heat buffeted her face and body, smothering her with a heavy, humid blanket of hot air. The six-block hike to home was not appealing.

By the time she reached her garage door, her body and clothing were drenched in perspiration. Uncomfortably she jiggled the key into the lock and fairly ran up the four steps inside the garage to her back entry, shoving the last barricade open. Coolness wafted over her immediately. Closing her eyes, she embraced the sudden change of temperature washing over her skin. "Thank you, God, for air conditioning."

A quick shower and a glass of ice water restored her amiable nature. Burrowing her back into the handful of pillows on the living room sofa, she unwound.

More often she referred to her bluish-gray bungalow as her "cottage," bestowing a quaint, cozy resonance on her one-level abode: living room, kitchen-dining combination, laundry room, two bedrooms, and an office. A makeshift futon gave the office a dual purpose in case Jacob and Autumn ventured home for a holiday simultaneously. Thus far, the reunion hadn't occurred.

Jasmine loved her snug, homey dwelling with the roofed porch looking out over a tiny fenced-in backyard where her old-fashioned flower garden bloomed a palette of hues and her vegetable garden had enough space for a half-dozen tomato plants and two hills of cucumbers.

The white privacy fence gave her exactly that: a retreat from the busy worlds of the school and community, a place to meet

God in nature when the weather allowed it and to engage in her preferred pastime: writing.

Jasmine Kirmis was a paradox. She had spent two years writing a novel and another twelve months trying to get it published. When a company accepted her manuscript and then mailed her a contract this past winter for a second book, she had done an Irish jig around her living room, praising the LORD for allowing her dream to take shape.

However, in order to meet the contract's deadline, she would have had to take a leave of absence from her teaching position. As much as she loved the sanctuary of her home, she realized her appreciation for the quietness came at the conclusion of a hectic day at school: answering a zillion students' questions, attending meetings, preparing lessons, correcting papers, and being available to parents. Only after she turned the key in the lock did the open arms of soothing tranquility greet her at the entrance of her cottage, inviting her to slip off her shoes and bask in the stillness.

If she chose to break the peaceful solitude by turning on a radio or television, listening to music, or even plugging in the vacuum cleaner, it was her decision, not a mandate from someone above her in the ladder of authority.

Ironically, her dream-come-true to be a published author now had its downside. Being an author would require hours and hours of alone time: hours to transcribe her thoughts into words, for the words to fill pages, for the pages to become chapters to pervade the space between two covers.

Her first book had been written during leisure time, a couple of hours on a weekend, a few days over a vacation, a month of summer days with no contract dictating a delivery date, no dotted line for her to sign.

It was one thing to experience quietness after an active day at school, but could she handle it day after day from morning until night? Would the four painted walls of her would-be-sanctuary begin to yell and scream at her, driving her nuts with the absence of live human beings to interact and work with? Would her darling cottage become a jailhouse sentencing her to the life of a hermit? There'd be no one pleading for her assistance, no one flashing her an unexpected smile or drawing her a crayon masterpiece.

In the end, she had requested an extension on the second book's deadline. Permission was granted, pushing the deadline back to August first of next summer. She would have to parcel off chunks of time in her evenings during the school year and use her weekends to make the words fly. Whatever she had left would be punched into the computer next summer after school closed in May.

And thus, whether she was on a road trip in her car, putting up bulletin boards at school, or at home washing dishes, a story was slowly unfolding in her mind, one that often sent her scurrying for a notepad to jot down another Roman numeral to her outline or to scribble a detail she didn't want to forget to include.

Rrring. Rrring. Rrring. Rrring. Rrring.

The soothing refrain of quietness was broken by the shrill pulsating of the discordant doorbell. Surfacing groggily from an unplanned siesta, Jasmine moaned at the interruption. Her eyelids voluntarily closed a second time, pleading for a few more stolen minutes of respite. The hum of the air-conditioner kicking in lulled her foggy head back to sleep.

Rrring. Rrring. Rrring. Rrring. Rrring.

Ugh! Why hadn't she had one of those melodious doorbells installed that played a jingle from a well-loved tune in place of this insistent bong?

Groaning, she turned over on her back, the dots of the digital clock informing the sleepy schoolmarm that her short rest had stretched into two hours.

Sometime during her nap, she had yanked the crocheted afghan off the back of the couch, where it been neatly folded in thirds. Now it covered her from neck to toe, warding off the chill of the blowing air. Chiding herself for being cold on a ninety-eight-degree cooker of a day, she made a mental note to up the temperature setting on the air-conditioner.

Rrring. Rrring. Rrring. Rrring. Rrring.

"Oh, Ryan, give me a few more minutes," she murmured lazily, savoring the minutes she shouldn't be wasting.

Without even peeking out the vertical blinds lining the front window, she knew it was Ryan. Most guests would press the doorbell once or twice, wait a respectable amount of time, and press it again. If there was no response, the assumption would be generated the occupant wasn't at home.

Not Ryan.

Ryan Benson had moved into the ramshackle house next door a year ago this past June, along with his relatively young mother, Tina Benson, and his high-school-aged half sister, Lacey Flicker. Chugging into town from a southern state in a rusty '84 station wagon, their bald spare tire had held together for the last hundred miles of the trip.

Everyone in town contemplated, *Why?* Why would a family living in a mild climate trade it for North Dakota's harsh winters? Why would Tina Benson choose a place in which she didn't know a soul to hang her hat?

Tina had the answer. "It was the cheapest house listed on the Internet." Jasmine speculated what the list price had been on the heap of weathered boards topped with a roof, still boasting its first set of shingles. Whatever the dollar figure, it had been too much.

Antiquated copper pipes sprung water leaks, prompting an estimate from a plumber. At the onset of the first cold snap back at Halloween, the furnace repairman was parked on the broken cement pad of what used to be a garage before a prior owner tore it down.

Townsfolk gathering at the local restaurants for coffee predicted Tina would have North Dakota in her rearview mirror by Christmas—if the car started—and if not then, by Easter. Nevertheless, the citizens gave her a warm North Dakota welcome, dropping off used furniture on her driveway, curtains to dress the windows, and dishes and canned goods to fill her cupboards.

However, the town had been wrong. Tina and her two children had survived a whole twelve months in Dakota and gave no indication they'd be packing up anytime soon.

Jasmine's introduction to the youngest member of the household came the second day after their arrival. On her hands and knees in the backyard, she had been spading a border between one of her flowerbeds and the encroaching lawn grass. Carefully fitting individual decorative bricks into the shallow trench she'd hollowed out, she patted each in place, painstakingly curving the cement blocks in an attractive setting. While she was leaning back on her heels to study her workmanship, a small pebble had hit her in the back. Looking over her shoulder, she saw no one. The gate in the fence hemming the yard was shut. Bending her head back to survey the branches of the clump birch tree shading the part of her flowerbed ideal for hostas, she hunted for a bird aloft on a white-barked limb.

Seeing only the triangular clumps of leaves quivering in the slight breeze, she went back to her digging. When she bent over to seize the loose grass tops, a definite spray of gravel spread over her back, softly falling in a semicircle about her heels in the mowed lawn. Eyeing the two largest chunks resting by her tennis shoe, she recognized them as broken cement.

It clicked.

Striking out purposely toward the white privacy fence, she detected a glimmer of movement in a crack where two of the fence boards didn't quite butt together properly. A child's cackle affirmed her suspicion. When she unlatched the gate, the rustle of footsteps running through the tall grass of the unkempt yard next door told her the culprit was heading for the hills, or at least a hideout.

A screen door slammed. Detouring to the front of the neighboring house flaked with peeling paint, she mounted the outdoor steps to a square landing cluttered with dead flower pots left behind from the last owner, a broken stool, and a stack of empty boxes. Jasmine knocked on the frame of a torn screen door and waited for an answering summons. All was quiet. She tapped a second time. A bed sheet draped over the front window parted slightly. Mischievous eyes appeared on top of a curved line of tiny white teeth momentarily before the makeshift curtain dropped back into place.

Probably the rascal was fearful of being reprimanded, yet his gleaming expression in the window did not indicate fright. Jasmine called out to him or anyone else inside the dwelling in a friendly voice. "Hello, anybody home? I just wanted to meet my new neighbors."

A series of noises escaping from the interior suggested she had an audience. Squeaking on rusty hinges, the inside door opened six inches, revealing the same dark-haired child, not more than three feet tall. For no specific reason, she christened the youngster a boy, even though his hair nearly brushed his shoulders and his bangs clouded his dark eyes.

"Hi, lady." Wearing a t-shirt, shorts, and a grin, he appeared elflike; twisting the doorknob, his brown eyes sparkled roguishly through the torn opening of the screen.

"Well, hi." She hadn't expected her predator to be of such small stature and as cute as a bug. "I'm Jasmine. I live in the gray house right next to you," she explained, pointing to her cottage.

"I know. I seen you." The chipmunk face bubbled in laughter.

Jasmine decided to skip the recognition of his naughty prank and aim for a better start. "What's your name?"

"Ry ... an." The name was dragged out into two long syllables.

"You must have spent lots of hours driving to your new home, Ryan."

"Yup. It was hot. Lacey wouldn't let me sit by the window." Tugging at the torn screen, he ripped the opening larger.

"And who is Lacey?" Jasmine moved to one side of the platform in case he decided to push the broken screen door open.

"She's my big sister, but she's mean." He giggled again.

"How old are you, Ryan?"

Spreading apart the fingers of one hand, he announced, "Five. I'm gonna be in kindergarten."

"Wow! That will be fun! Is your mom home?" It may have been an unnecessary question, for the old car was absent from the driveway.

Shaking his head, he informed her, "Nah, she went to buy some juice and cereal. I'm getting hungry." His big eyes generated drama.

"May I visit with your sister then?" Jasmine was not sure how much the child had been warned about talking to strangers.

"Lacey's in bed. She sleeps forever." Laughter crinkled up his face.

"I'll come back this evening when I can meet your whole family. Tell your mom I'll bring some supper over because she'll be busy unpacking your things." About to leave, the youngster stopped her.

"Mama's done." Having seen them arrive through her living-room window, three people in an out-of-state vehicle, she reckoned it could be true. There couldn't have been much room for luggage and boxes.

"Good-bye, Ryan. I'll see you later." She had returned to her job in the backyard. Sometimes she'd felt as if two dark eyes were watching her, but no more cement pellets blasted her backside.

Whack. Whack. Whack. Whack. Whack. A little kid's knock had replaced the tirade of the doorbell, and its location: the porch door off the dining room.

Surrendering her seclusion, Jasmine called out, "I'm coming, Ryan. Hold your horses." One last yawn escaped as she scooted off the sofa, hobbling to the French doors leading to the porch. Curtains gathered on rods at the top and bottom of the square panes shrouded the glass access from the eyes of the external world.

Unlocking the door, Jasmine tugged on the handle, admitting the cheery countenance of a flushed Ryan Benson and the scorching heat waves still visible in the late afternoon.

"I knew you were in here!" Ryan greeted her triumphantly.

"Come in, and I'll close the door," his neighbor coaxed, wanting to keep the parched air at bay.

Only too willing to oblige, he darted in and then, remembering the house rule, kicked his untied shoes off his feet.

"Guess what, Jasmine?" The sun-baked youngster with his mahogany tan was bursting with news. Not giving his neighbor lady a chance to reply, he babbled right on. "Mom and me went to school to see where my first-grade room is. And guess what!" Jasmine knew what he was about to say, but she didn't steal his thunder. He nearly shouted the big scoop. "You and me are in the same room! Isn't that good news?" His hand grabbed the air, his elbow pulling it down in a gesture of victory.

In spite of herself, Jasmine had to chuckle at his enthusiasm—to be so loved! When she had seen Ryan Benson on her class enrollment sheet, she'd been concerned. Discretion told her he should have been placed in Cynthia Burns's first-grade room instead of hers. Familiarity with a teacher outside of the school day could lead to a spunky boldness in the classroom. What had Principal Peterson been thinking? He had been aware of how many after-school hours Ryan had spent in her classroom during the preceding kindergarten year.

"Mom says I have to call you Mrs. Kirmis at school. Is that true?" He wrinkled up his face, wondering why two good friends would have to be so formal.

"Afraid so, Ryan. All of us teachers go by our last names with our students."

"That's weird." Even after a year, Ryan hadn't grown more than a half-inch and would be the shortest pupil in her class. "What if I forget and call you Jasmine?" His brown eyes couldn't conceal the impish shenanigans he always seemed to have stuffed in a side pocket ready to implement if he had a chance.

"You won't. Why don't you start practicing right now?"

"Right now? Even if we aren't in school?"

"If you climb on a stool by the kitchen counter, I'll gave you an ice cold Popsicle."

Dutifully he recited, "Thank you, Mrs. Kirmis," and then ruptured into a wild chorus of giggles, seating himself on the high, cushioned stool.

"See, I knew you could do it."

"It's a lot nicer in your house than ours. Our house is like fire!" Handily, he peeled the paper off the Popsicle before sticking the cool snack against his tongue and savoring the icy texture.

Guiltily, Jasmine admitted to herself he was undoubtedly correct. Fans on a sultry day couldn't compete with central air.

"Does your mom know you're here?"

"Yes, Mrs. Kirmis, and she said I can stay until you kick me out."

As their friendship had grown over the past months, Ryan had begun spending more hours at the neighbor's house than he did at his own home. His sister, Lacey, had shifted her living quarters to her boyfriend's trailer house, leaving Tina without a free babysitter.

Jasmine had never offered to replace her daughter for day care, but somehow it seemed to have happened. The teacher had grown fond of the youngster and worried about the lack of supervision next door.

"Then you'd better see what you can find in the toy box when you're finished with the Popsicle," she instructed.

After two trips to the back room, Ryan figured he had sufficient playthings to occupy himself on the kitchen floor. Since he
was engrossed with building a Lego bridge for the miniature cars
and trucks he'd found, the author in Jasmine took up her notebook and pen, and the two pored over their work side by side.

CHAPTER 9

Opening school day was an eagerly anticipated date by parents, students, staff, and Elton business owners, marked on the calendar weeks in advance.

Joel Linton wasn't a graduate of Elton High. School consolidations had weeded out the smaller village schools once located every eight to ten miles along the railroad tracks when class enrollments had tapered to a handful of pupils. Today, yellow school buses transported kindergarten through senior high students from a thirty-mile radius to the centrally-located public school in Elton.

Living twenty miles from town, Carson was the first pickup on bus number fifteen's scheduled route, driven by Richie Harris. Seven fifteen was mighty early for a first grader to have his teeth brushed and schoolbag slung over his back; however, Joel wasn't worried. The boy was used to being up at the crack of dawn to keep pace, in his estimation, with the smartest farmer in the world.

But the shrill ring of the school bell ordered a major alteration in Joel's farming agenda. A week of late nights remained for the wheat harvest; then at least a month-and-a-half break would ensue before the sunflowers would be dry enough to combine. To do well in his studies, Carson needed to be in bed by eight each night.

It was Arlene who came to the rescue again. Richie Harris would be dropping the first grader off at the Bautzes in the afternoon at the outset of the school year. After the evening meal, she would take the youngster home, tuck him into bed, and stay with him until Joel came in from his work in the field.

Foster care was a whole lot more complex without Melissa.

On this, the opening day of school, though, Joel had driven his charge into Elton, well aware with Carson's initial display of fear at anything new, there would have been no way he would have hopped on the bus. Arlene would retrieve him at the end of his first day. The second day of class would be soon enough for the groundbreaking of the yellow bus.

Joel smiled at the boy's determination to heft the laden schoolbag to his own shoulder, declining Joel's assistance. A steady stream of children and parents padded the sidewalk up to the brick building, passing by the "Welcome Back to School" sign. Kindergarten and first-grade rooms were located in the first corridor ahead. Joel and Carson could see an assemblage of people grouped about Mrs. Kirmis's open door at the far end. Paw prints ambled along the white cement blocks of the hallway wall, sometimes trekking up toward the ceiling and sometimes stroking the rubber baseboards, steadily treading toward the pair of first-grade classrooms.

Joel acknowledged a mother shepherding a toddler by one hand and guiding a school-aged youngster with the other. An occasional father tagged behind his kids, doing the first-day-of-school honors. Predominately, the parents were a generation younger than Joel, making him an older-than-average first-grade papa.

Carson's hand sought the secure sanctuary of the farmer's calloused hand grip, his blue eyes peering out from the blond hair, bleached white by the summer sun.

A paw print painted on the outside of Mrs. Kirmis's door ended the trail with a life-sized cartoon character of a bear sharpening a pencil. Coming to a halt in the doorway, Carson stared into the room at the children and parents milling about, his tanned face fading to a lighter winter shade, his slim body huddling close to Joel's hip.

An overprotective mother knelt in front of her perfectly curled and ribboned daughter, giving last-minute instructions. "Your sharpened pencils and erasers are on the ledge inside your desk. The puppy dog stickers you liked are in the new folder. If you have to go potty, just ask the teacher. I'm sure she'll let you go. Give Mommy a kiss and a hug." Dressed as a miniature model in a fashion catalog, the little girl dutifully complied and then walked into the room, not looking back. Her whimpering mother hung on to every movement she made, snapping a half-dozen digital shots before departing.

Mrs. Kirmis was across the room holding a desk lid open while a sandy-haired boy removed his school supplies one-by-one from his backpack. His mother visited with the teacher.

Joel eased Carson forward into the colorful world of first grade, noting a penmanship card taped to each desk with a child's name written in perfect manuscript letters. He spotted Carson's name in a tripod of desks in the first row. Propelling the frozen form to the appointed desk was no less laborious than getting a one-ton bull loaded into a stock trailer. Two adventurous little boys, not suffering from any form of bashfulness, had found a tub of toys on the shelf under the windows and were picking through the new treasures.

Lifting the schoolbag off the boy's stiff back, Joel coaxed, "Let's put your new notebooks and art supplies in your desk, Carson. You can arrange them the way you'd like them." Carson's eyes were on the other individuals moving around the room. Mrs. Kirmis was greeting still another parent and child.

Joel unzipped the bag for him, pulling out the box of crayons. He tried handing it to the mummified youngster, but Carson made no motion to accept it. Not knowing what else to do, he propped open the lid and tipped in the entire contents of the backpack.

Taking Carson by the hand again, he led him into the narrow cloakroom. Here too each hook had a student's name card above it. After hanging the bag on Carson's hook, Joel sat down on the bench below the hooks, gathering the stoic youngster into the space between his knees.

"Hey, buddy, you went to kindergarten last year. That was fun. First grade is going to be like that too. You'll soon know the names of all your classmates. You'll play with them at recess and learn with them here in the room. Each day when you come home, I want to hear all about it."

He looked deep into the blue eyes, trying to read what was going on inside his little Bantam chicken. There were no tears. No smile. Just a blank page. Squeezing him into a hug, the man whispered in his ear, "Love you, buddy. I'll be praying for you today." Carson's head rested against his friend's collarbone. If possible, Joel hoped some of his own strength was seeping into this fragile creature that had inconspicuously moved in and taken up residence in the farmer's heart.

A scruffy, dark-headed child wearing a cheery smile entered the end of the cloakroom swinging his schoolbag, letting it bump against his knees. No fear blanketed his countenance. Joel gave Carson a pat on the backside and slid him out from the hollow between his legs.

"Hi." The new first grader was not at all hampered by the presence of a broad-shouldered adult. Tiny in stature, the boy was a head shorter than Carson but a head taller in sociability.

"Hello there, young man. What's your name?" Joel addressed him, sticking out a hand.

Walking straight up to the man, the youngster stuck his tiny hand into Joel's larger one and pumped it hard. "Ryan. Who are you, mister?" A grin deepened, punctuated by sunken dimples.

"I'm Joel, and this is my son, Carson," he replied, clasping his thin shoulder.

Ryan's eyes shifted with interest to the light-haired boy, the contrast in coloring between the two classmates as evident as day and night. "Hi. How did you get white hair? Did ya dye it?"

Carson remained mute, sticking his hands inside his pockets. Joel smirked. *Dyed it?* "When God made Carson, he took a big bag of stardust and shook it right out of the heavens onto the top of his head."

"Cool," Ryan replied, accepting the answer as factual. "Mister, my name is sitting on your head."

Cranking his head around to the name tags taped above the hooks, Joel read, "R-Y-A-N, that's you? Excuse me for blocking your space." Rising to his full height, he moved aside.

Nimbly, Ryan hopped up on the built-in bench and looped a strap over the hook.

"You seem to know your way around here, young fellow." Joel watched as Ryan jumped to the floor again, his dark hair hiding his eyes.

"Yup, I'm Jasmine's helper." He clapped four chubby fingers over his mouth, his eyes widening. "Oops, I mean, Mrs. Kirmis."

Apparently the man was correct in his assumption. "Carson is new here. Maybe you could show him around."

The head bobbed. "Sure, come on." He marched toward the exit of the cramped cloakroom. Joel pushed Carson ahead of him, following their guide. New arrivals were scattered about the classroom. A mother with spiked auburn hair and pink high-lights kept Mrs. Kirmis captive, talking as fast with her hands as she did with her mouth. Catching Joel's eye, the teacher smiled a welcome before addressing the gal in tight stretch pants.

Ryan stopped his tour at his desk, a pudgy finger tracing each letter of his name. "See, this is where I sit. Where's your desk?"

Carson surprised Joel by pointing to the desk across the aisle. Raising his eyebrows, Joel stood back, wanting to witness the reception. Ryan hopped over to Carson's name sign. Touching each letter, he spelled, "C-A-R-S-O-N. I know all my letters."

"Me too." As if remembering he wasn't going to talk, Carson looked behind him for the security of Joel's presence. Stepping back, he stuck a finger into the man's belt loop.

The thin lady with the pink hair and coordinating magenta fingernails ruffed up Ryan's thick mop of hair. "You be a good boy for Jasmine, you hear?" Heavy makeup circled the lady's dark eyes. A definite resemblance linked her to the child.

"Mom, you said I can't call her that," Ryan corrected, ducking his head from out of her grasp.

She shrugged off the child's remark. "Gotta get to work. See ya, baby." Her high heels tapped a cadence as she left the room.

"Good morning, Carson. It looks like you're all set for first grade," Mrs. Kirmis greeted her new student. Steel-blue eyes bored into her.

Ryan took over. "Carson's new, Mrs. Kirmis, so I was showing him where to sit." Leaning his hip against the desk, he took on a stance of importance.

"That was nice of you, Ryan." The teacher smiled her approval. "Carson, you have fifteen new friends in this room waiting to meet you. This is going to be a fun year for all of us."

Carson's blank face didn't show any sign of her pleasant words having penetrated. His guardian shifted his feet, unsure whether to stay and help Carson through his anxiety or if it was better if he left. Baffled, he glanced over at Mrs. Kirmis for assistance.

Taking the cue, the experienced teacher grasped Ryan's hand and held her other hand out to Carson. "The first matter at hand this morning is to measure how tall each of my first graders are. Would you two like to be first?"

"Measure me, teacher. I bet I grew this much over the summer." Ryan held his hand high over the top of his thick, shaggy head.

Carson ignored her hand, but a hint of curiosity showed in his eye. "Okay, guys, let's head for the giraffe." Mrs. Kirmis led Ryan by the hand to the painted giraffe on the end of a tall bookshelf. A measurement stick ran up its tall leg and on up through its polka-dotted neck. Carson and Joel followed.

Immediately, Ryan backed up against the bookshelf, ready to see if he had indeed stretched over vacation. "Oh no, buster," Mrs. Kirmis exclaimed. "Shoes come off. I'm not going to give you any extra height you haven't earned."

Giggling, Ryan complied, pushing his right toe against the heel of his left sneaker. Seconds later, he stood in stocking feet, a hole in each toe. Laying a foot ruler on top of his head to mark his height against the measurement tape, the teacher announced, "Three feet, one inch."

"Am I touching the giraffe's back?" His eyes disappeared altogether under his shaggy hair as he tried to peer upward.

"Almost. By the end of the year, you'll be climbing on top of him for a ride."

"You're just goofing me. No one can ride *that* giraffe."

Winking, she admitted, "You've got me there." Recording his height on a tablet, she turned to Carson. "So what do you think? Are you tall enough to reach his back, or are you climbing up the spots on his neck?"

A tiny twitch at the corner of his lips gave him just enough courage to shyly back up to the bookshelf. Joel bent down to loosen the laces on his tennis shoes before removing them.

Eying up his blond classmate against the giraffe, Ryan exclaimed, "Gee, Carson, you can see over his back!"

"Yes, sir," Mrs. Kirmis verified. "Three feet, five inches!"

"Good going, Carson!" Ryan squealed, as if the thin child had anything to do with his stature.

"Hey, bud," Joel interjected, "you could be a sunflower growing in my field."

"You're taller than I be," Ryan pronounced, standing shoulder to shoulder with the new kid, "but I might grow more and beat you."

"If you two drink your milk every day, this giraffe won't be the only tall character in our room." Mrs. Kirmis added Carson's height to her list.

Sensing this might be an appropriate departure moment, Joel lowered himself to Carson's eye level. "I've gotta head out to the field, Carson. I will be waiting for a full report of everything you did on your first day." He wanted to engulf him in another hug but was fearful he'd have to pry Carson loose afterward. Instead, he cuffed him gently on the upper arm with his fist and stood up.

"See ya." He turned and walked to the door, where he paused for one last look. Blue eyes followed him. Their gazes locked.

Joel winked, tipping his index finger toward the child. He hesitated, wanting to stay, knowing it was best to leave.

Carson blinked both eyes back at him simultaneously, reminiscent to the lights flashing on a John Deere tractor.

A shrill buzzer broadcasted the commencement of the opening day, signaling to any remaining parents to be on their way. Mrs. Kirmis breathed a sigh of relief when she ushered the last reluctant mother to the corridor, leaving her alone with her sixteen protégées.

Grinning at the attentive children before her, Mrs. Kirmis scanned her audience. A sea of inquisitive faces watched her closely. Many sported fresh haircuts and new clothes purchased at a back-to-school promotion.

Expectantly, the students waited for the edified teacher to speak. Chubby Kaylee Edwards chewed on the end of a plaited pigtail. Stevie Dewayne pushed back in his chair, trying to balance on the back two legs, like he'd seen his older brother do. Joey Haun was distracted by the noise of a truck lumbering by on the street outside the classroom window. Lifting her childlike hand to the top of her head, Pixie Loman checked to see if the satin ribbon her mom had tied in her naturally curly hair was still in place. Her pleated plaid skirt and matching waist-length jacket gave her a college freshman preppy look.

Carson Reynolds sat petrified in his plastic chair, unsure of this new environment, while Ryan, in the tripod of desks across the aisle, gave Mrs. Kirmis a toothy smile, perfectly at home in his first-grade room. And why shouldn't he be? He'd already played with every toy in the room, sifted through the long rows of books on the shelves dozens of times, cranked the handle of the paper towel dispenser screwed to the wall beside the sink repeatedly, and practiced writing his letters and numbers on the whiteboard. All those after-school hours during his kindergarten year had been idled away in the first-grade room with his neighbor lady, Jasmine Kirmis. After Mrs. Kirmis's completion of preparations for the next day, invariably, the two had left the school together, walking the six blocks to their street, going their separate ways when they reached the front of Jasmine's blue cottage—unless the windows in the next-door Benson hovel were still dark and forlorn, a telltale sign that Tina Benson wasn't home nor even worried about her maternal duties.

Letting her eyes rest on each child individually, Mrs. Kirmis couldn't help but feel a deep joy bubbling up inside of her—the unbelievable privilege being gifted to her again this first day of a new term, to be granted these blessed children to teach for a whole nine months. And to think she had almost bypassed this school year.

"Good morning, boys and girls. I am Mrs. Kirmis. Welcome to first grade! I am so glad to meet all of you. Each day will be super special because you are here." Her eyes and lips danced in unison, allowing her friendliness and love for teaching permeate to the corners of the room. Her rollicking greeting and contagious cheerfulness relaxed the class as a whole, disposing of any first-day jitters.

After the recitation of the Pledge of Allegiance to the flag, Mrs. Kirmis clapped her hands to redirect the class's attention. "Let's form a giant circle in the back of the room." Scrambling to do their teacher's bidding, the youngsters quickly clasped hands.

"Stretch the circle." Moving outward, the circle widened until their short arms could reach no further. "Drop your hands. Sit down on the floor at the exact spot you are standing."

While holding a large, colorful plastic ball, Mrs. Kirmis situated herself on the floor between Hannah and Joey, who were only too happy to have the teacher sitting next to them.

"Now I need everyone to put on a thinking cap." Mrs. Kirmis pretended to set an imaginary hat on top of her chestnut hair, tugging it down to cover her ears. Her pupils followed suit, giggling as they envisioned themselves with headgear capable of thinking.

"Everyone listening?" Jasmine's eyes flowed around the circle of dimples and noses. "I am going to ask you a question. Each of you must think of an answer but hold it inside of your head until it is your turn to give us your reply out loud. I am going to roll this ball to one of you. If the ball comes to you, then you will pull your answer out of your thinking hat and tell us." She dramatized reaching deep into her hat to snatch up a retort waiting to be captured.

"Are you ready?" A ring of heads bobbed up and down, excited at the expectance of being the recipient of the kaleidoscope ball.

"Okay, here is the question—mouth closed—just think inside of your head. Why are you glad to be back in school?"

Flashing a colorful spectrum, the gyrating plastic ball moved toward Ryan's outstretched hands. He held it high over his head in a sign of triumph. "That's easy! I get to spend all day with Jasmine, every day! Oops!" Tossing the ball backward over his head at his mistake, he yelled, "I mean, Mrs. Kirmis!"

The teacher's heart warmed but also tore for the little guy who so very desperately needed the attention of a parent.

CHAPTER 10

Having tucked Carson into bed earlier, Joel used the next hour to catch up on what he nicknamed his "housewife chores." Melissa would have teased him of being a chauvinist, dividing work into *his* and *hers*. Ah, yes, Melissa had spoiled him. His sentiments softened at the thought. She would have said the same of him though.

Only now, it was just him.

He transferred a load of dark clothes from the washing machine to the dryer, spun the dial to thirty minutes, and pushed the start button. Soiled towels dropped into the washer next, followed by a cup of detergent.

Next, he tackled the sink full of dishes. No matter what anyone said, an electric dishwasher did not scrub fried eggs out of a skillet or scorched potatoes from a kettle. Opening his insulated lunchbox, Joel dumped out the remains of his noon meal.

Both he and Carson were adjusting to their new routine caused by the addition of a school day into their schedule. The conclusion of the small grain harvest of wheat and barley had made it possible for the yellow bus to drop Carson off at the Linton farm instead of at Ed and Arlene's. No matter what he was doing during the course of his many and varied farm chores, Joel, like clockwork, made sure he was in the yard at 4:15 sharp when Richie Harris cranked the steering wheel, swinging bus number fifteen along the edge of the slough and into the drive-way. A single towhead showed above the seat backs.

Carson was first on in the morning and the last passenger off on the return trip. Dust from the gravel road twirled in puffy clouds in the air when Carson flew out of the bus door, running full speed into Joel's waiting arms, crushing him about the rib cage, a smile smeared from ear to ear. Joel cherished this spe-cial ritual highlighting an ordinary afternoon. Hugging the child back, he thanked God for little moments.

Soapsuds disappeared down the drain.

Striding to his office, he winced at its conglomeration of papers, receipts, and farm books filling the bookshelves, the desktop, and the corners of the floor—another project to tackle someday.

Sliding a telephone directory and county atlas off his swivel chair, he lowered his blue-jeaned bottom into it. A click of the mouse brought the day's e-mails flashing on the monitor screen. Most of his messages were agriculture related. Joel's eyes trav-eled down the short list of entries to the bottom one.

What's this? Mrs. Kirmis? What would she be e-mailing me for? Did something happen to Carson in school today? Is he in trouble? His pulse quickened.

> Mr. and Mrs. Linton,
>
> Greetings from first grade! It is hard to believe that three weeks of the new school year have already disappeared. The class has been busy reviewing the concepts taught in kindergarten: the basic sounds made by the 26 letters of the alphabet, counting up to 50, and recognizing basic sight words, such as the colors.

Joel wondered if Carson's teacher sent a mass e-mail to all the parents of her first graders giving updates of what was pres-ently being taught. The thought reduced his initial anxiety over receiving an e-mail from the school. He continued reading.

Overall, Carson has maintained his timidity, preferring to be an observer rather than a participant in many activities, especially those outside of our classroom. His music teacher reports that while he is not a discipline problem at all, he refuses to sing or do the actions of the fun songs the rest of the class readily vocalizes and dramatizes. In gym class, Carson prefers to sit on the sidelines, watching the physically active games being played. At recess, he walks about the playground, observing the other children at play, and seems to enjoy seeing them having fun. When asked to join in, he always shakes his head.

So much for a mass mailing. This was about Carson. Carson alone.

Back in August, when you brought Carson for a pre-school visit, he fixed me with his blue stare. It felt like his gaze pierced right through me. You too recognized this behavior but assured me that once Carson felt comfortable, he'd come out of his shell. I see that happening when I work one-on-one with him. He readily will make the sounds of the letters and count objects for me. During free time, I have seen him sharing toys with at least one other student.

Some of my colleagues wonder if we should be pushing him more to interact with others. I disagree. Carson seems to be feeling out the new environment and will open the door to us when he decides we meet his security standards.

As his foster parents, I would appreciate your thoughts and observations at home. Does Carson come willingly to school? Does he talk about the school day? Do you have any suggestions of how we can better reach him in the school environment?

Thank you for being caring adults in his life.

Mrs. Kirmis

Joel breathed out, not realizing he'd been holding his breath, fearful of what the e-mail message would entail. The youngster was still finding his way. Although it hadn't taken Carson long to attach to the farmer's hip, for some reason he was more hesitant to allow other adults and peers into his safety net.

What had this six-year-old already seen in his short life? What had already been done to him? A young boy should be full of energy, ready to try almost anything, filled with laughter and anticipation. Childhood should be the best part of a lifetime of experiences—the years of no worries, no headaches, no big responsibilities. Yet Carson was scared of the very activities other youngsters looked forward to. Who or what had made him this way? A slice of his innocent youth had been stolen from him.

Oh, God, this is too big for me. Care for your child. Heal him on the inside.

Staring at the dark window of his office, Joel sought for the words to formulate a reply to Mrs. Kirmis. Somehow she was under the assumption that there was a foster mom in Carson's life. Joel fervently wished there was.

Guess he hadn't mentioned Melissa or the absence of Melissa. Oh well, it didn't matter. He was both Dad and Mom to the child. They were okay, weren't they? Melissa would have put the finer touches on their relationship with this midget—things he struggled with. Meals would definitely be better. Seasonal decorations would grace the farmhouse. A windsock would fly from the porch post, and plastic stickers on the windows would change with each holiday. She would know more about kids' books, movies, games, and clothes. Living with Melissa would have been a blast for Carson. And she'd know how to reply to a teacher's e-mail message.

Shifting in the padded seat, his eyes settled on the simple drawing tacked to the bulletin board above the computer. Carson had sketched it at the kitchen table while Joel had been paying bills, stuffing checks into envelopes. The elementary stick figures were typical of a first grader, except for the finer details. A tall stick man held the hand of similar stick boy. Both wore billed hats with grain elevator logos carefully printed on the forepart. In the man's front shirt pocket was a cell phone attached to a string tied to one of the shirt buttons. It kept the phone from accidentally falling out of the pocket, a precaution Joel used after losing his phone twice jumping up and down off of farm machinery. Clasped in the boy's free hand was a green and white water jug, their constant companion when working outdoors.

Tenderness descended upon the weary parent, relaxing his tight facial features. Carson may not be a famous artist, but this drawing was priceless to the recipient.

Awkwardly, his thick fingers hit a few keys on the keyboard. Oops! Backspace. He tapped out a few more letters. Pause. Gathering his reflections, he struggled to fit the words into adequate sentence structure. Writing a teacher wasn't the same as sending off a note to Ned. He hated to appear dumber than the average first grader. Joel grimaced. Backspace.

> Mrs. Kirmis,
>
> I appreciate you sharing your concerns for Carson as well as his triumphs. Having only shared four months of the six years of his life, it is hard to say what the little guy has witnessed or how he has been treated in the past. He may well have very good reasons for being extremely cautious in opening up. Thanks for your patience. I doubt if coercion would work anyway.

At home, Carson constantly talks about what has happened in school, all favorably. You can tell the music teacher he sings "The Wheels on the Bus Go 'Round and 'Round" in the shower.

Sincerely,
Joel Linton

"Teacher, Ryan broke my blue crayon." Pixie Loman pulled on her teacher's sleeve, bumping askew the manuscript printing Mrs. Kirmis was carefully writing in bold marker on individual reading cards.

Continuing to print, Mrs. Kirmis replied, "I'm sure he didn't mean to break your crayon. Sometimes when we color it just happens by accident." As usual, Pixie was dressed in designer clothes, a miniature fashion model on parade. Her big eyes were wide and serious with expression.

"Yes, he did, teacher. He broke it on purpose."

Broke it on purpose seemed to be a standard first-grade charge, a guilty verdict delivered with no chance of parole.

Changing her plan of strategy, Mrs. Kirmis tried complimenting the accuser. "It was nice of you, Pixie, to let Ryan borrow your blue crayon. Sharing is what friends do."

Pixie wasn't about to be distracted from her initial complaint of injustice. "He just took my blue crayon." She paused and then added, "Without even asking." That was a double whammy on Ryan, the classroom rascal.

Evidently Ryan had gotten into trouble numerous times in kindergarten. Sometimes he was given the blame for things he hadn't done—the class scapegoat. On the other hand, the condemnation was often justified, and it was being carried right into first grade.

Mrs. Kirmis sighed. Glancing to the pod of three desks where Ryan sat, she detected his hand flying back and forth across the drawing paper, coloring a blue sky above his autumn picture. A small stub of a crayon barely projected above his thumb and index finger's grasp.

Point scored for Pixie. Evidence: Ryan was holding a broken crayon.

Not wanting to overreact and have Pixie think it was her self-appointed duty to inform the teacher of Ryan's infringements, she said, "Hey, Ryan, your picture is fabulous! The blue sky above the orange pumpkins…looks like a perfect day to pick out a pumpkin to carve into a jack-o'-lantern."

Ryan looked up, his toothy grin spreading. Holding up his work of art for his teacher to see, he explained, "This is the pumpkin farm we went to at my old home. The daddy pumpkin in the middle is the one I picked." He poked a finger at the odd-shaped orange blob set amongst similar smudges of tangerine. How was Jasmine supposed to reprimand a budding Michelangelo when he was so enthusiastic about his creation? A broken crayon was minor compared to past antics he'd performed. Miss Hazeton, his kindergarten teacher, had been only too willing to pass him on to Jasmine's first-grade room.

Eying the pumpkin Ryan was pointing to, Mrs. Kirmis agreed, "Good pick! What kind of face did you give it?"

"A happy one; I don't like scary pumpkins." No doubt his Halloween pumpkin had matched the grin now displayed on his face.

Enlisting Pixie into the conversation, Jasmine asked, "Pixie, which of the pumpkins on Ryan's picture would you choose for a jack-o'-lantern?"

"I like little baby ones. I want the smallest one." Moving away from her teacher's elbow, she skipped back to her desk adjacent to Ryan's, examining his artwork.

"Here, you can use my special pencil to draw a face on it," Ryan generously offered, holding out a mechanical pencil he'd found in the hallway. Jasmine breathed a quick prayer under her breath, hoping Pixie would be distracted from her previous charges.

Satisfied, the curls bent over the drawing now sitting on her desk and began to carefully outline triangular eyes, a nose, and a bucktooth smile.

"Whew!" Jasmine muttered to herself. One classroom disruption was thwarted. Ryan seemed to be connected in one way or another to every first-grade eruption. Rough in play, quick and agile on his feet, he could invade a peer's territory, pull off a shenanigan, retreat, and disappear again before a wail of protest could climb up the victim's throat. An impish smirk would festoon his face, his eyes lit like Christmas lights.

Truthfully, he was not always the instigator of a ruckus, but he still was often given credit for its explosion.

At the dismissal bell, Ryan scampered past Jasmine's skirt as she supervised the pupils passing in the hallway. "I'm gonna play outside until you're ready to go, teacher."

"Okay." Sighing, she wondered why his mother didn't seem worried about his supervision after school. Tina worked as a cashier at the gas station along the bypass outside of town. On her scheduled days, she got off work at five thirty, but even on her days off, Ryan was at loose ends, never sure whether she'd be home or spending the day with a boyfriend.

But he knew where Jasmine was, and that's exactly where he chose to hang out. Shaking her head and lamenting inwardly, she glanced up to see Cynthia Burns, her partner in first grade, eyeing her from across the corridor.

"Hey, Mama Kirmis. What's it tonight? Supper? Bath? Bedtime story? And tucked in?" Cynthia was fully aware of Jasmine's quandary with the neighbor family.

Ryan did take up a lot of her hours, and yet what could she do? Guess that's why she was in the teaching profession. Kids could crawl into her heart, roll out a sleeping bag, and turn on a nightlight—and their parents took advantage of it.

Jasmine pursed her lips. "Hopefully I'll get by with an afternoon snack."

Leaning against the cool bricks of the hallway wall, Cynthia sympathetically stated the facts. "The kid's only in first grade. Without you, it would only be a matter of time before Social Services would step in and clean house. Are you going to play nanny until he graduates from high school?"

Ruefully, Jasmine admitted her friend's statements had merit. "Yeah, well, how long do you think Tina will endure North Dakota's frigid winters? She doesn't seem to be one who lets roots grow under her feet. She'll move on." Guiltily, she fathomed what would happen to Ryan at the next stop.

"Cheap housing and free babysitting. Heck, why would she want to leave? I wager she pulled out of the last state because bill collectors and social workers were knocking on her front door. She had to slip out the back quickly and hightail it out of the state." Cynthia's eyebrows shot up in a speculative know-it-all fashion.

"You might be right, Miss North Dakota, but if Ryan lived in your neighborhood, you'd do the same as me. It's what we do here: help every down-and-outer up. Our parents taught us too well."

Grinning, Cynthia hooked her arm through Jasmine's bent elbow. "Yup, we're two of a kind: dead meat for a roving coyote to prey upon. Two softies figuring we can change the world one child at a time. Fortunately, I live on the other side of the tracks, and dear ol' Miss Lydia lives next door to me. She only needs me to fetch her mail from the box on the street. And in return, I get a weekly plate of homemade cookies."

The blare of the intercom from Cynthia's classroom interrupted the banter.

Back in her own domain, Jasmine contemplated what she should tackle first.

She hadn't updated her computer with the memos she was constantly gathering on her students. These notes would be beneficial for the upcoming parent-teacher conferences. Arnie was making fewer reversals on his letters. Jeremy nodded off in class on September twenty-eighth and October fourth. Was he getting enough rest? Hannah surprised her by using the word *meandering* in her oral speech—a big word for a first grader! Ryan pushed a kindergartner off the swings on September twenty-seventh.

Clicking open the student folder on her PC, the class registry page popped up, an alphabetical list of her students with basic information. Noting a scattering of empty blanks, she typed in missing data she now had that hadn't been available or had changed since the start of the school year.

Scrolling to *Benson, Ryan*, she noticed the emergency home space was vacant. It wouldn't pay to ask Tina again for the name of a friend or neighbor the school could contact in the event Tina was not available during the school day. Jasmine knew Tina would assume the trusty Mrs. Kirmis would take care of her son. Pursing her lips, she moved down the list.

Lewis, Hannah: no street address. Back in September, the family was in the process of moving to a different home right here in Elton. The school secretary would be able to supply the new location.

Reynolds, Carson: still didn't have Joel Linton's wife's name. She may as well jaunt to the office and get the information right away. While there, she could run off some phonics and penmanship papers on the copy machine.

Entering the outer office minutes later, she waved to the secretary behind the desk. A high counter separated them.

Peering over the wire glasses perched on the end of her nose, June Max removed the pencil caught crosswise in her teeth and gave the first-grade staff member a hearty reception. "Hey, Mrs. Kirmis, first time I've seen you today. How goes it with the munchkins?"

June had filled the position of school secretary long before Jasmine had been hired on board twenty-three years ago. Her seniority kept Principal Peterson on his toes, reminding him of what ought to be done and when. Over a quarter century of school years had passed over June's desk. Having worked for two principals prior to Mr. Peterson, she was a library of information on educational protocol and procedure, families in the district, scheduling, and deadlines.

"Oh, the short people are doing just fine. Keeping me hopping, as usual." Jasmine leaned on the high counter partitioning the office into a workstation. "As always, it's me who needs your help, not the little people in my life. I'm missing some information on my roll data sheet."

June swung her mobile chair to her computer, clicking her mouse to upload the first grade. "Shoot."

"First off, do you have Hannah Lewis's new address?"

Again, June peered over the top of her spectacles, scanning the screen before her. "No, I still have the old one, but that would be easy to remedy." Sliding open her side drawer, she drew out the phonebook. "The Lewis family bought Joe Simpson's house when his family put him in the nursing home. I'll look up Joe's name. Here it is."

Having penciled the address onto her scratch paper, Jasmine proceeded to her second question. "Check out Carson Reynolds. What do you have for guardians? He lives with his foster parents."

Before she even reached his line on her spreadsheet, June replied, "That would be Joel Linton. He's a good twenty miles west of town. He and his wife, Melissa, started doing foster care about ten years ago."

"Good! That's what I wanted to know, his wife's name. Melissa. I haven't met her yet." Jasmine jotted down the name then stepped over to the copy machine, inserting the first original phonics sheet into the input tray.

"Why would her name be required on your data sheet? She isn't Carson's birth mother. The school only deals with the foster parents."

"Yes, I'm aware of that," Jasmine agreed, pushing the button to make sixteen copies. "But in case I ever have to call the Lintons, I might get her instead of Joel."

Chuckling, the secretary closed the phonebook and returned it to the drawer. "I realize with your faith, Jasmine, you may very well have a hotline to heaven, for that's exactly what it would take to contact Melissa."

A blank look crossed the teacher's face, not comprehending the secretary's offhand remark.

"Melissa died at least two years ago. Cancer. Years back, the Lintons had a sixth grader staying with them. What was that gal's name?" She tapped her pencil on the notepad lying beside the computer, her eyes frozen in a thought pattern. "Polly Wyatt. That's who it was. Don't you remember her? Tall, dark hair, kind of had a chip on her shoulder."

Color drained from Jasmine's face like a shade shutting out the sunlight. Her green eyes fixated on June's round face. What in the world was June talking about? The drone of the copy machine halted, having finished printing the set of papers. Jasmine didn't even notice.

"They had a little chap once too. Younger." Removing her glasses, the proficient secretary held them up to the light, squinting as she looked for smears.

"Of course, when Melissa got sick, they had to give up foster care. It was too much for her. She held on to the last child as long as she could. She didn't want to sever another relationship in the young man's life. Many foster kids don't experience much permanency. Either their birth parents don't want them, or the kids are taken away because of abuse or neglect. Sometimes a placement doesn't work out, and they have to be moved to another home. Melissa herself told me that one youngster they cared for had been in five different homes before theirs. Sad." Readjusting her glasses back on the tip of her nose, she peered over the rims up at Jasmine.

June's chatter entered Jasmine's auditory perception, but what she was hearing totally did not make sense to her. She wanted information on Carson Reynolds. Yes, he was a foster child—a child who lived with foster *parents*—not a *parent*.

Gripping the edge of the counter, the tips of her fingers turned a sickly white from the pressure. Slowly, she shook her brunette head. June was confused. Certainly the secretary had Carson mixed up with some other student—another whelp who had once attended school in Elton.

"No, June. I have Carson Reynolds in my class. I met his foster dad: Joel Linton—seems like a nice guy. But Carson has a foster mom too. He just has to." Her voice dropped off. Subtle panic was building deep within her. Carson had to have a mother. That's the way foster care worked, providing good parents for children who didn't have any or whose own family couldn't provide adequate care.

The dedicated teacher wanted loving, delightful childhoods for all her students. Ones in which big people cared for their offspring, nurtured their cubs' initiation into life with a cushioned nest of protection they could return to when the world slapped cold water on their miniature souls.

Startled, June recognized the change in her friend. She hefted her grandmotherly form out of the office chair and crossed the open space to the counter, standing directly opposite of Jasmine. Sympathy tenderized her voice.

"Back in August when Joel registered Carson for school, he apologized repeatedly for doing this on his own. He said his house was too quiet. It needed some noise. He didn't know if he could be a father and a mother, but he sure as heck was going to try. His eyes misted and his voice faltered as he sat right next to my desk filling out the registry forms. Joel Linton is a man, a single man—and, in my opinion, is making a darn good parent."

Jasmine's eyes stretched across the counter, held immovable by the truth generated in June's compassionate observation. Finally closing her eyes and digesting the facts, she leaned her elbows on the high counter, letting her chin drop onto her clenched hand.. Taking a deep breath, her eyelids flipped open, seeking June's appraisal once more.

Her voice came out as a whisper. "Why? Why would he do such a thing?" She shuddered inwardly, conjuring in her mind how the role of a single parent had been dumped on her unwilling shoulders four years ago—four long years ago when she had been left with a seventeen-year-old daughter and a twenty-year-old son.

"Her kids are almost grown," people had said. "Jasmine will do fine."

Fine? Was *fine* having a daughter with a year of high school left—a daughter so angry that every gesture of love shown to her she sent reeling back in a fist balled up in hate? Was *fine* sitting up at night waiting and praying for a defiant teenager, hours past curfew, to stumble in, knifing her mother's heart with ugly, slanderous accusations? Was *fine* putting her own grief on hold, endeavoring to fill the void blasted into her daughter's life at a tenuous age?

Nothing had been *fine*. To the depth of her soul, she believed that when a baby was born, God gave the tyke a mother and a father because He knew how hard the job of parenting would be, from the changing of the first diaper to waving good-bye after the high-school graduation ceremony. A father and a mother would be able to lean on each other, to gain strength from the other when the raising of an offspring became a battleground to blaze, when the independence and testing of the teenage years would hit like a suffocating, destructive Dakota tornado.

Single parenting? Yes, there were lots of single parents; parents who had been given the task through divorce, death, poor decisions, and even some by choice.

Would Jasmine Kirmis, at the age of forty, choose to be the sole guardian to two young adults on the brink of leaving the nest? Weren't the hard years already over? The difficult twos? Struggling through homework? Supervising practice sessions at the piano? Adolescence and puberty? Gaining the driver's license?

With every ounce of her being, she spelled silently, *N-O! No, no, no!* Being a single mom was absolutely the hardest thing she'd ever been forced to do in her life. And it still wasn't over.

She did not understand why anyone would want to go solo on parenting. "Why? Why would he do such a thing?"

The empathizing secretary clasped her in a tender hold. "I can't answer for Joel Linton, although I do think he has enough love in him to be both mother and father to Carson. Will he be a perfect parent? Heck no. None of us are. Carson needs love, something Joel has a whole lot of."

The two women stood momentarily paralyzed in the suspension of thoughts hovering between them. Blowing a huff of air upward, lifting her bangs, Jasmine broke the spell. "When did you become so smart, June? You exude wisdom." June gave her a lopsided smile, handing her the phonics papers from the copy machine.

"Well, hats off to Joel Linton, but you won't see me volunteering for the job." Jasmine's facial expression was hard and disapproving.

Pivoting on her heel to exit the office, she caught June's wink. "Oh yeah?" June threw back at her. "And who are you walking home with today, Mrs. Kirmis?"

The query hit her hard. Pausing, she squinted back at the wise old secretary whose shimmering eyes held a pointed speculation.

Ryan. The elflike neighbor with his toothy grin and skipping gait would be waiting for her. And yes, they would walk home hand-in-hand discussing such topics as, *Why does grass grow in the cracks of the sidewalk?* or *How do the birds know already it is going to be too cold in the winter?*

"Maybe you aren't so different from Joel Linton after all," June hinted, holding back a chuckle.

Heading for her classroom to ponder this turn of events, Jasmine didn't bother to answer.

But June was wrong. She was different than Joel Linton. Joel had a choice. She didn't—not with her daughter nor with the chummy chap living next door.

CHAPTER II

"Reach, Mommy. Reach harder! I need you." The urgency implored in the sweet toddler's voice goaded a deep maternal instinct within Jasmine to strain the stretched sinews in her arm even further beyond their endurance, extending her fingers toward the pudgy fingertips of her apprehensive daughter.

"Mommy, I can't feel you! Give me your hand, Mama!" the high cry shrieked beseechingly. Raw pain seared through shoulder tissue as the mother's outstretched arm lunged toward the wavering baby hand fluttering in the air before her. The spanning gap was narrowly close, a hair's breath, and yet too far. Tears rolled down the child's flushed cheeks, matched by the mascara gullies on her mother's face. Whimpering whines, like those of the coyote whelps heard howling in the night sky of the foothills, vibrated with terror. Mother and child each wanting but neither able to conquer the intervening chasm.

Elevating herself an inch higher on her scraped and bloody knees, Jasmine frantically extended her arm again toward Autumn's trembling rag doll position, gaining a mere millimeter of leverage, barely enough to illusively brush the soft fingertips of her baby. "Mommy's here, Autumn. Feel my touch."

The dear, angelic face she'd so often covered with feather kisses, the golden ringlets wet upon her forehead shimmered before her. How she wanted to cuddle her little girl, to rock her, and to sing evening lullabies in her ear and tell her everything would be all right.

"Mommy…" Autumn's call was weaker now.

Once more, Jasmine lunged with the force of her entire weight toward the miniature arm suspended in space, fighting for the child who meant more than life to her. Triumphal reward was bestowed on her like an athlete receiving the laurel-crown when the feel of her middle finger pressed against the velvety tips of two of the infant's tiny fingers. A baby smile lightened her child's countenance, the sun filtering through a stormy cloud. Mother and daughter reveled in the gift, the legacy of a faint touch shared between an infant and the woman who shared her life.

Seconds later, the contact was broken.

The sweet face of her daughter was ripped from her vision, obliterated by a hideous, disfigured form of a teenage girl glaring abusive hatred at her. Tattooed facial features produced slithering snakes venomously sprouting from the eyebrows, intertwining the purplish eyelids and dripping from the nostril holes before encircling the pointed chin. Fangs replaced the tiny, pearl baby teeth, vomiting out a swollen tongue perforated with jewels. Painted scarlet lips sneered evilly, framing the distended tongue, pus oozing from its infectious lacerations.

"My baby! Give me my baby!" Jasmine screamed at the grotesque image blocking her view of Autumn. "Get out of the way!" Her heart thudded against her ribcage, ripping open beat by beat.

Piercing laughter echoed through the black oblivion. "Some mother you are! You don't even recognize your own brat!" Scarlet lips lashed out at the overly distraught woman still demanding her baby.

Jasmine stared at the features of the witch sneering grotesquely at her—the high cheekbones, the green eyes, the heart-shaped face.

A heart-rending moan escaped from her. *No! Not Autumn.* Not her baby girl. Not the fair-haired child born in the fall at the height of nature's divinely colored autumn show. It was all a cruel joke—a freakish caricature of her sophisticated daughter, a sick artist's rendering of what was once strikingly beautiful.

"Get out of my life, Mother! I don't need you or your selfish God." Words of revulsion spewed out of the foul jaws like venom spouting from a serpent, killing the spirit of the woman wracked with tears of torment.

The director of music added his dimension to the horror movie displayed on the cinema's screen. Notes of a baby's lullaby cooed gently in the background, playing with the heartstrings of the parent drowning in her own pool of tears. Slicing his wand through the night sky, the tuxedoed maestro pointed at the bass drums and cymbals to interject their brazen clash into the timid nursery song. Tubas and saxophones followed suit, joined by the trumpets and trombones increasing the volume and tempo of the lullaby to a thunderous, earth-rattling, unharmonious jail wreck.

"*Stop! Stop it!*" Jasmine screamed, her bleeding hands pressed against her ears. "Give me my baby back!" The intensity of the music drowned out the continuous flow of hurtful condemnations of hatred thrown from the mouth of the teenage monster.

Lashing out toward the ugly creature, Jasmine's hand hit against something hard. "My baby, I want my baby," she moaned over and over. She struck again. Her knuckles hurt. A ringing sensation howled through the symphony's wielding discord, becoming louder than even the pandemonium of the out-of-tune instruments. Ringing and ringing and ringing.

Jasmine's hand flailed once more, this time connecting with the hard wood of her nightstand. Her body, bathed in sweat, suddenly sat up soldier stiff, her eyes tunneling into the darkness. Slowly, she detected the rectangular frame of her closet doors, the shine of the dresser mirror, and the straight-back chair beside the clothes hamper.

Another nightmare. Relief washed over her like the water from the shower spout, washing the terrifying scenes of the film

down the drain, but not out of her memory. Another dream ripping away her rest time, and yet not all of it was a fantasy.

Brrring!

Disoriented, it took her a moment to deduce the ringing was
no longer part of the nightmare. The sound vibrating from her
bedside phone startled her. Three minutes after eleven shone
from the clock radio. She'd only climbed into bed a mere half
hour ago. How could the thoughts nudged out of the way during
the daytime hours come forth in such revulsion once her eyes
closed for the night?

Clumsily reaching for the phone, the pictures of her daughter
still vivid in her mind, she croaked out a, "Ha-llo." Clearing her
throat, she tried it again. "Hello?"

Who would call her this late? Premature assumptions sent
her heart racing again. Had something happened to Autumn or
her son, Jacob? Jacob would never call at this hour. Or Autumn?
Autumn didn't call at all.

"Jasmine, this is Tina." Tina? Tina from next door? Raucous
laughter in the background made it hard to decipher her neighbor's voice.

"Jasmine, I just got called in to work." A male voice was talking to Tina at the same time. "Would it be okay if I sent Ryan
over to spend the night with you?" She giggled at something her
companion was doing.

Leaning back against the headboard, the washed-out woman
let out a tired sigh. She reached for the lamp setting next to her,
shutting her eyes momentarily as the darkness was dispelled by
the sixty-watt bulb. Four after eleven.

Incoherently, Jasmine attempted to push the nightmare's
imagery along with the fogginess of sleep out of her head in
order to concentrate on Tina's request. Why would she be called
to the gas station at this hour? Didn't it close at eleven?

"Jasmine, are you there?" No drowsiness coated Tina's words.

"Ah, yes, sorry, I'm here." Drawing her knees up, she planted her feet flat on the mattress.

Tina continued, "I know it's late, but I'm in rather a pinch." In the background, the same male voice uttered something indistinguishable.

What choice did she have? A six-year-old boy was at stake here. Tina's high-school daughter, Lacey, had moved in with an older boyfriend last summer after a fight with her mom. And Ryan? He was learning all about life, whatever version that might be, from the people closest to him.

"Sure, bring him over. I'll be at the door." Her hand crept up to cover her eyes.

"You are a lifesaver, honey. I'll make it up to you."

Replacing the receiver and swinging her feet to the floor, Jasmine wondered, *How?* It didn't matter that her sleep was disrupted. She needed to clear the bad dream out of her brain before attempting sleep again anyhow. But Ryan? Ryan mattered.

A rap at the door jolted her into action. That was quick! Surely the two must have run the intervening steps between the Benson house and hers or had been standing out on the sidewalk when placing the call. She unlocked the deadbolt and pulled on the knob, expecting to peer into Tina's heavily eye-shadowed lids.

No one. Dropping her gaze, her eyes fell on a disheveled youngster clad in his pajamas, wrapped in his favorite baby blanket, tattered from much love.

Kneeling at his feet, the compassionate teacher encircled the sleepy child with her arms, drawing him into the room and shutting the door behind him. His head immediately bumped against her shoulder.

"Didn't your mom bring you?" she inquired, bracing her feet to lift the bundle off the floor.

"Un-huh." A yawn widened his mouth before going on. "Burt wanted her to go with him."

So much for being called into work. Mrs. Kirmis, you've been had again, she silently chided herself.

Ryan's eyelids had already dropped shut, his breathing slowed. He was a lovely child. Maybe Tina wasn't the best mother, but she certainly produced an exquisite baby.

Nuzzling her nose against his cheek, Jasmine awkwardly carried her overnight guest to the spare bedroom. Tenderly she tucked the quilt up to his chin, with his baby blanket lying against the side of his face, guessing he would reach for it in his slumber.

A soft kiss landed on his forehead. Crawling beneath the covers of her own bed, with two pillows at her back, she pulled her Bible off the bedside table, reckoning sleep would be scarce now.

How did I come to be so all alone? Having had over two decades of married life, a husband to share her mornings and nights, two children to fill her quiver, along with a teaching profession and volunteering at the church, her life had always been busy—full to the max. Falling asleep had never been an issue then, rather a *lack* of sleep.

Evert had died in May over four years ago. She remembered the local police officer and her pastor materializing at her classroom door, her principal nervously volunteering to take over her class for the rest of the day as she was ushered down the hallway. Certainly the combination of the law enforcement and a man of the faith arriving simultaneously meant only one thing: death. The only factor missing was the "who."

An on-the-job accident had snatched Evert out of her life. Jacob was just finishing his third year of college at North Dakota State University in Fargo, four hours away. In many ways, he had already been gone, having worked summer jobs in Fargo during the intervening college years. The summer after his father's death, he had come back to Prairie City to grieve with his mom and sister. In the fall, he returned to NDSU, graduating the following spring and landing a job in Minneapolis.

Autumn had stayed the longest—but not willingly—having a year of high school to finish. Both of her children had been active in their local church in Prairie City, attending the weekly youth group gatherings and the camps in the summer. Autumn had helped in Vacation Bible School in prior years, but somehow when her dad died, her faith died too. She would have nothing to do with the pastor, refusing to come out of her room for his visits. The school counselor highly recommended a therapist in Bismarck, a hundred miles away. Jasmine couldn't even cajole her irritable daughter into getting into the vehicle, let alone into the counselor's office.

It was a miracle in itself that Autumn had graduated from high school at all—actually, more of a gift than an earned reward, bequeathed by sympathetic teachers who were Jasmine's comrades on the school staff.

Autumn lasted one semester as a university student, flunked all of her classes, and took off to set up her own agenda for her life, making it very clear she did not need nor want her mother's assistance.

And here Jasmine was—alone, dwindled from a family of four to a widow, living a solitary existence in a one-level bungalow in Elton, having moved from Prairie City two years after Evert's passing. Winter, prior to her relocation, had dumped record-breaking snow on the state, causing the fifteen-mile commute to work from Prairie City often to be perilous in the near-blizzard conditions created when the fierce winter winds tore across the prairie.

Traveling the icy route without Evert's assistance had scared her, scared her enough to move away from her closest friends in Prairie City, to leave the threshold of the home her husband had carried her over, to sell the tree-laced yard her children had played in.

Admittedly, her girlfriends were still in Prairie City. Didn't they still seek her friendship by inviting her to backyard barbecues, coffee at the Meeting Point restaurant, or to their daughters' bridal or baby showers? Of course they did.

The change was in Jasmine herself. Jane and Shelia were married to Evert's closest buddies. Both couples, the same as she and Evert had been. Somehow, she didn't feel quite as if she belonged anymore—not by anything they had said or done. Jasmine took the blame. There was no longer a *we* or *us* in her vocabulary, only an *I* and *me*.

Hugging her knees to her chest, Jasmine laid her cheek on the puffy comforter draped over them. If she was honest with herself, her coolness toward her former companions lay more in her effort to avoid questions about Autumn when the gals recounted glowing tales of their own children.

Life had sent the self-assured teacher and mother of two on a hairpin curve.

Mildly chiding herself for indulging in a pity party, she was reminded of Jacob's weekly phone calls, of her friends at school. Cynthia had taught her the ropes of first grade. June had been a confidant since day one of her teaching career. Laughter spilled in the teachers' lounge daily did her heart good.

And then there was Autumn. The nightmare threatened to return at the mention of her second child. She couldn't even go there. Her daughter's rejection hurt too intensely.

Refocusing on the cover of her Bible, her loneliness receded. Self-pity wouldn't help, but Jesus would. He hadn't left her. Together they'd journeyed the deep desolation of the valleys hand in hand, her doing the weeping and Him holding out the handkerchief. Somehow the hilltops always came into view once again, the greens a deeper verdant, the skies a translucent blue, the air purer than a Dakota breeze.

She flipped to the scriptures she frequently sought when nights were too long and sleep was not to be trusted.

> I sought the LORD, and he answered me; he deliv-
> ered me from all my fears.
> Those who look to him are radiant; their faces are
> never covered with shame.
> This poor man called, and the LORD heard him; he
> saved him out of all his troubles.
> The angel of the LORD encamps around those who
> fear him, and he delivers them.
>
> Psalm 34:4–7 (NIV)

Raising her eyes from the page, she repeated the next verse from
memory.

> Taste and see that the LORD is good; blessed is the
> man who takes refuge in him.
>
> Psalm 34:8 (NIV)

The words brought a cooling salve to her soul as she pictured
herself huddled in his arms. No, she was never alone. There
were always two of them marking the course.

In the quiet of the midnight hour, a child's nasalized breathing fluttered from across the hall.

Make that three. The thought brought a curve to her lips.

CHAPTER 12

The shared bag of sunflower seeds lay on the pickup seat between them. Carson carefully set a salted seed on edge between his front teeth, cracked it open, and retrieved the tiny meat sandwiched inside the dry-roasted shells.

Openly admiring Joel, he watched as the bigger man tipped a handful of seeds into his mouth, storing them in his bulging cheek like a pocket gopher. Then, cracking the seeds one by one, Joel used a paper cup spittoon to rid the shells from his mouth.

Carson wished he could eat sunflower seeds in the same fashion. He had tried it once. Somehow the shells and the inner meats had gotten all chewed up together, and he'd ended up spitting the whole glob out.

November was the month riding the fence line between the Indian summer days of October and the official start of winter in December as determined by the calendar. Bewitching in its personality, November could playfully let the warmth of the sun give farmers two additional weeks to finish harvesting late crops or to spread fertilizer for next spring's crop.

Or November could whip in with a fury, like uninvited goblins conjuring up an ice thriller for a Halloween masquerade party, refusing to be escorted out when the festivities are over.

Today was a combination of the two: a cold wind whipping out of the north, requiring the insulated winter attire to be extracted from summer storage closets, yet the white, snowy crystals were staying at bay.

Fully aware of the weather patterns to come, Joel didn't relish the thought of working out in the cold, weighted down by thickly-padded outerwear, heavy boots, fur-lined leather gloves, and head gear. Winter chores meant grinding corn and screenings for feed, hauling the feed and hay to the cattle, pushing trails through the snow with the loader bolted to the front of his tractor, and spreading straw to keep the animals warm and dry. No, this cattle farmer was not looking forward to the change of seasons.

On the other hand, his six-year-old comrade saw this day as perfect, the kind that produced a warm, fuzzy feeling inside his tummy, like when his teacher put a smiley-face sticker on his spelling paper. Riding with his most favorite friend in a pickup truck towing the stock trailer all the way to Bismarck—an hour-and-a-half distance—plus a day off from school, well, this was it! Christmas, birthday, and the Fourth of July all packed into one outing! Another shell hit the cup as Carson gave his lips a backhand wipe. This would be his first trip to a livestock auction to sell the six cows in the trailer behind them.

When he could spend an entire day with Joel, nothing bothered him, except Joel had told him their cattle would end up as ground hamburger. He was selling the half-dozen old cows that were too old to have any more calves. "Cattle are raised for their beef." He hoped Brush and Spit wouldn't end up between the two sides of a bun.

Pulling into the parking lot, two lines of cattle trucks and stock trailers were already ahead of them, waiting their turns to unload the stock they carried into the network of livestock pens outside the building. Nosing in behind a semi-truck with a license plate bearing the state of Nebraska, Carson watched wide-eyed, hearing the braying of cattle from inside the trailers along with those already captured in the corral fencing. It seemed there were cattle everywhere.

His anticipation equaled the expectancy he'd felt before attending the rodeo at the county fair last summer. Funny-dressed clowns teasing the bucking bulls had been really cool.

"Are the clowns going to be here?" Carson asked as the line of trailers slowly moved ahead.

"Nope. Clowns are only at rodeos to protect the cowboys from the dangerous bulls. Today, we want lots of buyers here. All of the cattle in these trucks and pens are going to be sold."

"How many cows are here?" Carson was perched on his knees to aid his view.

"I don't know. Why don't you count them?"

"There are too many to count, and they are too wiggly." Carson's eyes tried to follow the milling animals. Then, catching the humor shining in Joel's eyes, he boxed him with a playful punch. "You count them."

"Okay. One, two, three..." Joel pretended to point at each animal as he tallied up the count, his lips moving silently. "Three thousand eight hundred nineteen."

"Really?" Carson was amazed. He'd never counted that far in his whole life.

"Yup, exactly three thousand eight hundred nineteen." The rancher kept his poker face.

"Did you add our six cows?" The first graders were learning how to add in math class.

"Oops! I forgot them." Joel slapped his forehead. Holding up six fingers, he touched each one individually as he added, "Three thousand eight hundred twenty, eight twenty-one, eight twenty-two ... three thousand eight hundred twenty-five cows."

The truck driver in front of them now moved his two-tiered semi trailer up to the unloading dock. An attendant fastened a gate across Joel's front bumper, preventing the animals from roaming into the parking lot while empting the trailer. Carson scrambled to the seat across from Joel, his eyes glued out the front windshield. What a front row seat!

After unlatching the back door, the cattle attendant backed away, allowing the livestock to file down the unloading ramp. Joel prided himself in raising a strictly black Angus herd, but these animals were all colors and breeds: Charolais, Simmental, Tarentaise, Hereford, and even a couple black and white Holstein.

"Joel, how come we don't have any like those? They're pretty."

"I like black."

"We should buy some of those different ones." As an afterthought, he exclaimed, "Joel, you didn't count these ones!"

Poking the youngster in the ribs, Joel laughed. "It's time for you to take over my accounts."

When the last beast stumbled off the truck, the intervening gate was opened. The cattle attendant motioned for Joel to pull forward and then closed the gate again behind his trailer. Carson could feel the jostling of the trailer as the six cows exited. A sea of pens bordering both sides of their vehicle held bawling calves and cows captive. Bulls silently stood their ground, eyeing the commotion. Carson had never seen anything like it and was glad for the safety of the cab. Crawling ahead, Joel moved his empty rig out of the unloading area and advanced to the designated parking section.

"Look, Joel!" Carson screamed, his nose right up to his window. "There's my teacher!"

Skimming the parking lot with its row-on-row of cattle trailers in every size and model, Joel craned his neck trying to locate the car Carson had his eyes on.

"Where?" Joel asked, pulling to a stop alongside a cattle truck, frozen manure clinging to the sides of its trailer. The livestock barn's property reeked of animal waste, dulled at present by the freezing temperatures.

Carson's seat belt went flying.

"Hold on, buddy. You don't want to get run over." Their doors slammed simultaneously as the two met at the back end of the rig, Carson still excitedly waving an arm over his head to get his teacher's attention. Grasping his free hand, the older gentleman held the boy back as a dirty four-wheel-drive pickup passed in front of them, its muffler rumbling complainingly.

Still not catching sight of any teacher, Joel continued to scan the vehicles and the people walking hurriedly toward the entrance of the building, its bold-lettered sign attached to the roof proclaiming, "Livestock Auction Barn."

"What teacher are you talking about?" Joel's words were tossed in the wind.

Again he pointed with his full arm, his voice trilling with exhilaration. "There she is! Do you see her? Mrs. Kirmis! Mrs. Kirmis! I'm right here!"

Following Carson's gesture back toward the outdoor cattle pens fifty yards away, Joel could make out a semblance of a woman's form propped up on an wrought-iron fence enclosing one of the cattle pens. Denim legs straddled each side of the partition, a rump firmly positioned on the top rail. Joel couldn't tell at this distance who it was, but he strongly doubted that Carson's middle-aged teacher hung out at the livestock barn in her free time.

Propelled by the arm steering him back to the confined pens, Joel allowed himself to be led. A raw wind leaked tears into their eyes and swept down the neck openings of their insulated jackets. Flipping the hood attached to Carson's coat over his blond head, Joel clapped a hand to his own hat to keep it rooted in place.

If snow had been in the forecast, this day would have marked the first blizzard of the season.

Unperturbed by the cold and noise buffeting him, Carson manfully lengthened his strides, his eyes focused on the maroon stocking cap holding in the curls naughtily trying to escape the elastic band. "Hi, teacher!" Carson yelled, his words boomeranging back into his freckled face.

Even the barricaded fence didn't stop him. His gloved hands grasped the rods as the toes of his cowboy boots clambered up the bottom three rungs until his head cleared the top railing.

Hugging the top railing with his elbows, Carson grinned into the surprised green-speckled eyes of Mrs. Kirmis, perched on a parallel fence twelve feet away.

Her chin dropped an inch as she thumped the clipboard she'd been writing upon against her knee. Delightedly he laughed at his teacher's astonishment. "It's me, Carson."

Pinching the papers against the clipboard to keep the edges from taking flight, she greeted her pupil. "Oh, I know who you are. I just didn't expect to see you here." Her lips spread in a pleased welcome. Shifting her gaze to Joel, she saw the curiosity in his expression.

"See, Joel, I told you it was her."

"Who would have thought Mrs. Kirmis would choose such a crazy spot to correct arithmetic papers?" Having been proven wrong, the man clapped a hand on his charge's shoulder. Directing his next comment at the rosy-cheeked lady balancing on the fence railing, he asked, "Are you helping out here today?"

The clipboard baffled him. Detailed, accurate records had to be kept of the buyers and sellers of the cattle commissioned for the day's sale.

Clearly, Joel did not expect Carson's first-grade teacher, who lived a hundred miles away and was already employed by the Elton Public School system, to be moonlighting at the Bismarck sale barn. Noting her attire, the blue jeans and fashionable waist-length down jacket, he reasoned she wouldn't last thirty minutes before heading for a heated building or vehicle. Mrs. Kirmis might be a top-notch teacher in Elton Elementary with a roomful of youngsters crowding her knees, but she was definitely out of her league in the midst of this mooing sea of half-ton four-legged creatures, steam rising from their sweaty backs into the frigid air.

"No." She smirked, her frosty cheeks threatening to crack from the movement. "I'm getting an education. You've heard the old cliché: there is more to be learned than what is found inside a classroom." She winked at the pair.

"Our cows are over that way." Carson motioned to the livestock pens behind her. "They won't be mamas anymore," he announced wisely, geared with the information Joel had supplied earlier.

"Ah, did you fire them?" Jasmine nodded her head knowingly.

"They don't have no calves in them." He paused, contemplating whether he should tell her the rest. "They're going to be hamburger!"

"Sounds like Joel has been doing some educating as well." Her laughter floated within the white breath escaping from her mouth.

A sudden gust of wind flipped Carson's hood off his head, exposing his ears to the nipping frost. "It's cold out here, Joel." As if first noticing the winter bite, the boy jumped to the ground to use Joel as a windbreak from the gale.

Wrapping the shivering body in a Carhartt arm, he shook his head faintly at the huddled lady soon to be frozen stiff to the fence. "You are a paradox, Mrs. Kirmis. I'll try to bribe Carson into keeping your whereabouts on off days a secret, but I can't promise anything."

Opening and closing her leather-encased fingers to coax circulation to her extremities, Jasmine good-naturedly took his jibes. "In a few minutes, I'm going to be trotting along inside for a mug of coffee to hug."

Putting two fingers to the brim of his billed cap, Joel backed away. Head down into the wind, he raced Carson to the double doors marking the entrance of the livestock barn.

The entry spilled into a wide corridor, opening to a cattleman's restaurant on the left and glass-enclosed offices on the right. At the end of the tiled hallway, Joel ushered Carson up a steep stairway. Rounding the corner at the top, Carson stopped abruptly at the sight. They were standing on the top tier of a semicircle of seating cemented into descending layers, already occupied by a couple hundred people waiting for the sale to commence.

On the lowest level of bleachers, a railing protected the viewers from the ten-foot drop into the sales ring below. Joel explained to Carson that this pit was where the cattle would be brought in, a dozen or so at a time, for the buyers in the audience to view safely from up above. An auctioneer sat high in a glass cubicle on the opposite side of the ring where he could easily survey the cattle below him and the entire crowd across from him concurrently.

If a buyer liked the particular cattle in the ring, he would acknowledge the chant of prices pealing off the auctioneer's tongue by waving a card with his personal number imprinted on it or by raising a hand or giving a slight bow of the head. The auctioneer would continue raising the price until only one buyer was still bidding. Then he'd hit his gavel on the counter and call out, "Sold to bidder number five," or whatever the individual's number was. Attendants would herd the sold animals out of the ring and drive in a new lot of cattle. Depending on the number of animals commissioned for the sale, this procedure could continue all day and even into the night.

"Are we gonna sleep here?" Carson was ready for any adventure as long as Joel was a part of it.

"I sure hope not." Joel led the way down the cement seating to a middle section, acknowledging the strangers on each side. "We'll stay for a few hours. Hopefully our cows will be sold by then."

Carson hunched down beside the larger man, slowly letting his eyes meander the semicircle of cowboy hats and billed caps. Talk of cattle prices, weaning calves, and the cold onslaught of the weather swam through the bleachers. More folks kept filtering into the seating space.

"Ladies and gentlemen, welcome to today's livestock sale." Carson's eyes traveled back to the glass cubicle where the auctioneer was addressing the crowd. "At this count, we have one thousand eight hundred seventy-two calves to be sold today weighing anywhere from four hundred to six hundred pounds, nine hundred ninety-eight bred cows, one hundred twenty-six open cows…"

Carson's elbow nudged Joel. "Those are ours."

"...and a handful of bulls weighing in at eighteen hundred to twenty-two hundred pounds. Terms of the sale are cash. We will move along quite rapidly, wanting to get you folks home at a decent hour, so have your bidding number ready to wave. All the animals sold today have been inspected by our veterinarian, Louie Blieter. You can be assured you are getting top quality beef. We take bids by the pound, so do your math to determine the total price of a critter. Let's roll."

Three hired hands slid open a twelve-foot door on rollers. A dozen Angus heifer calves born last March raced into the sales ring wide-eyed, nostrils flaring, bumping into one another, milling about in the unfamiliar surroundings. Quickly, the door was rolled back into place. A screen overhead had their printed weights at 400 to 425 pounds.

Immediately, the auctioneer began his quick chant. "Ninety, ninety, ninety and a quarter, ninety and a half, ninety and three quarters, ninety-one now."

Mesmerized by the singsong drone, Carson's head swung from side to side as bidders throughout the bleachers nodded a head, raised a hand, or waved a bidding card.

The price climbed higher. Carson could hardly distinguish the numbers rolling off the auctioneer's tongue in a steady tempo.

"I've got ninety-eight, ninety-eight and a quarter, ninety-eight and a half, ninety-eight and three quarters. Thank you, sir. Ninety-nine." His voice continued to raise and lower in rhythm.

"Going once, going twice." *Bang!* His gavel came down. "Sold to bidder number thirty-six for a dollar ten. Fine bunch of calves you got yourself, sir."

Below the bleachers, the calves were being chased out of the ring through a second barn door before the next lot of white face calves bolted into the ring. The bidding began again.

For a full hour, Carson's attention went unbroken, spellbound by the action in front of him.

"Excuse me." A leather-vested rancher sprouting a straggly beard balanced a steaming Styrofoam cup of coffee in one hand while gripping a paper plate in the other. He squinted at Carson, who quickly drew his feet on top of the cement step to let the man slide past. The irresistible smell of fried potatoes and grilled hamburger wafted into the youngster's nostrils.

Leaning against Joel's shoulder, he raised his head to peer up at his friend. "You getting hungry, Joel?"

"Did the smell of that man's food tickle your taste buds?"

Carson vigorously nodded.

"Mine too, little buddy. Let's see what we can find to fill that hole." Leaving their jackets on the bench to hold their spots, they ascended to the top of the arena and then descended the stairway taking them to the ground floor.

A robust lady with an apron tied about her middle offered assistance. "What'll it be, sir?"

Using the wall menu as a reference, Joel ordered. "Hot roast beef, baked potato, fruit salad, and a piece of pumpkin pie and coffee."

"How about the little cowboy?"

Backing against Joel's denim thigh, Carson remained quiet. "How about that toasted cheese sandwich we talked about earlier?" Joel suggested.

Carson shook his head negatively.

"Do you want the same thing I'm getting?"

Another shake of the head.

"Come on, Carson. What'll it be? You said you were hungry." Joel was feeling the bite of hunger aroused by the tantalizing hot plate of food.

Jerking on Joel's sleeve, the child motioned for his friend to lower an ear. "I like Jell-O," Carson whispered.

Relaying the message, the foster father asked, "Do you have red gelatin?"

"That we do." She set a sealed plastic cup next to Joel's over-loaded plate on the counter. "Pretty lean vittles for a big guy like you." She arched her eyebrows at the little rancher.

"You have to have something else with it," Joel instructed. Finally, Carson agreed to a bowl of Knephla soup and chicken strips.

Hating to miss the sale of his half dozen cows in the sales ring and yet at the same time realizing it would be quite a feat to get their meals up the stairway and down the cement bleachers without a spill, he decided to take a chance on them not being sold while they ate. Indicating a table for Carson to put his feet under, he followed suit, with the waitress bringing up the rear carrying a piece of pumpkin pie and a tall glass of chocolate milk.

After a short blessing on the food, they dove into the home cooking like cats at the milk bowl, not wasting time on small talk. Carson dug a wobbly spoonful of gelatin out of the cup and shoveled it into his mouth.

"Hey, guys, I thought you said you'd come to sell some cows, but it looks to me like you're more interested in food," concluded a teasing voice above one of the empty chairs.

Carson's face immediately lit up. "Hi, teacher! Our cows are still ours."

"Unless they're being sold as we feast," Joel added.

Obviously the lady hadn't frozen to death. Her brown hair was pulled free of the woolen cap; her jacket hung open.

"Do you want to join us in some grub?" Joel gestured to the vacant chair.

"I already had some of that delicious Knephla soup to warm me up. You made a good choice, Carson," Jasmine replied, slipping into the seat, the clipboard deposited on the tabletop.

"Glad to see you didn't turn into an icicle." Joel's eyes twinkled as he took a bite of his roast beef.

"I hustled in soon after you guys did. You cattlemen are a hardy breed, caring for your herds in these bone-chilling conditions."

"Winter does add a new dimension to the occupation," Joel agreed.

"I help feed the cows." Carson wasn't about to be left out of this conversation.

"Don't you get cold?" Jasmine asked.

"Nah, the tractor is warm." Nimbly, he slipped another spoonful of gelatin into his mouth.

The love between the older man and youngster was as plain to read as the headlines in the newspaper. "I was just pestering the office personnel across the hall. Cattle business in North Dakota is a major part of the state's economy," Jasmine stated.

Summoning up the courage to ask her a personal question, Joel tiptoed into the topic with an introductory feeler. "So are you a buyer or a seller?"

Her laughter tinkled like the surface ice breaking on a corral's water trough on an early, frosty morning.

"Neither. I am exceedingly out of my realm. I'm not country bred. A livestock barn is definitely not on my list of favorite vacation spots. Although, I must confess, I am enjoying the day."

Observing Carson's meticulous scraping of the plastic gelatin cup coveting every last drop, she disclosed, "Cherry is my favorite flavor too."

"Actually, I'm doing some research." Jasmine surprised herself at revealing this tidbit of personal information. A Jell-O preference was one thing, her private life as an author quite another.

Her second manuscript was the unfinished story of an animal scientist and his wife taking in juvenile delinquents. Searching out background material for her book, she had already shadowed a veterinarian for a week last summer. During the county fair in Prairie City, she had toured the 4-H barns talking to school-aged kids about the farm animals they had entered in the fair.

"Not the usual place for a first-grade field trip," he commented. In his estimation, the conversation was not adding up to a plausible sum. In any event, her easy laughter made it fun to banter with her.

"Sixteen first graders turned loose in the cattle pens out back could be a real hootin' rodeo! I'm not sure parents would sign permission slips for such an excursion!" she agreed.

Not realizing the raillery was all in fun, Carson momentarily halted in his demolition of a chicken strip to confront his foster parent. "You would sign for me, wouldn't you, Joel? It would be a cool field trip!"

Both adults threw their heads back from the hilarity of the schoolboy's request. Mrs. Kirmis apologized. "Sorry, Carson, there will be no class trip to the sale barn, which means you are a very lucky young man having already been here with Joel. I am absolutely positive that you know way more about raising cattle than I will ever know."

"I can teach you." Carson sat up taller in his chair.

"And I accept." Her eyes locked with his blue gems, sealing the bargain.

Joel steered the discussion back to his original quandary. "Why do you want to learn about cattle anyway?"

Purposely being vague to ward off any further interrogating quests, she flung a hand into the air, nonchalantly saying, "My hobby, in the little spare time I have, is creative writing. I thought I'd try a bit of western prose. Nothing important, mind you, just for myself."

The rancher's face, a mirror of his inner thoughts, speculated the pretty lady was holding back. A tender, educated woman showing up at the capital city's Livestock Auction Barn when temperatures had dipped into the low teens wasn't any more plausible than a rancher taking up cake decorating in his nonexistent free time.

Saving his teacher from a follow-up question, Carson interrupted. "Hey, Joel, there's the auctioneer. Is the sale done?" The boy didn't miss a thing.

With his white cowboy hat still intact, the auctioneer was sitting three tables over, putting his jaws into a grilled hamburger.

"That's him," Joel agreed. "He must be taking a break. A cattle sale this size has to have more than one auctioneer. Which reminds me, we'd better get our butts back upstairs if we want to see our bossies being sold."

Jasmine, only too glad for the switch in the conversation, rose to her feet. "I want to hear the auctioneer's lingo too. I'll be upstairs a bit later."

"You can sit with us," Carson offered, not worrying about the propriety of the invitation. There was no lady he liked better than his teacher—well, maybe Arlene. But no one else. Joel could hardly repudiate the boy's harmless overture.

"Thanks, Carson. Save me a spot." She sauntered away.

Tossing the napkin onto his empty pie plate, Joel was anxious to head back to the sale. Carson stuffed the remaining chicken strip into one cheek. "I'm ... read—y," he said, his speech garbled with a full mouth.

Exiting the café, Joel caught Mrs. Kirmis sharing the auctioneer's table, busily adding more notes to the stack of paper caught under the clip. *Some hobby*, he mused inwardly. *Her husband must have lost control of her a long time ago.*

Back in their previous spots, Joel scanned the electronic screen over the cattle ring, relieved to see his cattle were not listed among those sold.

A dairyman was selling sixteen bred Holstein cows due to calve in February. The new auctioneer pulled bids from the buyers seated throughout the barn. When he raised his mallet to hit the stand, Carson simulated his action by bringing his clenched fist down hard on his open hand at the exact moment the man pronounced, "Sold!"

Feeling a light tap on his shoulder brought him back to a full sitting position. Mrs. Kirmis asked permission to scuttle past him to the slice of open seating on his far side.

Settling into the tight space, Mrs. Kirmis piled her jacket and cap on top of her lap, using them as a tabletop for her clipboard. "Okay, teacher," she addressed Carson, "explain everything going on out here." The first grader did a fair translation of what Joel had clarified for him at the start of the sale.

This time when the attendant rolled the heavy door open, six black cows jostled into the arena, their ears and dark eyes alert to the announcer's magnified voice. "Lot forty-six: six open Angus cows for slaughter."

"There they are! Those are ours!" In the excitement of seeing the half dozen critters who had ridden behind them in the trailer all the way to Bismarck, Carson forgot about the crowd of cowboys and gals encircling him when he jumped up and shrieked.

Hearty laughter scattered through the bleachers. Even the auctioneer gave reference to the little cowboy. "Who will be the first to bid on the young cowboy's cows?" He named an exorbitant opening bid, far more than the cattle were worth. After a good chuckle, the bidding started in earnest at a lower bid.

"Can I bid?" Carson asked.

"No way!" Joel pretended sternness, capturing Carson's hand against his thigh. "We don't want these bossies to accompany us home again."

"Why don't you bid?" Carson twisted to the right, focusing on Jasmine.

Caught off guard, she threw her arms up in the air in befuddlement, sputtering, "What would I ever do with six cows?"

"Make hamburgers!"

"Ma'am, was that a bid?" the auctioneer bellowed from across the way, pinning the unsuspecting schoolteacher to the bleachers. Flustered, her complexion burned a bright strawberry pink, with the attention suddenly shifting from Carson to her. A crowd of hats turned her way, easily picking her strawberry face out of the mass of onlookers.

"No! No, no." Her hands again took flight, this time to cover the embarrassment painted on her cheeks. Howls of hee-hawing ricocheted through the tiers of seats; a couple of younger guys whistled shrilly through their fingers.

Unable to contain his serious guise, the auctioneer chortled with the rest of the throng. Wishing fervently she could yank a trapdoor's rope, letting her disappear from sight instantly, Jasmine valiantly endured the cackling she'd caused.

A tall, husky rancher in the top row roared, "I'll help out the lovely lady by taking the bid away from her. I raise the bid to fifty cents." Applause thundered. Smiling sheepishly, Jasmine gave her rescuer a tiny wave.

"Ma'am?" The auctioneer had regained his microphone. "Don't wave at Pete, just sit on those hands. Keep them immobile." One last wave of banter washed over the stands before the auctioneer banged his gavel, announcing, "Sold to Pete for fifty cents a pound."

Relieved to have the sale move on, Jasmine sneaked a peek at Joel. His eyes twinkled back. "Sorry. Did I mess up your chance for getting a high price for your cattle?"

"Heck no." He chortled. "Those old girls are going to make some mighty expensive hamburger patties."

"You were great, Mrs. Kirmis! Wait till I tell the kids at school!" Carson extended his hand for a high five. Joel's lips twitched.

Grimacing, Jasmine reminded her first grader, "Forget the high five. I'm sitting on my hands from now on!"

Driving home in the early darkness, Joel mused over the day's proceedings. His six open cows had pocketed him a healthier check than expected—partially due to the aid of an inexperienced first-grade teacher. His funny bone was still shaking. *She'd best keep her day job*, he silently recommended.

Carson's head rested in the corner shaped by the back of the seat and the door. Lulled to sleep by the steady drone of the vehicle's motor, the tired chap was breathing heavily, his lips moving as he sold cattle in his dreams.

Almost six months had vanished since Meagan had brought the tyke to the Linton farmhouse. Churning in indecision, Joel had wondered if he was doing the right thing: taking on a foster child as a single adult, a male model only in the youngster's life. At times he still wrestled with the appropriateness of his resolution. Right or wrong, he would fight Meagan tooth and nail if she attempted to move Carson to a foster home with two parents. A half-year of waking up to the rascal and grappling him to bed at day's end had tightly entwined the two of them as close as a father and son could be.

Usually, foster children were entitled to supervised visits with their birth parents. In Carson's case, since termination of the parents' rights was being sought, the appointments had not been scheduled.

The court would make the ultimate decision; its verdict usually favored birth parents. Even if Social Services proved to the court the ongoing abuse and neglect in Carson's young life, a carefully screened adoptive family would be sought—one with two parents and maybe even some siblings.

Either way, the judge's decision would bring heartbreak to Joel's future. He pulled the blinds on such thoughts. The headlights burned back enough of the darkness for him to find his way home, a few yards at a stretch.

Life was the same. God provided just enough light for today. Tomorrow was traveled by faith.

An hour behind the Linton trailer, Jasmine too drove the same dark, lonely stretch of highway back to Elton. It had been a good day.

Beside her on the passenger seat was a binder packed full of facts, descriptions, and procedures gathered at the Livestock Auction Barn. She had interviewed dozens of ranchers, employees of the sale barn, and even an auctioneer.

Even driving into the frigid night air, Jasmine felt deliciously warm on the inside. An ounce of life had germinated within her soul in the last twelve hours, a smidgeon of a flame for living.

She had not experienced a true desire to live since Evert's accident four years ago. In fact, all the while she'd been busily jotting notes, asking questions, and taking in the sites of the cattle, the crowd, and the sale, she had not once thought of that fateful hour, the panic-swept minutes when the cop and pastor had somberly filled her classroom door and she had known.

Today, the haunts had given her a rest, a few hours off from their punishing cue cards. They'd be back—possibly even when she crawled between the sheets in a couple of hours. At least she'd had a reminder of what life could be like, what she needed to find again.

Her nose wrinkled as the comical bidding session replayed in front of her on the highway. What a fool she'd made of herself sitting in the crowd of farmers and ranchers. It was cleansing to laugh at herself and to feel the tightness within her nerves loosen.

The only cloud plaguing the day was Joel Linton, sitting with Carson Reynolds glued to his side. In every way possible, the pair appeared as close as a father and son could look—not by physical genes, but in dress, mannerisms, and touch—with Carson's knobby elbow sitting on Joel's knee, Joel's hand massaging the skinny back, whispered messages passed into each other's ear, and walking out across the parking lot hand-in-hand.

Granted, Carson was a mere six-year-old child, easy to fall in love with. The tough years were yet to descend on the duo. Years when Carson would no longer hang with rapture on to each word uttered by the older man, when Joel would be nicknamed rudely as the "old man"—out of touch with the times and especially the younger generation. What was hidden in Carson's past would erupt and destroy the relationship being cemented stone by stone at present. Tornadoes swept this prairie state, wiping out in seconds what it took years to grow or build. The same happened to relationships.

Yes, Joel Linton, enjoy this high plateau as a single father, for canyons are ahead—deep canyons.

Jasmine knew.

CHAPTER 13

Wrrrr! One single, sharp blast of the whistle signaled the rush of rubber sneakers alternately pounding and then squeaking in a reverse revolution on the polished gymnasium floor. Flying balls ripped the air aimed at opponents' lower extremities. High-spirited shrieks echoed off the hard surfaces of the floor and walls, adding to the revelry of the game.

Hank Perry, supervising the first-grade gym class, stood squarely in the middle of the playing floor, his eyes alertly followed the youngsters running pell-mell in every direction. "You're out, Arnie. Jeremy hit you with the ball." Dropping the ball he was about to fire at Kaylee, Arnie obediently headed for the sidelines to join the other teammates previously knocked out of the game by an opponent's careful aim.

An airborne sphere bounced off the instructor's shoulder. "Stevie, keep your throws low. If you hit someone in the head, you'll be out of the game."

Fidgeting in the folding chair against the wall of the gymnasium he'd occupied since the commencement of the school term, Carson gripped the alternating sides of the seat, pulling the chair forward and balancing on its front two legs. Initially, he'd parked himself in the metal seat like cars parallel parked on the street outside of the school—aligned and immobile. However, as the weeks trekked on, a string of fascinating games—kickball, clothespin tag, cat and mouse, and relay mazes—had drummed past the tips of his toes pressed against the white sideline painted on the gym floor, increasing Carson's wiggliness.

At the onset of each gym period, Mr. Perry would squat down in front of the boy, encouraging him to participate. Always, the blond head would waggle from side to side, refusing to give in to his inner urgings to run and play with his classmates instead of clinging to the iron chair as if it were a floatable lifesaver.

At Mrs. Kirmis's urgings, the staff had agreed to wait Carson out, coaxing him to join the class ventures but not coercing him. "Patience," she had implored at the roundtable discussion.

Caught up in the high-speed game from his sideline observation point, Carson cheered when Ryan's well-directed ball sent Arnie to the bench. He yelled lustily to Stevie to scramble for the blue ball rolling over the waxed floor in his path. In a jack-in-the-box style, Carson popped off his seat to grab the red ball near his feet and then flung it over the heads of the two closest opponents, dropping it into the hands of his best friend, Ryan.

"Get 'em, Ryan!" He whooped, letting his bottom fall back onto the chair, pounding his fists in the air.

Mr. Perry's whistle signaled the end of the game. Gesturing to the children sitting along the sidelines, he raised his voice. "Last time for today. Everyone's back in." A short toot sent the youngsters blowing to the four corners of the gymnasium, grabbing and throwing balls, dodging the rubber toys rocketing through space. No class period of the day could augment such intensity of enthusiasm in the short span of minutes between the start and end of a class period.

"Let's get Ryan out," Joey screamed, barreling across the centerline. His right arm bent back to discharge his ammunition. Quick and agile, Ryan dodged to the side, allowing Joey's ball to bounce on the hard floor before retrieving it.

Even in the midst of a wild frenzy of battle ball, Pixie displayed her ladylike coordination, trotting to Joey's battle cry, her tiny baby steps rotating with the speed of the spokes in a bicycle. Softly, she tossed the ball at her target. Ryan was in no danger from her dispatch, but her efforts gave Joey valuable seconds to scarf up two more balls.

Charging full speed back toward Ryan, Joey gleefully spiraled one of the orange weapons at Ryan's knees. In kangaroo style, Ryan jumped high as the ball rolled under his airborne feet straight into the open clutches of Carson sitting on the sidelines, well aware of Ryan's predicament.

Due to his hesitancy to participate in most class activities, Carson had also been slow in attracting friends. Not that any of his classmates disliked the new, tall student, for he hadn't given them a chance to discover the personality hidden under his fair skin. Only Ryan had repeatedly stopped at Carson's side to chat or observe whatever the quiet kid was engaged in. It was he who had shown the new kid the apple tree across the alley from the playground, where one could steal a mid-afternoon snack if the two teachers on duty were absorbed in a tête-à-tête. It was Ryan who volunteered to devour Carson's tuna sandwich for him when the lunchroom monitor said the shy child had to eat something before scraping his tray in the garbage can. And it was invariably Ryan who was the topic of the stories Carson told Joel over the supper meal steaming between them.

And now, Ryan was in trouble. "Watch out, Ryan!" Carson hollered a warning as Joey set loose the second ball, aiming higher than the first. Dropping flat on the hard surface, Ryan never felt the ball skimming the air above his wrinkled t-shirt. Joey bent over to snag another ball rotating across his path.

Without thinking—for if he had thought, he never would have had the courage—Carson bounded out from his solitary cell, the orange ball gripped in a hand, charging toward Joey in outright defense of his pal, Ryan. His skinny legs churned; the brand-new sneakers smacked loudly against the playing surface with every step he took.

Halting ten feet from Ryan's assailant, he flung back his arm, letting the ball twist out of his grasp, floating toward the caged light on the ceiling before plummeting downward again. Unpracticed, weak in force, Carson's throw was easy to sidestep, except Joey never expected the boy who rode the chair to be a threat. In fact, he never saw the ball coming at all until it lightly thumped him on the thigh.

Hank Perry, like Joey, hadn't anticipated Carson's entrance into the fray. His side vision had picked up the blur. Swinging about, his jaw dropped to witness the child who had riveted himself to a folding chair for eleven weeks suddenly burst from his cocoon and fly like a yellow butterfly hovering over the middle of the gym floor. Mr. Perry saw the uncoordinated throw, the orange ball looping skyward rather than a fast pitch covering distance rapidly. And unbelievably, he witnessed its gentle lob against Joey's thigh.

The cadence in the instructor's chest gave birth to a full sunrise on his face. Unbelievably, Carson was playing! His arms rose in triumph, as jubilant as a victor at the Olympics. Later at a faculty meeting Hank Perry was asked when Carson began participating in class. He knew as readily as Americans could spout out their whereabouts on 9/11, and right down to the minute: the second Thursday in November at 1:52 p.m.

"*Out!*" he roared, more loudly than necessary.

Dazed, Joey then realized who his attacker had been. "No fair! Carson wasn't playing!"

Even more surprised than the downed opponent was Carson. Staring at the lacings crisscrossing his tennis shoes, Carson cemented his feet to the gym floor. He was surrounded by a cheering mob of kids. Ryan's sweaty hand clapping him on his back, he praised, "Good job, Carson!"

Biting his lower lip, his already fair face faded to a lighter shade. What was he supposed to do next? Anxiety was back in Carson's abdomen.

The clock's face said it was time for dismissal. Wanting to verify the transformation the staff had all been waiting for in the youngster, Mr. Perry sought to seize the moment.

"Game's still going! Get moving!" Like calves turned loose in a lush meadow after being penned in the barn, the first graders turned tail and galumphed off, swooping up the abandoned balls and sending them into motion.

Resembling a tree planted in the middle of the meadow, Carson stayed rooted. Mr. Perry watched. Would the freed butterfly soar?

Through the maze of kids, Carson zeroed in on his seat of refuge, vacant on the sidelines. He wavered. Security lay with the folded chair; freedom lay on the exposed floor, unprotected and risky. Could he do it? Indecision mapped a crooked route, readable in his fixed stare.

The gym instructor waited silently.

Flying dark hair smashed into the rigid statue. "Here, Carson, take one of mine." Ryan thrust a ball into Carson's bent elbow. "Get 'em!" In a blink, the agile elf was gone, galloping into enemy territory.

Skepticism tossed under the chair, the towhead dashed after his rough-necked schoolmate, his shackles unlocked forever.

Mr. Perry was deaf to the programmed buzzer signifying the conclusion of the gym period. Third graders outside the door pressed their noses against the glass, questioning what the holdup was. His eyes focused on the first grader tearing across the floor having the time of his life. Mr. Perry allowed the game to continue until Carson was knocked out by Hannah's pummel.

A cog in Carson's gear mechanism had meshed into the right groove, metamorphosing him in entirety, literally all at once.

During the noon recess on the following day, Carson paced the sidewalk bordering a first and second-grade football skirmish. Without asking permission to join the game or inquiring which side needed another teammate, he inoffensively slid right onto the field. In the ten minutes remaining of play time, he never touched the football, but he ran and blocked and yelled right along with the rest of the team.

Five days later, Mrs. Retson reported he'd suddenly started imitating the actions for the song "The Wheels on the Bus Go 'Round and 'Round" right along with the other students. When reporting the improvement at the staff meeting, she confessed to being dumbstruck. "I forgot the next line of the song, even though it was same as the first line!"

Joel read the report on Mrs. Kirmis's e-mail, who was elated in the progress Carson had exhibited. "They wanted action," he mused. "I think they are going to see it now!"

The first scratch on Carson's personality makeover was a telephone call from Richie Harris, the bus driver. Fearful of anyone and everyone, Carson had sat in the first seat immediately behind the driver, until his reversal in behavior transpired. Now he was being assigned that very same seat until he could prove to Mr. Harris he could stay situated in one place for the duration of a day's trip.

Prior to his awakening, the most difficult behavior disruptions had happened primarily in Joel's presence—except for the dented car door at the Bautzes. Even then, it was Joel who Carson had been upset with for refusing to allow him to accompany him on an open tractor.

In Joel's estimation, it was easier to deal with a child's acting-out escapades when they occurred at home or at least in the parent's presence. Trying to control Carson's behavior in school or on the bus was like attempting to keep raccoons out of the sweet corn patch at night. Breathing out a heavy sigh, Joel reckoned his parenting skills were about to be tested severely.

Bowing his gray-tinted head, he took the matter to prayer.

If Carson could have vocalized the change within him causing such a stir amongst the adults, he would have best summed it up in two syllables: friendship. Racing across the gym floor or the scruffy grass of the playground surrounded by boys and girls his age was electrifying.

Crawling out of a skin of timidity had opened wide his formerly constricted environment. Now he was bold enough to leave his desk to sharpen a pencil or to use the bathroom without fearing his bladder would burst before he could dig up the courage to ask permission.

Riding the school bus had previously been boring, frozen behind the bulky form of Richie Harris. Not anymore! Bus code forbade switching seats while the bus was in motion, but the silly mandate didn't prevent him from playing seat tag.

Establishing a circle of comrades added a new dimension to his life. Not that his classmates and fellow bus riders were close friends, because they were not; however, the number of activities he could take part in had multiplied exceedingly. Before, he had imprisoned himself to solitary confinement, observing life from afar. These days, he was a part of the rhythm pulsing steadily throughout his environment. He could choose to participate in a group activity or page through a library book by himself. He had a choice. And he loved it!

Yet the very best part of this uninhibited freedom was the gift of someone his own age to laugh and play with, to be partners with in math, to share his carpet mat during story time. He had Ryan.

Ryan wasn't well liked by the other students in Elton Elementary, which didn't seem to bother him at all. He could crack funny jokes and think of cool things to do. He was a fast runner and smiled almost all of the time. Ryan liked to be boss, and that was okay because Carson didn't know how to be in charge.

And brave. Ryan was the bravest kid Carson knew. Once, barehanded, he had slapped a bumblebee daintily exercising on the edge of the outdoor receptacle. When playing pirate, Ryan pretended he was the sailor on duty high in the crow's nest of a vast ship. Standing on top of the highest pinnacle of the playground equipment where no was allowed to climb, he shouted in his roughest pirate voice, "Man the oars, you scallywags!"

Darting back into his toddler years, Ryan had often manned his ship by himself. Given long hours of unsupervised time, he had devised creative ways to amuse himself. He didn't necessarily need Carson for a buddy yet found the comradeship to his liking. Even though he had the stronger personality of the two, he was kind to his new friend, protective of Carson's insecurities.

Yes, first grade was definitely better than kindergarten ever was for the ragamuffin and his skinny tagalong.

Forever the early bird, Ryan patrolled the frost-covered playground before the supervisor's appointed hour for duty or any other children had filtered into the fenced enclosure.

Keeping his hands in his coat pockets to ward off the bite of winter, he hoped his mom would soon remember to buy him some mittens. Fortunately, his jacket sleeves were extra long, hiding his fingers as well.

Kicking a stone along the sidewalk entertained him for a while. Reaching the swing set, he dove onto the stiff rubber seat, his tummy hugging the seat, letting his feet and arms flail in the air. Tiring, he allowed his limbs to fall limp, a rag doll hanging from its middle.

From the upside-down position, he spied an abandoned soccer ball lodged in the bowl-shaped hollow under the far swing. Untangling himself from the inverted position, the urchin gravitated toward the forlorn object, as forgotten as he often was. He cradled the ball between his sleeve-clad arms, ambling in circles, no destination in mind.

He missed Carson. Having tasted friendship, he preferred company over his former antisocial existence.

Parking the ball against the side of the brick wall giving him a clear view of the bus zone, he balanced his butt on the movable ball, his back arched against the bricks, waiting for bus number fifteen to park at the curb.

Waiting was harder when old man winter threatened to turn a runny nose into icicles and uncovered ears to ice chips. Pushing his chin lower into the secondhand store's nylon lining, he wiped the snot dripping on his upper lip into its folds.

Loneliness gnawed at his inners more than usual. Mama had said she might be late again tonight. It was happening more often. "If Mrs. Kirmis can't take you, just smear yourself a peanut butter sandwich and turn on the TV," Tina had said, not noticing the downcast face on her son. "You're a good boy. I trust you to take care of yourself."

Yup, he was good at fending for himself. Sometimes he even preferred being alone—then he was the sole operator of the remote control and could pick whatever he wanted out of the refrigerator, except the pickings weren't very plentiful.

Humming a song Mrs. Retson was teaching the class for the Christmas concert in December, he resolutely endured the shivers sledding over the bumps of his spine. He decided he'd be tough like Frosty the Snowman, who danced outside all winter.

He wondered if Carson's bus had gotten stuck. But that was silly. There wasn't any snow. Last winter was his first experience with the white hills a snowfall left behind. Tumbling into the drifts, packing snowballs, and building forts had all been an unexpected eye-opener for the transplant from the south.

A bus engine's roar sliced through the freezing air, braking at the bus stop. Richie swung wide the double doors.

"Yeah! Bus number fifteen!" Warmth spilled through Ryan's body, dislodging the loneliness eating away at his small frame. Carson had arrived!

Fifth off the bus, Carson wore warm-bibbed snow pants under his Carhartt coat, a brown stocking cap, and matching gloves. His schoolbag hung over his right shoulder.

"Carson, over here! Look, I found a ball! We can play before the bell rings." Ryan's take-charge deportment elbowed to the forefront.

Shaking his head no, Carson walked directly toward the school entrance, motioning for Ryan to follow. Not accustomed to being Carson's shadow, the shorter fellow paused for a second, perplexed at what had come over his pal. Then, shrugging, his stiff legs complied.

Grappling with the door handle under the weight of his back-pack, Carson managed to slip into the narrow opening, using his body as a doorstop to hold it open for Ryan.

Carson dropped his backpack in the corner of the entry, strip-ping off the waterproof hand gear. Impatiently he knelt in front of his pack, tugging open the zipper.

"'Member teacher said we can bring toys for days when it is too cold out?" Mrs. Kirmis had informed her first graders that on bitter-cold days, they would remain in the room during recess. "Joel said I can keep these at school."

His arm disappeared up to the elbow inside the bag, his hand fishing for objects out of sight. Almost ceremoniously, he uncov-ered a miniature John Deere tractor, not more than five inches long, followed by a blue New Holland farm tractor. Gently he deposited the toys on the tiled floor. His hand tunneled in again, withdrawing a cultivator, an air seeder, and a combine.

"Cool, huh?" Carson murmured, enthralled with his own line of machinery, a matching set to Joel's farm implements used to plant and harvest a crop.

"Joel says these are the most important pieces I need to farm." Pointing at the cultivator, he explained, "This one digs up the dirt." Next he picked up the air seeder, showing it to Ryan and admiring its movable parts at close range himself. "This one plants the seeds." Carefully he transferred it into his friend's fingers so Ryan could scrutinize the tiny planter.

"And the combine harvests the seeds," Carson finished his explanations. "We can play farming on the cold days."

Farming? In Ryan's six short years, he had become educated with many aspects of life. Tina hadn't screened her babysitters well, so often Ryan had been entertained with R- and X-rated movies. Before the family of three moved up north, he'd had to accompany his mom to work when no babysitter volunteered. He'd spent many hours entertaining himself in the boss's office of the roadside tavern, using empty beer cans as toys.

But farming? He'd didn't have a clue what farming was all about. Carson talked about cows and sunflowers, vaccinating calves, and baling hay. His stories made farming sound exciting. Without imagery to illustrate the tales, it was hard for a child who had only lived in town to comprehend the home life of his rural friend.

Staring at the farm implements lined up along the tile seam, Ryan was fascinated. How did Carson play farming?

Squatting on his knees, Ryan was ready for his first lesson. "How do they work?"

"Like this. You back a tractor up to the cultivator and hitch the two together." Demonstrating the procedure, Carson vibrated his lips in a motor sound as he maneuvered the green tractor into reverse to connect it to the hitch of the cultivator. Zooming forward, the cultivator trailed the tractor wherever Carson rolled it.

"Let's pretend this corner is the field. You go back and forth digging up the dirt. I'll hook the blue tractor to the air seeder and plant the wheat," Carson ordered.

Engrossed in their farming operation, their jackets were soon flung on the floor in the vicinity of the open schoolbag and forgotten soccer ball. Students entering the outside entrance sidestepped the two farmers busily seeding their crop.

Having covered every inch of the marked tiles, Ryan asked the experienced farmhand, "Should I use the combine now?"

"No. I haven't finished planting the wheat. Then we let it grow."

"Oh. Then what can I do?"

"You can move the cows to the pasture. They like to eat grass."

"What cows?" Ryan did a quick side-sweep of the entry, wondering if the four-legged beasts were make-believe.

"In the side pocket."

Ryan scooted to the discarded backpack and dug out five plastic bovines: two cows, two calves, and a bull. Impressed, he set them upright on the flooring, but Carson objected immediately. "Don't let them in the field. They'll eat the wheat!"

Guiltily, Ryan snatched them back into his lap, searching for a better pasture. Spying the corner on the opposite side of the entrance, he suggested, "How about there?"

"Fine." Carson was intent on his planting.

The warning bell sounded. A rush of children from the playground tumbled through the doors, escorting the cold draft in with them.

"Don't step on my cows!" Ryan protested loudly as one cow fell to her side, bumped by a tennis shoe.

"Move 'em," an upper-grade boy shot back, showing no mercy to the budding cattleman.

Carson pretended to goose the throttle, swiftly parking his machinery against the wall out of the path of the trampling feet.

Stepping out into the corridor to supervise the last students passing to their rooms, Mrs. Kirmis caught sight of her two entrepreneurs engaged in their agricultural business. Smiling inwardly, she clicked her heels toward them.

"Boys, please pick up your toys and come into the classroom."

Holding up the long-horned bull, Ryan spouted triumphantly, "Carson is teachin' me how to farm."

Having been a prodigy of Carson herself at the ring sale barn, she had no doubt Carson was the man for the job.

"Carson, there is some land at the back of our classroom needing to be farmed. Would you consider moving your machinery off this roadway and working our fields instead?"

"Yes, ma'am. I just have to finish the headlands on this wheat field first."

Willing herself to be patient, she watched the farmer putter his tractor and air seeder back toward the first-grade room. "Ryan, put the rest of my things in my backpack and bring them," he instructed over his shoulder.

Dutifully, in the semblance of a responsible hired hand, Ryan completed the task, dragging their two coats along with the schoolbag down the hallway, dusting the waxed floors en route.

In appearance, the two boys were made from different molds: one tall and fair, the other short and dark. The teacher, a bystander of the impromptu parade, mused at the nonjudgmental display of friendship. Ryan, often the playground scapegoat, had unprecedentedly developed camaraderie with a fellow first grader, who by all demeanors reciprocated the rapport. Everyone needed at least one friend, someone to accept him as he was, someone to share his time and space; and if Ryan and Carson were that for each other, then she was happy the two had forged a bond. A lonely boy traipsing the playground at recess, rejected from all cliques, was a heart-searing sight for a teacher with a mother's heart.

At closer inspection, the two had more in common than being haphazardly assigned to the same first-grade classroom by a principal intent on keeping the sections even in number without duplicating any names. Both were products of dysfunctional families where responsible adults had failed to fulfill their roles, leaving the children they'd brought into the world to fend for themselves—vulnerable physically and emotionally. In extreme circumstances, neglected offspring were removed from their homes and dropped into a foster family. No matter how fine and loving these substitute parents were, the separation from the birth mother and father was a frightening split for a child.

Carson had weathered the upheaval of his family setting. He had found security in Joel Linton's shadow, copying every move the older gentleman made. But Carson's future was not mapped out. It would be decided by the whim of a judge. Curling his fingers into Joel's loving hand, he'd feel the pain when they were jerked apart again.

On the other hand, Ryan lived with his mom, a parent who was trying to relive her teenage years rather than caring for the child she'd been blessed with. Jasmine didn't doubt Tina loved the boy; she just loved her nightlife more. So who was better off: Carson or Ryan? It was a toss-up—an unfinished story. Fate would write the ending.

For now, the two rascals had each other. And momentarily Carson was in the leader's position in their ongoing game of follow-the-leader.

CHAPTER 14

Snow carpeted the town of Elton and the surrounding country-side barely after the Thanksgiving turkey was digested, painting the vast patchwork of fields and lots a stunning white. Eleven inches had fallen silently and reverently, bringing a majestic touch to the faded, worn-out landscape.

Jasmine's soul rejoiced at the shimmer of millions of crystallized diamonds sparkling off the laced veil hiding her porch furniture and dormant lawn.

Snow could mean hazardous travel until snowplows pushed the thick layer to the sides of the highways and streets. Jasmine had dedicated this long weekend to writing on her manuscript. With no travel plans to be apprehensive about, she could appreciate the sheer magic of the first snowfall.

Taking a break from the hours she had already spent at the computer, she dug in the closet for heavy snow pants and a hooded jacket. Why not shovel off the driveway even if the street was not yet plowed? The winter wonderland was beckoning.

Minutes later, the flat-edged shovel scooped up a foot of light fluff and whirled it to the sides of the cement pad. She steadily shoveled a trail from the garage to the street, the exercise invigorating her tight muscles.

"Hi, Jasmine! You don't waste any time getting your driveway open, do you?" The question floated in the fresh air from close at hand.

Pausing in her task to acknowledge her neighbor, Jasmine's green eyes took in Tina Benson's imitation leather blazer and high-heeled fashion boots. Smirking inwardly, Jasmine wondered how far her southern friend was going. Her station wagon, overlaid with a thick layer of snow bumper to bumper, could have been a child's birthday cake glazed with cream icing.

Chiding herself for poking fun at Tina's predicament when she had no garage to shelter her vehicle from the elements, Jasmine gave a cheery reply. "Merry Christmas, Tina! Snow has a way of elevating me into the holiday spirit."

Peering about her in distain at the white frost festooning everything she saw, the southerner commented dryly, "Yeah, well, I'm used to green Christmases and temperatures about sixty degrees warmer, but what the heck. This is North Dakota, right?" Tina rolled her eyes and then laughed.

Sympathetically, the older woman gestured toward the buried station wagon. "Need some help?"

"No. Burt said he'd dig me out. I just hope ol' Bertha starts."

"Maybe you should have a block heater installed under the hood so you can plug your car in at night," Jasmine suggested, speculating that colder temperatures than this would drop the mercury.

"Yeah, yeah. New tires, a muffler, a plugged drain in the bathroom, and a front door that leaks like a punctured balloon. My list for Santa Claus is long. Hope the old guy comes through." She briskly rubbed her hands together before tucking them into her folded arms. Jasmine noted Tina had something in common with her first-grade son: no mittens.

Not wanting to alienate her neighbor, she nodded kindheartedly. There was something important Jasmine wanted to ask her.

While she was walking home from school with Ryan before Thanksgiving, the chattering child had mentioned the bearded man also. Someone had told him if he wrote Santa a letter he'd get whatever he wanted. Spelling wasn't his easiest subject in school. "Will Santa be able to read my letter, do you think?" he had asked seriously. If Santa was into giving presents, Ryan wanted to be on hand, even if it meant practicing his spelling and penmanship.

Matching stride for stride, Mrs. Kirmis had hesitantly probed, "So you really like Christmas, huh?"

"Santa's the best! I like lots of presents!" His arms had flung open wide to encompass all the boxes his imagination held, stored under the tree.

"Do you know the Christmas story, Ryan?"

"I have the book. It has a picture of Santa on the cover with his reindeer. You can borrow it and read it to the class." His dark eyes had turned up to meet hers, pure generosity pouring out.

Ignoring his innocent offer, Jasmine had softly said instead, "Christmas is actually a birthday party for someone who loves us very much."

"Santa?" Expectation had fluttered in his black pupils.

"No, his name is Jesus. He was born at Christmas."

"Wow! It would be cool to have my birthday on Christmas. Then for sure I'd get tons of gifts!" The youngster had skipped the next couple of steps.

"Jesus is a gift. He is a gift from God, our heavenly Father who lives in heaven."

"How can a baby be a gift? Babies don't even know how to play." There was no way Ryan would have asked for a baby for Christmas.

"Ah, but babies don't stay babies forever. They grow up. Can I tell you the story of Christmas?" Jasmine had implored, hurting inside that people right here in the small town of Elton had missed the message of Christmas.

Ryan had bobbed his head earnestly.

"God peered down from heaven and saw everything He had made: the towns and farms, the plants and animals, the moms and dads, and children," she began, slowing her pace to give her enough minutes to reach the best part of the story before they would part ways in front of her house.

"Even me?" Ryan asked.

"Especially you. God gave us lots of good things to make us happy: food to eat, nice warm homes to live in, schools to teach us how to read and write, clothes to wear, games to play, friends—"

"Toys?"

"Yes, toys too. But after a while, when God looked down from heaven, he was sad. Instead of using his creation for good, people were using it to do naughty things. And worst of all, they had forgotten who had given them all these gifts. So God decided he would send his Son to earth to teach the people how to do what was right."

"Jesus is God's little boy?" His eyes widened in amazement.

"Yup! Did you know Jesus wasn't born in a hospital?" Crossing a street, Jasmine scanned the intersection for traffic.

"He wasn't? Where then?"

"In a dirty barn where cows and donkeys and sheep and spiders live."

"Yuck!"

"God chose a woman named Mary to be his mom and a man named Joseph to be his dad. Mary and Joseph were a long ways from home when it was time for Jesus to be born. All the motels were full, so a man gave them permission to stay in his barn."

"A barn? That's disgusting. He could have at least let them stay in his garage." Ryan's voice escalated at the preposterous notion.

"Back when Jesus was born, there weren't any cars or pickups. People rode horses and donkeys to get from place to place, and animals sleep in barns, don't they?"

Agreeing, he angled his face upward. "Did Joseph take a crib into the barn for the baby?"

"No, he cleaned out a trough that the animals ate out of and put a blanket in it for baby Jesus. Outside of town were some shepherds taking care of a herd of sheep. All was quiet in the black of the night. Suddenly, the heavens were filled with angels singing! But the shepherds were scared. They were used to defending the sheep from wild animals, but never had angels lit up the sky. Comforting the frightened men, an angel spoke, 'Don't be afraid. A baby has been born to you in the town of Bethlehem. He is God's Son, the Savior of the world!'" Her voice had risen in excitement.

"The shepherds decided to go into town and visit the baby. They were Jesus's first visitors."

"That's weird." Ryan had been perplexed.

"Later, some wise men journeyed to Bethlehem too. God had hung a special star in the sky for them to follow. Day after day, the star's brilliance lighted the way for them and their camels until they found the baby. They opened their suitcases and gave him gifts."

"On camels? Santa's sleigh would have been faster." Her wee escort listened attentively.

"Jesus was born many years ago, and yet every year we throw a big birthday party for him called Christmas." Jasmine concluded her simplified version of the biblical tale. Their houses were just up ahead.

"Did Santa Claus come to the barn?" Ryan's only association to the beloved holiday had centered around the man in red.

"No, Santa may give presents, but the very best gift of Christmas comes from God: Jesus."

"So Christmas is Jesus's birthday." Halting in Jasmine's driveway where they usually parted company, unless Tina's house windows were dark, Ryan had stood, absorbing the true meaning of Christmas for the first time.

"Yes, it is. In the Bible, it says that God loved us so much that He sent Jesus to earth to show us the way to heaven."

"How come we get presents if it's his birthday?"

"In a way, we are copying what God did. He gave us Jesus because He loves us. We give presents to others because we love them."

"Yeah."

And here was Tina, shin deep in the main ingredient for Sinatra's *White Christmas*: snow.

Jasmine steered a U-turn in the conversation. "Speaking of Christmas, the holidays are a mere four weeks away. If you wouldn't have any objection, I'd like to invite Ryan to be in the Christmas pageant at my church."

"Christmas pageant? You mean like a play?"

"Yes, the Bible narration of Jesus's birth. Ryan could be one of the characters in the rendition."

Jasmine prayed silently.

"I think my little trouper just might go for that sort of thing. He might cast better as a villain than baby Jesus though." Tina chuckled at her own joke.

Pleased at her ready concession, Jasmine offered an invitation. "He could ride with me and attend the morning service afterward. We'd be back home shortly after the noon whistle."

"Swell! I have to work the nine-to-five shift this Sunday. He'd like hanging out with you for the afternoon." Tina had sprung the trap, but Jasmine had provided the bait. Ouch! She really didn't mind having the chap's company. If only it was possible to work on her manuscript and listen to his chatter concurrently.

"Thanks, Tina. It sounds like a workable plan." God had to remind Jasmine that a child of God rated higher than some old book she was drafting. Lesson taken.

Thus the title of "bearer of the star" was bestowed upon Ryan. Dressed in black to signify the darkness of the night, he wore a headband festooned with a large, golden, glittering star. During the stable scene, his designated spot was standing on the mantle of the baptistery, his star shining over the makeshift barn. His smile alone was enough to light up the heavens, and this was only rehearsal.

When the hour for the wise men's arrival from the east came, his headband was rotated, the brilliant star radiating down his back. Walking slowly in front of the kingly gentlemen, he guided the royal visitors from the back of the sanctuary up to the manger setting on the front platform. Kneeling before the Christ child, the kings offered the babe a gold rock, a perfume bottle filled with water, and a sweet smelling bar of soap.

The miniature star clambered back up onto the baptistery sill, swiveling his cardboard star to the front, resuming his post overlooking the stable.

Ryan's enthusiasm mounted with each Sunday morning practice. He applauded the fifth-grade angels as they sweetly sang the message to the fourth-grade shepherds dressed in their bathrobes. Having listened intently to the many recitations, Ryan prompted mother Mary when she stumbled on her lines. A kindergartener in his wooly lamb costume meandered off from the rest of the flock. Playing the part of a falling star, Ryan jumped down from his perch to lead the lost lamb back to the stage.

Sitting beside Jasmine in the pew at the weekly church service, he drew the holy family on the back of a bulletin, always careful to place the star above the stable's peak.

Stacking plastic straw bales on a toy hayrack Carson had provided for their classroom farm, Ryan and his buddy chatted about the upcoming Christmas programs in their separate churches.

"I'm the innkeeper," Carson confided. "The guy whose inn was full."

"What's that?" Ryan frowned in confusion. His play didn't have one of those guys.

"You know, the guy who ran the hotel."

"Oh, him. I wouldn't want to be him. He didn't even save a room for Jesus." Ryan placed the last bale on top of the stack and putted the tractor pulling the hayrack toward the upside-down cardboard box serving as the barn.

"I couldn't kick guests out of a room I'd already given them." Carson's tone dripped with exasperation. "But it was my barn Jesus was born in. I let him use that instead." Pride replaced the irritation.

"Oh. I'm the star of the show at teacher's church." Ryan couldn't wait for Sunday night when the real show would be held.

"You are not," Carson objected sharply. "Jesus is!"

Figuring out what his friend meant, Ryan relented. "You're right. But I am the star in the sky showing everyone where to come."

"Hey, we could pretend this is the stable Jesus was born in, and this feeder could be Jesus's bed." Carson took the plastic feed trough out of the corral fencing they had set up for the cattle.

"Cool!" Anything to do with the Christmas story piqued Ryan's interest. "I have some robot people at home. They could be Mary and Joseph and the shepherds and wise guys."

"How about these cows for the donkeys and camels?" Carson asked, his mind running with his pal's ingenuity.

The idea of a classroom nativity scene was expanded even further in a joint effort by fellow first graders. Pixie had a wide, yellow hair ribbon she arranged in the manger to make the baby's bed softer. Stevie came with a pocketful of lambs borrowed from his farm set at home. Annie loaned the wise men her jewelry box to use as a gift for the baby. Most astounding was Arnie's addition of a glass baby Jesus from his mother's nativity set.

Scripture records Mary as pondering these things in her heart. Jasmine did the same. God was using two first-grade missionaries to enlighten the whole class on how He'd sent his Son to earth on the very first Christmas. Miracles were happening this Christmas as well.

Rumpled paper balls began littering the floor under Ryan's desk. Although a couple of times Mrs. Kirmis asked her student to clean up after himself—which he did—she didn't think to probe further into his activities.

It was the art teacher who unknowingly gave him the assistance with the missing dimension of the classroom manger scene during her weekly art lesson.

Rather than sketching on his paper, Ryan immediately began bending and folding the sheet at odd angles. Disheartened by the queer-shaped mayhem sitting in his workspace, he dropped his forehead to the table. It just wouldn't work. Frustration tickled the corners of his eyes.

A hand rubbed lightly over his back. "Hmm." The art instructor scooped up the deformed shape. "This must be a creation of the famous artist Picasso, moments before he showed his revelation to the critics, blowing them completely out of their chairs with his exquisite piece of art."

Peeking out from underneath his long strands of dark hair brushing the tabletop, Ryan spied the teacher, his misshapen paper sitting on her open hand like a parakeet about to trill for its master.

"A fold to the right, a fold to the left, and what doth appear, but a magical…"

Winking at the inquisitive eye not quite hidden under his bangs, she waited for him to finish her sentence.

"Star," he whispered.

"A magical star." Whipping a piece of shiny yellow paper off the supply shelf, she ordered the drooping dwarf, "Fold this piece of paper in half, sir." She oversaw his workmanship before giving the next direction. Almost magically the flat paper slowly turned into a three-dimensional star.

"How's that, Picasso?" It was definitely the star he envisioned.

"It has to have a string," he wistfully admitted, daring to plead for her assistance once more.

"Ah, yes." Using a paper punch to inject a hole in the top point, she then inserted a gold thread, tying the ends in a secure knot.

"Ta-da." The glossy star dangled from her index finger, twisting in the fluorescent lighting.

"Perfect!" His eyes fastened unbelievingly on the star of his dreams. "It's awesome, teacher."

After school, when the first-grade classroom was quiet except for the pecking of Mrs. Kirmis's fingers on the computer keyboard, Ryan crept to the back of the room. Kneeling at the nativity menagerie laid out on the floor, he studied the cardboard barn. He stuck his twelve-inch ruler out from a shelf above the scene. Then ever so reverently he looped the golden thread of the handcrafted star around the protruding end of the ruler. Backing up to evaluate the effect the spiraling star had on the pasteboard box and robotic figures below it, he hummed contentedly a song he'd learned at the church.

> Away in a manger, no crib for a bed.
> The little LORD Jesus laid down his sweet head.
> The stars in the sky looked down where he lay,
> The little LORD Jesus asleep on the hay.

Carson was lucky. He got to give his barn to baby Jesus. A thought struck him. It would be scary sleeping in a barn without a light. His star could be the baby's nightlight!

How was it possible for a paper star to give off such warmth that it penetrated right to the center of a little boy's heart?

CHAPTER 15

Stuffing corrected papers into the square pigeonholes designated for each child in her room, Jasmine was experiencing a shade of the January blues. Like the dry pine trees crammed in alley garbage cans, glittering with left-behind tinsel, the long anticipated two-week holiday break had disappeared, leaving crumpled wrapping paper in its wake.

Poking three additional school sheets into Ryan's mailbox, her thoughts settled on the little rascal, contemplating the joy emanating from the child's face the final night of the pageant.

Well-positioned lights reflecting off the glittering star on his forehead drew all eyes to the manger scene: Joseph tenderly helping Mary tuck the folds of the baby's swaddling cloths into the manger, the shepherds and wise men kneeling in adoration, the angels positioned prayerfully on each side of the star. Even the spotlight coaxing the star to shimmer and shine was no match for the beam on Ryan's face.

In his concluding message, the pastor had encouraged the parishioners to allow the light of Jesus to shine from the windows in their lives, pointing to Christ those with whom they came in contact in the same manner as the star of Bethlehem beckoned the wise men to meet their Savior. As if the pastor's words were a predetermined cue, Ryan unlocked his pose, gesturing hardily with both arms for those sitting in the pews to come. An *ahh* had filtered through the sanctuary at his adlibbing.

A six-year-old child, whose own mother wasn't among the proud parents and grandparents attending the performance, was doing the same. Tina had used the Christmas program as another night of free day care, casting aside her neighbor's overture to be her guest.

"Hey, Jazzy, you ready to take off?" Cynthia, framed in the doorway clad in her winter coat and gloves, jingled her ring of keys. "My turn to drive; your turn to buy," her coworker reminded her. For six weeks, the first-grade teachers were enrolled in a continuing education class given at the university in Norbert, an hour's drive away, one night a week.

On girls' night out, they allowed themselves an additional half hour to grab a quick sandwich before heading to the college. "I'm with you." Jasmine slipped on her down jacket.

An hour later, relaxing on the high swivel stool at the lunch counter licking mayo off her fingers, Cynthia sized up her partner. "So where is the devilish urchin tonight? Warming himself in a cardboard box under the bridge?"

Giving an exasperated huff, Jasmine gave a flippant retort. "The warming house at the ice-skating rink offers better accommodations."

"Smart kid. Does the city council serve hot chocolate at midnight to stock up votes for the next election?" Cynthia took another bite of her sub sandwich.

"No, silly. Kids can't vote." Jasmine made a face at her coworker. "Didn't you take civics in high school? Actually, I am positive, at this very moment, Ryan is snuggled up on the couch with Tina, practicing his reading, using the phonetic skills we outfit our students with to sound out unfamiliar words. No doubt, the two are bonding as mother and child, sipping frothy glasses of milk and nibbling on homemade chocolate chip cookies."

"Do I detect a touch of sarcasm in your tone, teacher?" Cynthia bent her head to the side, one eyebrow raised, giving her best impression of an undercover detective.

"Me?" Jasmine pretended shock. Dropping the guise, she returned to her role of overly concerned teacher and neighbor.

"Actually, when we decided to take this class together, I called Tina to inform her of my Thursday night obligation, making her fully aware I would not be able to keep Ryan. She thanked me profusely for letting her know in advance, making it possible for her to rearrange her work schedule."

Not easily convinced of the quick fix, having gotten an earful of Miss Hazeton's soap opera kindergarten nightmares last year, Cynthia was skeptical. "And she did?"

"Seems so. Last Thursday, Ryan's sister picked him up right from my room. Today, he took off toward home after the bell. Just to be certain he wasn't going to an empty nest, I gave Tina a buzz. She was home."

Shoving the paper wrappers from their light lunch into a bag, Cynthia checked her wristwatch. "Time to boogie. I really do hope you're right about Tina. Ryan is one of those kids who grows on you like a leech." She winked. "He deserves better."

Hours later, Cynthia dropped Jasmine off at her driveway. In a solitary stance on the cold sidewalk, the weary teacher's eyes washed over the tired, sagging dwelling rented by the Bensons. After missed house payments, the owner had taken the real estate back, allowing the family to stay as renters until a new buyer came along. A dim light shone from the rear of the house. Tina's station wagon was parked in the street. No other vehicles cluttered the curb. Good. Ryan had his mother to himself tonight.

"Sweet dreams," she whispered to his black bedroom window.

"Court was Tuesday. No one contested the case. Parental rights have been terminated for both of Carson's birth parents. It's the verdict Social Services strove for." Meagan's finger stabbed the indentation of her dimple.

Her declaration knifed Joel in the heart, a bull's eye, twisting the main artery into a tight knot of pain.

Seven short months ago, the light-haired boy had climbed his porch steps, hung the stick horse on the guestroom's doorknob, and crawled under Joel's armpit and into every breath he inhaled. Man, he could hardly remember life before the boy brought it back to him. Well, maybe he could, but he didn't want to. Life had been terrible back then, a mere shell of existence, mechanically managing his farm chores, seeding and harvesting the crops, the joy he once knew sucked out of him by Melissa's death.

Carson arrived with a mere trunk full of material items, and yet his energy and winsome laughter had filled the two-story farmhouse, jutting into every dark corner, expelling the gloom that had settled like suffocating dust over the furniture and fixtures.

Far from perfect, his charge had wet the bed, turned over a grocery cart, added chaos to the bus ride, rampaged through the house, and eaten up every second of Joel's spare time. Being a typical little boy, he had made Joel late for appointments, strewn the farm tools all over the shop, refused to eat his supper after insisting they have macaroni and cheese, and left the water hose running after watering his crops by the porch steps. The lake in the driveway was discovered hours later.

Wasn't the purpose of a foster parent to enrich the life of an underprivileged child, to give a floundering waif a second chance? Everything was backward! The beggar was feeding the rich; the helpless was aiding the rescuer; the youngster was giving the parent a reason to live. An uncontrollable quiver beat a cadence in the man's middle.

Foster care was a temporary setup: a few months, a year, possibly two. However, it always ended, like a hard frost killing the luscious growth the summer faithfully produced. Joel knew the next step: Carson would be put up for adoption. A six-year-old child was a baby in the adoptive world. He would be grabbed up by some childless family faster than the blanks on the paperwork could be filled. Babies were first choice, but there were never enough of them. A youngling like Carson would readily find a warm reception in a young mother and father's arms.

Invariably, the primary goal in foster care was to reunite the children with their birth parents, the heritage from which they'd come. Parents were given a set of requirements to complete in order to regain custody of their children. If they were slow in fulfilling the terms, the foster parents would nurture the children for an extended period.

If the rights of Carson's parents hadn't been annulled, then maybe, just maybe, Joel could have kept the youngster who had revived him for a while longer.

A spear in his chest steadily carved a hole, enlarging it until his whole upper trunk was on fire. Carson gone? Impossible.

Megan's voice penetrated his bleak outlook. "Finding the right fit for Carson will take some time, but we do have prospective adoptive parents who have finished the required training and paperwork. It is a matter of what age and sex they are interested in, and what would be best for the child."

Best for the child? Best for the child? What was best for Carson?

Carson was best for the widower. It didn't mean vice versa.

Resting his elbows on his knees, the man bent his head with a heavy heart. Selfishness. He had been selfish before—with Melissa. When the two of them couldn't conceive, she had plied the Internet seeking information on adoption agencies, American and foreign. She had studied photos of children, searching deep into their eyes for what their short biographies did not reveal. Printing off the picture of a four-year-old girl, his wife had mournfully surmised, "This one's window to her soul is the saddest of all." She'd propped the print-up against the windowsill above the kitchen sink, conversing with the image as she washed the dishes. Couldn't Joel see it, the forlorn plea, the dying hope? The nymph wanted a home so badly.

No, Joel couldn't see it. He'd told Melissa she'd better catch hold of her imagination before there were kids lined up on their porch steps like the stray cats fighting over the milk dish.

Without another murmur, the portrait had disappeared from the kitchen, the subject closed forever.

How could he have been so narrow-minded? She had been right: he was a stubborn old fool. He *was* capable of loving a child he hadn't sired. Carson was the proof.

And now he was repeating the mistake. Self-centered to the core. If ever there was a person who put *me* first, it was he. He thought only of his own wretchedness, his own loneliness. When Carson was placed in an adoptive home, the booming silence would return. He'd again be the solitary human being in the ol' house. *Stop!* What was wrong with him?

Didn't Carson deserve a father and a mother, and maybe even some siblings? Couldn't this be God's ultimate plan for his young life, with Joel being one of the stepping stones to get him to the designated family the LORD earmarked in his big picture window from above? The boy deserved a life more stable than what foster care could ever offer him.

Forgive me, LORD, *for being egotistical, for not loving the way you love.*

Ready to listen to the social worker's plan, he tuned her in again.

"This process will move slowly. We don't want to rush Carson. Too many relationships have been broken in his young life. We even hope that you may want to continue an affinity with him, providing his adoptive parents agree."

Meagan's eye contact was always too bold for him.

He was letting her read him like the daily newspaper, and headlines were popping up everywhere: his slouched posture, his diverted stare, the way he methodically rubbed his thumbnail, his unusually slow speech. There was nothing he could do to hide his disposition from her.

Not meeting her direct gaze, he mumbled, "Are you…are you going to tell Carson?"

"That he is up for adoption? Not right away. A social worker from the state adoption agency will begin meeting with him talking about adoption in general, what it means, and then compiling a 'Life Book' with him: pictures of Carson and his family when he was younger, getting him to verbalize about himself, his favorite colors, foods, games. That sort of thing."

At this new revelation, Joel's chin raised sharply, his low voice louder and quicker than was natural for him. "What! Another new social worker in his life? How many professionals does he need? He's already had a therapist, a psychiatrist, a pediatric neurologist, a judge, three sets of foster parents, and you." He felt the heat rising in him. Seldom did his irritation fuse into anger. Now, Joel's gray eyes purposefully blazed into Meagan's professional mask.

"What's wrong with *you* handling the proceedings? He's comfortable with you. Can't you tell him about adoption? What's so hard about that?" A glare accompanied his strong language, a glare Meagan didn't deserve. She was doing her job after all. Parental instinct was coming out in the man, a papa bear's growl to defend his cub.

His challenge left them both stunned, Meagan's eyes fastened on Joel's angry gray eyes, and this time, he didn't break the tight rope stretched between them. Stare for stare. Silence lingered.

"All right," the social worker conceded. "I can meet you there. Would you agree to me working with Carson on this end, helping him understand what adoption is and what it will eventually mean for him, while the agency's social worker notifies potential parents and works with them?"

"Only if you have a deciding majority in choosing Carson's parents." Joel wasn't backing up an inch. "You know him. You're familiar with what he likes: lots of room to run, animals, a swing in the backyard, parents who aren't too busy to listen to his stories."

Searching for the proper words to soothe the troubled waters, Meagan measured the impact her response would have. "Carson is young yet, fairly easy to mold, to adjust, to accept new environments. Right now, he is living in a country setting and loves it, primarily because of you. If placed in a small town or a big city, the same thing could happen to him as long as he feels secure and loved. You've turned the boy into a midget-sized farmer because he adores walking in your footsteps. However, I dare say he could also imitate a doctor, a teacher, a plumber, a mechanic, a coach, or whoever else is out there for him. Carson will fall in love with a family again, and hopefully, for the last time."

Her tenderly delivered words hit him like a slap on the face—only because they were true. Carson could love again. He could grow attached quickly to a man and woman who lavished him with attention, who tucked him into bed at night with hugs and kisses, who answered his endless questions. In his little mind, Joel would fade, his new father and mother taking precedence. The way it should be.

But oh, it hurt. His eyes thudded back onto the floor.

His calloused hand massaged his forehead and hairline, his throat tightening. Meagan quieted, fully aware how a grown man's heart could break.

Finding the control to push out the words, he made one last request. "Can you … can you make sure he gets parents who love the LORD?" His voice cracked on the last word. A tear in slow motion dawdled on the crest of the weathered cheekbone before trailing a path to his chin.

Wishing she could give promises and keep them, Meagan's professionalism faltered and then righted itself. "I can certainly take that into consideration when reviewing the files of prospective adoptive families with the team; however, I do not make the final decision alone. The team's foremost intention is to do what's right for Carson."

Nodding in agreement because anything he uttered might come out as a sob, Joel bowed his head, deflated.

Realizing she couldn't heal the wounded spirit grieving inside the foster father, Meagan closed her file and stood to leave. Stepping toward the rigid man oblivious to her exiting, she laid a hand on his broad shoulder. "Foster parents often become the adoptive home for a child in their care. Carson doesn't have to leave you."

Digesting her suggestion, the bereaved man refuted, "Yes, he does. He needs a mother too."

Wanting to argue with him but realizing he was looking out for the child, Meagan said instead, "Like I said, Joel, we will proceed slowly. It is still over three months until school adjourns in May. You can be assured Carson will finish his first-grade year in Elton." She gave his tough muscles a squeeze, buttoned her coat, and left.

"Knock, knock. Mrs. Kirmis?" A brunette thrust her head through the open door, offering a friendly smile to the woman scrubbing collected grime off the desktops.

Wringing out the rag in a pail of soapy water, Jasmine acknowledged the unexpected guest. "Hi, Sarah. Come on in."

"It seems a teacher's tasks are never done." Sarah watched the thorough cleaning job taking place.

"We had a rather messy project today, one of those where more glue ends up on the fingers and desks than on the Valentines being created. The glue companies love us."

Chuckling at the testimonial, Sarah Thern laid the binder she was carrying on the nearest clean desk. "Do you have a few minutes for a chat?"

Guessing it would have been presumptuous to assume the county social worker out of Prairie City had dropped in to swap recipes, Jasmine rubbed harder at a dried glue area, giving a quick dip of her head in agreement.

These discourses had occurred a time or two before, leaving Jasmine a bit on edge. Usually when Sarah came to visit about a student, she was doing it behind the backs of the child's parents—sometimes even pulling the child out of class to talk privately to the youngster. In small towns, these situations were often awkward, where gossip could spread faster than a prairie fire. She was especially wary after Autumn's reversal. Sarah had stopped in then too, not as a friend, but in her professional role.

"Who are you hitting on today?" Jasmine asked lightly, keeping her tone nonchalant. When she still lived in Prairie City, she had gotten acquainted with Sarah in the community as a fellow volunteer on city projects.

"I have been receiving some complaints on Tina Benson." Opening her binder and sifting through her notes inside as if she weren't already acquainted with the accusations written there, the brunette cleared her throat. I'd like to ask you some questions about Ryan."

Gritting her teeth, Jasmine feared the interrogation forthcoming. As a teacher, she was a mandated reporter of any suspected child abuse or neglect. Thus far, she was doing her best to keep the neighbor boy under her wing and out of harm's way.

Clicking the top of her pen, Sarah began. "Does Ryan appear to be in good health?"

Whew, this one was easy. "Yes, he has perfect attendance."

"Does he come to school physically clean, as well as his attire?"

Jasmine could respond positively to this question as well; Sarah didn't ask if his clothes were wrinkled or missized.

"How about tardiness? Is he late in the mornings?" Sarah jotted notations after each inquiry.

"Never. Actually, he's usually my first arrival." She could have added that he was also the last to leave; however, she thought she'd stick to the question.

It was obvious the social worker had come prepared, doing her homework ahead of the meeting. Moving down her list, she drilled, "Tired? Lays his head on his desk during class? Maybe he doesn't seem quite with it some days—out of focus? Anything like that descriptive of Ryan?"

"Some days I might wish he had less energy! Ryan is a bundle of activity." These questions were a snap. Some of her earlier apprehension began to ebb away.

"Any complaints of hunger?"

"No." Jasmine herself had wondered about this factor. Families on low incomes could receive reduced or free meals at school. Ryan always ate the school's food, never toting a lunchbox. Jasmine suspected he qualified for the federal subsidy. Each child was also given a container of milk at a midmorning break. Families took turns contributing a snack to go along with the milk. Tina had yet to provide a treat on Ryan's designated days. From experience, Jasmine kept extra boxes of crackers in her drawer for such emergencies.

"Does he ever make comments leading you to suspect things are not quite right at home?" Sarah's inquiries were becoming more direct.

"No." Jasmine suspected all right, but not from any complaints Ryan made. Her nerves were drawing tighter.

"How about Tina? Does she attend school functions conducive to Ryan's grade level, parent-teacher conferences, concerts, whatever?"

"His mother met with me for the fall conference. Our spring parent-teacher sessions are next month. I believe she was at the Christmas concert directed by Mrs. Retson. Back in November, I had my students perform a Thanksgiving play for their moms and dads. Tina works at the gas station on the loop. She couldn't get off that day." Perspiration was gathering at Jasmine's hairline, anxious to have the interview end.

"One last thought. Have you ever noticed bruises on Ryan or sprained ankles or wrists? Anything like that?"

Shaking her head, Mrs. Kirmis honestly reported, "Not anymore than any of the other kids. Some of those mishaps happen right here on our playground or during gym class."

Flipping her binder shut, Sarah relaxed, stripping off her job title. "We miss you over in Prairie City. We understand why you moved, but we still miss you."

"Thanks." Jasmine was glad to have the inquisition over. "It was a hard decision leaving all of you and the only home my family knew. And yet I think it was the right determination for me. Winter driving had me in a spin—no pun intended!"

Sarah gathered her purse and binder.

"Stop in again when you're not here on business." As Sarah was stepping toward the door, an unprecedented thought entered Jasmine's mind. "Oh, wait. I meant to ask you: what hoops would I have to jump through to become a county foster parent?"

Where had that come from? She had never considered being a foster parent with or without Evert. She was flabbergasted by her own query.

Halting in mid-step, Sarah donned a pleased demeanor. "This is rather ironic. There is forever a shortage of foster parents. At one time, I considered approaching you and Evert about the possibility of signing you up—and then the accident." Catching herself at bringing up the painful past, she shot on. "I'll mail you the lengthy application. You'll need some references and a home inspection, for starters. A background check is standard these days."

Whatever had come over her to make such an off-the-wall request?

"Don't rush. It was just a loose thought twirling around in my head," Jasmine added.

"What's the saying? Gotta strike when the iron is hot? Or something like that. I'll be on it. Thanks for your assistance with the Bensons." And she was gone.

Grasping the sides of her face, Jasmine couldn't believe what she had done. Foster care? She? A single parent who couldn't get a handle on her own daughter?

You're doing it with a roomful of children every year.

"Yes, LORD, but they don't come home with me," Jasmine refuted the inner voice.

Ryan does.

CHAPTER 16

After ceremoniously flipping the office calendar from January to February, the twenty-eighth square jumped out at Joel, having highlighted it in a bright rose color back in May: Carson's seventh birthday. It was a red-letter day, especially for a kid—a landmark worthy of a grand celebration.

If Melissa were here, how would she have marked the occasion? Melissa liked parties. For his fortieth birthday, he had come in from the field to find the dining area festooned with black streamers. Helium balloons hovered above a massive cake iced with the words, "Happy Birthday, Old Man." She'd shooed him upstairs to take a shower, and when he'd objected, pleading for information on what was going on, her eyes had sparkled, her lips sealed.

When he descended the staircase a half hour later, a chorus of "Happy Birthday" vibrated loudly, shaking the glass goblets stored in the antique hutch. Noisemakers blared, and confetti flew from a crowd of neighbors filling the dining area and spilling over into the living room.

Clem Schultz, wearing a welding helmet, clutched a small torch, alleging it was the only way to light four decades of candles. Everyone had laughed uproariously at the ol' man standing tongue-tied and red-necked stock still on the steps.

Snapping a string of pictures on her digital camera, his wife had winked at her uncomfortable husband. The photo on the dining-room buffet caught him endeavoring to extinguish forty trick candles, stubbornly relighting themselves after each puff.

Yup, she would have done Carson's birthday up big.

Now, three weeks later, the month had shrunk to a mere seven days remaining until February twenty-eighth. Procrastination had to end.

After the Sunday morning service, Joel cornered Suzy Taylor, imploring her for advice.

"For Luke's eighth birthday, we invited all of his peers entering the third grade to an outdoor swimming party at the park, with a hot dog roast afterward. Of course, his birthday falls in July." An apologetic wave passed over her face, realizing her idea was not feasible in February. "The year before, we treated his class to a pizza party at Naomi's Diner and then a movie at the theater."

Taken aback by the magnitude Pastor Lance and Suzy went to recognizing a kid's birthday, Joel stammered in disbelief, "The whole … whole class?"

Joel was blank. This birthday celebration was going to be harder than he'd anticipated. He almost wished Carson didn't know his birth date.

Straight away, Joel checked the weekly hometown newspaper. Limited to one movie a week, the theater's show for the coming weekend was rated R, for adults only. The movie idea was out.

How about a slumber party? Joel didn't think he could entertain a half dozen kids for a few hours, let alone overnight.

He had to be reasonable, simplistic, do what he could handle. Cut the guest list. One friend. He should be able to supervise Carson and a buddy.

Maybe that was too strict. Two friends. Two friends, and Carson would seem more like a party.

Next: the agenda. However, the ol' man was clueless.

Tucking Carson into bed that evening, Joel initiated the subject matter. "Pretty important week coming up." Sky-blue eyes studied the older man's face. "Anything special about this week?"

Lights illuminated instantly in the blue eyes. "Yup, it's my birthday. I'm going to be seven. It's the red box on the calendar."

No secrets here. "I imagine we should remember such an important day by doing something special. What do you suggest, partner?"

"Could you take the day off from work, Joel?"

"Well, your birthday actually falls on a school day, but if we'd wait until Saturday to party, I might be able to talk my bossies out in the barn into working out an agreement."

"You still have to feed the cows, Joel." The young farmer had learned a lot about raising cattle.

"Yup. How do seven-year-old boys celebrate getting older?" Joel wasn't just making conversation; he really wanted an answer.

"Hmm." Studying the shadowed ceiling, the youngster pondered the question. "We could have some company."

"Who would we invite?" Joel hoped their party ideas jived.

"Ed and Arlene would come."

"Sorry, bud. Remember, they're visiting their grandkids in Kansas."

"Oh yeah." Carson's gaze again concentrated on the ceiling.

"How about a friend from school?" Joel suggested.

"Only one?" The child no longer showed signs of tiredness. "How about two?"

"Two it is—plus you makes three. Perfect."

"You forgot to count you. Four. Perfect." Their hands met in a high five over the bedcovers.

"Who should I pick?" A puzzled frown darkened his face.

"It's up to you. You can choose any two friends you like."

"We're going to have a swell party, aren't we, Joel?" His eyes lit up once more.

"The best ever," he agreed. "What would you like to do besides eating ice cream and cake?"

Propping his lithe form on one elbow, he asked, "Could we look at equipment?"

Perplexed, Joel mimicked his charge's inquiry. "Look at equipment?"

"You know, like you and me do. We look at the combines and tractors and balers and cultivators and stock trailers. 'Member?"

Smiling, Joel did remember. Slowly patrolling the farm machinery lots in Elton and Norbert, meandering through the outdoor displays at the county fair, the two had done considerable window shopping for farm equipment. "You like that, huh? Me too." So much for Suzy's suggestions; farm guys had different ideas. "Then what?"

"How about you pull us with the tractor on the big sled?"

Not bad. The little tyke should work for a party company.

"You are a mastermind, young man! You have planned an ingenious party for a seven-year-old!" Joel nuzzled the soft cheek with his prickly chin after a day's growth. "And I'll be in charge of getting the ice cream and cake."

"And pizza," added Carson.

"And pizza. You're in charge of the guest list."

After finishing the night's closing ceremonies with a prayer and a hug, Joel switched off the light.

"Joel?" The high-pitched call carried through the darkness.

"Yeah, pal?"

"You are my very best friend."

The knife jabbed his heart again. "You're mine too. Love ya, Carson."

Slurping hot cereal shortly before the bus's arrival, Carson blurted out his guest list. "I'm asking Ryan for sure. We farm fields in school. I'm teachin' him about farming, and he shows me how to play ball."

It was no surprise Ryan's name came up. Although Joel had never met the classmate, Carson divulged the boy's antics daily. He'd e-mail Mrs. Kirmis for the names of Ryan's parents and a phone number.

"Do you have a second friend?"

The back of Carson's hand caught a dribble of milk tickling his chin. "My second goodest friend is teacher. She wouldn't want to miss my party."

Mrs. Kirmis? Choking on a wedge of toast, Joel hacked loudly, pressing a hand to his chest. Convulsed by persistent coughs, he thumped on his chest with his fist.

Still catching his breath, Joel objected. "Birthday parties are for kids, scamp. Ryan is an excellent choice. Isn't there another boy you could ask?"

Finished with his breakfast, Carson slipped from his place and pulled on his snow boots parked beside the outside door. "You had a party. I seen you in a picture." The boy was hanging tough.

Uncomfortable because he knew it was true, Joel changed his form of attack. "Mrs. Kirmis is married. Her husband wouldn't like it if she went to a party without him." Wouldn't that be the talk of the community: he touring machinery lots with a married woman. Even with the jam he was presently in, Joel had to smirk inwardly at the notion.

"No, she's not. I never seen no husband at school with her," Carson insisted.

"Of course not. He works someplace else. *Missus* means married."

"Well, why can't we ask him to come too?"

Handing Carson his jacket, the man sympathized. "Sorry. We agreed on two guests. That would be three." This was ludicrous, arguing with a first grader over a birthday gathering.

The tooting of a horn beyond the front porch made them both jump. A yellow school bus awaited a passenger. "I love you, Carson. Scout your class today for another good possibility."

The bus door slammed shut behind the rider. Exhaust fumes hovered in the biting air as the bus roared away.

Every school day was an adventure for Carson, especially since his evolvement into the mainstream.

Thoughts of his pending party drifted through his consciousness. If he had two friends come for his party, and then there would be Joel and himself—two plus two equaled four. That was an okay number. It would be a super party.

"Okay, class. It's time to practice our reading with a partner. I want you to reread the story about the bear and the fox we had yesterday," Mrs. Kirmis instructed from the front of the classroom.

Hustling to do their teacher's bidding, the children grabbed carpet squares from the stack to sit on. Inevitably, Ryan was paired with Carson. Crawling under the front table, the duo settled into their favorite hideaway. Their books open to the starting page, the colorful illustrations vied for attention with the printed words, and, even more so, the birthday party plans careening through Carson's head.

"Guess what?" he whispered to his dark-haired chum. "You get to come to my birthday party on Saturday."

"Cool!" Ryan's eyes lit up with the unexpected news. "I get to see your farm?"

"Yup, Joel says I can ask two friends to my party."

It gave Ryan a warm feeling inside to be chosen. "Who else is coming?"

"I don't know. I wanted to ask teacher. Joel says I can't 'cause she's married. He says her husband would get mad."

"She's not married."

"Yes, she is. Her name is *missus*. That means she is," Carson explained matter-of-factly.

"I've been at her house tons of times. She's got no daddy there," Ryan insisted emphatically.

"Then why is she a *missus*?" Carson was confused.

"Maybe that's what her mama named her."

"I'm not sure. Joel is smart. He would know."

Ryan shrugged his shoulders. "Ask her."

"Not me." The blond head waggled.

"Then I will." Without waiting until their reading assignment was completed, Ryan crawled on all fours out from their secluded cave.

Mrs. Kirmis was circulating amongst the reading buddies, keeping everyone on track. Noting Ryan's diversion from his reading group, she addressed him sharply. "Ryan, you are supposed to be reading the story with Carson."

"We have a question," he stated, not intimidated by her gruffness.

"How can you ask me to help you sound out a word if you didn't bring your book along?" she whispered.

In a raspy voice, the rascal implored, "Do you gotta daddy?"

Lowering herself until her skirt swept the floor, she demanded, "What does this have to do with the bear and the fox?"

Humping his small shoulders, he replied, "Don't know. Carson wants you to come to his birthday party, but his dad says your dad would get mad."

Sorting through the dads, Jasmine softened her expression. "I think you mean *husband*. I do have one; however, he doesn't live with me."

Ryan thought he understood. "That's me too. Mama says I have a dad somewhere. She just doesn't know where."

"Oh, I do know where my husband is. He lives in heaven."

The dark eyes widened like an animated cartoon character. "You mean with the angels that talked to the shepherds?" Ryan was thunderstruck on how anyone could be so lucky.

Nodding her head, her arm wrapped about his shoulders, squeezing him to her. "Yes, and even better, with Jesus."

"They live in the same house? I gotta tell Carson!" He trotted back to their hideaway, diving under the table to share the remarkable news. "Teacher's daddy is in the Bible. He lives with all those guys up in heaven!"

Carson processed this extraordinary revelation. "Do you think it's okay to ask her to my birthday then?"

With his first-grade intelligence, Ryan endorsed the suggestion. "Yup, the angels only come down from heaven at Christmas."

In the afternoon twilight, Carson tumbled off the bus, throwing his schoolbag in the general direction of the porch before bounding over the drifts, weighted down by his insulated clothes and boots. Joel was just closing the overhead door of the shop.

Never tiring of the enthusiasm his small friend poured into his after-school greetings each day, Joel's heart bruised. He was going to miss this.

"Guess what, Joel!" he started yelling before he'd conquered the final snow pile. Gasping for breath, he tried it again. "Joel, guess what!" Catching the padded body before he fell in the deep snow, the farmer scooped him up in a tight hug.

Chest to chest, Carson wiggled to bring his nose inches from Joel's red, cold one. Pointing his mitten-covered hand to the sky, he broadcast his announcement. "Teacher's daddy lives in heaven. She can come to the party!"

Letting the declaration soak in, Joel connected it to their breakfast conversation. A tangle of emotions descended on the man. "You mean her daddy or her husband?"

"Both! She'll come. I know she will." Carson was jubilant.

Relinquishing his tight hold, the child slid down to stand on his own feet.

Carson's teacher is a widow? Having felt the claws of death himself, empathy invaded his soul for anyone forced to travel through a similar fate. What he wouldn't give to have Melissa back.

"If her husband is in heaven, then Mrs. Kirmis must be pretty sad." Two and a half years had passed since he had followed his wife's casket to the cemetery, yet instantaneous pain could cut through the subsequent span of days like a saw blade, slicing right to the core of his being.

"Why?" The stubby nose turned up to study the elder. "You said heaven was a good place to be."

Last night, Joel had said his teacher couldn't come to his party because her husband wouldn't like it. Now there was no husband to be mad, but instead, his teacher was sad? A birthday party would make her happy. Wouldn't it?

"So can I?"

Joel didn't bother asking for clarification. Carson's mind was a train on one track today: Mrs. Kirmis coming to his birthday party.

Whatever. He'd send an e-mail invitation off to her to satisfy the boy. A teacher had more things to do than attend a birthday gathering for every student in her class. Inevitably, she'd nicely turn them down.

Tugging on Joel's arm, Carson steered him into the house, pushing him into his office chair facing the computer.

Opening his e-mail account, he typed, backspaced, and pecked away again:

> Mrs. Kirmis,
>
> Carson is having a small birthday party on Saturday afternoon and has been granted permission to ask two friends to the event. His first choice is a student in your class by the name of Ryan. I suspect Carson has already informed him of the weekend event; however, I would like to call the boy's parents. Please supply me with his parents' names and their phone number. Thank you.

His second friend is also in the first-grade class but not a peer. Carson is set on asking his teacher, no matter how I have encouraged him to choose another classmate. With your hectic schedule, do not feel obligated to accept.

His admiration of you, Mrs. Kirmis, does set me at ease in sending the tyke off to school each morning on the bus.

Sincerely,
Joel Linton

He clicked the send button. "Now, Carson, don't be upset if Mrs. Kirmis isn't able to come. She is a busy lady keeping up with all you first graders."

Smoothing the bedcovers up to the chins of the boy and his hare hours later, Joel brought up the topic of heaven again. "The Bible says heaven is the most wonderful place you can imagine. It is God's home. It doesn't even have nighttime because God's glory is so bright it blocks out the dark."

Carson contemplated. "That's where teacher's husband lives?"

"Anyone who loves Jesus gets to go to heaven."

"Are you going to go to heaven when you die?" His blue eyes were wide, seeking an answer.

"Yes, I am." Not only was Jesus waiting for him with open arms, but Melissa had a room in the LORD's mansion as well.

"How do you know?" For a six—almost seven—year-old, he was thinking way beyond what many adults contemplated.

"Because Jesus lives right here." Joel tapped his chest. "I was fourteen years old when I realized I didn't want to go through life alone. I mess up a lot, left to myself. Jesus forgave all my blunders and said He'd help me through. Acts 16:31 says, 'Believe in the LORD Jesus, and you will be saved.' I did, and He moved right into my heart and has been with me ever since."

Fingering the edge of the quilt, Carson processed the information. If even a big, strong person like Joel needed Jesus, then maybe he did too. Gently, Joel added, "Asking Jesus to live in your heart is the most important choice you will make in your entire life."

Carson was quiet.

Softly, Joel offered, "Would you like me to help you ask Jesus into your heart right now?" Love from this big-hearted man completely washed over the boy like the shower he'd taken minutes earlier leaving his tendrils still damp. Even with no blood kinship between the two, Joel didn't think it possible for a parent to love a child any more than he did this one.

Uncomfortable by the magnitude of the subject hanging above him and Joel's solemnest, Carson shyly shook his head no, purposely letting his eyelids fall shut.

Hoping he hadn't pushed the tyke too hard too quickly, Joel backed off. Their days together were numbered; so little time and yet so much to instill in the child. Sighing inwardly, he could feel he had stepped ahead of the Holy Spirit. *A rancher doesn't expect a cow to eat a whole bale of hay at one sitting either,* he chided himself.

Bending over, he planted a kiss on the boy's cheek. "If you ever decide you want my assistance, don't be afraid to ask. I love you."

Memorizing the tender look of the cherub at rest, he wished he could hit *pause* like he could on a movie to cherish this scene forever. And then he'd hit *reverse* and tell Melissa, *Yes, let's proceed with adoption,* the way she would have wished.

But life wasn't like that. No matter how one longed to hold on to the present or backtrack into the past, life kept moving on an assembly line into the future, where there was no Melissa or Carson either.

Father, lead me. I'm always stumbling.

A nudge within answered, *I work best in weakness.*

Reading Mrs. Kirmis's reply the following day, a film of nervousness moistened the foster parent's brow.

> Mr. Linton and Carson,
>
> Thank you for the kind invitations extended to Ryan and myself. As it happens, Ryan is keeping me company this Saturday afternoon while his mother, Tina Benson, is at work. I spoke to her, and she has given permission for Ryan to attend Carson's birthday party with me. Please give us the particulars. We anticipate an enjoyable afternoon in the country for this extra special event.
>
> Sincerely,
> Jasmine Kirmis

Three mouths cheered on the birthday boy, his cheeks puffed out like a tuba player, intent on extinguishing seven candles in one blow. Just as he was about to exhale a mighty blast of air, Joel cracked a joke. "Hey, everyone, hang on tight. Mr. Windy here is about to blow our socks clean off of us!" Joel squeezed his eyes shut, balking up for the onslaught.

Ryan giggled. Jasmine wiggled her bare toes, her wet socks drying by the heat register after her boots became wedged full of snow during the sledding party. "You're right, Joel. Mine are already gone!" Merriment pranced in her eyes.

A raucous, airy laugh escaped from Carson's rounded lips, destroying his attempt at sending seven flames up in smoke.

"Stop teasing, Joel, or I can't blow!" he protested.

Immersed in the gaiety warming the Linton dining room, Jasmine had felt refreshment creeping into her soul all afternoon from the initial minutes Joel had pulled his pickup into her driveway. The boys had scampered into the backseat of the extended cab, she given the honor of holding the birthday cake Joel had moments earlier picked up at the bakery.

Acting as a tour guide, Carson had transformed into a full-sized farmer describing each farm implement's function and how it worked as Joel slowly meandered his pickup truck through the lots of the two machinery dealers in the town of Elton.

Joel had done well integrating agriculture into Carson's base of knowledge, as the youngster rattled off the names of the equipment: tractors, cultivators, disks, manure spreaders, augers, combines, swathers, hay binds, rakes, mowers, and balers.

Jasmine herself had never toured a machinery lot in her whole life and was learning right along with Ryan. Her first-grade guide was a whole lot smarter than his teacher in the farming business.

Observing the camaraderie between the foster parent and his charge was heartwarming. She had witnessed it in the sale barn a few months ago, seeing the pair interact. A cemented closeness had grown in the adult-child relationship. Mr. Linton seemed to do well in his role as a single foster parent.

Here they were celebrating a birthday. A mother would have decorated the party area with balloons and streamers, had birthday napkins to match the plates and cups. Each guest would have received a bag of treats to take home, and her camera would have been snapping continually.

None of the usual décor was apparent here. Circular cardboards from the frozen pizzas still lingered on the kitchen counter. Coral dishes used for every meal in this farmhouse became festive china for the birthday lunch.

Being entertained by window shopping in a farm machinery lot and then being pulled on an old car hood across a snow-covered stubble field by a tractor was a contrast to the bowling and swimming parties or the gatherings at a fast-food restaurant typical of party agenda.

Jasmine was relishing the day immensely with the members of the Linton household again.

Sarah Thern's promised foster care packet had arrived promptly in the mail after her visit. Jasmine's first reaction had been to discard it in the wastebasket, but contemplating the relationship demonstrated by Joel and Carson, she had let it lay in her stack of mail that required some sort of response.

Discussing her dilemma with Cynthia on one of their weekly treks to Norbert, she again reiterated her frustration over being a single parent. "I can't imagine anyone choosing on their own volition to sole parent a child. Yes, there are millions of single parents out there, most not by choice, yet I concede some have made that decision." Joel Linton had immediately come to mind. "But why? Why would they punish themselves? Raising a child is hard work."

Having known Jasmine for years, Cynthia let her vent before forcing her to view the other side of the issue. "It's also fulfilling to be needed, to give love, and to receive love. It may not be the customary family unit portrayed in the old Dick and Jane readers or the TV programs like *Father Knows Best* or even *The Brady Bunch*, but it can work. Either way, children are being nurtured."

Admittedly, Cynthia was always more open to life in the twenty-first century than what she was. Jasmine pictured herself trying to paint pretty pink bows on the end of every story.

"Anyway," Cynthia continued, "foster care is a temporary situation. If you get your license, you're not tying yourself to a kid for the rest of your life. Rather, you're helping the child through a difficult phase." Noting the skepticism written like a textbook over her friend's face, she'd added, "And if a social worker calls and asks if your home is available, you can say no. It's kind of like substitute teaching."

The very next day, Jasmine had filled out the multiple pages of the foster care application, asked friends for references, and had her fingerprints taken at the local police station. Having stamped the manila envelope, she dropped it through the slot in the post office—out of her hands and into the LORD's.

Watching Joel interact with the pair of boys at his dining room table, Jasmine was more comfortable with her decision.

"Okay, Carson, on the count of three, blow your guts out!" Joel commanded. "One … two …"

Again, laughter spewed out from Carson's throat, destroying his second attempt at extinguishing the shrinking wax decorations. For all the trepidation Joel had experienced prior to this seven-year-old's celebration, he was now relaxed, having as much fun as the youngsters were. It felt good to laugh.

"I bet Carson can't blow 'cause we didn't sing to him!" Ryan propped himself on his knees on the chair to gain height.

"You might have something there, Ryan. You start it," the older man agreed.

Off key but expounding in exuberance, a fair rendition of the "Happy Birthday" song circled the table. Even Carson sang to himself. Tacking on the child's version ending, Ryan soloed, "You look like a monkey and smell like one too." Cackling filled the room, threatening to bring down the ceiling, when Joel elbowed Ryan, disputing the song.

"No, that's your own feet you smell!"

Jasmine's side actually ached from laughing; however, it was an ache she'd endure anytime.

"Look," Ryan exclaimed, "the candles are making puddles on the frosting!"

"They are melting quickly," Jasmine interjected. "Blow, Carson."

"Yeah, before we have to eat burnt cake," Joel added.

"Everybody help me," Carson excitedly pleaded. "One, two, three, blow!" As with four fire extinguishers, the candles were doused, the cake saved.

Between mouthfuls of ice cream and cake, Ryan suddenly remembered a priority for birthday parties. "Presents. Carson, you have to open your presents. Open mine first. It's really cool." His eyes were a pair of bright headlights.

After darting a look at Joel for permission, Carson tore the brightly colored paper from the small package. Before it even registered what the gift entailed, Ryan took it back out of his friend's hands, wanting to demonstrate the awesome features of the toy. "See, it's a pickup truck like yours and Joel's. See, the end gate flaps down, and the doors open. And what's really cool is the hood opens."

Openly admiring the new addition to their farming operation, Carson said, "Thanks, Ryan, you can use it too."

Next, he opened Jasmine's box. She had contemplated a long time at what to get a child whose mother was absent from his life. What would a man not think of? She finally decided on a colorful picture frame.

Not sure if he realized what it was, Jasmine quietly hinted, "You can put your favorite picture in this frame and then look at it every day."

Understanding, Carson slid to his feet and crossed the short space to the dining room cupboard. Gently, he set the frame erect beside the photo of Joel on his fortieth birthday. "We should take a picture of my birthday party." His gaze landed on Joel.

Instantly Joel knew he was caught. A camera? Melissa took pictures, not him. Her camera was in some drawer or cupboard, but which one? And even if he found it, the battery would be dead. He was doomed.

"Oh!" Jasmine exclaimed. "I always carry my camera in my purse. In first grade, we never can predict when there will be a Kodak moment." Hurriedly retrieving her purse, she appointed herself the photographer. "How about one of you and Ryan and the super pickup first, and then we will get one of you with Joel."

Sliding onto Ryan's chair, Carson draped an arm over his comrade's shoulder, both holding on to the miniature pickup truck. Two toothy smiles posed for the flash.

Joel had to admire the lady. Was it a female trait to take care of the details, to anticipate in advance what to expect, to prepare for the unforeseen? She sure had been a good egg that afternoon, climbing onto the car hood, taking turns with the boys, being swept in wide circles across the snow-covered fields. And even before the sledding. How many city-bred gals would tolerate a machinery display?

"You're next, Joel."

As Carson skipped over to Joel's lap, the man wrapped his arms snuggly about his little friend's middle. *Just like a father and son would do*, Jasmine surmised, centering them in the viewfinder.

"Will you give us a picture?" Carson asked his teacher.

"You betcha."

Behind Carson's head, Joel held up two fingers, silently mouthing the words, "Make it two." He suddenly realized that when Carson's departure day came, he would have no photographs of him to treasure, yet his heart would have scrapbooks full of beautiful memories.

"Aren't you going to give Carson a present?" Ryan's inquiry brought him up short. Yes, of course he was. He pulled a rectangular package wrapped in Christmas paper from a cupboard door.

"Sorry, scamp, it was the only roll of wrapping paper I could find in the house." Another one of those things Melissa took care of. A mother would do a birthday celebration right.

Carson reached eagerly for the gift. "I'll remind you the next time we're in a store." Not refuting the youth, Joel seriously doubted if he'd ever need birthday wrappings again.

As the yuletide paper fell to the floor, an eloquent box was uncovered. Lifting the lid carefully, Carson had an inkling this wasn't a game or a toy. This was something important, something valuable.

His premonition proved correct. Tracing his finger over the lettering of the thick book, he read slowly, *A Child's First Bible*. Embossed on the lower edge was his name, *Carson Reynolds*.

Setting the Bible reverently on the table, he flung both arms about Joel's neck. Moisture misted the gentleman's eyes, acknowledging that maybe he had done one thing right. "Now I can read about heaven myself and what a terrific place you say it is." Carson's muffled words were at his ear.

Burrowing his face into the boy's neck, Joel fought for control in front of the audience sharing the room.

Heaven. Yes, where there will be no more good-byes. He longed for that.

A flash of light—Jasmine snapped one more Kodak moment.

CHAPTER 17

March frequently gambols into North Dakota like a frisky, new-born lamb, spreading hints of warmer weather and greening pastures. Residents throw off their fur-lined hooded jackets and pack away the thermal underwear, only too glad to lighten the load and anticipate an early spring.

But not this year. March let loose an angry, roaring lion, the wind whipping the snow into near-blizzard conditions, the visibility a few feet in front of one's face. Winter was not loosening its grip yet. The mercury line clung to the low teens, reminding the hearty Dakotans that Mother Nature always has the last word.

Ranchers, deep into calving season, groveled long and hard to protect the newborn calves in their first hours after birth. Carried into barns or heated calf shelters to prevent their fragile ears from freezing, or worse yet, losing the new infant, the seventy-pound calves were tenderly cared for by the ranchers. A year from now, this brood of calves would be the ranchers' bread and butter. Long days and sleepless nights were worth the misery if the calf crop survived.

Along with his farming neighbors, Joel Linton operated with a few hours of rest, keeping a watchful eye on his pregnant mamas out in the corral.

Wide-eyed, Carson witnessed the birth of his first Angus calf, wet and matted, pushed out onto the straw bedding beneath the mother cow. Keeping a sturdy fence barricade between the boy and the overprotective bovine, Joel answered each of Carson's inquisitive questions.

"Why do the front feet come out first?"

"Was I born that way?"

"Why does the cow let her baby plop out on the ground?"

"Isn't it gross to lick the baby off?"

"How come the calf can stand up already?"

"How does it know where to get the milk?"

The miracle of the birthing process soaked into Carson's first-grade mind. "Wait until I tell the kids at school!" Smirking inwardly, Joel was confident Mrs. Kirmis could steer the next show-and-tell story appropriately. And if she couldn't, she'd blush a pretty shade of rose.

Sixty miles distant in Norbert, Jasmine and Cynthia sat through the wrap-up session of their six-week postgraduate class, having submitted the final written paper. Girls' nights out had been a welcome diversion during the dark winter months, but now they'd move their coffee cups closer to home.

Turning out of the parking lot, the teachers headed back to Elton in the bitter cold of the March night.

While dropping Cynthia off an hour later on the far side of town, Jasmine's whole body pleaded for rest. She wasn't a night owl. Friday mornings were inevitably payback time for staying up past her self-imposed curfew on school nights.

Traffic was nonexistent as she slowly slipped by the dark windows of the sleeping town. A wide-mouthed yawn filled her lungs with oxygen, keeping her awake to maneuver the last corner to her street. Giving way to a second yawn, she was caught up short by a dazzling beacon burping out surges of illumination halfway down her block. Her teeth banged together, her body instantly alert.

"What on earth?" She stared at the out-of-place scene, her heart already gaining momentum. "Did a neighbor have a medical emergency?" Art and Alice Linstrum lived in the forest greenhouse across from Jasmine's bungalow. They were elderly people.

Creeping to her driveway, she found the cop car parked at an odd angle, monopolizing her entrance, leaving barely enough space for her to edge onto the cement pad.

An unidentified automobile tucked in behind the sheriff's unit sat directly in front of the Benson residency. Every window under its sagging roof spilled out a square of yellow onto the snow-covered yard. Tina's dilapidated station wagon was noticeably absent.

Doom sat heavily on the teacher's shoulders. A cop car at midnight did not bring good news. She thrust the car door open and sucked in the cold. Blocked by the snow bank obstructing the slice of lawn between the neighboring homes, she stepped out onto the street before struggling through the deep snow in Tina's neglected walkway. The steps to the Bensons' front door were almost impassable, but imprints of footsteps before hers formed a hard-packed slippery trail.

Carefully thrusting her foot into each deep depression, she wobbled to the leaning wrought-iron handrail. Grabbing it firmly in her gloved hand, she drew herself up the snow-laden steps.

Banging repeatedly on the broken screen door with her fist, she yelled, "Tina, are you okay?" When no immediate answer intoned back to her, she screamed, "Ryan! Ryan, are you in there?" Frigid air whirled about her. Fear itself acted as a burning fire, making her oblivious to the icy fingers of frigidity raking at her back. Pounding with both fists, she insisted on being heard.

Unceremoniously, the inside door was jerked open, the sheriff's bulky body silhouetted against the interior light. He recognized her immediately. "Mrs. Kirmis, we're sorry to have awakened you. Everything is under control here."

Yanking the screen door partway open, she brushed away his words like crumbs off a table. "Did something happen to Ryan? Where is he? What's going on?" Frantic trepidation turned her words into staccato notes of a horror movie. Her eyes darted past the officer's uniform to the disheveled room behind him. Tina didn't waste much time on housework. Another person came into view.

"Sarah! What are you doing here?" A cop and a social worker. Jasmine feared the answer to her own question.

Al Forman stepped aside to allow Jasmine to talk through the tight opening. Carrying a bulky garbage bag, Sarah met her at the door. Scanning the house from her limited viewpoint, Jasmine demanded, "Where is Ryan?"

"He's warming up in the police car out front. By morning, he could have frozen to death in here." Sarah's words were short and angry. For the first time, Jasmine realized no friendly warmth met her, neither from the vexed social worker nor from the interior temperature.

"Ryan has been sitting in this cold house since school was out?" Jasmine asked, dazed, guilt stabbing her conscience. Assuming Tina had remembered her Thursday night class, she hadn't checked with the irresponsible mother to verify that Ryan's after-school hours were supervised before leaving for Norbert.

"The living room thermostat reads forty-two degrees. What would have it been by morning?" Sarah stuffed a pair of small shoes and boots into the garbage bag. "Evidently the fuel tank to the furnace ran empty. Tina didn't think to check it."

"Where's Tina?" Jasmine's eyes swept the room behind Sarah a second time, willing the neglectful mother to appear, to lighten the charges her carelessness was about to avalanche upon her.

"Don't know. She was scheduled to work today but didn't show up. Her car is in the parking lot of the filling station where she works. Water pump problems. Someone gave her a ride home yesterday. We've tried her cell phone, but she evidently didn't pay that bill either."

Officer Forman was on his cell phone with the owner of the Bensons' rental house, informing him of the situation. By morning, the water pipes in the house would burst if heat wasn't restored to the dwelling.

Jasmine's head was racing for explanations. "Ryan's sister, Lacey, lives in town. Maybe she knows where her mom is."

"Doesn't answer her cell phone either. Al checked out her boyfriend's pad. No one home." Sarah scribbled a note to Tina, leaving it on the cluttered kitchen table, in case the neglectful mother would return sometime during the night. Then she lifted the bag and squeezed out onto the doorstep.

"Let me have Ryan for the night," Jasmine begged. "Tina would expect to find him with me." How scared the dark-haired youngster must be.

"You might be right, but Tina went too far this time. It's out of your hands, Jasmine." Sarah was furious. "That's why we are taking Ryan to a safe, warm home sanctioned by the county."

Emergency foster homes or shelter beds acted as a safe haven for children until a decision was made in a court hearing within ninety-six hours of the child's removal from his home. Jasmine had no choice as the fuming social worker propelled the slippery steps ahead of her. Sarah hugged the bag of clothes to her middle, carefully watching her footing in the deep snow. Behind them, Officer Forman secured the house door.

"Sarah, be reasonable. Ryan knows me. I'm his neighbor and his teacher. I'll keep him safe," Jasmine pleaded, trudging through the deep snow beside the determined social worker. Fear had warmed her minutes earlier. Now the fervor was replaced by an uncontrollable shaking.

"You had your chance. You protected him all right," Sarah snapped. The officer climbed into the driver's seat of the cop car.

Sarah followed suit with hers, banging the door behind her. In the rear passenger window of the cop car, attended by another policeman, a sad little face peeked out from the quilt wrapped snugly about him. His dark eyes peered out at Jasmine, his palm and fingers pressed against the glass.

The plea in his brown eyes wiped her breath away. She had always been there for him when his mother was not. This time, she too had failed him.

She couldn't prevent the tears from freezing to her cheeks as they spilled over the embankment. Her heart burst.

Their stares held until his face faded in the darkness.

Standing transfixed in the freezing cold, Jasmine buried her face in her hands. What had she done? The impish rascal had somehow wrenched off a piece of her heart as he was escorted away in the backseat of an officer's car. After Evert's death and Autumn's rejection, she hadn't thought any heart remained.

Had she protected Tina only to hurt Ryan? Families needed to stay together, didn't they? No matter what the cost?

Reality soaked in along with the frigid air seeping through her wool jacket. Social Services wasn't the enemy but rather the savior when the family unit failed.

What if no one had found the boy in the cold house tonight? His chair in school would have been vacant in the morning. Would she, as his teacher, immediately have been on the phone checking out the situation? Or would she have waited, hoping her little pal was home nursing a nasty cold?

Ryan may not have needed a foster home at all had the police officers arrived a dozen hours later than they did. A funeral director would have been the recipient of the summons instead.

Shuddering at the fragility of life, she sunk to her knees in the cold snow, suddenly overwhelmingly appreciative of Sarah's profession. Ryan's life had been spared because Sarah cared. Yes, Jasmine loved the boy more; however, sometimes love was an enabler. Jasmine had unwontedly aided Tina in placing a higher value on a social life than on the precious urchin she had borne.

Overhead, a star-studded sky lit up the heavens. Lifting her face to her maker, she wept songs of praise-filled worship to his providential hand in caring for Ryan Benson. She was so small and weak, her LORD almighty and powerful.

"Teacher, it's my turn to get the milk, not Arnie's." Pixie's insistent whine grated on Jasmine's already taut nerves.

Patience was as brittle as skim ice on a spring pond. Sleep had been nonexistent. Ryan's desperate eyes had stared at her writhing form from the shadowed ceiling above her bed. Straining to hear motor sounds throughout the cold night, she'd waited for Tina's frantic knock on the door. None came.

When she stepped out of the garage to commence her daily walk to school, her eyes had instantly taken in the Benson premises. The windows were dark; no puffs of smoke emanated from the brick chimney. Tina's usual parking space in the street was still empty, except for the telltale tracks left behind by the midnight visitors.

Jasmine was struck dumb. Her neighbor hadn't come home at all! What was Tina expecting? Did she assume Jasmine would act as a mother hen, gathering the neighbor child under her wing whenever Tina's social calendar had no room for a son? Not a note, an e-mail, or phone call to verify Ryan would have someone to tuck him in at a reasonable hour.

The realization ignited an anger burning within, keeping her steaming all the way to school. Storming into Cynthia's classroom, she'd dumped her load on her friend's attentive ears. Enragement at Tina eventually gave way to tears of frustration. She blamed the negligent mother; she blamed herself for trusting Tina's maternal practices. Guilt ate away at her, even though Cynthia's reasoning told her she wasn't responsible for everyone.

Wasn't she supposed to be concerned about her neighbors, or at least her first-grade students? Instead of being cooperative when Sarah Thern had come seeking information on the Bensons, Jasmine had been protective, almost secretive, not giving out one more syllable than she had to—guilty on two accounts.

And now, Ryan's tiny desk sat empty. His classmates assumed he was sick. And they were right. He was heartsick and homesick, cared for by strangers. What must be going through his innocent mind this instant?

Had he come through the snow after school yesterday tapping at her door when his mother failed to show up? The bungalow's door had been locked. No heat seeped under the sill to encircle his shaking limbs and frostbit nose in a warm embrace. Had he forlornly tramped back through the deep snow to burrow under a pile of quilts in his own dwelling?

A sharp jerk on her cardigan plummeted the teacher's focus to Pixie's round eyes, critically demanding an audience. "Teacher, you made a mistake. I'm supposed to get the milk today." The six-year-old's bottom lip pouted prettily, framed by springy curls controlled by a rust-colored ribbon tied on the crest of her head.

Impatience whittled a crack in Jasmine's usual professional composure. She spun the spoiled little girl in a hundred-and-eighty-degree circle, marching her toward her desk. Mrs. Kirmis snapped a retort. "It's Arnie's birthday. He gets to be my helper all day. Sit down, Pixie." Mortified by her teacher's reprimand, the student did as directed.

It was the longest teaching day Jasmine had ever endured. Secretly, she hoped Sarah Thern would call, keeping her abreast of the situation.

However, no summons came from the office.

Cutting short the lengthy preparatory hours after school, Jasmine hurried homeward, thankful it was Friday. Tina would certainly have reappeared by now and be out of her mind agonizing over her son and furnace problems—hopefully in that order.

An unsettling thought pervaded her twisted emotions. If Tina hadn't bothered to come home last night, assuming Jasmine would perform her free nanny service, why would she be worried now? She'd assume Ryan had gone to school with his teacher this morning, giving her another day without the responsibilities of parenthood. Ugh!

Almost afraid to investigate, she marched past her own sanctuary to give her full view of the Bensons' tiny rental. Disappointment pinched out the tiny flame of hope still gallantly wavering.

Dark, vacant windows, unshoveled steps, a cold chimney, and an empty street—no sign of any life. Sharp raps on the screen door's broken frame brought no sounds of footsteps, a door opening, or any other hint verifying an occupant. Only the echoes of the town filled her ears, dousing completely any smoldering hope wanting to explode into sparks.

Carrying a heavy heart, she retraced her steps, letting herself into her own haven. Her purse and schoolbag landed on the kitchen counter as she grabbed the phone, pressing the digits to the Social Services office in Prairie City. Her back slumped against the wall, sliding down its smooth surface until her rump hit the floor, her head against the cool wall.

"Sarah Thern here. How can I help you?" The voice was aloof, void of friendliness or empathy.

Feeling like she was eating crow, Jasmine filled her lungs with air. "Sarah, this is Jasmine. Please tell me what's happened since last night. Is Ryan okay? Have you gotten a hold of Tina? I really want to help." She knew she was blubbering. Her heart thudded hard against her ribs.

A lengthy silence followed and then a sigh. In measured words, slowly and articulated, Sarah replied, "As a teacher and neighbor, I can understand your concern. However, you, being a professional, know that such information is confidential."

It was like a slap in the face. Jasmine felt the sting over the airwaves. She didn't care; she could lower herself to groveling. "Sarah, many days I spend more hours with Ryan than his mother does. Have you seen him today? Tell me how he's doing." Her voice wavered, the last words coming out in a squeak.

Relenting a centimeter, Sarah gave a short synopsis. "I talked to his foster parent briefly. He is fine. Until we contact Tina, he will have to stay put."

"You mean Tina hasn't been found yet?" Certainly she couldn't be that far away. What were the authorities doing?

Sarah caught the accusation in Jasmine's tone and quickly donned her professional mask again. "I really can't say. Thank you for your concern, but there is nothing else I can share. Good-bye." The line went dead.

"Oh, LORD, do something," was all she got out before the sobs broke the dike she'd carefully kept plugged all day in front of her class. Droplets of frustration and grief wallowed from deep inside of her, emptying her guts of all she could not do. Nothing was within her grasp.

And that's when the LORD can work the best, when human frailty admits defeat.

Sunlight filtering through her lace curtains cast an intricate lattice shadow along the ceiling of her bedroom. Opening her eyes on Saturday morning to the sunny room decorated with its dainty edging momentarily erased the foulness of the last two days. Sheer exhaustion had finally dipped her into sleep in the early morning hours and had blessedly allowed her to slumber until almost noon. Rest didn't alleviate the problems next door, yet it gifted her mind to work in reality instead of on an emotional tidal wave.

If Tina had figured Jasmine would step in and help her out on Thursday after school, even in so much as keeping Ryan overnight and letting him tag along with her to school on Friday, why didn't she show up last night? Did she somehow get wind she was in trouble? Had something else happened? Why couldn't her daughter, Lacey, be reached either? And what about her job at the station?

Endeavoring to shake her head clear of the plague of questions, Jasmine crawled out of bed and wriggled into a pair of jeans and a worn sweatshirt.

From inside of her refrigerator, she selected a grapefruit, rolling it around in her hands to soften its skin before peeling it. Propping herself on a kitchen stool, her gaze floated out to her snowy backyard. The white landscape breathed purity and simplicity. Why was life so hard and complex?

She'd given these problems to the LORD a hundred times last night, and yet every thought seemed to be dragging them back into her lap.

No, LORD, take them. I can't make sense of it all. You know where Ryan is—and Tina. Work it out, LORD; work it out.

Rinsing her hands at the sink, she decided this was the day to get started on the individual photo albums she gave to each of her students on the last day of the school year in May. After dumping the boxful of pictures she had developed thus far onto her countertop, Jasmine began sorting them into piles for each girl and boy.

Picking up a photo of the classroom farm, Jasmine frowned. Carson and Ryan were astutely proud of their agricultural setup in the back corner. Two totally different children but somehow headed in the same downhill spiral.

If any child had transformed since the first day of school, it was Carson. First, he was a frozen statue refusing to take part in any activity; then he miraculously emerged from his shell, wholeheartedly delving into the class dynamics. Now, he had become almost too acclimated, erupting from his desk during work time, often interrupting her teaching and having to be reminded repeatedly to use his quiet voice. Joel Linton had warned her of the fine line between a kitten and a lion.

Below the photos cropped and taped onto colorful pages, she added pertinent captions to narrate the pictures. Shadows on the walls had lengthened when the last picture was secured to its background.

Growling in her stomach reminded her she had skipped lunch. Remarkably, it was already past four o'clock in the afternoon. The day was slipping by.

The aroma of hot cheese and a grilled chicken breast soon rose from her stovetop.

One bite into her sandwich, the ringing of the doorbell chimed simultaneously with an insistent rapping on the kitchen door.

Along with the cold air, a bedraggled Tina breezed in, staring out at her from the remains of heavily-applied eye shadow and mascara, now smeared and patchy. Her usual spiked hair had lost its altitude and bent lamely to the side. Always dressed too skimpily for the weather conditions, she held her waist-length jacket across her chest with a clenched hand rather than zipping it.

Shocked to see the prodigal she had been praying would find her way home, Jasmine let out a startled, "Tina! Where on earth have you been?"

Sweeping the kitchen dining area with a quick scan, Tina demanded, "Isn't Ryan here?"

"Ryan?" Jasmine blubbered in confusion. "Why would he be here? He's your son." Jasmine could feel her defenses rising.

How could this woman, who called herself a mother, dare to come barging in three days after sending her child off to school and ask if Ryan was here? Was she nuts?

"Well, I expected you'd have kept him until I got home!" Tina's eyes shot accusations at her neighbor.

"Got home? You haven't been home for three days. You didn't even go to work on Thursday. I was in Norbert after school that day for my graduate class. Where were you?" Anger was rising in Jasmine's chest, her voice gaining intensity.

"Class? You're still going to Norbert for that? I thought that was long over." Tina's voice dripped with disdain. "Did you see what I got?" Holding out rumpled papers Jasmine hadn't noticed her clutching, she spewed, "I'm not home ten minutes, and I get visited by our mighty town cop serving papers on me!" Her hand visibly shook as she held out the copies she had crushed in accordion folds in her agitated state.

"He said Ryan was at a safe house. I figured it was yours." She let out a garbled scream. "Where have they taken him? Is that snoopy social worker behind this?" Tina couldn't stand still. Her eyes continued to frisk about as if she suspected Jasmine of hiding Ryan from her. Nervous twitches on the side of her face accented her anguish.

Roping in her own quick retort to keep the situation from elevating out of control, Jasmine surmised her neighbor's reaction to the court summons was compounded by the alcohol on her breath.

"Come have a chair. Have you eaten anything lately?" Jasmine quieted her own voice with the invitation. She needed to talk this out with Tina. No matter what she thought of the lady or her maternal capabilities, Tina was still Ryan's mother.

Noting Tina's indecision, Jasmine beckoned for the distraught lady to follow her as she returned to the dining room table, pulling a chair out for her guest to drop into. Twisting the papers even tighter, Tina followed, waving her maroon-painted nails in the air. "No food. My stomach is in such a knot it couldn't possibly hold anything." She dropped the papers and rested her elbows on the table, her fingers digging hurtfully into the sides of her face.

At the sink, Jasmine filled a mug with tap water and a sprinkling of coffee granules before placing it in the microwave. When the timer dinged, she carried the coffee to Tina, setting it on the table before her.

Tina's long fingers circled the mug like a drowning swimmer clinging to an inflatable life preserver. The once-manicured nails were scratched and cracked. Her disheveled head bent over the table like a child saying her prayers, although Jasmine doubted the woman cared about the LORD's ways, or at least had never been introduced to the love of a heavenly Father.

Swearing under her breath, Tina looked up but focused on a point past Jasmine's face. "Where in the heck did I go wrong?" Jasmine wasn't sure if the words were directed to her for a response or if Tina was sorting through the jumbled messages in her brain.

In carefully measured words, Jasmine suggested, "Let's go back to Thursday. Weren't you scheduled to work at the gas station that day?"

Tina's eyes stayed riveted on the wall somewhere behind Jasmine. A hundred different images flashed across her face, but no words fell from her mouth. Not sure if her words had penetrated, Jasmine sucked in her breath, unsure of how to proceed. Her sandwich lay uneaten on the plate.

As if circling the bases and finding each one covered, Tina's dark lids closed, waiting for the umpire's words, "You're out!" Dragging her eyelashes upward, she momentarily caught Jasmine's worried complexion.

Rubbing the folds of skin on her neck, she admitted, "I was supposed to work on Thursday, but a friend suggested a tempting rendezvous. I got Lucy to take my shift, and we headed out of town."

Sarah had said Tina hadn't shown up for work. Jasmine let the inconsistencies in the stories lapse.

Jasmine supplied the name. "With Burt?"

"No, not Burt. New blood." Her voice rose in volume. "Ain't I deserving of some fun once in a while? I work hard, put up with a lot of backlash, and don't have much to show for it. I can't live your boring life!"

Glaring across the table, she abruptly dropped the sneer. "Ah, don't listen to me; what do I know? My life is certainly a blast. I have cops pounding on my door, my child kidnapped right from my own home, social workers chasing me down the street, and a judge summoning me to court. Boredom has its merits."

Even though Jasmine knew her troubled neighbor was venting, seething at being backed into a corner by the legal system ready to hang her with red tape, the bitter summation of Jasmine's life condensed into one word, *boring*, hurt. Was that the way her faith, moral code, and values appeared to an outsider? She purposely shrugged off the satirical jibe, concentrating on the more pertinent problems at stake.

"We all need a day off once in a while," Jasmine agreed, venturing to appease the flighty female perched at the table. "How did you plan this excursion?"

"Plan? I didn't. My friend did it all. I liked his plan. Get out of town for a while, have some laughs, just the two of us." Jasmine knew the woman across the table was younger than her, but at the moment, she appeared to be years older.

"And what were your plans for Ryan?" She tried to keep the inquiry light, but underneath the words, the teacher was as hard as rock.

"Ryan? Oh, I figured he'd walk home with you after school as usual, and when you saw I wasn't home from work yet, you'd invite him in." Her glazed eyes shifted uneasily and then studied a torn fingernail. It was just as Jasmine had expected—use the servant lady next door.

Letting out a loud expletive, Tina then retracted her words. "Ah, heck, I don't even remember thinking about the kid at all. I was hot to trot. Give me a man with a cowboy hat and boots, and

I'm gone." In anguish, she turned sideways in the chair, as if to get up and run from the prison bars she already felt banging shut on her. Instead, she closed her eyes, pinching her upper nose to ward off a stream of tears about to capitulate and follow the lone droplet zigzagging a muddy mascara trail down her cheek.

"I know. I blew it." A wretched sound choked out her last word, sending it to a high pitch as she virtually crumbled into a heap of cheap clothes and painted façades that couldn't camouflage the scared lady underneath. Even in her wretched state, she wouldn't let herself disintegrate into a pool of tears.

Empathy spilled over in Jasmine. What did she know about this woman's past? How young had she been when she had Lacey? Had there been a mother for her in those early days of motherhood to teach her? Broken relationships, toughing it out on her own with two kids in tow, traveling far from her roots. In a lot of ways, she was gutsier than Jasmine ever would be.

Easing off her seat, Jasmine didn't quite know how to comfort the grieving woman pinned between the edge of the table and the chair back. She reached out to rub the two boney shoulders of the silently sobbing woman, massaging the tight muscles, showing compassion to a neglectful mother she easily could have strangled the night before. Minutes crept by. Had it not been for the grace of God, Jasmine reasoned she too could have committed mistakes weighted with heavy consequences.

Twisting her head, seeking Jasmine, Tina flung a hand to her own shoulder, catching the massaging fingers. "Come talk to me."

Jasmine gave the thin shoulder a final squeeze before retrieving a tissue box from the bathroom. Again she reached out to hold Tina's trembling hand across the table.

"What am I going to do?" Tina whispered, all of her earlier venom diffused. Her carefully painted face had slipped to expose the vulnerable human being inside.

"Take one little step at a time." Jasmine pressed her fingers gently. "Something you can handle."

"I don't think I'm up to handling anything. Everywhere I go, I mess up." Nervously, she tapped her feet under the table.

"Why don't you start with a good night's sleep? You look exhausted. It's hard to think clearly when we are operating on a low tank. How about using my guest bedroom tonight, and we'll talk in the morning?"

Jasmine wasn't sure why she was extending the invitation. Ryan was the one who used the room the most often, and now she was fluffing the pillows for the woman who was the cause of Ryan's removal. Was she an open doormat to people? Could anyone come in and wipe his muddy shoes on her face and then ridicule the standards she lived by? Jasmine wasn't sure this was exactly the right arrangement, but God always seemed to be nudging her to do the servant work.

"Nah. I've got a warm bed just a stone's throw away. I'll sleep better there anyway." Tina made no effort to give up her chair.

"It's warmer here. You best stay here until you can get the furnace running again."

Tina's streaked head came up abruptly. "Furnace trouble? What are you talkin' about? My house is warm." A biting edge attached itself to her words.

Taken aback, Jasmine stuttered, "The po—police came. I mean, Ryan was freezing to death."

Suddenly, Tina breathed new energy. She snatched her hand from Jasmine's clasp as she stood up. "Freezing to death? Are you out of your mind?" Her eyes narrowed into slits.

Jasmine was confused. Was Tina not aware of the empty fuel tank? This conversation was not making sense. "That's why you could be charged with child neglect. You not only left Ryan home alone but in a house with no heat when the temperature outside was below freezing."

Tina's jaw dropped. "I wouldn't do that! I might not be voted mother of the year, but I certainly would have the decency to protect my son from the frigid elements!"

"Tina, the fuel tank in your backyard is too small to hold enough fuel oil for the entire winter. Have you filled the tank since last fall?" Momentarily, Tina was speechless, giving her neighbor a chance to implant another thought. "Didn't you have the fuel truck come in the middle of the winter last year?"

Color drained from Tina's makeup-streaked face. "Yes, no! I don't know! But I was just at my house. It's as warm as yours." Moving toward the door, she stopped in mid-step.

"That's why there is an electric heater in the kitchen and another one in the living room. My landLORD must have put them there." Running a hand through her oily hair, she groaned. "I didn't have time to think about anything before the cop was banging on my front door, shoving these papers in my face. And then I hightailed it over here." A look of total terror emanated from her face.

"I am a terrible mother. The worst. First, I leave my son alone, and then I let him sit in a freezer. I'm done for it. I'll never see him again!" Wrapped in her friend's arms, the slow mollification process started over.

CHAPTER 18

Nerves stretched tightly. Tina fiddled with the straps of her purse sitting on her lap.

Outside the windows, a continuous stretch of white landscape reeled past, dotted with an occasional farmyard snuggled in a knot of trees close to the highway. Every mile appeared monotonously the same, reeling her toward her date in court like a fishing pole reeling in its catch.

Taking her eyes off the road, Jasmine noted Tina's transparent discomfort. No doubt she needed a cigarette. Jumping beans were doing a dance in her own stomach as well. Fumbling in her bag on the floor with one hand, she drew out a pack of gum, offering a stick to her companion. "Whatever happens today, I am assured the LORD's hand will be in it, doing what's best for both you and Ryan."

Tina grunted a noncommittal response but took the offered gum. Having folded the spearmint chewing gum into her mouth, her hand crumbled the wrapper into a miniature ball, rolling it around and around in her fingers. Nervous and disgruntled, Tina muttered more to herself than to her companion. "Why didn't I leave town when I still had a chance? I knew better than to stay more than a year at the same address."

The dazzling white scenery out her window could have been prison walls.

"Rural life here in North Dakota grew on me: friendly people, simpler lifestyles, neighbors, like you, who took an interest in me." She crushed the wrapper flat again; her teeth grated enamel on enamel.

Alarmed at Tina's solution to her problems, Jasmine intervened. "Running wouldn't help Ryan."

As if not hearing her friend's words, Tina swore. "Every state has a Department of Human Services ready to butt in where they're not wanted."

Jasmine wasn't sure she'd be welcome at this hearing. After a juvenile's emergency removal from a home, the legal system demanded a closed hearing to be held to access the situation.

Before leaving Jasmine's kitchen on Saturday evening, Tina had begged, on the brink of hysterics, for her neighbor to accompany her to the hearing on Monday morning. Predicting her inability to hold herself together, yet alone to comprehend the legalistic terms bantered back and forth in the courtroom, she'd grasped both of Jasmine's hands in hers, imploring her assistance.

Two pools of desperation had formed on Tina's lined face, obliterating any trace of objection Jasmine might have formulated. Thus, instead of singing the ABCs with her first graders today, she was chauffeuring her neighbor to Prairie City—the neighbor whom had taken advantage of her repeatedly. What was one more time if her presence at the hearing helped Ryan in any minute way?

As the two were ushered to the courtroom on the second floor, Tina's strapless heels echoed on the hardwood floors. Her heavy makeup was back in place, her nails repainted a forest green to match her eye shadow. Jasmine had inwardly winced when she first climbed into her car, wishing Tina had downplayed the cosmetics for her day in court and had donned the appearance of a down-to-earth, humbled parent.

Interrupted by the clicking taps against the floorboards, both Sarah Thern's and the state attorney's heads came up synchronically from the papers they were discussing. Sarah raised her eyebrows slightly before extending a greeting. "Good morning, ladies. Thank you for being prompt, Tina."

Tina nodded curtly, sliding into a wooden bench two rows from the front.

"It seems we meet again, Mrs. Kirmis. You do realize this is a closed hearing." Sarah wasn't wasting anytime on niceties.

Tina slipped an arm through Jasmine's, holding on to her tightly. "I want her here. She stays; you already took my son."

Sarah sent a pointed look at the state's attorney, who remained expressionless. He too was acquainted with Jasmine from the years her family members were residents of Prairie City.

Gary Murie leaned across the front pew to shake hands with the women. "It's nice to see you, Jasmine. I'm sorry, but hearings of this nature involving children are usually closed to the public, unless you have testimony that would help in the court's decision."

Sharply Tina cut in. "She does. She is going to testify on behalf of Ryan."

Mr. Murie looked from Jasmine to Tina then back to Jasmine. Nodding his head in resignation, he backed away.

Jasmine sat quietly, letting a million thoughts slip through her head while Tina fidgeted beside her. She noted Officer Forman sitting off to their right. What would happen today? Would Tina be given a second chance? If not, how severe would her reprimand be, and for what duration? Child neglect was serious; judges didn't take kindly to the subject.

"All rise for the Honorable Judge Krammer." Jasmine pulled Tina to her feet as she stood up.

As the judge took his high seat at the front of the courtroom, the rest followed his lead. "The state of North Dakota versus defendant Tina Benson. Attorney Murie, would you please identify the people present in the courtroom?"

"Yes, your honor." Mr. Murie came to his feet. "Tina Benson, Officer Al Forman, social worker Sarah Thern, and Jasmine

Kirmis. Tina Benson has requested the presence of Mrs. Kirmis here today. She is Ryan Benson's first-grade teacher and a neighbor to the Bensons in Elton."

Nothing ruffled Judge Krammer's disposition. Transferring his directive back to the state's attorney, he asked, "Do you have any objections, Mr. Murie?"

"No, sir."

Resting his eyes on Jasmine in turn, he said, "You are welcome to stay."

"Let us proceed."

Leaning his forearms on the podium, he directed his words toward the defendant. "Tina, it is obvious you do not have representation in this court. You do have the right to an attorney. If you cannot afford one, an attorney may be appointed for you if you fill out the proper paperwork. Or you may waive that right altogether. Do you understand?"

Nodding her spiked hairdo, Tina shakily consented, grasping the wooden seat on each side of her knees as a mainstay.

"For the court records, would you please answer verbally?" Judge Krammer kindly requested.

"Yes." Her eyes affixed themselves at a point halfway up the judge's high desk, unable to look the man in the eye.

"Would you like to seek representation, or do you want an application for a court-appointed lawyer?"

Again, she shook her head and then remembered to speak audibly. "No."

"No, you do not have representation, or no, you do not want a court-appointed lawyer?"

"No to both." Tina's slim body shook like a loose window rattling in a Dakota wind.

Slipping on a pair of reading glasses, Judge Krammer took up the court papers in front of him. "Go ahead, Mr. Murie."

Clearing his throat, the state's attorney stood at an angle to the judge and the apprehensive ladies sitting side-by-side in the pew. "I, in turn, would like to call on Sarah Thern."

"Your Honor." Sarah rose to her feet, a sheaf of papers in her hand. "In front of you, sir, you have a list of the dates and alleged offenses of child neglect involving Tina Benson in connection with her six-year-old son, Ryan Benson. They are mainly infractions of negligence in being inconsistent in providing the child with nutritious food, adequate clothing for the winter, and supervision when she is at work or on personal outings.

"I would like to elaborate on this final point, which brought us to the emergency removal of Ryan Benson from his mother's home last Thursday, March fifth of this year. Ryan was found in the home by himself at eleven thirty in the evening. The oil furnace in the dwelling had gone out due to the depletion of the fuel tank. To our best calculations, the child had been in the house alone since coming home after school was dismissed at three fifteen. A court order was requested over the phone and given. Officer Al Forman and I went to the home to retrieve the child. The temperature in the home at the time was forty-two degrees Fahrenheit. Attempts were made to contact Tina Benson on her cell phone, at her work number, and at her daughter's residency. No connections were made. Very little food edible to a child was found in the home. Ryan is temporarily being cared for in a foster home, waiting upon the court's directives."

At Judge Krammer's nod of understanding, Sarah resumed her seat.

Next, the state's attorney sought Al Forman's input. "Officer Forman, were you the officer who delivered Tina Benson's court summons? If so, please elaborate."

Al Forman strolled to the front. "Yes, sir, I was. I delivered the envelope to her on Saturday, March seventh, at four fifteen in the afternoon. The police department had continuously attempted to contact Mrs. Benson by phone and at her door, both unsuccessfully, until this time."

"You mean, two days had passed since Ryan was left sitting in the cold house alone before his mother could be contacted?" the attorney asked.

"Yes."

Turning to Tina, who sat with her head bowed, the state's attorney continued his questioning. "As the mother of this six-year-old child, can you tell us where you were?"

Clenched fists lay in her lap. Moisture gleamed on her cheeks. Tina was making an effort to hold herself together. "I—I was out of town, and my cell phone doesn't work."

"For more than two days you were out of town without lining up child care for Ryan?" The state's attorney pushed her further.

"I didn't know I was going to be gone that long." Her voice dropped to a mere murmur; she rubbed her bent knuckle under her runny nose. Jasmine passed her several tissues.

"What about Thursday after school? Were you fairly certain you wouldn't be home when Ryan was dismissed from school for the day?" Other than Tina's sniffles, the courtroom was utterly quiet. Water dripping off the eaves made the stillness more poignant.

"Mrs. Benson, would you answer the question, please?" The judge kept his voice at an even tone.

A sob broke from her throat as she forced out a reply. "Yes, but I thought he'd go to Jasmine's house like he usually did if I wasn't home." Her tears came in full force now. Jasmine put an arm about her shoulders as Tina bawled into a wad of tissues.

Waiting a few minutes for the woman's composure to be regained, Mr. Murie addressed Jasmine next. "Jasmine Kirmis, would you tell the court what relationship you have with Tina and her son, Ryan, and why she would presume Ryan would have gone to your home."

"Yes, sir. I am Ryan's first-grade teacher along with being a next-door neighbor to the Bensons. When his mom is at work, Ryan tends to linger after school until I am done with my preparations for the next day's classes, and then the two of us often walk home together. We have both grown rather fond of our walks together."

Bushy eyebrows peered over the rim of his glasses at Jasmine. "Had Tina Benson arranged with you to babysit her son in the intervening hours between the end of school and when she gets home from work?"

With Tina fastened to her side, it was hard to honestly explain exactly how wobbly a setup existed between them, if indeed there was one at all. Now was the time to be truthful. She had tried to cover up for Tina once before, and it had only ended up hurting Ryan. "No, sir. It kind of happened out of habit. At first, when we reached my driveway, he always skipped on home, and I proceeded into my house until I realized he was going home to no one. Then I would sometimes invite him to keep me company until his mom was done with work."

"Then why wasn't the boy with you last Thursday night?"

Glancing at Tina's slumped posture, she continued, "I was in Norbert. For the last six weeks, I have been taking a graduate class at the university on Thursday nights."

"Was Tina aware of your schedule?"

"Yes, I had informed her." Jasmine whispered inwardly, *Please,* LORD, *your will.*

Noting that Tina had quieted, the attorney inquired of her, "Tina, if you thought Jasmine would again befriend Ryan last Thursday night like she had on previous occasions, did you also assume she would keep the youngster overnight both on Thursday and Friday nights? And when you still did not materialize on Saturday morning, that she would care for him indefinitely until you decided to return and resume your role as his mother?"

Never raising her head, however realizing the judge would expect a verbal response, Tina garbled, "I wasn't thinking at all."

Judge Krammer intervened at this point. "Tina, I understand you are a relatively new resident to our state of North Dakota. For those of us who have grown up here and have lived our entire lives in this seasonal state, we, for the most part, like it here. But we do have severe winters, which make life a bit more difficult during these months of the year. I can comprehend you forgetting to check the fuel tank outside your home. Some of us have done the same and are quickly reminded when the temperature in the interior begins to drop quickly.

"That mishap I can understand and even forgive, but not providing for the supervision of your young son for three days in succession no matter what the weather components were is another issue—a very serious issue. It is a life-and-death matter when it happens in the winter. It is hard to fathom what could have been so important to keep you from providing for the well-being of Ryan." Letting his words soak in, he paused at length.

At last, he signaled to the state's attorney. "On behalf of Ryan Benson, what is the recommendation from the state?"

"Sir, we recommend that to ensure the safety of Ryan Benson, the county be granted custody for a time not to exceed six months."

For the first time since the hearing started, Tina's spine took shape, each vertebrae standing at attention. Beside her, Jasmine could feel the transformation taking place.

Jumping to her feet, Tina placed her hands on the top edge of the pew in front of her, pushing herself up on the tips of her toes. "No, you can't take my baby from me! Yes, I made a mistake, but I won't let it happen again!"

Stunned by the outburst, all eyes zeroed in on the mother, who moments ago whimpered like a pup and now was ready to go to battle for her cub.

Judge Krammer addressed the respondent again. "Ms. Benson, I truly believe you love your child. In my estimation, you have your priorities out of order, which has inadvertently led you to make some unwise choices. Had things turned out differently Thursday night, Ryan could very well have frozen to death. That mistake is something this court is not willing to take a second chance on just yet."

He spoke to the county social worker next. "Mrs. Thern, I agree with the state attorney's recommendation and ask that you seek a permanent foster home setting for Ryan for the length of sixty days, providing a petition for extension be filed within thirty days."

"No, I beg you, sir! Please! Please don't give my baby to a stranger!" Tina didn't know court protocol, and she didn't care. She was interrupting a second time.

Judge Krammer was a patient man. He spoke reassuringly to the distraught lady. "Ma'am, foster parents are well-meaning folks who are willing to take children into their homes and love them for whatever days or months they are needed. Ryan will be in good hands."

Tina was not so easily pacified. "You don't know Ryan. We have moved numerous times in his life. The only thing that has stayed the same for him in his six young years is me. I will do whatever you say, if you just put him in a home where he already feels comfortable," Tina pleaded, holding her hands out toward the man who had the power to separate her family.

"Social Services is willing to seek a suitable relative in place of a foster family," Sarah interjected, addressing the judge.

Stomping a foot in agitation, Tina vetoed the suggestion immediately. "There are no suitable relatives, and anyway, they'd be far out of the state. But there is Jasmine," Tina suggested, pointing to her companion. "She's been the best friend Ryan and me have ever had."

Jasmine's jaw dropped. She stared up at the backside of the lady who had just spun a complete three-hundred-sixty-degree circle in her disposition.

"Ryan loves being with her. She has taught him so much at school, and now the other kids like him too. He doesn't get into fights near as much as he used to. At Christmas, she took him to practices at her church, and for the first time, he was in a church pageant. You'll probably say that her house is too close to mine, but I will follow all the rules. I'll do whatever you say. Just don't give my baby boy to an unfamiliar family!" Her plea ended with her voice reverting to tearful weeping.

Gaping at the woman standing beside her, Jasmine wondered if Tina was finally internalizing how much she, as his mother, really did care for her son.

"This is rather an unusual turn of events." Judge Krammer tapped his pen against the desktop. Letting his attention fall on the teacher sitting in the pew, he asked, "Mrs. Kirmis, have you ever entertained thoughts of becoming a foster parent?"

Six months ago—even a mere four months ago—Jasmine would have been adamant in her steadfast stand against single parenting. Parenting was one tough job. Who would ever want to do it solo? And now, here she was at the crossroad: Tina pleading on one side, a judge staring at her from his high podium, and a social worker disconcerted at how her carefully laid plans were suddenly being knocked askew.

Jasmine's own daughter, Autumn, still needed parenting. Only the LORD knew how that story would unfold. With Jasmine's track record as a mother, she hardly seemed the one to take on the nurturing of another woman's child. And yet it wasn't just any child's future sitting in limbo; it was Ryan's, the little guy who had already moved into her classroom, her home, and her spare bedroom.

Judge Krammer misconstrued Jasmine's loss of words as a denial. "I apologize to you, Mrs. Kirmis. It is unfair to put you on the spot, expecting you to answer such a heavily loaded question without giving you time to deliberate on it long and seriously. Foster parenting is a calling, just like many other vocations. It means working with children twenty-four-seven, a job you are already experiencing as a teacher."

Refocusing on Sarah Thern, he inquired, "Is there a vacant foster home available suitable for Ryan's needs?"

Before Sarah could reply, Jasmine found her voice, sliding off the hard seat to stand next to Tina. "Actually, sir, I have thought about it, even to the point of submitting the paperwork to the county office and having my fingerprints taken as part of the foster parent application." Swallowing hard, she wondered what she was saying.

Surprise splashed across the judge's face.

"Over the years, in my teaching profession, a lot of children have passed through my classroom door. Earlier this winter, Ms. Thern encouraged me to consider becoming a foster parent, to keep that avenue open in my life in case a situation such as this one ever presented itself. At the time, I was hesitant, but after some careful consideration, I decided to pursue her recommendation and thus submitted the application."

"How long ago was this, Mrs. Kirmis?" the judge asked.

Trying to think back through the maze of weeks, Jasmine wasn't sure. "Maybe a month ago I dropped it in the mail."

Turning back to the social worker, Judge Krammer asked for clarification. "Ms. Thern, I take it you have received the application. At what point in the review process is Mrs. Kirmis's paperwork?"

Squirming a bit at this change in events, Sarah admitted, "Mrs. Kirmis has completed her side of the application. I need to do a home study on her dwelling and then send the paperwork on to the state headquarters for approval."

"In your determination, how long would it take to adequately finish up her application?"

Tinting an unnatural shade of pink, Sarah winced, aware of the direction Judge Krammer was subtly headed with his questioning.

"Juggling my schedule a bit, I could have the home study done this week if Jasmine's calendar would allow it." Sarah did not look Jasmine's way.

"Mrs. Kirmis?" Judge Krammer waited for a response.

"Yes, I can be flexible."

"Just to make sure we are all on the same page, Mrs. Kirmis, is my understanding correct in that you are agreeing to the placement of Ryan Benson in your home as his foster parent?"

Jasmine nodded. "Yes, sir."

"And you will proceed with the final phase of getting your foster care license?"

Once more she nodded. "Yes, sir."

"Ms. Thern, are you in mutual approval of this plan?"

"Your Honor." Sarah pressed her lips together in a thin line. "I am sure you are aware that the county Social Services places children in homes previously approved for foster care. We seem to have the cart before the horse today."

Leaning back in his leather chair, Judge Krammer acknowledged her concern. "I understand what you are saying. But isn't it also true that you not only seek to find the least disruptive environment for a child but further endeavor to match the child with the foster family best able to turn this bump in his life into a success story? As a foster child in Jasmine Kirmis's home, Ryan will be able to continue as a student in the Elton Public School system. His first-grade year will not be disrupted with a change of schools or by having to establish new friendships. There will be no interlude in his studies while a new teacher evaluates what he has already mastered and what he has not. An unusually strong bond seems to already exist between Mrs. Kirmis and Ryan. Ryan is at a precarious point in his young life. Let's catch him before he falls."

Sarah brought up another concern dismissed by Tina. "And what about the proximity of Jasmine's and Tina's homes? How is Jasmine supposed to parent if Ryan can run home to Mama whenever he feels like it?"

Fastening his eyes on Tina, who stood with her shoulders back, staring directly back at him, the judge spoke firmly, "As I said before, Tina, I do believe you have the makings to be a good mother. As part of your treatment plan, I am requiring you to enroll in a lengthy parenting class to equip you with some fundamental guidelines and techniques to help you in your parenting of Ryan.

"Meanwhile, you will be living next door to your son and his foster mom. She, along with Ryan's astute social worker, will make the rules. It is up to you to abide by them. I see no reason why Ryan shouldn't be able to spend a couple of hours a day with you. Obviously, those times can't be when you are scheduled to be at work; however, they can be at any other hour—even if that means you have to cancel some of your social events. Jasmine Kirmis is not your babysitter. She will need some time to herself as well. Working out a feasible schedule between the two of you will be to everyone's benefit."

Adjusting his glasses, the judge went on. "Tina, you have been freeloading on Jasmine, using her as a free day care. Foster care is not free. The court expects you to abide by each and every guideline set up. Is that understood?"

"Yes, Your Honor, and thank you." She exhaled audibly. For the first time since Saturday afternoon when Officer Forman served papers on her, a hint of a smile touched Tina's face. The tight facial muscles notably relaxed and smoothed out.

Driving home later, Tina and Jasmine were each submersed in their own thoughts. Not until Jasmine brought the car to a stop in her garage did Tina speak.

"You really believe in your prayer thing, don't you?"

Jasmine inclined her head in agreement.

"Guess there must be something to it. You said you were confident your LORD would work things out in a way that was best for both Ryan and me." She pushed against the door latch and placed one high heel on the cement flooring of the garage. "He did. He gave us you. Thanks."

Never in a hundred centuries did Jasmine suspect the hearing's outcome would christen her Ryan's foster mom—the very role she swore she'd never take. She had just become a single parent to a first grader.

Tina was right. This had to be from the LORD, for left on her own, she would have given Judge Krammer a flat no.

Jasmine wondered whether God was chuckling down at her right now from his heavenly throne.

Did she hear a deep bass *amen*?

CHAPTER 19

Leaning against the hallway wall, Mr. Perry awaited the first-grade class. Every youngster loved his physical education class and could hardly wait to cross the line onto the gymnasium floor where running was permissible. "Care to join us for a little game of kickball today, Mrs. Kirmis?" Mr. Perry teased as her line of students passed between them.

Jasmine smirked at her fellow educator, fully aware his proposal was only in jest. "I think I'll take a rain check."

"Bye, Mrs. Kirmis," Joey Huan called to his teacher as she turned to leave. Carson and Ryan had somehow maneuvered their way to being the cabooses of the line.

Mimicking Joey, Carson too yelled out, "Bye, Mrs. Kirmis." After bestowing a smile on each of them, Jasmine proceeded in the direction of her classroom.

Ryan trotted after her, catching her unexpectedly in a hug from behind. "Bye, *Mom*." His dimples punctuated his impish grin, his twinkly eyes dancing at his cleverness.

In many ways, she had become his mother, now that he had moved into her spare bedroom. His dirty clothes lay on the floor near, just not quite into, her clothes hamper. Now he not only walked her home from school but came with her in the morning as well. Together they shared meals, stories, and the kitchen counter. All in all, Jasmine wondered if in Tina's narrow estimation, the wayward mother actually preferred this new arrangement. Tina no longer had to worry about Ryan's whereabouts each day; she just had to be there for his visitations—in the time slots convenient to her.

While roughing up his dark hair, still worn longer than most of his peers but neatly trimmed since living in the Kirmis house, Jasmine winked, before walking away. The little mite had a way of crawling right inside of her. Tina was missing out on a heck of a lot, even if she didn't know it.

Upon reaching her room, Jasmine used the intervening minutes to shove the desks into pairs and to pour a pile of geometric shapes onto the tops in readiness for the day's math class.

Hearing a low mumble of distant voices in the hallway, she stepped outside her door to supervise her first graders from afar, who were a zigzagging line shuffling toward her. "Teacher, kickball is really fun! You should have seen the ball Arnie kicked. It went way up in the bleachers!" Jeremy kicked his foot out forcefully to show his teacher what he meant.

Entering the room and noticing their desks in another new arrangement, the first graders quickly found their places. Frowning, Mrs. Kirmis observed two empty desks.

"Where are Ryan and Carson?" she asked her class.

Always ready to be the informant, Pixie Loman popped up from her chair. "They got in a big fight and couldn't play the game. I think the gym teacher sent them home."

Before Pixie could surmise any more possibilities for the two little renegades, Mrs. Kirmis cut her off. "I'm sure they will be along soon. We will start our math lesson without them." Clearly, if two of her students had been suspended, she would have been notified.

She picked up the pen to the Activboard and wrote *triangle* in bold print. "Has anyone ever heard of a shape called a triangle?"

Hands shot up like bottle rockets in an Independence Day sky.

Jasmine's thoughts shifted between her lesson at hand and the boys missing from her classroom. Something was amiss. If ever two boys stuck together like peanut butter and jelly, it was the two of them. Pixie must be right about the fight, for it was obvious they weren't here.

"Find a triangular shape on your desktop," she continued.

The boys were only first graders. How bad could a disagreement get between two first graders? Had not her duties as a teacher demanded she stay with her class, she would have checked the situation out. In another half hour, school would be out for the day. Surely they would be back before another thirty minutes transpired. Hank Perry, or possibly Principal Peterson, was lecturing the boys on proper conduct in gym class.

"How many sides does a triangle have?"

"Three," Joey supplied.

"Yes, three. Let's move on to four-sided shapes."

Minutes crawled by. Unbelievably, the so-called duo had not returned when the final dismissal bell rang.

Pivoting on her heel to beat a fast staccato to the office, she was brought up short by Mr. Peterson's voice echoing over the intercom.

"Mrs. Kirmis, please report to the main office."

Her heartbeat raced ahead of her lengthened strides. What on earth could have happened?

Almost panting by the time she reached the wall of windows opening into the main office, she didn't perceive anything amiss. June Max, talking on the phone, waved the teacher on into Mr. Peterson's personal office. Nervously, Jasmine crossed the few steps to the open door. Peering in, she saw her two first graders sitting on opposite ends of a couch. Ryan's shadowed face was clouded in remorse, but a fierce determination set Carson's lips in a hard line. His eyes, now a dark navy blue, dared anyone to wrangle with him.

Most out of the ordinary was the rugged form of Joel Linton, attired in his work clothes, sitting erect in a straight-back chair beside Carson's end of the couch. Had he been summoned as well? Glancing up at Jasmine's entry, his eyes held hers for a second. Principal Peterson indicated with a hand movement for her to take a seat beside Ryan as he closed the office door. Immediately, the child snuggled up to her hip.

Seating himself behind the highly-polished desk, Principal Peterson picked up a letter opener and twirled it in his fingers. "Joel, I am sorry to call you away from your work and force you to drive all the way into town. I felt with the backgrounds of both of these young children, it was necessary for them to have the support of parents. Both you and Mrs. Kirmis are in the same position caring for children not born to you but in all forms acting as parents, so I and Mr. Perry implore your help."

For the first time, Jasmine noted Hank Perry sitting in the opposite corner of the room.

"Mr. Perry, could you please give us a summation of what occurred during your gym class?"

Mr. Perry shook his head, lifting his arms in bewilderment. "I really don't know what started the tussle. Mrs. Kirmis, you brought your class to the gym door. We said a few words. You left and I walked into the gymnasium, closing the door behind me. I blew my whistle for the class to line up on the back line so I could give instructions for the kickball game we were about to play. Like always, the first graders responded as I'd asked, except for Carson and Ryan. They were pushing and shoving each other, oblivious to what I had directed them to do. I called their names sharply, but they didn't even hear me because they were so intent on their argument.

"Suddenly, Carson dove for Ryan's legs, and they both hit the gym floor, punching and slugging it out. I pulled Ryan off Carson, but Carson dove at him again. I had to hold Carson back with one arm, keeping Ryan tucked in the other. I told them each to have a chair and sit out of the kickball game. Their fists doubled up again as soon as I released them. I had to ask Mr. Peterson to talk to them while I conducted my class."

Twisting the letter opener in his hands again, Mr. Peterson took up the explanation. "I brought the boys to my office, but they were as mad as two wet hens, glaring at each other as if they were enemies instead of the two fast friends I have witnessed them to be. The story finally came out. And that's when I called you, Joel."

Changing position in his chair, the principal looked encouragingly at Carson and Ryan. "Okay, boys, can you tell your teacher and Mr. Linton what caused this squabble?" Shifting his surveillance from one youngster's face to the other, he waited for a response. Like a perfectly timed dance act, the two boys dropped their eyes to the tips of their tennis shoes and grasped the overstuffed arms on the opposite ends of the couch. Stoic frowns met the man's inquiry.

"Who'd like to go first?" he tried again. "Carson?" Carson's features were molded in cement. Slowly, Joel raised his arm and rested it on top of Carson's thin hand clutching the upholstery. The frail child shook visibly and yet hardened his jaw line, refusing to speak.

Turning to Ryan, Mr. Peterson leaned across his desk, using his best persuasive tone. "Why did Carson get upset with you, Ryan? Did you do anything to him?" Glued to Jasmine's side, Ryan appeared to be just as firm as Carson. "Did you take something that belonged to Carson? Did you cut in line in front of him?"

Ryan shook his thick, dark hair slightly. Sniffling, he softly gave a short explanation. Even Jasmine beside him missed his hushed words. Placing her arm about his narrow shoulders, she gently urged, "Ryan, I couldn't hear you. Tell me again so we can get this all straightened out."

His eyes ascended from his shoes into Jasmine's concerned face. "I said, 'Bye, Mom' to you when you took us to the gym."

At first, Jasmine didn't understand this declaration. What did his saying good-bye to her have to do with a fight involving Carson? She knew when he had clipped a quick, "Bye, Mom," at the gym door, he was trying to be cute. Yet it had warmed her, bringing them a notch closer.

With everyone holding Ryan in their vigil, they missed the signs of defiance sizzling into an explosion at the other end of the sofa, until it erupted in a child's angry outburst. "I told you she's not your mom! You can't call her Mom!" Carson was on his feet, his black eyes burning with the fierce intensity of a prairie fire about to whip across the close space to engulf his so-called friend in flames. A vein on the side of his head visibly throbbed.

Had not Joel's stronger arm rested on Carson's weaker one, the fuming seven-year-old may have renewed his attack on the smaller first grader. "You can't have two moms!" Carson shouted at Ryan, his fingers tightening into two fists.

Joel's strong arms engulfed the boy, backing him into the space between his open legs, hugging his bony back against his own broad chest. "Shhh," Joel whispered into Carson's ear, swaying slightly back and forth with his prisoner. Although six people occupied the room, Joel blanked them out, holding the boy he loved. Squeezing his eyes shut, he willed Carson to feel the love he was pressing into him. *A mom.* Carson was angry because Ryan had called Mrs. Kirmis *Mom.* Did Joel need any more proof that Carson not only needed but wanted both a mother and a father?

A picture of Joel's own parents passed before him mentally. Would he have wanted to choose between having a mother or a father? Heck no! He loved and needed them both. Working alongside his pa, he had learned what hard work was all about. A man's word should always be good. Ma had been the tender parent, forever bubbling with empathy for others. Had it not been for the faith his ma and pa demonstrated, Joel doubted if he would have become a Christian himself.

No matter how strong Joel's feelings were for the boy, it was not enough. God's ideal setup for a child was a family—a mother and a father. A widower by himself was only half the package.

Carson's muscles were hard and stiff, his body unbending. Joel hummed softly, his head lying against the light hair, praying inwardly for the fierce little tiger cub to withdraw his claws.

This had happened before. Joel remembered the day Carson had wanted to stay at home and play farm in his room instead of doing Joel's jobs outside. Then too, the bigger man had wrapped his arms about the child, breathing tranquility into the out-of-control rascal.

"Hey, pal," he whispered, rocking him like a baby in a cradle, "I'm here for you. Shhhh."

Anger drained out of Carson as water flows down a drain. And as his frustration dissolved in the arms of love, tears trickled down his cheeks, dripping off his nose. He was spent.

No one else uttered a sound, watching the portrayal of a father-child relationship painted with all the strokes and feelings of a master artist. Moisture wet Jasmine's cheeks as well. If ever there was a person who could be a father and a mother to a child, it was Joel Linton. He simply did what came naturally to him, while she felt totally inadequate to the task. Clasping Ryan to her side, she inwardly pleaded, *Oh*, LORD, *help us.*

Minutes slipped by, healing the fragmentations of the unusual conflict between the two youngsters. It was Joel who finally broke the spell. He slipped a dark blue farmer's hanky from his pocket, wiping the boy's eyes and nose. Then, setting the child on his right knee, he looked Carson in the face when he spoke.

"Life isn't fair, son. I wish it was, but it isn't. I don't have a wife, and you don't have a mom. I wish it was different for both of us. Yet we can't blame someone else for what we don't have. It doesn't help." His thumb tenderly stroked Carson's arm.

Laying his head on his foster father's shoulder, the blond head nodded.

"But one thing we do both have is friendship. You and I are the best buddies ever, wouldn't you say?" Again, Carson's head bobbed. "And that isn't all. We have other friends as well. You've told me you really like your teacher, Mrs. Kirmis. She is a swell lady, wouldn't you say?" Steel-blue eyes moved to the lady sitting at an angle from them. Her jaw softened.

"And then there is Ryan. School wouldn't be near as fun if you didn't have Ryan. Do you think?" When Carson lowered his focus to Ryan's face, the usual happy watermelon grin sliced across his friend's face. Carson's lips hinted at a smile.

"You and I, being men, sometimes have to admit when we've made a mistake and apologize to those we've wronged. Do you think you owe your friend here an apology?"

Ryan, always being quicker in his actions than Carson was, ducked out from under Jasmine's arm, sliding to his feet. Bumping into Joel's other knee, he blubbered out the words, not wasting any time thinking, "Carson, teacher isn't really my mom, just sort of my mom. She can be your mom too. We can share her!" His eyes lit up as if he had come up with the best idea ever.

All three adults hesitantly smiled, unsure if it was the correct solution or not. They let it pass.

Carson reached out to his fellow first grader. "Sorry, Ryan. I shouldn't have gotten so mad." Eager to forgive, Ryan held his hand up for a high five. *Smack!* Their two hands met in the air between them.

Relief flooded through Joel. He hadn't been sure Carson was going to fold this time. "Since you guys messed up my day's work and I'm in town anyway, would there be two young whippersnappers who'd like to accompany me to Naomi's Diner for some hot fudge sundaes?"

The two youngsters jumped and shrieked with anticipation. Joel directed his next words to Ryan. "You forget something," Bewildered, the dark-haired urchin peered up at the farmer, who motioned with his head toward Jasmine. "Don't you have to ask permission?"

"Oh yeah." Ryan giggled. "Mom, can I go with Carson and his dad to get ice cream?" The midget-sized tadpole always had one more witty epigram up his sleeve.

Catching on after a moment, Carson's eyes lit up. "Dad? Yeah, *Dad*, let's get some ice cream." And he too gave a toothy smirk.

Giving assent, Jasmine let the honorary titles lodge within her to ponder later.

Ryan and Carson's friendship had been restored for the time being, but a lasting separation was in the works.

Water dripping off the roof awakened Jasmine. Spring had seeped its warm fingers into the snow covering the roof, melting it into rivulets dribbling down the shingles, filling the eaves. Sunshine streaming through the lace curtains invigorated her. This was her day: a day off from school to devote to her writing. Working on her neglected manuscript without any interruptions was long overdue.

Tina's visits with her son didn't follow any set pattern. Understandably, her work schedule at the filling station had to be considered. Although the judge had clearly stated Jasmine was to set up a schedule conducive to her own timetable, it wasn't turning out that way. Jasmine had become the full-time babysitter Tina could never find or afford before.

Last week, Tina had promised Ryan they'd spend Wednesday evening together after she got home from work. When the station wagon had pulled up to the curb a few minutes after six, Ryan had scampered over to his mom's place. Within an hour, he was back again, saying his mom had to go somewhere.

Having thrown the covers aside, Jasmine padded to the bathroom, peeking into Ryan's room on the way. She decided not to wake him, as his mom was not an early riser, especially on her day off. He'd have the rest of the day to do something special with Tina.

Dressed in some comfortable clothes, she carried her notebooks, Bible, and thesaurus to the dining room table. Peeling an orange to nibble on while rereading her previous chapter of the manuscript, the written words quickly carried her back to the rural South Dakota town where her main characters were wrestling with the challenges of a juvenile delinquent denying their authority. Caught up in the story, Jasmine began to write; her pen flowed, filling the pages. Or was her own daughter, Autumn, the real person camouflaged into the description of the seventeen-year-old juvenile? How would Autumn's story twist and turn to an end someday?

Autumn was in captivity, and until she acknowledged the LORD, her life would be a bobber on a stormy sea. She could turn a cold shoulder to God, but she couldn't stop her mother's prayers for her. Did the distraught teenager in her story have someone praying for him? Someone who would never give up? Someone who would always be waiting for the return of a son or daughter?

Meow, meow. Unconsciously, Jasmine reached one arm under the table to pet the kitty while flipping in her Bible to Jeremiah with the other hand. Thoroughly she scratched the fur on its head. The cat purred and rubbed its fluffy coat against her leg. *Meow.*

Abruptly, it occurred to Jasmine that she didn't own a cat. In alarm, she hiked up her leg and peered under the table fearfully. Ryan's laughing eyes met hers.

"Oh, you rascal, you!" she exclaimed, rolling him onto his back and tickling his sides. "You sneaky little cat!"

Screeching hilariously, Ryan righted himself and scampered away in his pajamas, taking a flying leap for the couch. Jasmine sprang after him, rolling her pet kitten into a ball in the afghan and nuzzling him with her nose.

"Would the nice kitty want a bowl of milk for breakfast?"

Licking her nose, he flipped his hair in a negative fashion. "French toast."

"Now, Garfield, that doesn't sound like kitty talk to me, unless you are French cat. But I will grant you your wishes if you get some clothes on first."

Chuckling, Ryan crawled down from the couch on all fours and padded to his bedroom. Amused, Jasmine crossed to the kitchen, retrieving eggs and milk from the refrigerator. Two slices of French bread were sizzling in a frying pan upon his return.

Climbing onto the high kitchen stool, Ryan waited patiently. "Don't I get to spend today with Mommy?" he asked, already aware of the answer.

"You sure do." Jasmine neatly flipped over a slice of bread in the frying pan. "Maybe you and your mom can go for a walk, and you can try out your mud boots in all the puddles." Another minute and the French toast was ready. She set the browned slices before him. "There you go, pussycat."

Out of habit, Ryan folded his hands and prayed, "Thank you, God, for the French toast. Let my mommy be fun today. Amen." Sagging a bit on the inside, Jasmine poured the maple syrup generously over the fried bread.

"Will Mommy be out of bed yet, do you think?"

"When you're finished and have washed up, you can run over and check it out." For his sake, she hoped it would be a super day. A sunshiny morning was certainly a good omen.

Summoned by the ring of the telephone, Jasmine wiped her hands on the dishcloth before picking up the receiver. "Good morning." Winking at Ryan's sticky face, she gave her attention to the caller. "Hi, Tina. We were just talking about you. Are you ready for a guest?" The sun slowly set in Jasmine's face as she listened to yet another excuse.

Turning her back on Ryan, she made a face looking out into her backyard. How could Tina keep doing this to her son?

"Well, Tina, he's right here. I'll let you tell him." Before Tina could hang up, Jasmine handed the phone over to Ryan. "Your mom wants to talk to you." Steam was rising within her. What kind of parent always put her social life before her own son? When Tina had thought Ryan was going to be taken away from her, she had acted pathetically contrite; however, the old selfish Tina had returned.

Downcast, Ryan pushed the phone back to Jasmine. "Guess it's not such a good day after all," he mumbled.

"Sorry, buddy." Jasmine leaned her elbows on the counter, her chin sunk into her palm.

Picking at the last chunk of syrupy bread with the fork, he traced a wayward path through the pool on his plate. His sad eyes raised to Jasmine's. The usual sparkle snuffed out. "You wouldn't want to walk in mud puddles, would ya?"

Her eyelids dropped. A banner from Jeremiah accosted her vision. "For I know the plans I have for you" (Jeremiah 11:9, NIV). Plans? Yes, that's what they were. Today, His *plans* were for her to tramp through spring puddles with her little friend.

"I can't think of anything I'd rather do on a warm, spring day," she emphatically replied, closing her notebook.

And they did.

CHAPTER 20

"Will that be all, sir?" the parts man at the farm dealership in Norbert inquired, typing the last transaction for a hydraulic planter hose into the computer. Joel was purchasing extra parts for his spring seeding equipment to have on hand in case of a breakdown.

With the land still too wet to drive on, Joel did not harbor any of the self-imposed stress he heaped upon himself every spring. By the calendar, it was early yet. Even if he didn't begin seeding wheat until the first of May, the crop would still be in the ground in a timely fashion. After throwing his purchases into a heavy cardboard box, he paid for the items and left.

Climbing into his pickup cab, he knew it was too soon to return to the Social Services office. After taking a slow, meandering tour through the machinery lot, he braked at the exit. What next? Loitering in the parking lot at the foster care office didn't appeal to him. Maybe a walk in the city park would clear his head.

Norbert's park was heavily shaded by a canopy of oak and elm branches stretching over a network of walking paths trailing the Souris River. Black squirrels frisked close by, undaunted by human invasion. Birds called to each other, swooping through the flowerbeds at his feet before soaring overhead to nests camouflaged amongst the fluttering leaves.

Pausing at the fork of the intersecting walking paths, the troubled man scanned the natural setting. He needed direction from his heavenly Father to sort out the jumbled emotions tangling within him.

When Joel picked Carson up from school an hour before the usual dismissal bell, the boy had sensed this was not an ordinary meeting with Meagan in Norbert. No one had told him any differently, but he was aware of a change in Joel—more subdued, less talkative; the youngster followed his hero's lead. The seventy-minute drive had been quiet, except for the songs on the country music station.

When the Social Services office loomed ahead, Carson's inkling was confirmed. He had been seeing an awful lot of Meagan lately. She always wanted him to do more schoolwork—well, not schoolwork exactly, but it did seem like that to him. "A Life Book," she called it, pictures from his past, asking him crazy questions he never thought about before. His therapist also wanted to talk about a word called *adoption*. Silly guy. Carson knew what adoption was. Sometimes Joel had to trick a mama cow into adopting another cow's newborn calf if the real mommy didn't have enough milk for her baby. Didn't these people understand that he and Joel had more important things to do than writing down a list of his favorites or drawing a picture of a make-believe family?

As was customary, Meagan had greeted them cheerfully, teasing Carson about the larger-sized shoe he had grown into. "Do we have to work in the book today?" Carson whined.

"Absolutely not," Meagan exclaimed emphatically. "I think it's time you treated me to a hamburger at McDonald's."

Carson's eyes lit up at the mention of his favorite eating place, a winsome smile replacing the frown. "Really? To the McDonald's with the play place?"

"I was hoping you would suggest that one."

His next eager plea was directed to Joel. "Will you crawl through the tunnel with me and climb in the boat?"

"Ahh." Caught off guard, the man tripped on his words. "Well, I—I don't think I'm invited." Meagan had corresponded with him earlier in the week. A prospective adoptive couple was driving the seven-hour road trip from Minneapolis to meet Carson. For this initial meeting, they would be introduced to Carson as friends of Meagan's, taking any undue pressure off both the child and the new parents. Each would be able to get acquainted with the other and then decide later if proceedings should continue to the next level.

Hastening up the departure, Joel questioned Meagan, "Two hours?"

"Two and a half. That should be long enough for us to slurp down a chocolate shake and maybe some chicken nuggets and fries."

Quickly turning on his heel, Joel had pushed open the office door and strode to his pickup. One more moment in front of the youngster and his social worker, his voice would have cracked. He couldn't have forced a chunk of hamburger past the hard rock in his chest. Was he like King Darius in the Bible handing Daniel over to the lions?

Standing at the fork of the walking paths, his left foot pointed straight ahead, while his right foot set at an angle aimed toward a trail hidden by an overgrowth of honeysuckle bushes. Whenever in doubt, young man, go *right*, as if such a minor decision could magically transform his bleeding heart.

For purely selfish reasons, he had returned to fostering kids, namely Carson. And he had received abundantly more than he had given. He knew he had to let the child go, to let him experience the love of a mother and a father.

True love did that—released the hold to let the loved one fly. But how? Mist momentarily blurred his eyesight. *Please*, Lord, *when the time comes, give me the strength to smile and wave good-bye.*

His mind flitted to the couple from Minneapolis—a colossal city compared to Norbert. What were they like? Did they already have children of their own, or was their home empty, like his? Not that it mattered, but what did they do for a living? Did they have time for a seven-year-old boy? Meagan had been very close-lipped about the candidating couple. Were they only worried about whether Carson met their stipulations, or were they concerned at how they could enrich his life? Granted, the couple had driven a long road trip for a two-and-a-half-hour visit, probably missing a day on the job. And not everyone wanted to adopt someone else's child. He had been guilty of such an offence himself. So, granted, they could be swell people with big hearts who would make the perfect family for Carson. And all would live happily ever after—except Joel.

Why was his life full of good-byes? Those closest to him left. First Melissa, and now Carson. The trio would have made a loving family unit. Why didn't life ever work out?

Kicking a twig off the paved path, he was suddenly contrite. *Sorry,* Lord, *I came here to let you talk to me, yet I'm monopolizing the conversation with my complaints. Help me to listen.*

Sometimes it was hard to pray, to stop the mind from galloping at full speed, snooping in every crevice instead of allowing the Lord to control his thoughts.

A soft breeze shook the leaves above him. Coming through the pink and white honeysuckle blossoms, he saw a young woman a stone's toss down the path raise a hand to greet an older man with a friendly hello. The simple gesture slapped Joel in the face.

Hello.

In order for there to have been *good-byes* in his life, there had to have first been *hellos.* Beginnings. Starts.

And there were.

Initially, he had met Melissa at a concluding Vacation Bible School program given at his church in Elton. As a service project, the Christian college she attended sent out teams of five members to conduct week-long Bible-based kids' day camps. Being a bachelor at the time, Joel didn't have any children to send to the camp, but he had attended the program at the end of the week. The fair-skinned woman teasing the strings of a guitar accompanying the children's action-filled tunes had attracted his attention immediately. It had taken a lot of guts to amble his way up to her during the social hour following, but it had turned out to be the best *hello* he'd ever extended.

And then there was Carson. Ah, yes. It would hurt to see him go, but Joel wouldn't undo his step back into foster care. In another month, it would be all of a year since the little guy and he had said *hello*. What a rich year it had been.

Giving God a wink through the patch of an azure sky peeking through the overhead branches, Joel spoke out loud, "You got me there, Lord. My life hasn't been a deep pot of misery. Sorry."

Then God brought to mind verses from Ecclesiastes.

> There is a time for everything, and a season for every activity under heaven: a time to be born and a time to die. . . . a time to weep and a time to laugh, a time to mourn and a time to dance.
>
> Ecclesiastes 3:1, 2, 4 (NIV)

In less than an hour, he would be retrieving Carson from the office, and the two of them, like always, would be heading back to the ranch. Carson wasn't going anywhere, except with him. Yes, there would come the day when another family would choose to love Carson and take him home with them. But not today. Not this month, maybe not next month, or the next.

Joel had been mourning and weeping when the hour of grieving had not yet arrived. Now was the time to laugh and to dance, to make more memories, to crack a zillion more jokes, to give oodles of hugs, and to live the days God was pouring generously upon them.

A new briskness entered his step, turning it almost into a jig. Robins and kingbirds harmonized; the branches slapped in rhythm. This was a cantata to celebrate, a bunny hop to dance—he and Carson together.

Every day they still had left.

The celebration began on the highway back to the country. Giggles and funny tales, make-believe creatures, and preposterous alliterations filled the cab of the truck.

"Try this one," Joel enunciated distinctly. "The big, brown bear ate the big, brown bug baked in a bubblegum biscuit."

Giggling from the onset, Carson chanted, "The big, brown bear ate the big, brown bug and barfed!"

Joel steered clear of any serious talk until they had turned onto the last ten miles of gravel road.

"So did Meagan really make you pay for your supper?"

"Nah. I didn't have any money with me," Carson said, snorting.

"Anyone who eats McDonald's food and doesn't pay has to wash dishes," Joel teased.

"Well, I didn't have to."

"How was the play room? Did you get Meagan to go through the tunnel?" Joel hated having to pump for information.

"Nah. There were other kids in the game part. I played with them."

"See anyone you knew?" Joel kept his voice light and nonchalant.

"A kid who went to head start with me when I lived in Norbert."

"Oh. That was nice you had a friend to play with. Did you leave Meagan sitting at the table all by herself?" He tapped his thumb on the top of the steering wheel.

"She found some guys she knew there too. She hung out with them." Carson seemed totally blind to the situation.

"Hmm. Did they talk to you too?" He glanced over at the boy digging through the box of parts he'd purchased.

"Nah."

Obviously, the couple hadn't made any big impression on him. Closing the subject, he gave the boy something else to think about.

"What do you want to do on Sunday after church? You get to pick."

"Me?" Carson squeaked.

"Yup, it is your turn to choose."

"We don't take turns."

"We do now!"

"Hmm." Joel expected him to have to put much thought into the open-ended adventure; however, he was brought up short when his friend came up with an idea immediately.

"Camping."

Camping? Joel hadn't gone camping in decades. Where did the kid come up with these notions? "Camping, huh?"

"Yeah. One time when we were up in the attic, I saw you had an orange tent. We could use that."

"A tent? You did?" Shaking his head, Joel tried to think of what could be in the attic that resembled a tent.

"Even though the days are warm, the nights still dip below freezing. You don't think we'll freeze our ears off sleeping outside in a tent, do you?"

"Nah, we'll use sleeping bags," the boy reassured the adult.

Sleeping bags? Had he seen those with the orange tent? "Okay, camping it is. You got a campground in mind?"

"In the backyard."

"The backyard?" Joel hadn't suspected such a convenient location.

"That way we have the yard light for light, and we won't have to worry about a skunk or a bear or a coyote attacking our tent."

"Lions, tigers, and bears, huh? I can see your point. The back-yard would also be close to the bathroom and the refrigerator."

Grinning, Carson nodded. "It will be cool. Just you and me."

The laughing and dancing were on a roll. The mourning and weeping could be stored in a box in the attic for later.

After escorting Carson to the school bus the following morning, Joel filled a five-gallon pail with fencing supplies and strapped it behind the seat of his ATV. In a few weeks, the cattle would be moved to the pasture for summer grazing. Winter snow and wild deer usually played havoc with the electric fence surrounding the meadow. Today, he'd check the fence lines.

Hours later, he felt his cell phone vibrating in his pocket. Checking the number, he set down his tools. He'd expected the social worker's call.

"Hey, farmer Joel, where am I catching you today on that vast estate of yours?" No matter what the issue, Meagan was always upbeat.

"Oh, just doing a little fence maintenance." He settled back on the ATV.

"Ah, yes. That time of year, is it?"

Certainly she hadn't called to discuss ranching with him. His heartbeat quickened, but thinking of his discussion with the Lord yesterday, he forced himself to stay calm. When he didn't comment, she got to the point.

"I thought I'd give you an update on Thursday's proceedings, although Carson has probably given you his version."

"Actually, he didn't have much at all to report," Joel replied. Hopefully, she didn't either.

"Well, the visit went quite well. The Ottersons were already at the restaurant waiting for us. They had met at my office a couple of hours prior to your arrival to go over quite a bit of preliminary information. Jane Freshner, from the adoption agency, joined us as well.

"Eric and Carol seem like pretty down-to-earth people, most sincere in their search for a child. They were very open with their lives and in full agreement in letting the adoption move forward slowly, giving Carson ample time to get used to the idea.

"As I told you earlier, we did not tell Carson these people were interested in adopting him. It was only a meeting to get acquainted. I introduced the Ottersons to Carson as a mom and a dad, so if the relationship works, it will be an easier transformation later."

Joel simply listened, letting the summarization sift over him.

"They were attracted to Carson's personality; however, they didn't push him to give more than he was willing."

Her musical chuckle vibrated through the line. "You know how direct Carson can be. When I said, 'This is a mom and a dad,' he asked, 'Where are your kids?' Of course, they told him they didn't have any. Then he asked, 'How can you be a mom and a dad if you don't have any kids?'"

Inwardly, Joel lauded, *Good for you, pal!*

"He also told them he didn't have a mom but he did have a really nice dad."

Closing his eyes, Joel breathed in. Surrounded by the racket of chirping crickets, the *killdee, killdee* calls of the killdeers, and the melodious tunes of the meadowlarks, he heard nothing except *really nice dad*. Compressing his lids tightly, he murmured, *I can do this*, LORD. "*I can do everything through him who gives me the strength*" (Philippians 4:13, NIV).

Meagan's dialogue continued. "School will be out in another three weeks. The Ottersons agreed to postpone the next meeting date until summer vacation—end of May or beginning of June. How does that suit you?"

"Sounds like a plan." For Carson's sake, he had to be in agreement. Whatever was the least painful for the little guy.

"We'll be in touch then. You get back to fixing those fences, farmer. I don't want to hear on the news that some rancher's cows got hit on the railroad tracks."

Good old Meagan. She was a fine social worker, even if he didn't like what the future held.

On Saturday, while spending the bulk of the day sharing the cab of the tractor trailed by a corn planter puttering up and down in the black soil, Carson and Joel discussed in detail the upcoming campout. In fact, with school on Monday morning, they had decided to move their tenting excursion to Saturday night.

Barely taking time to set the water jug and the lunchbox by the kitchen sink, Carson scrambled for the closet door hiding the staircase to a walk-up attic. Out of sight, Joel heard him grunt. Smirking, the older man stopped to wash up at the sink before exploring the cast-offs in the upper level.

A muffled, "Joel! I need a little help here!" filtered through the open doorway. Scrounging in the top freezer of the refrigerator, Joel ferreted out a package of hot dogs and a bag of buns to thaw in the sink. Entering the stairwell, he grinned up at the miniature arm muscles straining to lift the horizontal, hinged piece of plywood covering the opening to the attic.

"You need a little help, huh? Where are those biceps when you need 'em?" the bigger man teased.

Joel mounted the steps and pushed one hand up alongside of Carson's, swinging the board onto its hinges to stand upright. A sixty-watt bulb cast shadows over a conglomeration of boxes, old furniture, wreaths, and dusty storage containers. Joel winced at the sight. When Melissa was here, she kept everything carefully organized and labeled. But after she became sick, he had a tendency to simply chuck articles into the attic to remove them from sight.

Beside him, Carson's eyes widened in expectation. "Wow!"

"So where exactly did you see this orange tent?" Joel gazed in bewilderment at the piles of junk.

"Over by the bushes hanging from the ceiling." Carson pointed a finger. Following his gesture to the dried bunches of baby's breath and goldenrod tied to nails protruding from the rafters, Joel was reminded of Melissa's flair for decorating.

Brushing a cobweb out of his way, Joel moved in the suggested direction with Carson hot on his trail. A stack of old wallpaper books, a box teeming with odd-sized flowerpots and baskets, but a tent? Quick and agile, the youth dodged between Joel's legs straight to the tent roll slid in between two Christmas boxes. Beside it was even an old canteen. Freeing them from the surrounding clutter, Joel made a quick survey for anything resembling sleeping bags. He wasn't in the mood for a massive search.

"We can use some quilts from the linen closet, Carson. They're almost like sleeping bags."

Carson agreed, clutching the prized tent bag to his side.

Thirty minutes later, the tent was propped up halfway between the house and the shelterbelt of ash and pine trees lining the front lawn, a pile of blankets and pillows shrouding the net entrance.

Carson dragged two chairs off the porch to add to the scene. Foraging in the tree rows, the campers found a great supply of dead twigs and branches to keep their campfire alive.

"What are we missing?" Joel surveyed the campsite.

"*Food!*" the boy announced, feverishly hopping from one foot to the other. "I'm starving!"

"Me too," Joel agreed, enthusiasm stirring in his blood as well. "Let's get the fire burning, and then we'll see what we can dig up for grub." Breaking sticks for kindling, the man used his dormant Boy Scout skills to teach his comrade the proper way to build a campfire. Soon, a flame was licking at the crisp branches.

Back in the kitchen, Carson filled the canteen from the spigot as Joel threw supplies into a clothes basket: hot dogs, buns, relish, ketchup, graham crackers, marshmallows, chips, cans of pop. "Hmmm, no candy bars."

"We can have some cookies instead," Carson suggested.

"No way. For a cookout, we make s'mores. For those, we need chocolate candy bars." Joel opened the cupboard above the stove.

"What are s'mores?"

"That's when you roast marshmallows over the fire until they're bloated like a dead cat lying in the sun." Wrinkling his freckled nose in disgust, Carson refuted the colorful description. "Then while they are still hot, you squish them between two graham crackers with some melted chocolate. You are going to love them! You'll be aching for some more!" Joel plucked a package off the shelf. "We're in luck! Chocolate chips will work as a substitute. Here, catch."

Dangling the branches Joel had whittled to a point over the hot coals, the pair slowly roasted their sizzling hot dogs. Impatient to bite into a bun dripping with ketchup, Carson thrust his hot dog into the open flames. In seconds, the skin turned a charcoal black. A shift in the breeze sent the smoke reeling into their faces. While shielding his eyes with his bent elbow, Carson's nose crinkled into folds. "Whew! The logs are puffing at me!"

"Your dog is about as black as you can eat it. Let's get it in a bun away from this smoke." Joel positioned their chairs at a ninety-degree angle from the offending fumes. Hungrily, they loaded their plates with chips and hot dogs smothered in relish and ketchup.

Slurping on a can of root beer, Joel showed the youngster how to roast a marshmallow golden brown until it was soft and gooey before stuffing it between graham crackers and chocolate chips.

Relaxing in the heat from the campfire, the cool breeze sneaked up on them as the sunset faded. Stars dotted the heavens. Without cloud cover, it would be an even colder night.

The two talked about whatever topics the seven-year-old camper initiated. "How do gophers know when to come out of their holes after the snow?"

"What should I plant in my fields by the porch steps this year?"

"Were there bullies in school when you went?"

"Did you have a social worker?"

As candidly and honestly, Joel attempted to discuss whatever questions his buddy put to him.

"How come Ryan gets to live with teacher?"

Joel answered this one with a reverse question. "Would you like to live with Mrs. Kirmis?"

Moving off his chair and into the farmer's lap, Carson thought about the hypothetical situation. Would he like to live in town with his teacher? If he did, he'd get to play with Ryan every day, and he'd get to climb on the playground equipment after school instead of taking the bus for the long ride to the farm. Nestling his head against Joel's armpit, his thoughts drifted into the starry sky.

A sigh escaped from Joel's lips as he tucked an arm over the sleepy form.

"If I lived with teacher, I wouldn't be able to bottle-feed the calves or ride with you in the machinery. I wouldn't get to sleep in a tent tonight or eat s'mores."

"No, but kids in town get to do things you don't do. In the summer, they can ride their bikes to the swimming pool, and they can see their friends more often." Joel was trying to be fair.

After a long pause, Carson picked up the conversation. "Maybe both places are good."

"I think you're right," Joel agreed.

"I was mad at Ryan 'cause he lived with teacher. But he doesn't get to live with you."

Tightening his hold on the child, the man bent his head to kiss the cool forehead. There was no place he would rather be at this moment. Softly, he started to sing in his deep voice, "Jesus loves me, this I know."

Carson's sweet, high voice joined him. "For the Bible tells me so."

In a few hours, the evening temperatures would drop to the freezing mark, yet the warmth of sharing this campground on the front lawn would burn in the older man's heart long after Carson had moved to Minneapolis.

As the last notes of the song faded into the night air, a pack of coyotes hiding in the distant edges of the county began a chorus of, *Yip, yip, yeow*. Had he been outside by himself, Carson would have hightailed it to the porch steps, his heart hammering against his chest. But in Joel's arms, there was no fear, rather complete confidence and lasting security.

"I'd only live with teacher if you lived there too," he murmured.

Kissing the forehead a second time, Joel roused himself. "We'd better crawl into the tent before we freeze solid out here."

Crawling on all fours into the low tent, the two giggled, trying to spread out the quilts without bumping butts. Finally tunneling between the folds, Joel groaned as his back and legs stretched out upon the hard ground. Wiggling to find a comfortable spot, Carson followed suit. "Hey, you wiggle-worm, lie still, or we'll find ourselves folded up in a collapsed tent." Snuggled against each other, the snickering died away, displaced by slow, even breathing.

Sounds of the night hummed outside the tent.

Shivering from the cold in the dead of the night, Joel found himself wide awake. Every muscle and bone ached. Feeling the stiffness in his nose and cheeks, he floundered about to tug a quilt to fling over his head, only to find he had no blankets at all. In his sleep, Carson had turned and twisted until he had wrapped all of the thick quilts into a cocoon around himself, like a bun encasing the hot dog they'd eaten earlier. "Snug as a bug in a rug." In spite of his agony, Joel's face cracked into a smile.

Clumsily, he hoisted himself to a sitting position then maneuvered himself to the tent's zipper on the screened netting. Quietly

as possible, he rolled out of the tent into the early morning crisp-
ness. His sore back and hips cried out loud as he lumbered to his
feet, padding through the shadows to the house silhouetted by
the yard light.

Once inside, he grabbed his thickest pair of insulated coveralls and a stocking cap. Feeling like the abominable snowman,
he waddled back to the tent extremely appreciative that no video
camera was catching him on film.

CHAPTER 21

Parents and grandparents packed the parallel bleachers attached to the opposite sides of the gymnasium, spilling over into the folding chairs lined up on the basketball floor. This, the finale of the year—the elementary spring concert, brought out every mom and dad, toddler, and crying baby.

Dressed in their fanciest clothes, the girls in curls and the boys' rooster tails flattened with water and hairspray, the squirming students stood side by side on the tiered semicircle of risers at the front of the gym.

Having marched her sixteen first graders to their designated spot on the bottom row of the risers, Mrs. Kirmis joined the other teachers in the bleachers to enjoy Mrs. Retson's spring rendition of tunes, evolving upon a summer vacation theme.

Studying her class from above, Jasmine was amazed as always by the growth and maturity exhibited by her almost-second-grade brood in a mere nine months. Stevie stood next to Carson, the two agricultural experts, dutifully keeping their eyes pinned on Mrs. Retson's baton. Jasmine's motherly eyes slid down the line, attracted to Ryan's elfish face. Even if he wasn't a particularly talented singer or reader or farmer or ball player, he always delighted in whatever he was doing. A grin stretched across his lit-up face, one elbow nudging Joey beside him. Seemingly like a cat tracking a mouse, Ryan had tended to be one up on his peers all year, staging the next comical escapade.

Through the impromptu applause following the introductory number, Ryan riveted his sights on the gym door. Having carefully scanned the crowd filling the bleachers and the floor, Ryan had already concluded his mom had missed the opening song. Watching the open doorway, he still hoped for her debut.

Jasmine was intensely aware of his scrutiny. Every day for the past week, he had asked her if she thought his mom would come to his concert.

An hour ago when the two of them were having a light supper before dashing off for the spring program, Ryan had prayed, "Thank you for the sandwich. And Jesus, could you please tell my mom to come and hear me sing tonight? Sometimes she forgets. Amen."

Jasmine had subconsciously been doing an inventory of the audience as well, yet no Tina had thus far made the guest list.

Two days of the school term remained. Jasmine was eagerly anticipating her three-month break. Endeavoring to write on her manuscript while accommodating her school schedule had been unrealistic. Balancing two careers was nearly impossible. Her summer months would be devoted to finishing and editing her book.

Ah yes, and to Ryan.

Sarah Ternes, Ryan's social worker, had talked to her more than once about being firm with Tina. As Ryan's mother, Tina needed to not only complete a mandatory parenting class, which she had thus far failed to enroll in, but also to exemplify a significant desire to maintain a close relationship with her son. With the proximity of the Kirmis and Benson homes, Tina should be able to easily reserve a segment of her day for Ryan and cut the excuses. If Tina didn't take the judge's orders seriously, Ryan's six months in foster care could extend into a year. Jasmine grimaced. What kinds of thoughts must the miniature fellow roll around in his head?

Across the auditorium, Joel Linton slumped on a bleacher bench, his attention resting on Carson. The two remaining days of school plagued him. As long as school was in session, Social Services and the adoption agency had stalled the adoption proceedings to prevent Carson from being uprooted from one school and dropped into another during his first-grade year. Changing families would be enough disruption in the little guy's life. However, with school's dismissal, the wheels would churn full speed ahead.

Safeguarding the LORD's revelation given to him in Norbert's park, Joel had maintained his resolution to laugh and dance with Carson in their remaining days. On occasion, it came from his heart; however, on other days, it was a façade for his little friend's benefit alone, his laugh and dance hollow. While he was observing his blond-haired love from the hard seat of the bleachers, it was difficult not to slip back into weeping and mourning.

A hush fell over the crowd, the muting drawing both Jasmine and Joel back to the musical entertainment. In a sweet soprano voice, a sixth grader lifted her voice to sing of her homesickness while attending summer camp. The kids on the risers joined in on the chorus, pretending to call their parents on make-believe cell phones. Summer camp was not at all what they had expected it to be. The lyrics of the song were catchy and cute.

The intrusion could have been part of the program, its timing written right into the script, so perfectly was it staged. Even Principal Peterson, acting as a sentry at the entrance during extracurricular events to foresee any negative behavior brewing, faltered in recognizing the unwelcome demeanor.

A jovial shriek split the air, erupting from the gymnasium's entrance. A female's shrill whistle emanated between two fingers in her mouth, answering the choristers' mournful plea.

"Hold on. I'm comin' to get you, baby!"

As if on cue from the script, the audience's eyes rolled off the choir of lively children begging their moms and dads to come and get them from the dreaded camp to the thin lady in skintight, slinky black slacks. Strutting across the polished floor in clickety-click high-heeled boots and a low-necked, blazing-orange midriff shirt, she became the spotlight. People in the chairs twisted about, trying to discern what the commotion was all about.

Extending her arms over her head, the intruder waved wildly, like tree branches bending in a summer thunderstorm, at the platform of kids. "Here I come, baby!"

The kids started giggling. This certainly hadn't happened at rehearsal! Gleefully chortling, the younger children pointed their fingers at the funny lady.

Glancing at her director, the confused soloist wasn't sure whether to keep singing or to stop. Mrs. Retson, her back to the scene, totally submersed in following the musical score in her director's book, was oblivious to the side act dramatized at the rear of the room. Her baton kept pounding the air, propelling the vocalist on.

Principal Peterson too hesitated at the bizarre sight, not wanting to intervene in Mrs. Retson's planned program, if this indeed was the plan. Indecisively, he remained fastened to his lookout post.

Only Jasmine knew instantaneously what a fiasco this night could turn into. Swaggering up the middle aisle, clapping wildly to the music, the silly woman stealing the spotlight from the soloist was none other than Ryan's mom: Tina! She had shown up for the concert after all, weaving from one side to the other, making a complete spectacle of herself.

Slapping a hand to her mouth, Jasmine half rose off the bleacher seat then flopped back down, groaning in horror. Tina was drunk! *Stop her,* LORD*!* An upward prayer was all Jasmine could do to remedy the situation.

As if Tina had heard Jasmine's inward groan, she saw an open chair halfway up the aisle and toppled herself into it. She laughed out loud, continuing to clap her hands to the refrain and antics of the children. Her feet flew off the floor and then hit the gym tiles again, totally caught up in the entertaining comical program.

And by all outward appearances, she was.

Even while the accompanying choir behind the sixth-grade singer broke up in laughter, the soloist stayed true to her director, singing her musical selection right to the last note. Tina doubled her applause, pounding her palms together like rubber shoes flapping the pavement, reminding the crowd to applaud as well in appreciation for the performance.

Convinced this invasion was not part of the program, Principal Peterson followed the steps Tina had meandered, finding an open chair in the row behind her. Not wanting to disrupt the concert any more than it already had been, he would be ready to remove the offending guest only if he had to.

Surprisingly, with the preliminary tones of the next song, Tina quieted noticeably. Listening intently, with black-lashed eyes glued on Ryan, she imitated every choreographed movement the children's choir made: leaning to the right then to the left, hand on the hip, tapping a knee. Mesmerized by the music of the children, she kept her seat and refrained from blurting out any more rejoinders.

Until the end. As the children fanning the risers bent forward in a universal bow, Tina was on her feet, one fist batting the air, yelling, "That's my boy, Ryan! You did good!"

Ryan was in ecstasy, bouncing up and down. His mom had come to his program! As he filed off the risers with his class, the line of children wove right through the aisle next to Tina. She caught Ryan by the hand, planting an orange lipstick kiss on his cheek. "You're going to be a rock star someday singing like that!" she boomed. Pleased with the compliment, Ryan waved to her as he continued across the floor with his class.

Principal Peterson escorted Tina safely out of the building. Social Services would be getting a call.

Hand in hand, Joel and Carson climbed the steps of the church. Inside the vestibule, Joel handed him off to Mrs. Saar, his Sunday school teacher. Attendance in the morning Bible classes and worship service were diminished over the summer months with families off on vacations and kids at camps. Carson peered curiously into the small room used for his class, hoping to see Eric or Sam or Spencer.

"Where is everyone?" he asked Mrs. Saar, checking under the table.

"It looks like it's going to be just you and me today," she replied, deftly assembling the felt characters in front of the flannel board in readiness for the Bible story. "Is that okay?"

Feeling a bit awkward at being the only student in the class and yet fully aware of the terrific stories Mrs. Saar told and the fun crafts she kept hidden in the cupboard, he wavered. He spied a half dozen juice boxes setting on the back shelf. M&Ms polled the deciding vote.

"Sure."

Rubbing a felt man onto the display board, Mrs. Saar launched into her lesson. "Carson, meet Paul."

"You told us about Paul before." Carson recognized the bearded man with the brown dress sticking to the flannel graph.

"Oh, you are a smart one. What did I tell you about Paul?"

"You said he was a mean man until God caught him. A big light got in his eyes and made him blind." During story time, Carson was always spellbound. On the way home after the church service, he could always repeat the story to Joel.

"And then what happened to him?"

"Then he became a good guy and told everyone about Jesus."

"Exactly." Placing another figure on the flannel graph, she proceeded with the story. "This is his friend, Silas. Silas loves Jesus too. The two men travel from town to town telling the folks how Jesus died on the cross to cover the naughty things they did." She handed a felt crowd scene to Carson, letting him smooth it onto the board.

"Did the people listen to them?" the boy asked.

"Some did and believed. Others didn't like Paul and Silas and got them into trouble. The two men were thrown into prison."

Mrs. Saar replaced the three figures on the flannel graph with pictures of Paul and Silas being beaten and chained in prison. Adding a jailer, she continued, "The jailer was ordered to guard them in case they tried to run away. He locked them in chains.

"Because these men loved Jesus, they didn't even let being locked up in jail stop them from worshiping the LORD. The Bible says they sang songs and prayed throughout the night." She added still another picture to the scene illustrating more prisoners in stocks and chains. "The other prisoners in jail with them listened to what Paul and Silas told them about Jesus.

"Suddenly, in the middle of the night, the jailhouse began to rock and shake." Mrs. Saar gripped the edge of the classroom table, shaking it as she narrated this portion of the story. "It was an earthquake! The walls rattled! The bars on the windows rattled! The locked door rattled open! Even the chains and the stocks rattled! And *bang*, they fell apart! Paul and Silas were free!"

"Yippee!" shouted Carson, pounding his palms on the table. Faces of happy men praising the LORD peered out at Carson from the flannel board.

"Who do you think sent the earthquake?" she asked.

"Jesus!"

"Everyone was happy except the jailer. He was scared. It was his job to make sure no one escaped from the jail. Now he would be punished. He drew his sword and was about to kill himself when Paul stopped him. He said, 'Sir, we are all here. No one has run off.' The jailer rushed in to see for himself, and sure enough, all the prisoners were still there."

Placing her last picture on the board, Mrs. Saar shared the best part of the story. "The jailer fell at his feet and exclaimed, 'What must I do to be saved?' Paul and Silas told him he must believe in Jesus. And the jailer did. Not only him, but he had Paul and Silas tell the wonderful story to his family as well. And they believed too!" Mrs. Saar clapped her hands together, her exuberance filling the tiny room. "Wasn't that wonderful? A whole family becoming Christians!"

Carson's unblinking eyes riveted on hers, wrinkled with crow's feet but shining like stars. *God's light*, he figured.

Still staring, the boy asked, "Does Jesus live behind your eyes?"

At first, she was struck dumb by his question, but then God's wisdom revealed his inner quest to her soul. Her short, gray waves slowly bowed in thanksgiving; her lips moved in silent prayer. She sought his clear-blue stare that had not lost its intensity.

"Yes, Jesus lives all over inside of me."

"How did he get there?" Carson was remembering the conversation he'd had with Joel.

"I asked him to live there. I told him I was sorry for the bad things I had done and that I believed he'd died on the cross for me."

"And then he popped right inside of you?"

Smiling, she wasn't quite sure how to respond. "Kind of like that."

"And then he put stars in your eyes?"

"That's Jesus, baby. That's Jesus shining through me."

"Can you get the lights for me too?" Wistfulness coated his words. Joel had told him asking Jesus into his heart was the most important decision he'd ever make. He was ready to make the decision.

"It would be a blessed privilege to pray with you." The older lady's words were soft like the breath of the Holy Spirit blowing into Carson's being as he closed his eyes. Repeating the words his Sunday school teacher prayed, the child asked Jesus to live in his heart too.

And the Savior gladly stepped in.

Sharing the enclosed pickup cab with Joel on the way home from church, Carson's eyes were even bluer than usual. His angelic smile glowed brightly.

Joel noted a purer resonance about him. "What's up, buddy?"

The blue eyes sparkled with a thousand stars; his cheeks puffed upward as his grin dipped deeper. Shyly, he announced, "I did it."

He didn't have to explain. The beautiful countenance beaming on his face explained the three words. Joel's eyes widened into full circles. He hastily steered the vehicle to the side of the paved road and parked. Sweeping Carson into a bear hug, he squeezed the mite until he screamed in delight. "Praise the Lord," the father yelled out his window into the heavens. *There is a time to dance.*

The pickup cab was too confining; the two tumbled out onto the road, dancing a rhythmic hop and skip on the deserted highway. Joyfully laughing and raising their arms heavenward in thanksgiving, the man and the boy shared the celebration of another child coming into God's family.

Carson's travels might take him to Minneapolis; however, Jesus would be riding on the hood, navigating the trip.

CHAPTER 22

Backing the tractor onto the cement pad in front of the shop, Joel switched on the radio for a distraction as he fixed. Sometimes he got tired of himself, the continual parade of old thoughts and pictures traipsing through his mind, like hitting the remote for the old reruns on TV. If it would only play yesterday's scenario instead of delving into the archives—or worse yet: the future.

Yesterday's adventure was the pinnacle, the absolute highest tribute of thankfulness a father could pour out of his heart: Carson's step of faith, a tiny baby in Christ who would need a continual supply of spiritual food to grow. But the seed planted in his soul had sprouted. The process had begun.

What a joyful Sunday the two of them had had.

The week prior, Joel had taken Ryan and Carson fishing. Neither of the boys had ever held a fishing rod nor experienced the thrill of its tip abruptly dipping forward, signaling a nibble on the line. The outing had ended in a thorough baptismal dunking of all three of them struggling to untangle lines and unsnag hooks.

After their highway dance yesterday, Joel had reminded his partner that it was his turn to pick the day's itinerary. Fishing had been Joel's choice the week before. Somehow, Carson had the uncanny ability to come up with ideas the adult mind never entertained.

"Let's visit Brush and Spit. I haven't seen them in a while." Brush and Spit, along with all the other cattle, had been hauled to green pastures for summer grazing. These two bottle calves from a year ago had grown into seven-hundred-pound heifers kept over for breeding. Next spring, they would have their first calves.

With a makeshift lunch in the cooler, the pair of ranchers had done just that.

When he reviewed the pleasant hours in his subconscious, it was easy to dismiss the future, to rip the calendar off the wall, to never turn the page to the next month. The rancher could pretend the world consisted only of Carson and him, living here on the farm, tilling the soil, and letting the sun's rays color their skin a deep shade of brown. When Melissa died, had Carson been theirs, this is exactly how it would have been—father and son. However, Carson wasn't his child by birth or adoption. He was kind of borrowed, yet it seemed like he was his—until the phone would ring.

And it had.

Early this morning, Jane Freshner had been at his porch step to transport Carson to Norbert. The Minneapolis couple was making their second appearance. Meagan Ritter would return the child this evening.

Setting to the task at hand, the farmer dropped the plug on the oil and screwed out the filter. Every two hundred hours, Joel changed the oil on his tractor.

To his figuring, the social workers were keeping a wide chasm between him and the prospective adoptive parents, in fear of the interrogation he might give them. Would he? Like a father interviewing his daughter's fiancé, would he blatantly ask the questions heavy on his mind? Or would he trust the social workers to choose the best parents for Carson?

It was happening again; his mind was on a runaway mission. Reaching up to the radio, he rotated the knob to full volume.

Meagan was planning to tell Carson about the Ottersons today—the real reason behind their visits. Blowing the air out of his lips like a child letting go of a half-blown balloon, he yanked the oilcan closer to the piece of machinery.

Carson wasn't very cooperative at making small talk with Jane Freshner. His answers to her constant stream of questions were one syllable at best. For one thing, he didn't know her, hardly at all. And second thing, she smiled too much. He liked happy grown-ups, like teacher in school. Meagan was okay too, but there was nothing to smile about today.

He wanted to help Joel change the oil on the tractor. Did he get to? No way. Jane had to wreck everything. His little nose hovered at the base of the passenger window, staring at the land-scape swiftly running past. Brushing a tear away with his fist, he stopped replying to her inquiries.

When he reached the Social Services office, the tightness in his tummy lessened. Meagan was here. He liked her better because she had given him Joel. Nimbly Carson raced away from Jane's car, yanked open the heavy door of the building, and slipped inside.

Jane followed him.

"What are we gonna do today, Meagan?" he asked, hoping it wouldn't include Jane. "You wanna play ping-pong with me? I bet I can beat you this time!"

Laughter behind him spun the boy in a ninety-degree arc. He froze when he saw the same couple who had been at the McDonald's restaurant last time.

"How come your friends are here again?" Carson tilted his head back to look up at Meagan.

Lowering herself to his eye level, she explained, "Actually, this mom and dad are hoping to become your friends as well. We thought we'd all spend the morning in the conference room looking at some books they brought."

Carol Otterson patted the colorful handbag sitting by her feet. "Carson has a book he has been writing to show you too." Meagan appraised the reluctant child's demeanor.

"Hey, that's great," Eric Otterson spoke up. "What kinds of pictures did you put in your book, Carson?"

Bewildered, Carson didn't have an answer. Meagan eased the group into the next room around the table. Sandwiched between Meagan and Carol, Carson scooted his chair closer to Meagan's. Jane brought Carson's Life Book from her office, setting it on the table between Carol and the child.

"Why don't you go first, Carson? You have lots of exciting things in your book," Jane suggested. Carson's hands remained hidden in his lap. He was giving up a day of helping Joel to do this?

Gently, Carol used one finger to lift the corner of the cover, flipping it open. A large photographer's photo of Carson as a first grader grinned back at her. "My, who is this handsome boy?"

Her husband rounded his lips into a soft whistle. "Hey, what a cutie! Looks like the young man must be about ten years old."

Meagan reinforced the Ottersons' playful attempts. "Ten years old? Are you ten in that picture, Carson?"

Smirking as he cowered at her side, he shook his head. "Seven."

"Seven? You wouldn't be joshing me, now, would you?" Eric's eyes grew as huge as basketballs in disbelief.

The group studied the pages, commenting on Carson's first-grade penmanship, his drawing of a farm tractor, and the photos Mrs. Kirmis had taken of him at school. They lingered over the page listing his favorites.

"You like gummy worms?" Carol asked. Carson bobbed his head slightly. "That's my favorite candy too," she exclaimed. "Sometimes I make dirt dessert and put gummy worms in it."

Eric made a face. "Don't ever eat her dirt dessert. That's exactly what it tastes like: dirt."

"He's just fooling you, Carson. It's really made from Oreo cookies and chocolate pudding." Carol gave her husband a tender look.

Carson laughed out loud. The Ottersons were gaining ground. Having reached the concluding page, Carol reached down to her bag. Unearthing a photo album, she apologized. "My book isn't near as nice as your book, Carson. You are a true artist. But if you excuse my poor job at scrapbooking, I'll show you where we live."

Curiously, Carson inched closer to Carol. In an effort to see better, he propped himself up on his knees on the seat, his elbows on the table.

Under the cover, a map of North Dakota and Minnesota vividly illustrated the locations of Norbert and Minneapolis. Marked in red was a jagged line connecting the two cities, showing the route the Ottersons had traveled. "See," Carol explained, "our states are neighbors. We aren't really so far apart at all."

"Where's Joel's farm?" Carson wondered, tracing the red line with his finger.

Meagan's pink nail pointed to a spot not far from Norbert below the colored line. "About here."

Carson sighed in relief. "I'm sure glad he's a lot closer, or it would take a long time to get home tonight."

Dismissing his remark, Carol continued to turn the pages. "These are photos I took of our home and our backyard." An attractive split-level home, bricked halfway up on the front, edged with shrubs and flowering plants, reflected back at them. Attached to the back was a roofed portico. "We often eat outside in the summer."

"Do you have a swing?" Carson was sizing up the small lawn.

"No," Eric admitted, "but there is a city park a few blocks from our home with playground equipment and bike paths."

"Are we going to do anything else today?" Carson asked Meagan, beginning to lose interest in the pictures.

Carol flipped the pages faster to accommodate his waning attention span. Pictures of their cat, Peaches, Eric's job site, and the traffic on their street flashed past. "There are lots of fun things to do in Minneapolis," Eric pointed out, tapping a number of pictures in succession. "See this? This is the Mall of America. Kids love it here. You can visit an aquarium with every underwater animal imaginable—say, fish, turtles, otters. There's a roller coaster, a miniature golf course, huge Lego models, and lots of stores."

"Cool." Carson fastened his attention on an otter frisking in the underwater showcase. "Is there an auction barn for cows?"

Carol and Eric looked perplexed.

"You know, where the man in the cowboy hat goes, 'Forty, seventy, ninety-five, one hundred. Sold to bidder ten!'" the seven-year-old explained, trying to copy the auctioneer's chant.

Amused at his pretensions, the Ottersons chuckled. "The Mall of America is so immense that we haven't seen everything there is to see." Eric sidestepped the quizzing and did some of his own instead. "What interesting places do you have right here in Norbert?"

Carson shrugged his shoulders as though there weren't any. Jane restated the question. "Sure there are, Carson. What have you done here that's fun?"

"The waterslide. And the zoo."

"How about the museums and the skate park?" Meagan added.

"And McDonald's!"

Jane chortled. "Bet you can't guess where his favorite place to eat is!"

"Whoa, it is almost lunchtime," Meagan commented, glancing at her wristwatch. "I have an appointment with another one of my kids." Meagan let her gaze fall on Carson. "Hmm, what should we do about you? I can be back at the office by four o'clock to give you a ride back to the ranch, but that's a good four and half hours from now." Strumming her fingernails on the polished tabletop, she appeared to be mulling over the situation.

"Well," Eric suggested, "we're going to get something to eat. How about if he joined us? Maybe he could show us one of Norbert's hotspots while he's at it."

And that's exactly how Carson ended up spending the afternoon with the Ottersons, first gorging on chicken strips and fries at McDonald's before giving them a detailed tour through Norbert's City Zoo. He led them past the pelican sitting at the opening gate to the Canadian geese waiting for a handout, along the grizzly bear's cage, and to the bench to sit and watch the silly antics of the penguins. The threesome traipsed uphill to the zebras' pen, stopping to marvel at the giraffes extending their long, spotted necks to munch on a leafy branch.

However, the majority of their hours at the zoo were spent across the walking bridge at the farm scene monopolized by its red and white barn and little shuttered house. Chickens of every breed and color scuttled in the dry dirt, pecking for a mid-afternoon snack. White leghorns, the same as Ed and Arlene Bautz raised in their coop, intermixed with exotic strains; some had clumps of feathers hugging their feet, resembling a plodding Clydesdale horse. Carson was intrigued with the brown-speckled fowls with no feathers at all ringing their necks.

"Those aren't North Dakota chickens," Eric concluded. "One good blizzard and they'd freeze to death."

Giggling, Carson fathomed a solution. "Not if we made them scarves to wear!"

In the barn, the stalls held a pair of miniature ponies, a braying donkey, and a cow being milked by one of the zookeepers. "That's a Holstein cow," Carson informed the Ottersons. "You know how I can tell?"

"How?" Carol was fascinated at his knowledge.

"Its black and white spots. Joel and me have black Angus cows. They're all black. But we don't milk them. We let their calves do that."

"You sure know a lot about cattle. I think this is the first time I've been this close to a cow." She appeared a bit nervous.

"Do you want to touch her?" Carson asked, sliding in beside the zookeeper sitting on a small stool dutifully squirting milk from the cow's udder into the pail.

"I'm fine right where I am," Carol replied.

Nodding without upsetting his rhythmic tones hitting the bucket, the zookeeper assured her, "A certain amount of fear with any animal is healthy. Old Betsy here is a gentle old milk cow, perfect for a kid's zoo."

Having wheeled himself up to Betsy's head, Carson scratched the fur covering the hard bone between her eyes. "Where's her calf?" he asked, reaching up to feel the horn tips barely sticking out of her head.

"Died," the man replied. "That happens sometimes with young animals."

"Yup," Carson stated matter-of-factly. "My dad pulled a calf, and it still died." Twisting around to see Carol, he explained for her benefit, "That's when we have to help the mama have her baby 'cause she can't do it by herself."

Glancing at Eric, the man asked, "How many cows do you run?"

Carson interrupted before Eric could answer. "He's not my dad. We have a hundred of 'em."

With a last tug on the teat, the zookeeper stood, picking up the pail of frothy milk. "You sound like a good farmer, young man."

Carson's chest swelled with pride. Yup, he was going to be a farmer, just like Joel, someday.

Meagan had the return trip to the Linton ranch to broach the subject of adoption with her passenger—not adoption in general, but Carson's adoption.

"So you had a good time with Mom and Dad Otterson?"

A thin shoulder shrugged before Carson suddenly sat alertly, staring out the passenger window. "Hey, that guy's still spreading anhydrous on his field. Fertilizer helps the crops grow healthier." Looking over his shoulder, he wanted to make sure Meagan saw the tractor pulling an air seeder and a long, white anhydrous tank.

"He is," she acknowledged. "The Ottersons would like you to come out to Minneapolis and see what it is like there." She gave him a sneak look through her rearview mirror to witness his reaction.

His inquisitive eyes swung back to meet hers. "They do? What for?"

"Remember how we've been talking about adoption? How you need a family all of your own? A forever family? One where you won't have to move from one family to the next anymore?"

"I have one. Joel is my family."

Meagan inhaled before going on. "Joel is a foster parent. He takes care of kids for a short time until they find a real family. Joel is a very good foster parent. You have felt safe at his house, right?"

Carson's blond head gave affirmation.

"And now we want to find you a forever family that is just waiting for a great young man like you."

Carson was listening silently, his eyes focused on the highway.

"The Ottersons want a son. They want to be some child's forever family." Holding her breath, she waited for his response.

"Why does it have to be me?" Habitually, he began chewing on the inside of his lip.

"We don't know if it is going to be you. We want the best for you and the best for the Ottersons. They have come to Norbert twice to get to know you. But it wouldn't be fair unless you would get to go to Minneapolis and see what their home is like."

His reply was firm. "I want to live in the country."

"That's because you live in the country right now with Joel. You don't know what living in Minneapolis is like. What if you tried it and you found out it was even better than the country?" Excitement expanded her voice.

When he didn't answer, Meagan continued. "Carson, adoption is a good thing. It means someone wants to love you so much that they are willing to give you their last name and make you a part of their family for always. Isn't that pretty cool?"

"Kind of."

"A family comes with relatives: grandpas and grandmas, aunts and uncles, and oodles of cousins."

Quietness settled over the youngster as he reviewed the information Meagan was giving him. His therapist had read a book to him about a mom and dad choosing a boy and a girl to be their very own. In the book, they had to go to a courthouse, where a man wearing a dress sat in a big chair with a hammer thing he pounded on the desk. Then they ate ice cream and cake.

"Do I have to go in front of the judge?"

"Not right away." Meagan explained the details. "I'd like you to visit the Ottersons in Minneapolis, just for a weekend, and see what this big city life is all about. Then I want you to come back to Elton, and we'll talk about it. Together we'll decide if this would be a good move for you and them or not. Maybe you'll need a second weekend in Minnesota to figure it out. You don't have to decide right away. I want you to be happy, Carson. That is the most important part of adoption."

Watching the rear end of a semi-truck in front of them, Carson let Meagan's proposition filter through his mind. He knew some kids at school who were adopted. One girl told Carson she got to have an adoption party when her family adopted her.

Adoption. The word rolled around in his head. It would be nice not to have to move from one place to another ever again. To have his own parents. To have their last name instead of *Reynolds.* Joel's name was Linton, not Reynolds. Would he like his name to be *Carson Otterson?*

"Do I have to go by myself to Minneapolis?"

Meagan was pleased he was warming to the idea.

"No, of course not. The Ottersons would come and get you and bring you back. You know them, don't you?"

"Kind of." His teeth resumed biting on his inside lip.

"Would you feel safe with them?"

The words were spoken slowly. "Yeah, but I would miss Joel."

"Yes, I believe you. But Joel would be waiting for you." She winked at him in the rearview mirror.

Adoption must be a good thing if Meagan says it is, Carson reasoned. Even better than Joel's farm. If that was so, it must be awesome.

"Suppose I should tell Joel I might get adopted?"

"Yes, he will be very excited for you," she replied, giving him a broad smile. Maybe he wouldn't be exactly *excited*, but he would do everything in his power to give Carson a smooth transition into a permanent home. Meagan could count on Joel.

Joel was still tinkering in his shop when Meagan's tires crunched over the gravel in the driveway. Bypassing the farmhouse, she pulled up beside the tractor in front of the shop. Carson tore out the door to give Joel the customary hug. Wiping the grease off his hands with a rag, Joel barely had time to prepare for the onslaught.

Kneeling on the dirty floor, he wrapped his sweaty arms about Carson's middle. For a second, the blond hair rested on his shoulder. Impulsively, Carson struggled loose, stealing Joel's billed cap and flopping it on his own head. Circling the tractor, he asked, "Did you get the oil changed?"

"Sure did." Joel loved the interest the little farmer showed in agriculture.

"Guess what, Joel?" His eyes were shining brightly, an odd smirk on his face.

Not sure what was coming, the man shook his head in short jerks. Briefly, he studied Meagan and then flashed back to Carson.

He lifted and then dropped his hands in a gesture of complete bewilderment. If this was the moment he'd been dreading and subconsciously preparing for, he should be ready. No matter what emotions he was carrying around inside of him, he'd be able to conceal them from a thin skeleton of a kid.

Joel lowered his weight onto an overturned empty five-gallon pail, figuring he might do better sitting down, if this was what he thought it was. He sucked in his breath and waited for the announcement.

Carson let all of the words fizz from his lips in a rush, like carbon dioxide escaping from an unsealed bottle of soda. His blue stare held Joel's gray eyes at gunpoint.

"Guess what, Joel—I'm getting adopted!" His grin expanded from earlobe to earlobe, awaiting his hero's blessing.

Throughout the long hours of the day, Joel had practiced his congratulatory response until he had it just right, his emotions locked up tighter than a deadbolt lock. He had memorized exactly the words he'd use when the news was manifested.

Identical to an actor on opening night on Broadway, after the curtain slowly ascended, the spotlight fell on him. The audience awaited his opening line. Joel knew what he was supposed to say. Something about being happy for him and proud of the young man he was growing into. And how lucky the new mom and dad were going to be to get a son like him.

He worked his jaw, but the brain shut down, refusing to impart cue cards for the actor's lines.

The man's frozen smile turned downward; the gray eyes flooded. Not able to hold his breath any longer, he exhaled a giant heart-rending sob. His chest heaved; another lament followed, even louder than the first one. His face crumpled. It was the opening debut, and Joel Linton had failed. The five-foot-ten muscular rancher bent over in a pool of misery, tears raining down his tanned cheeks, the last chunk of his heart breaking in sorrow as his chest wafted again and again in shuddering convulsions.

Only once before had he felt this way, had he lost total control of himself, like a runaway horse unable to be reined in—when Melissa breathed her last breath.

Carson's wide eyes never blinked, his stance chiseled into a rock formation. Images of Joel scaring a wild coyote away from the calf shelter or commanding a one-ton bull to move into a corral gate flashed in front of him. His foster parent was the closest man he'd had to a real father. In his childlike estimation, he envisioned Joel strong enough to do anything; nothing could beat him. If there was a person he could trust, it was Joel Linton.

Yet the boy had never seen the man—tougher than a rusty gate and gentler than the touch of a monarch butterfly—cry. Once, he thought maybe Joel was crying when he felt the back of his own shirt getting damp, but he must have been mistaken because he'd heard somewhere that real men didn't cry.

In a way, it scared him, not making him afraid of Joel; however, he wondered about this word called *adoption*. If it was such a good thing, then why was Joel crying? Shouldn't he be cheering?

Lifting his eyes to Carson's, the grieving man motioned for the boy to come. In baby steps, Carson obeyed, no longer wearing a clown's demeanor. When he was within reach, strong arms enveloped his slight frame, pulling the youngster into a tight embrace. In Carson's confusion, ponds formed on his own face. Why was Joel acting this way? Joel's ragged breath fanned his ear.

Professional Meagan's composure had washed away like a sandcastle at high tide at the first gut-wrenching sob erupting from the man's throat. Love radiated from Joel Linton the way the sun's rays warmed the earth. If ever a pair belonged together, it was Joel and Carson. But Joel loved the boy more than himself. His gift to Carson would be a family, with both a mother and a father, a complete forever family.

When Joel reached a hand into his back jeans pocket for his red handkerchief, Meagan dug in her own bag. After wiping his face, he folded the hanky in half and blew his nose in a loud, piercing trumpet toot. Balancing his chum on his knee, he apologized. The words hidden before now flowed readily, straight from his heart. "I'm sorry for crying, Carson. Sometimes news is so good, so beautiful, I can't take it all in. My heart was full to the top." Tapping his chest, he continued to swipe at wayward droplets. "I had to make room for your adoption news. And now I'm ready. Tell me all about your adoption."

A veil of shyness had crept over Carson with Joel's breakdown. Peeking at Meagan, the boy grew strength from her dark, curly head waggling encouragement to him.

Hesitantly, he gave Joel a brief summation. "There's a mom…and a dad…in Minneapolis who might want me." He toyed with the button on Joel's cuff.

"Isn't that great news!" Joel exclaimed, squeezing the boy to his side, shutting out any reentrance of the warring factions in his middle. "They are going to absolutely love you. You are the most terrific kid I know." When Carson didn't reply, Joel prompted him, "Have you gotten to meet them yet?"

A slight incline of the head answered the question.

"Pretty nice people?"

"They took me to McDonald's and the zoo," Carson admitted, unbuttoning the cuff.

"Hey, that's cool. McDonald's is your favorite!" Joel rubbed a knuckle across the soft cheek. "You've been to the zoo quite often. Did you show them all the animals?"

Again, the head bobbed. "They liked Betsy the best." From Carson's short narration, Joel could surmise where the boy and the Ottersons had spent the majority of the afternoon. Ranching may not have been a gene he was born with at birth, yet he sure had acquired it in the past year.

"Yeah, old Betsy is a winner. So when do you get to see this family next?" It was all Joel could do to get the question casually past his front teeth.

Falling back against the strength of Joel's arm, Carson said, "They want me to see their house."

The thought of his buddy being seven hours away hurt, but he wasn't going to melt into a pile of mush again. "That would be a good idea. Kind of check the place out, huh?" Joel's gaze dropped to the boy's tennis shoes.

"Guess so. They said they have a big tank with fish and otters in it." His nimble fingers were attempting to button the cuff again.

"Really?"

"Yup, and lots of stores with kids' stuff."

"That'll be something to see." Joel flexed his other hand.

A little of the old fighting spirit still within him, Joel gave Meagan an impish look as he fished for any possible spiritual connections. "Did they say anything about you going to Sunday school?"

She frowned slightly, but Joel didn't care. She hadn't danced a jig with the boy last Sunday afternoon on a vacant highway.

Carson's eyebrows scrunched together as he tried to recall his conversations with the new mommy and daddy. "Do you think Jesus lives in Minneapolis too?"

Placing two fingers on his friend's frail chest, Joel reassured him, "Since he's in your heart, he will live wherever you go."

Even in Minneapolis.

Never will I leave you; Never will I forsake you.

Hebrews 13: 5b (NIV)

CHAPTER 23

"Hi-yah, hi-yah." Ned and Rae Ann sang the chant in unison, allowing their voices to drop with each second syllable as they trailed the Schultzes' herd of calves into a pen, swinging their sorting sticks to keep the young cattle moving forward. Joel slammed the gate shut after the last dogie passed by him, locking the herd inside the enclosure.

Clouds of dust drifted upward, spun from the milling hooves of the braying animals. Waiting at the fenced alleyway, Ned's dad, Clem, hollered above the racket, "Try to take ten at a crack, and we'll squeeze them in the alleyway!"

Cutting a group from the herd, Joel, Ned, and Rae hustled as a team to guide the milling, bawling calves into the narrow corral built just wide enough to form a single file line of calves. "Hi-yah, hi-yah." Together they raised their arms to scare the young calves forward. Ned touched one on the rump with his sorting stick, who was preventing the others from pushing forward. Another gate banged behind the last calf, capturing the batch into the narrow enclosure.

The compressed corral provided safety for the ranch hands yet gave them access to the calves by standing outside the fence when administering the vaccinations.

Clem already had syringes filled with enough vaccine to shoot below the skin of each animal in the first lot. As soon as the vaccinations were completed, the first lot of calves was released and another group chased in. Once the calves were done, the cows would follow a similar treatment. It was a full day's operation. By evening, everyone would be dragging.

With the process moving like clockwork, Rae switched positions and began filling syringes for Clem, helping him to keep up with the steady flow of calves moving through the alleyway.

A large portion of the day had been eaten away when the crew moved on to the cows, giving each a shot and pouring the animal with a liquid to ease its fly irritation. When each lot of cows was released, the mamas went looking for their calves, who had been separated from them for most of the day. The hungry offspring came searching for their dinner, nuzzling the mother cows' milk bags.

Joel was feeling the effects of the long day. Working cattle was hard work. There was a lot less zip in Ned's and Joel's strides as they brought up another batch of cows, pushing them into the alley. "Hi-yah, hi-yah."

"Where's Carson when we tire out?" Ned blocked a cow with a sorting board before it could back out of the alley. "He always has lots of energy!"

Just the mention of the boy's name brought a tightening to Joel's chest. When Clem had asked if he could give their operation a hand on Friday working their herd, he had welcomed the diversion.

Today was the commencement of Carson's outing to Minneapolis. Meagan had picked him up again this morning, taking him to meet the Ottersons in Norbert. It was a very hesitant young man Joel had deposited in her backseat. Having horse-whipped himself thoroughly for wrecking the child's introduction into adoption, the man had been forcibly positive about the trip to the twin cities. "Lots of kids live in the big city, Carson. Chances are, you are going to have playmates right in your own neighborhood, maybe even next door." A small hand had waved to him down the driveway and continuously all the way around the slough until the grove of trees blocked their view. By now, the two of them were seven hours apart—too far to make an emergency run if Carson cried in the night or was embarrassed about waking up wet in the morning.

Ornery cattle and a handful of cowboys boxing it out in one corral left no thinking time. Physical exertion coupled with a steady stream of humorous parley kept Joel's mind from turning down any emotional trek.

But he sure hoped Carson was doing fine.

Irene Schultz always treated anyone who chanced to be on their farm at mealtime to her homemade cooking. Entering her sunny, hospitable kitchen, Ned joked, "Hey, Ma, I hope you cooked Joel's favorite: hot dogs! Or was it pizza?" He slapped the older man on the back.

Irene fondly scolded her son. "If you'd move out on your own, you wouldn't do any better." Shooing them to her bountiful table, Irene's face wrinkled in puzzlement. "Didn't I count right? How could have I set one too many places?" As if leading a math lesson in school, she had everyone mentally counting the white dinnerware edged in pink prairie roses.

Patting his wife's arm, Clem said, "That's all right, honey. Just means there is more food for the rest of us!" Chairs scraping against the floor brought all eyes to rest on the scalloped pota-toes, ham, and side dishes.

Perplexed, Irene exclaimed, "Carson! We're missing Carson. I knew I had counted right." Her eyes circled the table.

Joel had told Clem that Carson wouldn't be with him today; evidently, the message hadn't been passed along to his wife.

Not wanting Carson's pending adoption to become the topic of the meal, Joel downplayed her direct quest by saying, "He's on a visit today." Even before it was past his front teeth, he was certain Irene wouldn't let the matter drop so easily.

"A visit?" the farmer's wife repeated. "Who would he visit?"

Joel couldn't conceal the curtain of pain flitting across his face from the woman. He watched as her face turned a pasty white.

"He's not being adopted, is he?" Alarm ringing in her tone clanged in Joel's heart. Her hand stopped in midair, holding the basket of bread she had been about to pass to Ned.

Confidentiality prevented a foster parent from explaining the circumstances, but he didn't have to. Agony burning in his facial features told her it was true.

"They can't pull that boy out of your home, Joel!" A spirit of fight flared from her nostrils. "He practically worships you, the way he has to do everything just like you do. Anyone who doesn't know you two would swear you were father and son." The woman's posture stiffened.

Feeling the heat threading its way up his neck, Joel was uncomfortable being the focus of the supper table discussion. Stomach muscles knotting in his abdomen choked out the appetite he'd worked up earlier.

Seeing his discomfort, Rae Ann came to his rescue, thwarting Irene's next torpedo. "Foster care doesn't last forever. You've done a remarkable job getting Carson ready for his new parents, Joel. How excited they must be!"

Assenting grunts ringed the table. Ned took the bread out of his mom's hand. Clem changed the subject to crop emergence, but even then, Joel could only go through the motions of eating the delectable dishes Mrs. Schultz had spent hours preparing, now flat and tasteless.

It was another two days before Carson would return from his trip to Minneapolis.

Only to leave again.

With a rosy-pink sky as a painted backdrop, Joel was up at the first peek of dawn walking his emerging wheat fields.

It was these early morning solitary hours that the country boy inborn in Joel loved the most. Some journalists described the rural setting as quiet. However, it was nothing of the sort. A full concert choir of wildlife rehearsed on the prairie from dawn to the break of day the following morning. Birds of every color and song twittered, bees buzzed, crickets hiccupped, and mosquitoes hummed, accompanied by the howling of the coyotes creeping from their hidden dens. Joel sucked in his breath at the expansive beauty of the tinted heavens touching the rolling shades of emerald green patchwork fields butting up against the horizon line miles in the distance.

And yet, even in this paradise, his mind refused to rest. Yesterday, he had the banter of Ned, Rae, and Clem to keep him occupied as he tried to keep up with the fast-paced cattle. There were few minutes to entertain thoughts of the fleeting days he had left with Carson.

But today, his mind still had enough open space to color his vision with the frail framework of a blond-haired, blue-eyed heartthrob.

Joel took to praying out loud. "Heavenly Father, you see me here, just a dirt farmer loving what I do, and in your awesome power, you also have Carson in your specs. Forgive me for always indulging in self-centeredness, for wanting to keep the boy here just to keep me from being lonely. I pray for the Ottersons that they fathom what a gift this precious child will be to them. Help me to let go. Thank you for the months you have given Carson to me."

There was no concluding, "Amen," for the prayer was ongoing as he continually lifted his little friend up to his loving heavenly Savior.

His mind-set continued into the afternoon, when he pulled the tarp off his table-saw shoved in the corner of the shop.

When the final good-bye came, he wanted a special gift to give Carson, something worthy of the fine young man he was, one that would last through his childhood and maturation into a man.

His grandfather had done the same for Joel when he was about Carson's age.

A treasure box. Anyway, that's what he called his: a wooden box about two feet square with a hinged lid. When he was a youngster, his treasure box had held things like a jawbone of mice teeth he'd found when digging with his toy shovel by the grain bin or a rock almost as round as a baseball.

As he progressed into his teenage years, his prized possessions evolved into school memorabilia and the title to his first pickup truck. Even now, as a man, his chest held the letters Melissa wrote him when they were dating from a distance.

Immersed in the fine wood shavings and powdery dust from sanding, his hands lovingly measured and cut the boards, fitting them together like a jigsaw puzzle. Creating this gift with his own hands was a soothing balm to his bleeding heart. Slowly wiping his hand over the smooth lid, he could visualize Carson doing the same. The carpentry eased away the anxiety of the past weeks.

Maybe the Ottersons would let him act as an uncle to their son. Having had most of the relationships in his young life severed, maybe the one he had with Joel could remain intact, just in a different form.

When his cell phone jingled, he didn't even jump or think the worst, or even that it might somehow be connected to Carson. But it was.

"Hi, Joel, this is Meagan. Sorry to call you on a Saturday."

Even the realization the social worker was calling on her day off didn't ruffle his inner stress level. "No problem, Meagan. This is your day off, not mine." Above his workbench was a small cardboard box holding hinges. He opened it and found what he needed. "What's up?"

"Jane and I have a bit of a scheduling snag. When the Ottersons were here yesterday morning, we agreed one of us could meet them in Fargo on Sunday evening to pick up Carson and bring him the rest of the way home. Fargo is about halfway.

That way they wouldn't have to spend so much of their visitation time with Carson in a vehicle." Her lilting voice paused.

"Makes sense, I guess," Joel agreed.

"Anyway, now it doesn't work for either of us to make the trip." Meagan's words ended on a high note.

"Oh? So now what?" Joel dug under the workbench for his drill and case of bits.

"I thought I'd check and see what your Sunday plans were." Her voice trailed off as if she wasn't sure she should be asking him.

Joel's heart picked up its pace. "Fargo? You want me to go to Fargo?" Was he hearing right? He always thought Meagan was fearful he would spoil the placement. His hand dropped to the bench.

"Only if it isn't interfering with your schedule." Almost a wistful plea coated her words.

Interfering? Heck no. Any additional time he could have with Carson, he was in! Keeping his voice at its usual slow drawl, he teased, "Thought you wouldn't let me within a mile of those city slickers."

"Whatever gave you that idea?" Meagan chuckled, pretending the thought was preposterous.

Fargo was a good three and a half hours from the farm, but that was three and a half hours sooner he'd see Carson than what he had anticipated.

Having punched in the appropriate buttons on the self-serve fuel pump, Joel thrust the nozzle into his gas tank. After attending the Sunday service in Elton, he deemed driving the twenty miles back to the farm an unnecessary detour when he'd be headed in the opposite direction in a couple of hours.

Joel had fought with himself to stay focused on Pastor Taylor's sermon rather than drifting off to Fargo prematurely. Half of him had sat in the wooden pew examining Annie Tulof's unusual flowered hat from his rearview position as the strains of "He Leadeth Me" filtered through the air from a duet.

"Lead me, LORD. Thy will, not my will," he had murmured before letting the other half of him skip across the miles to Minneapolis, pondering if the Ottersons and Carson were likewise worshiping in a local church. As thankful as he was that the child had made a commitment to Jesus, he also knew that in order for his new faith to grow, it needed to be watered. It was a tiny shoot bravely emerging above the distractions of this world, one that Satan would love to snuff out with the heel of his shoe. Without a godly environment to provide nourishment, Carson's thrill at the prayer his Sunday school teacher had led him through would fade into dormancy.

For the past year, Carson had been his shadow on Sunday mornings, becoming quite a favorite amongst the small band of parishioners. His notable absence on this particular day caused quite a stir, as Joel was aware it would. Unabashed amazement percolated the faces of his church family. He'd braced himself for the onslaught of curious questions. Wetness gleamed in Mrs. Saar's eyes, recalling the sacred moments she'd had with her student. Suzy Taylor squeezed his arm and said she'd pray for the transition. Bill Vance was the most direct. "Well, Melissa's death almost wiped you out, Joel. Giving up the boy should finish you off."

Joel had no comeback.

The scripture reading by Pastor Taylor had jolted him back into the hard church bench. "Reflect on what I am saying, for the LORD will give you insight into all this" (2 Timothy 2:7, NIV). Keeping facts and emotions separated was as difficult as distinguishing salt crystals from sugar granules mixed in a glass jar.

Yet somehow the words gave him the assurance that he and Carson would both come out stronger in the end.

A short horn toot snapped Joel's head up to recognize the driver braking at the fuel pump across from him. Jasmine Kirmis's lithe form slid out from behind the steering wheel, extending an amiable greeting. "Hi, Joel. This is a pleasant surprise." Reaching for the gas nozzle, she tossed him a smile over her shoulder. "You clean up nicely."

Warming to her smile, Joel threw one back to her.

"Thanks. I do get off the farm once in a while." Although the absence of foster sons was clearly obvious to both of them, neither of them commented. Calendar squares marking appointments, meetings, and home visits were the norm in foster parenting. "Looks like we're both headed out on road trips today."

"Not me." Jasmine twisted her fuel cap off. "Since I'm a town driver, my tank doesn't drain as quickly as yours, but every so often, I have to replenish her. Kind of like the refrigerator." Her soft laughter refreshed him, like a dip in the lake on a sizzling day.

Joel had this unprecedented overwhelming desire to spend the day with Jasmine. Her gentle speech, her unassuming ways, her love of kids appealed to the tightness in his chest straining for permanent release. The long drive to Fargo would roll under his wheels more rapidly with her company.

Yet the mere thought of asking a woman to join his camaraderie was unsettling. Over two decades had lapsed since he had drummed up the courage to talk to Melissa the first time.

"You got that right." Joel removed the window-washing squeegee from its holder to stall for a few more minutes in her presence. Pushing it across the front windshield, he felt the sweatiness of his fingers against the handle. *This is ridiculous*, he chided himself.

"So you're headed out of town," she commented, checking the number of gallons the machine had pumped into her tank.

"Yeah, I don't venture too far—mostly day trips. I'm on my way to Fargo but will be back home by nightfall." He ripped off a length of paper towel and wiped the moisture off the squeegee's blade.

"Whoa. That's quick. You have some rubber to burn." She retrieved her purse from the front seat and headed inside to pay her bill.

Once his own windows were completed, Joel crossed the intervening space to her waiting vehicle. With the dripping squeegee he rubbed at the bugs and spots on her windshield before flipping the tool over to the rubber blade, giving the glass a spotless shine. Jasmine caught his act of chivalry on her return.

"Well, thank you, sir. I don't remember the last time someone cleaned my windows for me," she exclaimed, admiring the effect.

Masquerading as a station attendant, Joel politely inquired, "So, ma'am, are you just traveling through these parts?"

She readily played along with his performance. "No, sir. I aim to settle down right here in Elton."

"Then let me be the first to welcome you to our little town of Elton; population: one thousand eight hundred sixty-three residents, the latest up-to-date count after cousin Lucy gave birth to infant Alexander just last night." Gallantly, Joel swept the air with the squeegee, the windows completed.

"So I take the census count doesn't include me."

"Don't worry, ma'am, I will be sure to notify the auditor to update the records." Opening the car door for her, he motioned for her to enter.

Settling herself in the seat, she looked up at him and said, "You know, I think I'm going to like this town."

Then Joel summoned the courage he didn't think he had, catching her completely off guard. "And if the lady would have the afternoon free, perhaps she'd like to accompany this station attendant to the grand city of Fargo, where he will be picking up a young man named Carson."

Her eyes widened in surprise. "Are you asking me out on a date?"

"If you call spending seven hours driving in the enclosed cab of a pickup truck a date, ma'am, then yes, I am." Waiting for her response, his heart skidded into a wild, untamable rhythm. Even at his age, rejection would be similar to falling from a windmill.

"Actually, it would work for me. Ryan is spending the night with his sister, Lacey." She paused, an impish look scooting across her face. "That is, if the station manager here will let you off work." Her eyes twinkled at the fine-looking man loitering at her door.

Winking, he replied, "I think I can talk him into it."

Without the presence of a pair of hyper boys to chatter through the lulls in conversation, Joel had been a bit apprehensive about filling the hours between Elton and Fargo with meaningful discourse. He need not have worried. Having already established a friendship by having a parent-teacher relationship, along with the unexpected meeting at the Bismarck livestock sale barn last fall and Carson's birthday party celebration, gave Joel and Jasmine a large chunk of common footing to set the two at ease.

A hundred miles down the road, they were ready to admit to each other that they had skipped the midday lunch. Chancing upon a quaint western café beside the highway, they shared an outdoor picnic table on its front porch.

"This décor looks like your kind of place," Jasmine commented, sizing up the horseshoes ringing the outside door and the horse collars hung between the windows.

"Me?" Joel snorted. "I don't own a horse, but then again, you might. Any lovely lady found hitched on top of the sorting pens at a sale barn in the dead of winter, mind you, surely has a quarter horse staked in her backyard."

Jasmine laughed out loud. "I'd hoped you had forgotten about that."

The man swallowed a swig of coffee. "What were you doing there anyway? Buying a classroom pet?"

She wouldn't have expected him to know she was an author. Having only one book published—and not exactly the type of book he'd pick to read anyway—hardly distinguished her as a well-known novelist. Somehow she'd always felt it would be boasting if she called herself an author. It seemed one had to earn the title by having a dozen or more books on the library shelf.

"Ah, not exactly. For a hobby, I dabble in journalism. I was doing some research for a piece I planned to write." Jasmine made a face at him. "Weird, huh?"

Internalizing her confession, he figured there was more to it, but he let it go. "Guess we each have our own idiosyncrasies that add up to the complex beings we are."

The lady dabbed her lips with a napkin. "You have some of those odd traits yourself."

Leaning back in his chair, his meal finished, Joel gave the lady his full attention. "I do, huh? Like what?" Was she referring to his hermit lifestyle or the pickup truck he drove everywhere, even with its poor gas mileage?

Jasmine bluntly pinpointed the character trait she found perplexing, catching him completely off balance. "A bachelor signing on as a foster parent."

Never would he have foreseen this direct hit coming. His chest burned as if struck by lightning. Shifting uneasily in his chair, he attempted to hold the smile on his face in place, preventing her from seeing how her appraisal accosted him. Did she too reason a single parent couldn't do justice to the difficult task of raising a child? Was she insinuating Carson was notably lacking emotionally or physically from being in his home? The relaxing meal they had finished off was beginning to solidify in his stomach.

Stalling to collect his thoughts, he passed a question back into her playing field. "You're also a single foster parent. Do you feel yourself inadequate to meet the demands of the role?"

Not letting more than a second lapse before responding, she locked her eyes on his, her gaze unwavering. "Yes, totally." Instead of attacking him for being a single parent, she was revealing an inadequacy deeply hidden in her soul. The hard rock in his middle dissolved as he realized how she was cutting herself open for him to see.

Sitting up straighter, he moved the dirty dishes to the side of the tabletop and lowered his forearms onto the smooth surface. "In what ways?" He really wanted to know. This was the very reason he thought Carson would do better with the Ottersons.

Puffing her bangs in an exhale of breath, she made an effort to form into words the numerous ways she'd felt horribly incompetent in parenting Autumn and in the end had failed miserably.

"Children don't follow a precise set of instructions. Giving them food and clothing, a nice bedroom to call their own, a haircut every six weeks, and keeping up on their inoculations is the easy part. The hard part is figuring out what is going on inside of them. Parents are to help guide and mold their offspring into unique creatures, instilling in them self-confidence, work ethics, empathy for others, and a love for God. It all sounds rosy and easy, but it isn't. Kids come with differing measures of stubbornness, open defiance, and teenage hormones! When I try opening my arms and loving them, I get rejection and am blasted with everything I ever did wrong. If I try to be the tough-love parent, I'm accused of being hardnosed and stringent."

"Evidently, you are speaking from experience." Joel was a good listener. They had all afternoon.

"Without a spouse to act as a soundboard on the infinite parenting issues cropping up or to share the wild ride of emotional teenage waves, I failed miserably." Abruptly, Jasmine stopped, her eyes landing in her lap, pretending to study her fingernails.

Joel's sights settled on a car in the distance disappearing into the horizon. He'd thought her shortcomings in parenting would come alongside his; however, they didn't. Maybe Carson was too young yet to put his parenting skills to the kind of tests she'd been through. Then again, maybe not.

Gently, he asked, "If you feel this way, why did you take Ryan in as a foster child?" Somehow she wasn't making sense. From what he had witnessed of her relationship with Ryan, it appeared to be a mutual bond, the same way Carson adored her as his teacher.

Sighing, her eyes disengaged from her lap. "Ryan is an absolute doll. An ornery one, maybe, but mostly pure delight. I actually think we're doing quite well." Her lengthy pause stretched into a bird's-eye hold on a musical score sheet as she struggled inwardly at how much she should reveal. Giving in because she was tired of concealing this shadowy part of her life, she released her daughter's name.

"It's my daughter, Autumn." From there, she told him of the downward spiral of her second child after Evert's death: her senior year of defiance, dropping out of college, and now shunning her mother from her life. "I don't even know where she is right now," Jasmine softly admitted, moisture blurring her vision. "Evert was always able to break through her spells of moodiness, to get her back on our side."

Grieving—Joel knew all about grief, yet he reckoned the woman across the table from him did also. "We all grieve in different ways and at different times." He recalled how motivation had completely oozed out of him with his wife's death, not even caring about the golden crop standing ready for harvest out in his fields. Even now, a sun did not set without Melissa drifting into his tender memories.

"Somehow I don't think you've seen the last of your daughter. Train up a child in the way she should go, and she will return to you. A verse in Proverbs says something like that."

Her green eyes softened. "Yes, 'Train a child in the way he should go, and when he is old he will not turn from it' (Proverbs 22:6, NIV). I've memorized it. Her father passed away five years ago. It seems a lot longer."

After checking her watch, she quickly stood up. "Joel, the narration of my pitfalls in life is going to make you late for Carson. We need to get moving."

Inspecting his own timepiece, he was nonplused. "We still have an hour to spare, but we can boogie on. Maybe we'll find another place to explore."

Quietness settled inside the cab as the flat North Dakota prairie slid by the windows. While he drove with one hand on the steering wheel, the lady studied his profile. Skin the shade of a baked potato darkened by hours in the sun, brown-speckled hair trimmed close to the ear and neckline, high cheekbones. He turned and caught her scrutiny. And a John Denver smile, she decided.

Breaking the solitude, Joel asked, "Cat got your tongue?"

Her emerald eyes crinkled. "I thought I'd give your ears a rest. Actually, you never told me why you became a foster parent."

"Pure selfishness."

She blinked, not comprehending.

"I became a foster parent out of selfishness."

"Now, that doesn't even make sense. Foster parents are usually cast as people having a genuine love for kids, who would take in all of the underprivileged children in the world if they could."

"That's not me. I was looking out for number one—me only."

Jasmine looked for a hint of humor in his eye, but there was none.

"The first year after Melissa died, I wanted to die too. I was so utterly lonely, so tired of the silence on the farmstead and in my big, old house, I swore I could hear the ants marching quietly underground. Everywhere I turned, I was by myself—at home, in the field, in the pickup, sitting by myself at church and community functions. I was tired of my thoughts, my shadow, my face in the mirror."

Listening, Jasmine realized her initial grief as a widow had been tangled up with the exertion of struggling with Autumn. Although sometimes there had been silence, more often there'd been shouting and doors slamming.

"It wasn't that foster care was anything new to me; Melissa and I had done it together when we discovered we couldn't have children." Inwardly, he cringed at this revelation. "When a second year of desolation followed the first, I decided to renew my foster parent license. Don't get me wrong, that was an inner battle too. Was I capable of caring for a child without my wife's help? I was taking a big chance with a child's life."

"But it's working."

"Only by the grace of God—and by the gifted help of Ed and Arlene Bautz."

Jasmine couldn't let it rest. "You are different from me. When I first found out you were a single foster father, I was appalled. Why would anyone choose such a position? I knew firsthand what single parenting was all about. Then I saw you in action. From the very first day you introduced Carson to his new classroom, I could tell there was something unique about the two of you. You and Carson are a perfect match."

Not convinced, Joel refuted her reasoning. "For now."

"And you'll never know if you lose him." Jasmine's intuition summarized this jaunt to Fargo. He hadn't told her of Carson's pending adoption, yet she knew it instinctively. "From my meetings with Ryan's social worker, Sarah Thern, I'm under the impression foster parents are given the first opportunity to adopt a child."

"Yup, the key word is *parents*. You confirmed my beliefs earlier. A child needs both a father and a mother. To give him one without the other is cutting him short. Carson deserves the best. Self-indulgence brought him into my life; I won't be greedy again." Firm resolution coated his declaration.

"So what is Carson missing out on by not having a mother?"

"Lots. If Melissa were alive, she'd have painted his room some bright colors or wallpapered a border of sailboats and trucks about the perimeter. She would have baked him homemade cookies and had a cup of hot cocoa waiting for him when he hopped off the bus after school. His seventh birthday would have been done up in little boy fashion: streamers and balloons, a carefully-decorated chocolate cake with gooey frosting. She'd have compiled a photo album this thick." Separating his thumb and index finger, he displayed the thickness of the imaginary scrapbook. "I haven't taken even one picture of him since he came a year ago. Moms just have a way about themselves that make everything nicer and sweeter and softer."

Softly, Jasmine murmured, almost to herself, "I did all that for Autumn…"

…And she isn't here.

She hadn't said it out loud; however, both of them finished the sentence internally.

Wanting Joel to consider both sides of the picture, Jasmine continued on. "Foster children often come from deprived backgrounds with dysfunctional families. They have seen situations no child should have to witness, whether it's drugs, alcohol abuse, physical fights, or improper displays of sex. Courts tend to give parents every chance to redeem their children, while months and years fly by. Kids get bounced between foster homes and their parents' ever-changing addresses, their skin getting thicker and thicker, eventually becoming a shell tougher than a turtle's back—impossible to crack."

Joel grunted. "You're painting Carson's picture. I'm his third foster home."

Inclining her head in affirmation, the woman went on. "Maybe I'm wrong, but I don't think a child who has been jerked from home to home, who has experienced what we only see on television, cares if his bedroom is decorated or not or if his cake and cookies are homemade or encased in a cellophane wrapper from the grocery store. He wants stability. He wants an adult he can count on when he is naughty and when he is good. He wants an address and relatives and friends that stay the same. On the bottom line, he wants love."

"You heard Carson that day in school when he and Ryan had the fight. He wants a mother," the foster father objected.

Jasmine Kirmis was an enigma. First, defiantly acclaiming the negative aspects of being a single mom, and then doing an about-face by encouraging Joel to hang on to Carson as a single father. Having discussed this subject as far as he could stomach, Joel switched directions. "So what is Ryan's future?"

A disheartening sigh escaped from her lips. "The law doesn't let kids have prolonged placements in foster care. Tina isn't exhibiting any effort to accomplish her court-mandated requirements; thus, I suspect the judge will give Social Services another six months at the next hearing.

"Long term?" Jasmine paused and then answered her own question. "Tina will get her son back. The day the gavel hits the sound block, she'll throw her belongings into the back of her rusty, old station wagon faster than the clerk can file her case. One heavy foot on the accelerator will have her out of this state by nightfall."

"Sad." Joel tapped a fingernail against the steering column.

"Yes, it will be." She'd miss the rascal.

"Remember, as foster parents, we are a temporary window in a child's life. Hopefully, we give them the love and encouragement they need to climb the next hill."

The first billboards along Interstate 94 advertising sites in Fargo loomed ahead.

"I asked you to come along today to help the time go quicker. It has." His mood lightened at the thought of being able to hold Carson in his arms soon.

"Sorry, I let the air get rather heavy. A travel companion should stay within the boundaries of proper afternoon discourse."

Reaching across the seat, he folded his rough fingers around her smaller ones and squeezed briefly before releasing. "When it is all said and done, I think we understand each other. We're parked at similar crossroads, just have to figure out which way to go." He held her eyes a second longer than necessary, restoring their friendship.

So they didn't see eye-to-eye on foster care and adoption. He would have to live with the decision he made, and he was man enough to do it—with God's help.

Taking the exit ramp, Joel commented, "We're a shy early. Would you like to do something else first?"

"No thanks. I think I'd prefer to be in the parking lot when he arrives. Wouldn't want him to be apprehensive if he doesn't see your sleek pickup truck right away."

Had Jasmine read his mind? Those were his exact thoughts.

Now that the time was getting close, his heart soared, beating an erratic tempo. A giddiness lifted his spirits. *A time to laugh and a time to dance.*

The instant the dark-blue van's turning signal flashed, Joel instinctively perceived this was the one out of the hundreds of vehicles whizzing past or turning into the busy truck stop that held Carson. Fastening his sights on the highly-waxed exterior, he waited for it to approach, to get his first glimpse of the passenger in the middle seat. The Ottersons wouldn't recognize him, nor he they, but a blue-eyed, blond-haired youngster would be the link between them.

Checking the excitement building within him, Joel reminded himself this was the Ottersons' weekend. The goal of this visit was to facilitate a bond between the adoptive parents and Carson. In his overwhelming eagerness to snatch the boy up into a giant hug, Joel forced himself to tread lightly, to follow Carson's lead.

For the last twenty minutes, Jasmine and Joel had sat side by side on the open-end gate of his truck, sizing up every automobile passing through the station. Noting his fixed stare, Jasmine followed his mark of attention. Drumming fingernails on the metal tailgate spoke volumes on how difficult this transition was for Joel Linton. Jasmine couldn't determine where the right placement for the boy was. She had messed up the family tie she'd once had with her daughter. Who was she to have an opinion?

Jumping off the end gate, Joel took a step toward the traffic, waiting for the navy van to pass in front of him.

Joel saw his friend first—a worried little man sitting tall in his seat, his chin thrust upward, peering through the opening between the two front bucket seats then rotating to check the passenger windows in the middle bench seat. Joel wondered if the tyke knew who was picking him up.

Carson looked long and hard out of his left window then scooted across the seat to check the right side.

And there was Joel. Elation flooded the freckled face like a brilliant morning sunrise bursting through the hazy purple shadows. Blue eyes opened wide; a toothy smile stretched like a rubber band to monopolize his face. Jumping up and down, Carson waved at the person he loved more than any other. Yanking on the door handle, he was obstructed by the electric locks that wouldn't budge until Eric parked the vehicle in an open spot a few spaces past Joel's truck. Then out tumbled the boy, his legs pumping up and down. Clad in a brand-new, red nylon jogging suit with a matching hooded jacket, he was a blur of legs and arms as he leaped into Joel's waiting embrace, the boy and man a knot of arms clinging to each other for a full minute.

Jasmine sat mesmerized by the demonstration of unrestricted love by a man and his foster son. Tears stung her eyes and pinched her heart; she was unable to fathom how the two would endure separation.

Carol and Eric Otterson witnessed the reunion as well as they slowly approached the duo. Feeling their presence, Carson slid down Joel's front side to stand on his own feet. "Come on, Joel, let's go home," he pleaded, tugging on Joel's arm.

"Just a second, big guy." Spying his teacher leaning against the end gate of Joel's truck, Carson couldn't believe his good fortune: the two most favorite adults in his whole life. He sped off in her direction, giving Mrs. Kirmis a hug as well before climbing into the truck's backseat.

Reaching out a hand to shake first Eric's hand and then Carol's, Joel introduced himself. "I'm Joel Linton, Carson's foster parent." Motioning for Jasmine to join him, he added, "And this is Jasmine Kirmis, Carson's teacher this past year."

Exchanging polite pleasantries, Eric explained, "Meagan called us and let us know there was a change in plans."

"So, ah, how did the weekend go?" Joel asked, feeling like he was taking on the role of the social worker.

"Ah, good … good." Eric nodded his head but didn't elaborate. "These things take time. Slow goes the turtle and gets the prize." His smile didn't appear to reach his eyes. "I'll get Carson's bag out of the back." He hurried back to his van.

Carol looked like a nice lady, the kind who would make a good mother. Her tired face held sadness but understanding. "I can see what he was missing." She peered up at Joel. "He was really homesick, crying both nights at bedtime and being listless during the day no matter what activities we suggested. I even thought we might have to cut the visit short. Eric is sure if we take it slow, the child will come around, but truthfully, I don't think we'd get him back into the van for another visit to Minneapolis. His heart belongs to you."

Joel's Adam's apple swelled as he swallowed. Jasmine gently pulled the lady into an embrace, whispering, "You have a mother's heart, Carol."

Interrupting the scene, Eric handed Carson's bag off to Joel. "Guess we better be on our way. We both have miles to travel before we sleep."

Joel agreed. Signaling to Carson in the cab, he called, "Come out here, Carson, and say good-bye to the Ottersons." In reply, the child shook his head, shrinking out of sight. Seeing his reluctance, Joel took a step toward his pickup to get the youngster.

Laying a hand on his arm, Carol stopped him. "It's okay. He's home now. We understand. Thank you for being the kind of foster parent you are." With that, she turned quickly to hide the emotions transparent on her face. Eric raised a hand as he followed his wife to their vehicle.

Facing Jasmine, Joel marveled. "I never expected it to be like this. Carson was hurting as much as I was, and I couldn't do anything to help him."

"You both survived. Let's take him home." ′

Soft snores floated up from the backseat before the truck even had Fargo in its rearview mirror. "Tuckered out. If Carol admitted he was homesick, he must have really had a bad case of it." It broke his heart to picture his buddy crying into a wet pillow, his yellow hair matted to his head.

"If this adoption is going to move forward, it is going to have to be reined in to a walk. Meagan and Jane have to require the next handful of visits to be in Norbert or even at the farm. Maybe the Ottersons need to camp out in our state for a few weeks." Indignation amplified his conjectures.

Agitation pricking under his skin surfaced as external fidgeting. Shifting his weight, rubbing the back of his neck, messing with the buttons on the dashboard—he resembled a snake trying to rid itself of too tight a skin.

"If I didn't know better, I would classify you as a first grader with a bad case of ants in the pants. Want me to drive?"

"No," he said, glancing over at his companion. "I have the white dog and the black dog battling it out in here." He tapped his middle with a closed fist.

"Who's winning?" A trace of humor fringed the question.

Smirking at her, the frustrated foster parent confessed, "I can't tell."

"May I?" she asked, placing three fingers on the radio button. "A change in the atmosphere might help."

"Sure, anything's better than a dog show."

Music replaced the conversation in the cab the rest of the way to Elton. After dropping Jasmine off at her home, Joel continued to the farm with his sleeping companion.

Carson awoke as Joel was grappling with the screen door, balancing the dead weight of the slumbering child in his arms.

Disoriented, the boy awoke in a panic, fighting the arms that held him safe, screaming Joel's name out loud.

With the toe of his boot, Joel swung the inside enclosure open then dropped his knees to the linoleum flooring, fearful the struggling child would yet fall out of his hold. "Shh, Carson. You're okay. It's me, Joel. You're safe at home, with me." He planted the child's feet on the floor as well, holding him upright in a loose embrace. Sweaty from his nap, his hair lay in wet clumps, like a chicken caught out in the rain.

Climbing up out of a bad dream, the thin arms in the nylon jacket flailed the air. A mournful wail clambered up the scale in a bellowing crescendo. Pointed elbows dug into the man's chest in his eagerness to get free of whatever bound him.

"Carson, open your eyes. Look, honey, you're home with me," Joel cooed by his ear.

The boy's eyes peeked open a slit, then wider. Swallowing the shriek still in his throat, he froze, staring at the familiar table and chairs, the cupboard doors, and the kitchen window. Slowly twisting like a corkscrew, he rotated his slim body to see the man holding him.

The whites of his eyes expanded to two round saucers as he comprehended where he was and who was holding him. A new waterfall of tears poured over the dam. Throwing his body at Joel's chest, his arms encircled the neck in a fierce never-let-go hug.

Shutting his eyes tightly, Joel reciprocated the fierce grip, pressing the child to his heart. Awkwardly getting to his feet, he carried his precious cargo to the reclining chair in the living room, depositing the two of them into its soft leather. All through the rest of the night, they continued to cling to each other. No matter what happened, at least they had this lasting expression of love.

Tumultuously, a child's voice pleaded at his ear before drifting off to sleep again, this time for the entire night. "Don't you *ever* send me away again."

CHAPTER 24

Bacon sizzling in the open iron skillet diffused a smeary spray of grease across the top of the stove. A half dozen eggs frying on the griddle and a couple of slices of bread browning in the toaster permeated the old farm house, sending a trail of tantalizing aromas rising to the top floor.

Buried in foaming bubbles in the bathtub and singing at the top of his lungs, Carson was tempted to cut his soaking with his sponge toys short. Gnawing in his tummy was a pertinent reminder of the supper meal he'd slept through the prior evening.

Slapping the bath water repeatedly, Carson watched the suds mount into billowing clouds of froth, licking his back and arms. Giggling in delight, he pummeled his legs against the tub floor, whipping the soap bubbles into higher peaks of meringue.

All of the apprehension and shuddering qualms throbbing through his thin body the preceding days had been washed away—not by the bubble bath treat, which he did like immensely, but by the safe harbor of Joel's arms and the return to this trusty house where just the two of them lived. Yup, him and Joel—best buds.

Flipping eggs in the kitchen alternately with stirring the hard lump of frozen orange juice in the pitcher, Joel hummed to the tune Carson was screeching filtering down from the upper level. Carson sang with a gusto of pure joy brought on in his eyes by Joel's heroic rescue.

Joel's low crooning was more of an ominous foreboding of what the next phone call might bring. And Meagan or Jane would be calling both the Ottersons and him.

Splotching a wet footprint on each step as he descended the staircase in his bare feet and denim jeans, Carson was thrilled to find the breakfast table plentifully piled with mouthwatering dishes instead of the usual choice of cereal boxes. Joel was feeling the pinch of hunger in his middle as well.

"Hey, guy. You are about to devour the most scrumptious, sweet-smelling, delectable breakfast you have ever eaten in your entire lifespan of seven years, cooked to your satisfaction by none other than these two very hands." Spreading ten fingers in the air, he wiggled them at Carson sprouting wet rooster tails on the back of his hair. "Cereal first and then bacon and eggs? Or eggs and bacon accompanied by strawberry jam slathered thickly on a piece of toast?" After setting the pitcher of juice in the middle of the table, Joel sat down in his chair, only to bounce up again. "Forgot the milk."

Cocking his head to the side, Carson eyed the fried egg lying flabbily beside the toast. "Mine looks like it's kind of burnt on the edges."

"Burnt?" Joel masked profound disbelief. "That, my fine young man, is a perfectly fried masterpiece, a tough outer ring preventing your yellow yolk from oozing all over your plate, infiltrating your bacon, and turning your toast into a soggy newspaper left on a doorstep in the rain." Crossing his eyes and sticking his tongue out, Joel had his pipsqueak charge chortling.

"I was just joshing you, Joel. You're a good cook." Carson pierced the soft yolk with a prong of his fork. "I'll pray this time."

"Okay," the man agreed, adding the milk carton to the menagerie of dishes and foods. "I suppose you're afraid I might poison you with my food."

Dutifully folding his hands, his eyelashes lying on his cheeks, Carson prayed, "Thanks, Jesus, for teaching Joel how to cook."

He opened his eyes a sliver to check if the man across from him was listening. When Joel peeked out of one eye to see what the pause was, he met the youngster's saucy grin. Closing his eyes again, Carson continued, "And thanks for showing him how to get to Fargo to find me. Amen."

Joel sighed inwardly.

Launching into the meal, the two did not mention the visit to Minneapolis. It was a time to laugh instead.

Stacking the dishes in the sink after their stomachs were satisfyingly stuffed, Joel said it was his own turn for a shower.

"Good," Carson agreed. "I gots some farming to catch up on in my bedroom." Trying to take the steps two at a time, he raced to the top, only stumbling twice. Smirking, Joel followed behind him.

Later, Joel stuck his head into Carson's bedroom, pleased to see the urchin lying on his side on the floor, moving his four-wheel-drive tractor hitched to the air seeder across the braided rug. The foster dad had some business to take care of in his own room.

He lowered his frame onto his bed, propping himself up on the pillows piled against the headboard. Joel reached for his Bible on the nightstand, opening to the Gospel of Mark. For the last few days, he had sought direction from Christ's own words in the books of Matthew and Mark. Pastor Taylor's scripture for Sunday's sermon had been simmering on his back burner: "Reflect on what I am saying and I will give you insight" (2 Timothy 2:7, NIV). Boy, did he need it!

Moving down the pages, he absorbed the Word, letting it sink into the corners of his soul. Continuing from chapter eight into chapter nine, his eyes stopped on the thirty-sixth and thirty-seventh verses. Rereading them, his heart skipped a beat, arrested by the clear implication the verses had for him—Joel Linton. It was as if Christ were sitting right there in the room speaking only to him.

> He took a little child and had him stand among them.
> Taking him in his arms, he said to them, "Whoever

welcomes one of these little children in my name
welcomes me …"

Mark 9:36–37a (NIV)

Could it be that to welcome *Carson* was to welcome *Christ* into his
family? Was this the answer he had been seeking? Was he not supposed to give Carson up at all? Didn't a child need a mother? Or
was it more important for him to have unprecedented acceptance
and love, which again and again had been stolen from the child
as he moved from his birth home to foster home to foster home?

The man mulled it over. Not give up Carson? Not send him
to an adoptive home? He wouldn't be guilty of selfishness if he
hung on to the boy? *Whoever welcomes one of these little children in
my name welcomes me.*

It was such a fresh solution, a simple answer, one that would
please them both. Was this truly what the LORD wanted, or was
he, Joel Linton, trying to read himself into the verse?

His knees hit the floor beside his bed; his upper body bent over
the quilted coverlet as his hands smothered his face. An audible
groan escaped. No way did he want to step out of God's plan.
"Father," he begged, "not my will but thine." For long minutes,
he knelt at the feet of Jesus, imploring his guidance, struggling
to accept what the verses seemed to imply. In silence, he waited.
"What would you have me do, LORD? Please, give me a sign."

Noise in the next room was followed by footsteps tapping down
the hallway. "Hey, Joel, aren't you gonna do any farmin' today?"
A small hand on his shoulder reclaimed his attention. Opening
his moist eyelids, he found himself staring directly into the clear,
celestial eyes on Carson's face, not six inches from his own.

"Don't you think we should check the fields and see how they're
doin'?" The blue eyes glowed with complete trust and love.

Tears trickled over the uneven cheekbones of the man's face.
Man, did he love this kid. Folding the youngster against his
chest, he couldn't find the words to say, so he simply nodded.
Struggling to right himself, Carson wondered about the tears.

He had always thought real men didn't cry, but that must not be true, for Joel was a real man.

With a handful of tissues from the box on Joel's nightstand, the boy blobbed at the wet marks on his friend's face.

A juicy kiss landed on the boy's fair skin. Joel drawled, "You are an angel. Help this old man to his feet, and we'll do whatever you say, boss."

Transferring the wad of tissues to Joel's outstretched fingers, Carson yanked on the arm as the man fought to regain his balance. Seeing his friend was upright and following him, the boy let go and darted ahead. "I'll get my boots!"

Joel detoured into the bathroom to throw some water at his face. Dropping the fistful of tissues into the wastebasket beside the sink, Joel glanced down. The most beautiful sight met his eyes, the sign he had asked for. Stuffed into the garbage can was a brand-new red jogging suit and its matching jacket.

Carson's blond head popped inside the door. "Are you comin'?" Seeing what the man was staring at, he explained, "I'm not never ever wearing those again. You and me wear blue jeans!"

Meagan's phone call came mid-afternoon. Joel was ready for it. "So how did Carson's visit with the Ottersons go?" she asked, pleasantly as always.

The man got right to the point. "Carson's not going anywhere. He is staying right here on the farm with me." Joel was equipped for battle. There was no way he was going to put the young chap through another miserable weekend like he'd just endured.

"Well, glory be!" Meagan yahooed. "It's about time you saw the light, cowboy! I'll start working on the adoption papers immediately."

Although she couldn't see his face, Joel was beaming. Thinking to himself, he reflected, *I always said she was a good social worker*.

Six Months Later

Jasmine's prediction had been wrong…and right. She hated them both.

She hadn't been invited to attend Ryan's six-month hearing either by Social Services or Tina. But the wayward mother had been more prepared this time than she had been at her son's initial hearing, having asked for a court-appointed lawyer. Even though the budding attorney's pay had been minimal, he had done his homework and given Tina as much attention as a case paying him five digits.

Sarah Thern had called Jasmine with the outcome. Ryan was to be returned to his mother. The six-month extension of foster care Social Services had asked of the court had been denied.

A child did belong with his parent. Even though Ryan's sleeping quarters would shift to next door, Jasmine could still have a lot of influence on his young life. In many ways, life would return to what it had been before Ryan had been admitted to foster care—except, hopefully, that Tina would take her role as a parent more seriously. Jasmine could have handled the court's decision if she hadn't been skeptical about Tina's willingness to do so. Ryan would be the one who would pay for his mother's shortcomings. Her heart ached.

The following Saturday, a feeble knock came on her kitchen door. It was Ryan. But not the Ryan with the toothy smile. Not the Ryan with a prank up his sleeve, nor the Ryan who was a whirlwind of activity. This Ryan stood solemnly, barely holding back a floodgate of tears, the corners of his mouth pulling painfully downward.

Immediately his former foster mother was on her knees pulling the child into her arms. "Honey, whatever is the matter?"

The sympathy in her voice was the breaking point for the elf-like tyke. Tears tumbled down his cheeks like rain cascading off a roof during a fierce summer thunderstorm. Jasmine had never seen the child cry before, not even the night she viewed his somber face through the backseat window of a police car.

Sobs and hiccups prevented the child from verbalizing his distress, but instinctively, Jasmine knew the cause of his turmoil: Tina was moving.

Jasmine had been painfully right. Watching the beat-up brown station wagon, loaded to the ceiling, pull away from the curb and head out of town was bruisingly final. It hurt even more than Autumn's breach of relationship with her mother.

Because Ryan didn't want to leave.

Frustration burned through Jasmine. She was even more convinced than she ever had been before: single parenting was not for her.

Skeleton trees lining the cement steps of the county courthouse, lifted their bare branches into the sky. A V-shaped pattern of Canadian geese flapped their wings overhead, their necks outstretched, honking to each other as they steadily moved southward to their winter home.

North Dakota weather was as changeable as a mannequin's outfits on display in a store window. Some years, winter burst in uninvited with a cold, snowy blast on Halloween night and took up immediate residency, not losing its grip until April.

But this November was a sweet gift, a sprinkling of extra blessings from above. A lingering autumn cast balmy temperatures and gentle breezes on the prairie state.

A fatherly hand rested on Carson's shoulder. Their faces shone like the sun blazing in the fall sky. Yet a dreary day would have been no less bright, for today it became legal and binding. From this day forward, Carson would be the son of Joel Linton.

The courthouse lawn had succumbed to a brown dormancy, dying outwardly to sleep through the coming winter. In contrast, a man across the street stood aloft on a ladder taking advantage of the Indian summer days to string Christmas lights along the roofline of his house in preparation for the advent season. Liking what he saw, Joel's heart lifted. He and Carson would dazzle their porch with lights for Christ's birth, the way he used to do with Melissa.

In Joel's heart, the spirit of Christmas had already arrived in the miracle of becoming a father to a seven-year-old boy. Gray, lonely days of the past were replaced by a deep, penetrating joy, a desire to live, to breathe in and out, to serve the LORD with wondrous appreciation and gladness.

A time to laugh, a time to dance. He'd thought the hourglass was running out for him, that he would slide into the time to mourn, the time to cry, on bruised and bloody knees. He'd wave good-bye to his little chap; the loneliness he'd lived through after burying Melissa would return, only worse—blacker and darker.

But he had it all backward. The hourglass was filling, not emptying. He wasn't descending into another valley; he was clambering up the far side of the canyon, grabbing each clump of grass, each protruding root, pulled by the tight grasp of the LORD's hand folded over his, lifting him out of the valley of grief and despair, out of the mourning and crying. Each step he climbed was taking him toward a new mountaintop where the laughing and dancing were just beginning.

Would there be other valleys? Certainly. But for now, he was going to enjoy the thrill of the lofty peak.

Wrapping a thin arm about the man's hips and hooking his thumb into a belt loop, Carson tilted his head backward to peer up to the full height of Joel Linton. Mischievous sparkles flickered like fireworks in his stare. "Let's go home, *Dad*." Stressing the title, he waited for a reaction. Once before, the youngster had called Joel *Dad*—in Principal Peterson's office when he had been upset with his friend Ryan for referring to Mrs. Kirmis as

Mom. But then it was just pretend. Now, it was real. Joel Linton was Carson's dad.

Joel hugged the boy to his side. "Let's do that, *son.*"

Everything about the day was brighter and clearer than usual. Tiny stones of gravel disappearing under the pickup truck seemed more distinct. Burnt ditches bordering the road in preparation for the winter storms were blacker and bolder. Clouds drifting in a celestial sky held a paint-by-number effect.

Glancing at Carson in the rear seat, Joel vowed to hold this day fixed in his memory forever, every tiny detail of it.

As the vehicle slowed to rumble around the curve bordering the slough leading to their driveway, Carson was the first to notice. "What's tied to our mailbox?" Moving his upper body forward as far as the seat belt would permit, he squinted, endeavoring to focus on the tails and dash of yellow swinging in the breeze. "It looks like a butterfly."

"Pretty big butterfly," Joel commented, he too perplexed at whatever had been caught by the mailbox, flying in the wind from its wooden post.

As they closed the gap, Carson kept changing his speculation. "It's a shirt. No, a balloon. It's something with strings on it."

The shifting jig of yellow finally took a precise shape, distinguishable to the new family occupying the cab. Yards and yards of six-inch ribbon had been looped back and forth then secured in the center, forming the most gigantic bow either of them had ever seen. "It's a present!" The younger Linton excitedly bounced on the seat. "It's a present!"

The vehicle came to a full stop. Two sets of eyes took in the sight. In their absence, someone had removed the old nameplate screwed into the bracket above the mailbox—the one that had read in plain chiseled lettering *Joel Linton*—and replaced it with a newer metallic plate reading *Joel and Carson Linton*.

"My name's on the mailbox! Look, Dad, my name is right beside yours!" The seat belt snapped loose as he dove through the opening between the bucket seats to slide into the front seat next to Joel. His nose smudged the windshield. "Cool, huh? Cool!"

"Well, what do ya know!" Joel let out a low whistle. "Somebody had an inkling of what we were up to today. It looks good, doesn't it? Joel and Carson Linton."

Taking his foot off the brake pedal, Joel let the pickup roll past the mailbox and the slough, giving them an open view of the Linton farmstead in front of the hood ornament.

"Whoa!" the father and son exclaimed in unison. The mailbox was only the prelude for what was ahead, for their whole yard was festooned with golden ribbons—tree branches, corral fencing, swing poles, shed doors, even the chore tractor parked beside the shop was marked with a magnolia streamer swooping from the cab's roof.

His eyes wide in astonishment, Carson couldn't take it all in. "It's Christmas everywhere!" His gaze traveled the yard. "Why did somebody do this?" His voice died to a faint, whispering awe.

Joel too was struck by the scene before them. Not only was the yard transformed by an artist's splattering of mustard paint but by dozens of automobiles parked along the corral fence and the sheds. Neighbors and friends milled about the dry lawn and the open area at the base of the porch. Lawn chairs and picnic tables dotted the farmstead. Everyone was waving at the approaching pickup truck, like the participants in the Fourth of July parade.

It seemed every man, woman, and child from a twenty-mile circumference stood in the crowd, including the Schultzes and Jeannie, his cleaning lady and her family. Ed and Arlene Bautz raised their arms from the porch swing, his nephew's family pumping the air behind them. Rae Ann lifted the pitcher of lemonade she was carrying to a loaded table set up on the porch. Friends from the church in Elton let loose a hearty cheer: Lance and Suzy Taylor, kids from Sunday school, and dear Mrs. Saar. Bill Vance, visiting with Ben Fillmor, gave them a salute. Even Carson's bus driver, Richie Harris, and his wife rose from a pair of lawn chairs to welcome the Lintons. One hip propped on the top railing of the porch was Meagan Ritter, both hands clapping over her head. And next to her, Jasmine. Momentarily, Joel's eyes rested tenderly on her beaming face. God willing, he and Carson would find a heap more reasons to be spending hours with her.

Bright yellow helium balloons fixed to the porch columns accentuated the long sign flapping above the railings between the poles.

Joel killed the motor and reached an arm across the enclosure to lift his son next to him. Even Carson was subdued by the surprise outpouring of love manifested on the farmstead he could now truly call *home*. Hugging the blond head to his shoulder, Joel thanked his Father in heaven for bringing this all to pass.

Gazing up at the calligraphy written beautifully across the sign, he clarified for the boy the mass of golden ribbons embellishing the farmstead. "Yellow ribbons have a special connotation. All of our friends are gathered here to help you and me celebrate us becoming a family. See what the sign says?"

Dazzled by the bright lettering, the child nodded in assent. " 'Welcome Home, Carson!' "

He was home, once and for all. No more foster homes, no more court hearings. Carson Linton was home to stay.

Coming years would be intermixed with life's struggles, potholes in the road to the future, but amongst the trials and the tears, there would be immensely more time to laugh and to dance in his new family.